Mr. Darcy's Refuge

ABIGAIL REYNOLDS

WHITE SOUP PRESS

Mr. Darcy's Refuge

www.pemberleyvariations.com
www.austenauthors.com

To
Sharon Lathan and the Austen Authors,
fantastic writers and fabulous writing buddies,

and to

Jane Austen

who inspires us all

THE PEMBERLEY VARIATIONS
by Abigail Reynolds

WHAT WOULD MR. DARCY DO?

TO CONQUER MR. DARCY

BY FORCE OF INSTINCT

MR. DARCY'S UNDOING

MR. FITZWILLIAM DARCY: THE LAST MAN IN THE WORLD

MR. DARCY'S OBSESSION

A PEMBERLEY MEDLEY

MR. DARCY'S LETTER

MR. DARCY'S REFUGE

Also by Abigail Reynolds:

THE MAN WHO LOVED PRIDE & PREJUDICE

MORNING LIGHT

Chapter 1

THE BREAK IN the rain seemed like a sign. It meant Darcy could ride to the parsonage and discover what was troubling Elizabeth. Her friend Mrs. Collins had said she was ill, but his cousin averred that he had seen her but a few hours ago, and she seemed well then. Darcy would have thought Elizabeth would stop at nothing to come to Rosings tonight, his last night in Kent, and her last chance to ensnare him. Instead she had remained at the parsonage, leaving her friend to make her excuses to his aunt, Lady Catherine.

She must be avoiding him. There could be no other reason for her absence. But why? She had every reason to wish to be in his presence, unless she had decided that winning his love was a hopeless cause. Perhaps that was it. Perhaps his failure to declare himself had left her believing that he was simply toying with her. Perhaps she thought it would be too painful to see him tonight, knowing it would be for the last time. Darcy's mouth curved a little with the thought. Dearest Elizabeth! How happy she would be to receive his assurances of love.

Just at that moment, the pounding of rain against the windowpanes finally began to slacken as the thunder faded off into the distance. His aunt's attention was focused on rendering unwanted advice to Mrs. Collins while Richard was attempted to engage Anne in conversation. He could slip away unnoticed. It was definitely a sign.

Once he had escaped the gloomy sitting room, he lost no time in making his way to the stables. In a clipped voice he asked a sleepy groom to ready his curricle.

The man squinted up at him. "I don't know if that be such a good idea, sir. With those wheels, 'twould be a moment's work to find yourself stuck, the road is that deep in mud after all this rain."

"Then I will ride," Darcy said firmly. He would not allow bad roads to keep him from Elizabeth's side, not tonight.

Yawning, the groom went off to saddle his horse. Darcy helped himself to a riding crop from a shelf, then tapped it impatiently against his leg until he heard the clopping of hooves. The air hung heavy on him, thick and full of moisture. Much more of this rain and the crops would rot in the fields before they even had a chance to sprout. He would have to speak to his aunt about relief for the tenant farmers, but now was not the time to think about such matters.

Soon he would be in Elizabeth's presence, where he would finally be the recipient of her dazzling smiles and hopefully even more. Elizabeth would not be *Miss-ish*, certainly. It was not in her character. Yes, he had every reason to assume she would allow him to taste those seductive lips that had been tempting him almost past the point of sanity. His body filled with fire at the mere thought. He would finally feel her warmth in his arms and hold that shapely form against him, her shining energy at last his, only his.

He could not afford these thoughts, not now, or he would be in no condition to be in Elizabeth's presence. He disciplined himself to think of something else, anything else – the weather, his aunt's latest rant, his horse. He swung himself into the saddle, ignoring the groom's proffered assistance.

The groom had been correct about the condition of the road. The horse's hooves squelched and spewed out droplets of mud. Darcy kept to a slow walk, since he did not want to be covered with mud when he paid his addresses to Elizabeth. The pace seemed interminable, leaving far too much time for thought and memories.

Memories of his father, telling him he must marry an heiress because Georgiana's dowry would cut into the Pemberley coffers. His mother, taking him aside so that his father would not hear, reminding him that he was an earl's grandson. She had married beneath her because it was the only way she could escape from the fate her brother had planned for her, but once she had hoped to catch a viscount at the very least. Her voice still echoed in his ears. "Pemberley does not want for money or land. You must find yourself a titled lady to bring honor to the family name."

Then there was his aunt, Lady Catherine, who was determined that he marry her daughter. Darcy snorted at the thought of Lady Catherine's insistence that it had been his mother's wish for him to marry Anne de

Bourgh. His mother would not have thought her own niece good enough for her son and heir.

For all these years Darcy had been determined to choose a bride who would have pleased both his mother and his father, but he had yet to meet an aristocratic heiress he could tolerate for an evening, much less a lifetime, and here he was, about to completely defy his parents' wishes by proposing to a lady whose breeding was questionable and whose fortune was non-existent. The scandal of it might even hurt Georgiana's chances at a brilliant match. How could he do this, knowing he was failing in his duty to his entire family?

His decision to follow his heart and marry Elizabeth had been the hardest of his life, and even now he had his doubts. He was being a fool and he knew it, but for once in his life he was in the grip of a passion beyond his control. He could not help himself. At least that was his excuse, though he could just imagine his father's scorn and the curl of his mother's lip if he had ever dared to say such a thing to them.

For a moment he considered reining in his horse and returning to Rosings free of the encumbrance of a distasteful alliance, but the memory of Elizabeth's sparkling eyes and the way the corner of her lips twitched when she was amused spurred him on. He had to have her. There was nothing else to be done, at least not without dishonoring himself more than he already was by making this proposal. The wild young men at White's would have some very different ideas about how he should slake his lust, caring nothing for who might pay the price as long as their own desires were fulfilled, but that was not for him. It was such things that made Darcy prefer Bingley's company over that of his peers. Bingley had been foolish to fall in love with Jane Bennet, but at least he had never considered dishonoring her. It had been marriage or nothing for Bingley, and it was the same for Darcy. But how would Bingley feel when he discovered that Darcy was marrying the sister of that same woman he had insisted was not good enough for his friend? He was a hypocrite as well as failing his parents' wishes, but Elizabeth would be his.

The sucking sound of the hooves in deep mud gave way to the thud of horseshoes striking wooden planks as he crossed the bridge. The flood waters rushed loudly beneath him, the usually peaceful, meandering river now a raging torrent after the last month of pounding rain. Even in the darkness he was certain that the water must be over the banks by now. The wind was picking up again, starting to lash against his coat.

A flash of lightning split the night sky, causing his horse to shy. Darcy automatically quieted him as the rolling rumble of thunder seemed to make the very air tremble. His skin was tingling, a certain sign that another storm was in the offing. Yes, it was far better to think about floods and rain than to hear voices from the past railing at him.

By good fortune he reached the parsonage at the top of the hill just as the skies opened. Dismounting hurriedly, Darcy led his horse into the slight shelter of the eaves and tied his reins to the waiting ring. Silently he made his apologies to the horse who deserved better than the drenching he was about to receive. Under normal circumstances he would never treat one of his mounts in such a shabby manner, but tonight was not normal, and the shelter of a stable was a quarter mile further along.

He thanked his lucky stars that the front entryway was covered. Already a cold trickle had found its way down the back of his neck, sending a shiver down his spine. He rang the bell loudly, hoping someone would come quickly. No one would be expecting callers, and it would be hard to hear anything over the drumming of the rain and the rolling thunder.

The door was opened, not soon enough for Darcy's taste, by a timid, half-kempt maidservant holding a single candle. Clearly she had not expected her services to be needed tonight. He set his hat and gloves on a small table and brushed the remaining drops of rain from his coat. His valet would have fits were he to see his normally immaculate master in such disarray, but there was nothing to be done for it. He had a mission, and he meant to accomplish it. "I wish to see Miss Bennet," he told the girl in a clipped voice.

He did not notice her reply, his entire being concentrated on the knowledge that in just a few minutes, Elizabeth would be officially his, putting an end to his months of torment imagining a lifetime in which he would only see her in his night-time fantasies. Half in a daze, he strode past the girl into the sitting room where Elizabeth stood, a pile of letters on the small painted table beside her. She was noticeably pale and did not smile at the sight of him. Perhaps she was in truth unwell?

Suddenly nervous, although he did not know why, he made a correct bow. "Miss Bennet, your cousin informed me that you were too ill to join us at Rosings. May I hope that you are feeling better?"

"It was nothing but a slight headache." Her tone was decidedly cool.

He took his usual seat, trying to make sense of her serious

demeanor. Surely she must know why he was there? She should be delighted at his presence! Then it hit him. She must have been expecting his addresses these last several weeks, and his reticence had injured her sensibilities. It was only natural. What lady would not feel wounded when an eligible suitor seemed unable to make up his mind about her? In sudden generosity of spirit, he decided he must be completely open with her. He would tell her his dilemma and why he had delayed so long, and how his love for her had overcome all barriers. He would help her see that it was not a reflection on her charms or the depth of his feeling for her. On the contrary, the extent of his struggle showed the strength of his devotion. But how to begin? She seemed reluctant even to look at him.

His agitation of spirit could not be contained, so he left the chair to pace around the small room, searching for the words to express himself. He wanted nothing more than to pour his heart out at her feet, but first he must tend to the injury he had unwittingly inflicted upon her. What a fool he had been to wait so long to claim her as his intended!

He could not wait another minute. He approached her, coming as near as propriety would allow, and the words began tumbling forth. "In vain have I struggled. It will not do. My feelings will not be repressed. You must allow me to tell you how ardently I admire and love you."

What a relief it was to finally say the words! He had Elizabeth's complete attention now; she was almost staring at him, her cheeks becomingly flushed, apparently at a loss for words. Telling her was the right thing to do. With greater certainty, he continued, "I have admired you from almost the first moment we met, and it has been many months since I have known that my life would be incomplete without you in it. You may wonder why I have been silent until now, and question the strength of my devotion, but I can assure you it had nothing to do with the depth of my love. I had not known myself capable of a passion such as this. For the first time in my life, I have understood what it was that inspired the greatest poets to produce their masterpieces. Until I met you, I thought their words of love were but a form of artistic hyperbole, and I could not believe that any man would actually find himself so overcome with violent love. But in you I have discovered what it is to need another as I need the air to breathe."

He paused to collect his thoughts as thunder briefly drowned out his ability to speak. "Indeed, I should have made this offer to you long ago, had it not been for the disparity in our stations in life. My family has a long and distinguished history, with the expectation that I would marry a lady of rank and fortune, and you do not fall into either category. Your lack of dowry could perhaps be overlooked, but my parents would have been horrified at your low connections. Your father is a gentleman, although of a rank inferior to mine, but your mother's family must be seen as a degradation. I had no choice but to fight against my attraction to you with all the strength I could muster, my judgment warring with my inclination. I do not have the words to describe the battles I have fought with myself, but in the end, in spite of all my endeavors, I found it impossible to conquer my attachment to you. My sentiments have proved powerful enough to overcome all the expectations of family and friends. My devotion and ardent love have been fiercely tested and emerged triumphant. May I dare hope that my violent love for you will be rewarded by your acceptance of my hand in marriage?" He gazed into her bright eyes, awaiting her affirmative response.

Elizabeth, seeming at a loss for words, unfolded her hands, but at his eager look, she hastily refolded them. She inhaled deeply and said, "In such cases as this, it is, I believe, the established mode to express a sense of obligation for the sentiments avowed, however unequally they may be returned. It is natural that obligation should be felt, and if I could *feel* gratitude, I would..."

Loud pounding from the front of the house interrupted her words. Elizabeth's brows gathered as she looked over her shoulder towards the door of the parsonage.

A deep shout from without all but rattled the windows. "What ho, the house! For the love of God, let us in!"

Darcy frowned furiously in the direction of the racket. How dare anyone interrupt him at this tender moment and in such a manner? The voice betrayed low origins. Could there be footpads abroad on such a night as this? He could make out the sound of crying children now. Where was that maid? Just then a brilliant flash of lightning flooded the room with light, accompanied by an ear-splitting crack of thunder and a resounding crash. A child's scream pierced the night, and the pounding began anew.

Darcy strode to the window. Through the rain streaming down the window he could make out the shape of a fallen tree limb. The giant chestnut tree had been split down the middle, smoke rising from the ragged stump. A cluster of shapes huddled nearby.

Light footsteps behind him alerted him to Elizabeth's presence. She stood just behind him, her hands covering her mouth. The whiteness of her face stirred him into action. He gripped her arm lightly, even in the crisis marveling at his right to do so, "There is nothing to fear. Lightning struck the tree outside, but we are perfectly safe. I will deal with this."

He walked purposely toward the front door, discovering the maid cowering in the entryway. Frowning at her, he threw open the door to reveal a roughly dressed old man, soaked to the skin, with perhaps two dozen others, mostly women, behind him.

The man said, "Please, sir, the water's rising somethin' fierce! It carried off Smither's cottage and his wife and children with it, and half the village is knee deep in water. We never seen the like of it, never! You have to help us, sir!"

For a moment Darcy wondered irritably if they thought he had the power to stop the river, then he realized the parsonage and church occupied the highest ground on this bank. They had fled to the safest spot they knew.

A high keening reached his ear as a woman appeared, tugging at the man's arm. "It's Miller's Jenny. She's trapped under the tree, and we can't lift it!"

Darcy swore under his breath, then turned to the maid. "Take the women and children to the kitchen and build up the fire." He frowned at the pouring rain. There was no help for it; he would have to go out.

The fallen chestnut was no more than a score of steps away, but cold rain was already trickling down Darcy's neck when he reached it, following the sound of a child's wails. He could barely make out shapes pulling at the fallen tree trunk. It was large enough that he would not have been able to wrap his arms around it. One of the figures slipped on the wet grass and fell hard, swearing in the shifting tones of a boy whose voice was starting to turn. Darcy's vision was beginning to adjust. It was nothing more than the old man and two lads trying to shift a limb far beyond their weight. Darcy crouched down by the small child whose legs were trapped, examining the position of the fallen limb.

"We'll need a lever," he said decisively. "You, boy – run to the house and tell them we need a crowbar or something like it, whatever they have." He pointed to the other boy. "You must find some other branches, big ones. Where are the other men?"

"In t' village still, tryin' to save what they can," the old man said.

"Sent me with t' women, they did."

Darcy nodded, then turned to the little girl. "You must be very brave and listen carefully to what I say. We are going to find a way to move this, and when I give the word, you must pull yourself out from under it as quickly as may be. Do you understand?"

"Ye...Yes, sir," she whimpered. "Please, it hurts so much!"

"We'll have you out of there as soon as we can." And Elizabeth would be waiting for him, like the treasure at the end of a knight's quest. With a warm feeling inside despite the cold rain, Darcy pushed a lock of sodden hair out of his eyes, then broke a branch from the trunk and began wedging it under the fallen wood.

Elizabeth hurried upstairs to the closets so carefully arranged according to the direction of Lady Catherine de Bourgh. It was simple to find the blankets she was seeking, but there were not as many as she had hoped. She added the blanket from her own bed for good measure, then returned to the kitchen and began distributing them, encouraging the women with young children to wrap the blankets around them for warmth. The fire was as high as the maid had dared make it, but the soaked refugees still shivered.

An older women was standing alone, her chapped hands outstretched to the fire. Elizabeth approached her and said, "Can you tell me of the situation in the village?"

The woman shook her head. "You can't believe how high that water is, and the current strong enough to pull a man off his feet. There won't be much left by the time it goes down." Her voice trembled a little.

Elizabeth bit her lip. While Mr. Collins and his wife Charlotte were at Rosings Park, it was up to her to make arrangements for all these people. She had no idea what food stores were available or where they would sleep, but she could hardly send Mr. Collins's newly-homeless parishioners out into the storm with nowhere to go.

The kitchen door swung open to reveal Mr. Darcy, his dark curls sodden and dripping into his face, carrying a young girl in his arms. He called across the kitchen, "Miss Bennet, a word, if you please?"

She drew in a sharp breath. What was he still doing there? She had expected him to be long gone after she refused his startling offer of marriage. After that insulting proposal, she despised him more than ever, and as her rejected suitor, he must be furious with her. He had clearly expected her to accept him. What unlucky fate had forced them to be together, especially under these circumstances?

Still, she had no choice but to follow him into the hallway. The last thing she wanted to do was to meet his eyes, so instead she turned her gaze to the limp form in his arms. "Is she injured?" she asked.

"I believe her leg is broken. It is fortunate for her that she fainted when we tried to move her. What is the best place for her?" Mr. Darcy sounded remarkably calm under the circumstances. His tone carried none of the anger she had expected.

If he could be civil, she would as well. "Could you bring her upstairs? I will show you the way." The simplest thing would be to put the child in the room she shared with Maria, since the bed in the spare room was not made up.

He inclined his head. The gesture lost a great deal of its aristocratic air owing to the water dripping from his hair. Elizabeth barely controlled a smile as she fetched a candle from the sitting room and led him up the dark staircase to her room. She set the candle on the vanity and found a towel to spread across the bed.

The little girl moaned as Mr. Darcy set her on the bed, taking great care to move her as gently as possible. One of her legs was bent at an unnatural angle. Elizabeth tried to remove her shoe, but stopped as her action provoked another moan from the child. She only hoped the girl would remain unconscious long enough for her wet clothes to be removed.

Elizabeth dried her hands on a corner of the towel, then looked up to find Mr. Darcy's dark eyes fixed on her. She realized with a shock that, apart from the unconscious girl, she was alone in a dark bedroom with a man who claimed to be violently in love with her. To her utter astonishment, he smiled slightly.

"But you are quite wet, sir! Mr. Collins's rooms are just down the passage. I am sure he would not object to the use of some of his clothing. After all, he would be mortified if you were to take a chill while in his house," Elizabeth said, aware that she was babbling.

"An excellent idea," he said, but made no move to go.

"And I must find this child's mother. She will need comfort when she awakens." Elizabeth began backing out of the room, anxious to depart from his unnerving presence.

He picked up the candle and held it out to her. "Do not forget this. I would not want you to trip on the stairs."

His courtesy was unnerving, but she would not allow it to intimidate her. "I thank you, but I have been down the stairs many times, and you will need the light in Mr. Collins's room."

"I could not possibly..." Darcy paused, then his face lit up with a smile. "Perhaps a compromise is in order. I will see you downstairs with the candle; then, when you are safely ensconced there, I will return with it to Mr. Collins's room, if you will be so kind as to indicate where I might find it."

Was this a battle of wills to see who could show the most courtesy? "Very well, sir. An excellent idea."

He bowed and swept his free hand out, indicating the door. "Also, there would be no point to dry clothes before I find shelter for my horse. The shed in the garden – would it be large enough to accommodate him?"

Elizabeth nodded numbly. "Perhaps there will be a break in the rain soon and you will be able to return to Rosings." It could not happen soon enough for her.

He shook his head. "I cannot possibly leave you here alone under these circumstances. Besides, there will be no need for a break in the rain. No doubt Lady Catherine will order her carriage for Mr. and Mrs. Collins, and I will return in that conveyance."

"As you wish. Now, if you will excuse me, I must find out how many guests we must provide shelter for." Anything to give her an excuse to leave his company. She started down the stairs.

His voice continued from behind her. "However many there are here now, the number is likely to increase. Apparently some of them are still attempting to rescue their possessions, and they will most likely arrive later. I have already instructed the men outside to settle themselves in the church. Fortunately, it is not a cold night, so blankets and hot bricks should be enough to keep them warm until morning."

Trust Mr. Darcy to assume command of any situation, regardless of whether he had any rights in the matter! Elizabeth fumed, not least because she had not thought of that solution herself. She did not trust herself to answer him in a temperate manner, so she said nothing. She would not waste her energy on Mr. Darcy when there were so many others who needed her assistance.

Chapter 2

DARCY STRIPPED OUT of his soaking attire as quickly as possible, but he had to wrestle with his tightly fitted topcoat, which was snug enough that it usually required his valet to remove. Being saturated with water did not help matters. If only he could ask Elizabeth for her assistance – how he would enjoy having her remove his clothing!

His wet clothes made a puddle on the floor as he toweled himself dry as best he could. The friction of it warmed his cold skin a little, but not anywhere near as much as Elizabeth could just by looking at him.

Her recent behavior was puzzling, though. She had seemed almost skittish just now, unlike her usual self. Perhaps she was worried about failing to handle this crisis with the aplomb he would expect from the mistress of Pemberley. That was no doubt the cause; it was so like his sweet Elizabeth to be already taking her future role so seriously! He would have to make a point of telling her how well she was doing. Later, perhaps, he could give her some pointers on how she should have behaved. It was generous of her to attempt to help the villagers herself, but she should not have been in the kitchen as if she were one of them.

The clothes in Mr. Collins's wardrobe were dry, but that was the best that could be said for them. Some appeared freshly pressed – he supposed he could thank Mrs. Collins for that – but others were rumpled, and all were of coarse fabric he would never dream of wearing under normal circumstances. Although Mrs. Collins had no doubt done her best, his shirts were no longer the pristine white Darcy usually required. Making a face, he picked out the one with the least mending and shook it out. It was passable, he supposed, wrinkling his nose. Like the entire room, it was imbued with the stink of sweat that he associated with Mr. Collins.

He did not mind if Elizabeth wished to continue her friendship with

Mrs. Collins. Although her father was in trade, Mrs. Collins was a nicely-mannered woman and would not embarrass either of them, at least as long as she did not mention her family. Mr. Collins was another story. Darcy had no intention of having that fool at Pemberley even for a day. It was hard to believe that he was related to Elizabeth, not that most of her family were much better, of course. Fortunately, there would be little need for her family to interact with his, and Darcy supposed that for Elizabeth's sake he could somehow manage to tolerate the Bennets in brief doses.

He paused, his arm half-way into the shirtsleeve. Elizabeth was *his*, by God! Even wearing disgusting borrowed clothes and being forced to deal with the riff-raff from Hunsford could not diminish his sense of triumph that it was finally settled. No more second thoughts or doubts; it was done. And if he had anything to say about it – and he intended to say a great deal about it – they would be married as soon as the banns had been read. He would have liked to hear more of Elizabeth's reply to his proposal, but that was not the important thing. They were engaged. And he still planned to steal a kiss once he had everyone settled for the night. If Mr. and Mrs. Collins were not yet returned, it might be even more than a kiss. Now there was an idea to improve his mood! If he was very, very lucky, the roads would be completely impassable and he would be forced to spend the night at the parsonage.

He pulled the shirt over his head and looked in the mirror. Ill-fitting, of course, but the smile he could not repress made up for it.

Several hours later, some thirty villagers had been settled in the church. Elizabeth had rationed out the few available candles, while the cook took stock of their food supplies, muttering gloomily about having to feed such a crowd in the morning. In the parsonage, a few young children rested on blankets in front of the hearth in the larger sitting room, their mothers beside them. Mr. Collins would not be pleased by it, but Elizabeth had no intention of allowing the children to fall ill simply for his convenience. She had been unable to find the parents of the girl with the broken leg – apparently they were still in the village trying to salvage whatever they could - so Elizabeth had assisted two of the village women in splinting her leg, a nerve-racking experience since the girl screamed in agony whenever they touched it. Fortunately, an older woman offered to sit with the girl afterwards.

Elizabeth peered out the window of the small sitting room for the what seemed like the hundredth time, as if she would be able to make out anything in the ongoing deluge. The single candle, barely lighting the room at its best, flickered each time the wind rattled the windowpanes. It was past midnight, and Mr. and Mrs. Collins still had not returned. Would this day never end? It seemed like weeks since she had walked with Colonel Fitzwilliam in the garden, totally unaware that Mr. Darcy admired her. She leaned her forehead against the window frame.

She could never forgive the part he had played in separating Jane and Mr. Bingley, but in all fairness, he had handled her refusal remarkably well. She would not have thought him capable of even basic civility under these circumstances, but he had been polite and had shouldered responsibility for their unexpected guests.

As if the mere thought of him caused him to appear, she heard his footsteps behind her. She closed her eyes, silently willing him to go away. Instead, the footsteps continued to approach her, stopping only when he was so close behind her that she could practically feel the warmth radiating from his body.

"Miss Bennet, you must rest. It is very late, and there is nothing more you can do tonight," he said quietly.

She shook her head. "I will not be able to sleep until Mr. and Mrs. Collins are back safely."

"They will not return tonight. According to a villager who just arrived, the bridge is out. It is hardly a surprise; it was in need of maintenance, as I have told my aunt on several occasions. But you need not worry; the Collins' will stay the night at Rosings Park. In the morning, it may be possible for them to travel upstream to the next bridge."

Elizabeth sighed. "Then I had best make plans for breakfast, if Charlotte will not be here."

"You need not trouble yourself. I have spoken with the maid, who has recruited two of the village women to assist the cook in the kitchen in the morning. The fare will be simple, but no one will go hungry. All will be well."

She hated to admit it, but she was relieved that he had dealt with it, relieved enough that she did not immediately realize the source of the comforting warmth around her waist. But she could not miss the brush of lips against the side of her neck, especially since it created a riot of sensation far beyond the immediate stimulus. In a moment of weakness, she was half-tempted to lean back against the strong body behind her, but that very desire brought her to her senses.

She pulled his hands off her waist and slipped under his arm. Once she had reached the safety of several paces away, she whirled to face him. "How dare you, sir! I had just been noting that for once you seemed to be behaving like a gentleman, and now I discover it is nothing but an attempt to take advantage of my situation."

He had the gall to look puzzled. "I apologize for distressing you. You seemed in need of comfort, and under the circumstances I thought you would not object."

"Under the circumstances that I am stranded with you and have no other choice?"

"Under the circumstances that we are engaged to be married, Elizabeth. I know you are fatigued, and perhaps it would be better to speak of this in the morning."

"I am most certainly *not* engaged to you, and I have *not* given you permission to make free with my Christian name!"

He inhaled sharply. "I am sorry if I overstepped my bounds, but I cannot believe you wish to call off our engagement because of that."

She stared at him in astonishment. "There is no engagement! In case you were not paying attention earlier, I was in the process of *refusing* you when the villagers interrupted us!"

He paled, taking a step back. "That is nonsense. You were hoping for, no, *awaiting* my addresses. You have no reason to refuse me."

"No reason! Do you think that any consideration would tempt me to accept the man who has been the means of ruining, perhaps forever, the happiness of a most beloved sister? You dare not, you cannot deny that you have been the principal, if not the only means of dividing Mr. Bingley from her, of exposing one to the censure of the world for caprice and instability, the other to its derision for disappointed hopes, and involving them both in misery of the acutest kind."

She paused, and saw with no slight indignation that he was listening with an air which proved him wholly unmoved by any feeling of remorse. He even looked at her with a smile of affected incredulity.

"Can you deny that you have done it?" she repeated.

With assumed tranquility he then replied, "I have no wish of denying that I did everything in my power to separate my friend from your sister, or that I rejoice in my success. Towards *him* I have been kinder than towards myself."

Elizabeth disdained the appearance of noticing this civil reflection, but its meaning did not escape, nor was it likely to conciliate, her.

"But it is not merely this affair," she continued, "on which my dislike is founded. Long before it had taken place, my opinion of you was decided. Your character was unfolded in the recital which I received many months ago from Mr. Wickham. On this subject, what can you have to say? In what imaginary act of friendship can you here defend yourself?"

"You take an eager interest in that gentleman's concerns," said Darcy in a less tranquil tone, and with a heightened colour.

"Who that knows what his misfortunes have been, can help feeling an interest in him?"

"His misfortunes!" repeated Darcy contemptuously; "yes, his misfortunes have been great indeed."

"And of your infliction," cried Elizabeth with energy. "You have reduced him to his present state of poverty, comparative poverty. You have withheld the advantages, which you must know to have been designed for him. You have deprived the best years of his life, of that independence which was no less his due than his desert. You have done all this, and yet you can treat the mention of his misfortunes with contempt and ridicule!"

"And this," cried Darcy, as he walked with quick steps across the room, "is your opinion of me! This is the estimation in which you hold me! I thank you for explaining it so fully. My faults, according to this calculation, are heavy indeed! Perhaps someday you will do me the honor of telling me what manner of falsehood Wickham is spreading about me now, and for what reason you have chosen to believe whatever he said in the complete absence of proof!"

"I saw enough proof with my own eyes! Your manners, impressing me with the fullest belief of your arrogance, your conceit, and your selfish disdain of the feelings of others, were such as to form that groundwork of disapprobation before I ever met Mr. Wickham; and I had not known you a month before I felt that you were the last man in the world whom I could ever be prevailed on to marry."

"Now it is all clear! You disliked my pride, so clearly any manner of slander attached to my name must be true. I ask you again, what *proof* did he supply of his so-called *misfortunes*?"

"And I might ask you what proof you can offer that his claims are untrue!"

"None, in as much as I do not know what claims he made, but I can produce more than enough evidence of his deceitful nature. It is clear there is no point in doing so, however, since you clearly have already determined not to believe a word I say. Forgive me for having taken up so much of your time. I will hope for the good fortune of an end to this rain so that you need not tolerate my presence in the morning."

With these words he hastily left the room, and a moment later Elizabeth heard a door bang shut.

Covering her face with her hands, Elizabeth sank into the nearest chair, tears of anger and fatigue filling her eyes. What a disaster! She did not know which was worse, his ridiculous assumptions or her intemperate behavior. Even if he had misunderstood her earlier, she should have simply been firm with him about her refusal. There had been no call whatsoever for her to lose her temper with Mr. Darcy, but exhaustion and shock at his unseemly behavior had taken a toll of her composure. His forwardness had been disturbing, but was understandable enough given his misapprehension. Still, his abominable pridefulness surprised even her. That he should think she had been hoping for his addresses! And that she would agree to marry him, for no other reason than that he wished it! She would have found it comic if she had not been so very tired – and if she did not have to face him in the morning. And to think her opinion of him had been improving since he had been so helpful and polite to her once the refugees had arrived! It was only because he believed he had prevailed. Vexing man!

Somehow she must get some rest. Swaying slightly, she trudged up the stairs, but stopped short at the door of her bedroom. The girl Jenny lay in her bed, while the elderly woman who was watching her would likely be asleep in the bed Maria Lucas used. Elizabeth leaned her head against the doorframe, forcing herself to think. There was Charlotte's room, but that had a connecting door to Mr. Collins's bedroom where Mr. Darcy would spend the night. The mere thought was enough to banish sleepiness. No, the smallest bedroom, the one that had been used by Sir William Lucas prior to his departure, would be her best option, even if the bed was not ready.

At least the small room had been aired out already, the bare mattress resting on the bedframe. She considered hunting for linens, but she could not face the effort, nor the possibility that she might once again encounter Mr. Darcy. It did not matter; the counterpane sat folded on the windowseat, and she could simply wrap herself in it for the night.

She would have to sleep in her shift in any case, since her nightdress was in the other bedroom. Undoing the buttons on the back of her dress presented something of a challenge, but somehow she managed it. As the muslin slid down her body, her hands paused on her hips as she unexpectedly recalled the sensation of Mr. Darcy's hands around her waist. Her skin tingled oddly, a disturbing sensation which made her step out of the dress with less care than she might have otherwise. She tripped over the skirt in the darkness, and the sound of ripping fabric made her wince.

Elizabeth shook her head at her own clumsiness. It was just one more sign of this disastrous evening. Tossing the dress carelessly over a nearby chair, she took the counterpane and climbed onto bed, hoping for sleep to come instantly. It might even have done so had the memory of Mr. Darcy's lips on the sensitive skin of her neck not intervened. Her hand crept up to touch the spot, and she fell asleep with her fingers covering it.

Chapter 3

THE SUN WAS already high in the sky when Elizabeth awoke. The strange bed reminded her instantly of the events of the previous evening, and she burrowed her face under the pillow in hopes that it would somehow all go away if she just did not look at it. Unfortunately, life seldom cooperated in these matters, and now that she was awake, she could not understand how she had slept so late with children's shouts punctuating the clatter from the kitchen, not to mention the rain thrumming against the window.

She could not stay in bed with so much to be done. Apart from making certain that everything was in order before Charlotte and Mr. Collins returned, she should check on the injured girl. It made sense to do that first, since she would need to go to her room for fresh clothing and her hairbrush in any case. Yesterday's dress had a narrow rip running several inches up from the hem. Still, she had to wear something, so she slipped it back on, managing to fasten all the buttons except the one in the very middle of her back.

Fortunately, the passageway was empty, and the door to her usual bedroom at the opposite end stood wide open. Hoping to avoid notice while wearing her wrinkled and torn dress, she hurried in. To her dismay, the last man in the world she wished to see was sitting beside the little girl's bed, talking quietly to her.

Darcy's voice broke off in midsentence. With a chilly expression, he stood and bowed in greeting, but said not a word. Elizabeth mentally cringed as her belated curtsey served to reveal a full view of her ankle through the tear in her skirt, just as she realized that he was once again in *her bedroom*. The presence of one small injured girl could not change that fact.

To make it worse, that one small injured girl had tears running down her face, something Elizabeth could not ignore, even if it meant speaking to Mr. Darcy. Elizabeth crossed to the far side of the bed before laying a comforting hand on the girl's arm. "Does it hurt so very much?" she asked gently.

The girl's voice quavered in response. "It's terrible bad."

"I'm sorry to hear it. Is there anything I can do to help?"

The girl turned pained eyes to her. "Can you find my mama, Mrs. Darcy?"

Elizabeth turned a look of betrayal on Darcy, but before she could correct the girl, Darcy said, "Jenny wants her mama to sit with her, but her mother ran into the water after her brother, and she has not seen either once since then."

"The river was taking him away, so she had to catch him. We're not supposed to play in the water, but he just slipped," Jenny said, her calmness a certain indicator that she did not understand the implications.

"Jenny has been waiting for her ever since," Darcy said gravely.

Their eyes met in mutual acknowledgment that their own quarrel had no place in the presence of tragedy. Darcy said, "I was about to make inquires as to the whereabouts of her parents."

"That is kind of you, sir," Elizabeth said, meaning every word.

His lips thinned. Without a word, he left the room.

Elizabeth, feeling oddly as if she had been chastised, did her best to distract Jenny, asking the girl's opinion on which of her several dresses she should wear and requesting her assistance in putting her hair up. She did not care to think of how she would look, but Jenny seemed delighted with the opportunity, so she resigned herself to whatever lopsided hairstyle resulted from the experiment.

As she returned the favor by brushing and braiding Jenny's thin hair, the girl began to open up, telling her about her father's mill and the doll she had left behind in the flood. "I put her way up high in the rafters, so she'd be safe no matter how high the water came."

"That was very clever of you," said Elizabeth, hoping that Jenny's doll had in fact survived the flood. She was likely to need to comfort of her familiar toy soon.

Afterwards, Elizabeth realized she had never corrected Jenny's error about her relationship to Mr. Darcy. Well, what did it matter if a little girl she would never see after tomorrow thought they were married? It might be easier to allow her to believe that than to explain why they were both in the same bedroom.

When hunger finally sent Elizabeth downstairs in search of some sort of breakfast, she was relieved that Mr. Darcy was nowhere to be found. It looked like the rain had finally stopped, so with any luck, he might have taken his horse to wherever the next bridge might be and found his way back to Rosings Park. The kitchen was in chaos, with six women working in a space sufficient for no more than three. It was fortunate that Charlotte could not see what had become of her well-organized domain.

She helped herself to a bun, deciding that the prospect of a hot drink was hopeless. It was not worth the effort to try to make herself heard over the din. She sought out refuge in the dining room where she startled the maid who was carefully counting the silver.

"Oh, Miss Bennet, you made me jump! I thought I should see that everything is here, with all the comings and goings, and Mrs. Collins sure to be furious if anything goes missing. I'm thinking I should take the valuables upstairs where they'll be less in harm's way."

"A wise idea," said Elizabeth. She did not doubt that Mr. Collins's parishioners would be trustworthy under normal circumstances, but some of them had just lost all their possessions, and temptation might get the better of them. "I take it they cannot yet return to their homes?"

"Mr. Darcy says not, but he sent some of them to stay in the barn at Brown's farm over the hill. Old Tom Brown was happy to take them in, but he doesn't have anything to feed them, not this time of year. I don't know what we're going to do, miss, if this keeps on. We've already gone through most of the provisions here."

Elizabeth chewed a bite of the cold bun thoughtfully. "We will have to send someone to a nearby town to buy more food, then."

It was her turn to jump as a familiar deep voice came from behind her. "It has already been attempted, Miss Bennet, but without success. The road to the east has been washed out, and the men I sent to Tunbridge Wells returned empty-handed because the shopkeepers there would not extend them credit." He turned to the maid. "There is a manservant here, is there not?"

"Usually there is, sir, but John lives on the other side of the river."

"Pity. I will need you to press my clothing as soon as possible, then."

"Yes, sir." The maid scurried off to do his bidding.

Elizabeth turned slowly to face him. She had not noted his appearance earlier, but he certainly lacked his usual impeccable style. The coat he wore, made for the heavier Mr. Collins, hung off his shoulders, and his cravat was limp. She hardly thought that ironing his clothing was a matter of the highest priority in a situation such as this, but apparently it was to a man of such pride and vanity. "So you are returning to Rosings, then?" she said.

"No. Lady Catherine can be of no help to us here. It would take a day, if not more, to reach Rosings. I would have to ride most of the way to London to go around the floods. I am going to Tunbridge Wells. They will not refuse credit to Lady Catherine's nephew, but I will need to look the part if I am to convince them." He looked down ruefully at his rumpled appearance.

She quickly revised her opinion of his foolish vanity. "It will be a long trip for you if the rain begins again."

He shrugged, his lips thinning. "There is no other choice - for either of us," he said pointedly. "You will, of course, have to accompany me. I regret the necessity of exposing you to the elements." He did not have to add that he regretted exposing her to himself as well; it was clear in his expression.

"I have stayed here without Mr. and Mrs. Collins before, and there is no reason why I cannot do so again," she said sharply.

"It is not the absence of your cousins but the presence of so many strangers that is the difficulty. Regardless of what you may think of me, I cannot and will not leave you here unprotected, so either we both go to Tunbridge Wells or we both remain here while all these good people go hungry tonight. The choice is yours. I have asked for Mr. Collins's mare to be saddled for you."

She swallowed with difficulty. "I am not a horsewoman, sir."

"You *can* ride, I assume."

"A little. I have no particular skill in that regard. Could we not take the cart?"

"The cart is stuck axle deep in the mud less than a mile from here. Horseback seems our only option."

"Then I had best tend to my own appearance." Elizabeth touched her half-fallen hair. "I discovered this morning why four-year-old girls are never hired as lady's maids, but Jenny did enjoy playing the role." For a moment she thought he was starting to smile, but then it turned into a frown. "Were you able to discover anything about her parents?"

"Her father was last seen trying to free the mill-wheel. Her mother and brother were carried off in the flood. She has an aunt who is in service at Rosings and an older brother, thought to be twelve or thirteen years old, who is apprenticed to a miller near London. One of the women has agreed to take her in until her aunt can be contacted, but until she can be moved, it seems a moot point."

It was what she had expected, but Elizabeth felt a deep pang for the bright-eyed girl who would never see her parents again. She wondered who would tell her the sad truth.

Mr. Darcy tugged at the loose cuffs of the coat he wore, examining them as if they were of great interest. "In any case, we should leave soon if we are to have food here by nightfall. Can you be ready in half an hour?"

She hesitated, then said, "I do have one question. Why are you doing this? You have no responsibility for these people."

He gave her an incredulous look. "*Why* am I doing this?"

"Yes, why? You cannot possibly wish to ride to Tunbridge Wells in the rain, especially in my company, yet you insist upon it."

"It is my *duty*, madam." His voice was icy. "Did you think I would shirk it? No, please do not answer that. I would rather not know. Even your dear friend, George Wickham, will tell you that I *always* do my duty. It is a characteristic, I believe, that he holds in some scorn."

Elizabeth lifted her chin. "I did not mean to imply anything of the sort. I have never seen you show such interest in the welfare of those so far beneath you. That is all."

He seemed not to have heard her. "Of course, I have many habits he holds in scorn. I pay my debts. I speak the truth, even when I would rather not. I do not gamble more than I can afford to lose. I do not take advantage of young women with no one to protect them. I have no doubt that George Wickham would find an excuse to sit indoors and drink all your cousin's brandy rather than ride in the rain in search of food, but *I* will not. These people are my aunt's tenants, and in her absence, I am responsible for them – and for you. Whether I *like* it or not is irrelevant."

Elizabeth felt as if she had stepped off the edge of a precipice with no idea of what lay below. She had never seen Darcy – or anyone, for that matter – in such a cold rage. She would not have been surprised to see icicles forming around him, but she would not let him intimidate her, so she met his eyes steadily.

He had the grace to flush. "I will see you in half an hour, madam." He turned on his heel without even a proper bow and left the room.

Chapter 4

DARCY DISCOVERED QUICKLY that Elizabeth was not being modest when she described herself as a poor rider. Her back was ramrod straight, but given the death grip she had on the pommel of the sidesaddle, it was more likely out of fear rather than an attempt at proper posture. He had already instructed her twice to give the mare more slack on the reins, and again she was making the horse restive by pulling them too tight. If she continued to sit that way, she would be stiff and sore tomorrow. She would need to improve her seat when... he cut off the train of thought before it could begin. It was better not to even think of the future.

At least the rain had stopped for the moment. The road was in sorry shape, pitted with mudholes and covered in deep puddles whenever it dipped into the valley, but it was passable. No doubt it added to Elizabeth's anxiety, though. His own horse was sure-footed, but Darcy kept a close eye on the mare who had stumbled more than once.

He could not believe he had lost his temper with her yet again this morning. There had been a few hours last evening when he had thought they had a happy future ahead of them, and he had been shaken into fury that night when he discovered his error. As he lay sleepless in Mr. Collins's bed, he had resolved that in the morning he would calmly explain the truth about George Wickham to Elizabeth, and she would see reason. But when he finally had a moment to speak to her alone, it had taken only one ill-timed question from her to turn him into a raging beast again. His goals were more modest now. Maintaining a distant politeness seemed the best he could hope for.

It took over two hours to travel the five miles to the town, which they spent in silence apart from his occasional suggestions about her riding. He had taken his cue from her when she came downstairs ready to travel, but apparently quite unable to look in his direction or to say more than a bare minimum for the sake of civility. The pathetic thing was that it had *hurt* that she would avoid dealing with him. How much a fool could he be?

Once they reached the turnpike road at the top of the ridge, the last mile went quickly, and for the first time since leaving the parsonage, they seemed to have reached an area unaffected by the flooding. Coaches passed them going in both directions, and Darcy was acutely aware of the stares they were receiving from some of the passengers. Fortunately, Elizabeth seemed not to notice that she was the recipient of most of them, riding Mr. Collins's swaybacked mare beside his own thoroughbred hunter. He hoped no one would recognize him.

In town, Elizabeth finally seemed to take an interest in the surroundings, peering down lanes of workshops and houses. Darcy found the way to the provisions shop that the maid had recommended without difficulty. At least Elizabeth was willing to accept his help in dismounting; that was something, he supposed.

Darcy found Elizabeth looking over shelves hung with dried herbs. "We have a little time while they load the saddlebags. Would you care to stroll the Parade while we wait? There is a colonnaded walkway if the rain should start again."

To his surprise, she gave him one of her bewitchingly arch smiles. "That would be lovely."

What had changed her mood? Raising an eyebrow, he gestured toward the door. He decided it would be wisest not to offer her his arm, given the likelihood that she might refuse it. "It is just around the corner."

She cocked her head. "Well, sir, you have convinced me of one thing."

"What is that?" He hoped she was teasing, whatever it was.

"You are not in the habit of asking for credit."

"Was it so obvious?"

She paused, her eyes sparkling even if her face was solemn. "Three repetitions of the name of Lady Catherine de Bourgh would likely have been sufficient to establish your credentials, but no doubt a dozen were even more effective."

He bowed slightly. "I shall keep that in mind if the occasion should ever arise again."

They entered into the Parade. Elizabeth, unlike most ladies of his acquaintance, seemed to take more interest in the elegant architecture than the shop windows filled with Tunbridgeware and other luxury goods. She seemed oblivious to the fashionably dressed ladies and gentlemen enjoying the promenade.

She said, "One would not even know that people have lost their homes to the flood, yet we are only a few miles from Hunsford."

"The town caters to those who wish to take the waters and to partake of polite society. They would not wish any ugliness to enter here."

She gave him a surprised look, then seemed caught by something in a shop window. "Would you mind if I looked in this shop?"

"Not at all," he said automatically. It was a stationer's shop, and he wondered what interested her there. He held the door open for her. Not wishing to hover, he pretended interest in a display of inlaid wooden boxes while Elizabeth spoke to a clerk and pointed to a section of toys. She rejoined him a few minutes later carrying a wrapped package.

"For Jenny?" he asked.

She nodded. "She was telling me about her doll that had to be left behind. She put it in the rafters of her house and hasn't seen it since. I thought she would need something to hug." Her voice caught slightly on the last word.

Darcy was seized by a lunatic urge to grab her hands and beg her to marry him. He was saved by a clap of thunder that made them both turn immediately toward the window. A few raindrops splattered on the glass, and then started to beat a fierce tattoo against the paving stones.

Elizabeth sighed deeply. "Our good travel weather appears to be at an end."

Darcy looked at the pelisse Elizabeth was wearing, then out at the downpour. "It would be best if you stayed here while I see if the horses are ready."

"It hardly matters. I will be soaked sooner or later in any case."

"Perhaps the rain will stop by then." It was not a lie, at least not technically. Anything was possible in this weather.

She gave him a limpid look of disbelief. "Perhaps so."

⌘

Elizabeth crossed her arms and glared at Mr. Darcy. "No. Absolutely not."

"This is a matter of simple practicality, not a gift. I do not wish you to become ill from exposure to the rain." He held out the woolen cloak to

30

her once more.

"Indeed it is not a gift, for I will not accept it."

"Miss Bennet, it is as much for my sake as yours. If you refuse to take it, I will have to insist that you wear my greatcoat to stay dry, and then I will be soaked. Now, will you wear it, or shall we stand here and argue until it becomes too late to travel back to the parsonage? If you think accepting a cloak from me could be a problem, how will you explain spending a night here with me?"

Had he truly said that? Of course, he *wanted* to marry her, so he would not care if they were forced to marry because they had been stranded for the night together. She snatched the heavy woolen cloak from him and wrapped it around her shoulders, tucking the package for Jenny underneath it.

"Thank you," said Darcy tiredly. He reached out and raised the hood, settling it over her bonneted head with more gentleness than she had expected, his hands lingering for a moment near her temples. "Shall we go?"

Once out from under the protection of the colonnade, Elizabeth was grateful for the heavy cloak, although she would have preferred to suffer endless torments rather than to say so. She tried to be gracious about accepting Darcy's help in mounting the mare, and was glad he was there to steady her when the wet leather of the sidesaddle proved to be slippery.

She found the riding to be treacherous even on the turnpike road. The mare, who had cooperated well enough on the ride there, disliked the pounding rain and now had to be coaxed every step of the way. Once they had turned off onto the dirt road to Hunsford, it became even worse as the mare struggled to keep her footing in the mud and shied from every low hanging branch. Elizabeth could barely keep her seat. Once she only managed to stay on by grabbing onto the edge of the heavy saddlebags, and her heart pounded with fear of falling. Beside her, Darcy seemed to be having no difficulty, which only made her feel worse.

After half an hour, during which time they seemed to make little progress, Elizabeth began to wish they had stayed in town, even if it meant having to marry Mr. Darcy. Despite her best efforts, the cold rain had found its way inside the cloak and ran down her neck, and she felt thoroughly miserable. Even worse, the light was starting to fade. But there was nothing to do now but to go forward.

She was conscious of Darcy casting concerned glances in her

direction, and once or twice he asked her if all was well. Somehow she managed to answer in the affirmative. Then, as they crossed through a large patch of mud and puddles, the mare caught her foot in a hidden hole and lurched to a stop.

Elizabeth could tolerate it no longer. She slid down the side of the horse, miraculously landing on her feet in mud that immediately covered her half-boots.

Instantly, Darcy dismounted and was by her side, water pouring off the capes of his greatcoat. "Are you hurt?"

She shook her head. "I cannot do this. I will walk the rest of the way." She knew even as she said it that between the condition of the road and the late hour it was impossible.

Darcy was silent for a moment, then he disentangled the mare's reins and tied them in a knot. "My horse is more surefooted and can keep a better pace. You can ride before me."

"What about her?" Elizabeth gestured to the mare.

"She will most likely follow us back to her stable, and if not, someone can be sent for her later. She is hardly likely to run off in these conditions." He turned to his horse, easily two hands higher than anything Elizabeth had ever ridden, and made adjustments to the saddle. "Come."

He lifted her to the saddle as if she weighed nothing, despite the sodden cloak. She grabbed the slippery leather, but the horse stood perfectly still, even when Darcy mounted behind her, as gracefully as if he did the maneuver every day. She did not dare breathe as she felt Darcy's hands on her waist, shifting her position slightly forward, then pressing her legs between his knee and the horse's shoulders. She could feel the shape of his other thigh behind her.

"There. Are you comfortable enough?" His voice sounded rougher than usual.

"Are you certain this is safe?" She did not want him to know how much the closeness of his body to hers disturbed her.

"I have done this often with my sister when she was younger. She used to love to ride with me, even after she learned to ride on her own." His arm came around her from behind, circling her waist and holding her firmly against him. "I have you, and you cannot fall. Stormwind is the most sure-footed horse you will ever meet."

Without warning, he nudged the horse into a brisk walk. Elizabeth stifled a gasp, unable to keep herself from clutching his shoulder. He said nothing, but his face beneath his hat rim was stern, so she forced herself to release her hold on him.

"Relax, Elizabeth. Sit back and let Stormwind do all the work." His warm breath brushed her ear.

How could she possibly relax? Not only was she atop a very tall horse, but Mr. Darcy was effectively embracing her. She tried closing her eyes so that she would not have to see the distance to the ground, but that only increased her awareness that the entire side of her body was pressed against him. It sent chills down her spine, just as it had when his lips had played along the back of her neck. She tried to pull herself upright and further away from him, but that did not help either.

"You may find it easier if you lean against me. That is what my sister did."

What did it matter, anyway? Her position could not be any more improper than it already was. She tried following his advice, and it did make her feel more secure, even if the pounding of her heart threatened to drown out the rain. "I am sorry. I am not usually so *Miss-ish*." She felt pleased that her voice sounded so even.

"No, you are not," he agreed. "I am sorry to have put you through all this trouble. I know you thought it unnecessary, and I should have told you then that I was not merely being arbitrary. I have been assisting my aunt's steward in dealing with some lawless behavior on the part of a few of the men from Hunsford village. I could not have left you there safely."

"I see." That was some consolation, especially since their little junket had turned out to be even more compromising than staying alone would have been. She should be grateful that the rain kept everyone indoors so there was no one to see them now. She closed her eyes again, this time appreciating the feeling of security in being held so carefully.

They rode in silence for several minutes, then Darcy said, "Elizabeth, what did Wickham accuse me of doing?"

She tensed, but realized he sounded more tired than annoyed. "He said that your father left him a living in his will, and that you did not honor the bequest." At the moment, the story did not sound as sensible as it had in Meryton. After all, a will could not be ignored, could it?

His chest moved in a sigh. "That again. I suppose he did not tell you the part where he informed me that he had resolved never to take orders and requested some sort of pecuniary advantage in lieu of the preferment. Nor, I imagine, did he tell you that I gave him three thousand pounds, in exchange for which he resigned all claim to assistance in the church."

Elizabeth bit her lip. "He said he asked you for the living and that you refused to give it to him."

"That is true as well, but it happened some three years later, after he had dissipated away the earlier sum I had given him. He said then that he was absolutely resolved on being ordained if I would present him the living in question, of which he trusted there could be little doubt. As he told you, I refused to comply with his request, for reasons which I hope you understand."

His explanation threw Elizabeth's mind into turmoil. It fit with Mr. Wickham's story in all but the one crucial detail. In truth, she knew nothing of Mr. Wickham's past but what he had told her himself; she had never heard of him before his entrance into the militia. There was no particular instance of goodness on his part that she could recall, only that he had enjoyed the approbation of the neighborhood based on his countenance, voice and manner. He had not told his story to anyone but her until after Mr. Darcy left the area, when it became generally known. Could she have been so very wrong? The idea made her feel ill.

When she did not reply, Darcy spoke again, this time with seeming reluctance. "Unfortunately, that was not the last of our dealings. My sister, who is more than ten years my junior, was taken from school last summer and given into the care of a Mrs. Younge, in whose character we were unfortunately quite deceived. She had a prior acquaintance with Wickham, and with her connivance, he was able to recommend himself to Georgiana. She recalled his kindness to her as a child, and was persuaded to believe herself in love with him, and to consent to an elopement. She was then but fifteen, and unable to imagine that Wickham's chief object was her fortune of thirty thousand pounds. No doubt he also hoped to revenge himself on me. Had I not discovered their plans by happy accident, his revenge would have been complete indeed."

Elizabeth could not help gasping. It was so completely unexpected and horrible, but she could not conceive of Mr. Darcy making up such a tale about his own sister.

"I do not imagine my word is worth a great deal to you, but for the truth of this I can appeal to the testimony of Colonel Fitzwilliam, who can verify every detail. I will ask him to make himself available to answer any questions you may have." Darcy's voice was now toneless.

Attempting to muster her scattered thoughts, she said in a shaky voice, "I... that will not be necessary." She no longer doubted his version. He had no reason to lie, and every reason to hide the truth.

Even through her cloak and the heavy greatcoat he wore, she could feel the tension leave his body. "Thank you," he said quietly.

Elizabeth sank into a miserable silence, remembering Wickham's sudden change of allegiance when Mary King had come into her inheritance, his flippant behavior with Kitty and Lydia, encouraging them to run wild, and the impropriety of confessing his secrets to her on their first meeting. Flattered by his attentions to herself, she had been willfully blind to it all and had fallen into the snare of his lies as if she had no more wit than Lydia. She had blithely dismissed Mr. Bingley's assurances that there was another side of the story, as if her slight knowledge of the principals were more valuable than his years of friendship with Mr. Darcy.

To crown it all, she had not even had the sense to keep her thoughts to herself – no, she had to make a fool of herself with wild accusations to Mr. Darcy's face. After all he had suffered at Wickham's hands, she had compounded the injury, and even enjoyed the knowledge that his tender feelings for her would make him that much more vulnerable to her words. The recognition of her vanity, her lack of insight, and even her cruelty pierced her deeply.

All that time she had thought herself so clever and perceptive! If only she could hide herself away from the world, and most especially from the one man who had the most reason to resent her – the one who at this very moment was sheltering her in his arms. At least he would never know that tears of humiliation were running down her face; it would just look like that much more rain.

She did not even realize the horse had stopped moving until Darcy said gently, "Elizabeth, we are here." He swung himself down, somehow managing to keep a steadying hand on her arm. He lifted her down from the saddle, his hands lingering on her waist as she stood in the narrow space between his body and the horse's flank, but her mortification was such that she could not bring herself to look into his face.

He led her inside as if she were a child. She stopped on the doorstep to wring out excess water from her cloak, and found she was still clutching the sodden package from the toy shop. The ink on the package had bled on her hands.

"You should warm yourself at the fire," Darcy said. "I will return shortly."

Numbly, she watched after him as he disappeared into the rain. It was only then that she realized he had addressed her by her Christian name.

Chapter 5

ELIZABETH WAS ENORMOUSLY relieved to be out of her wet clothes and into a dry dressing gown. Even with a bonnet and the hood, her hair was soaked. Wringing as much water out of it as she could, she plaited it, then scrubbed her hands. The thin paper wrapping of the parcel had almost dissolved off, leaving traces of ink residue on her fingers. The carved dog had to be dried with a towel, its painted areas carefully blotted.

She took her wet garments into her old bedroom, suspecting correctly that there would be a fire in the hearth in front of which she could hang them to dry. Upon discovering that little Jenny was sitting on the floor beside her bed, her broken leg extended in front of her and her face scrunched with pain, Elizabeth dropped the clothes heedlessly and hurried to the girl's side.

"What happened? Did you fall out of bed?" She brushed back a lock of the girl's hair, exposing a tear-stained cheek.

"No, miss," Jenny whispered. "I needed the chamberpot, and I didn't know it would hurt so much."

"There was supposed to be someone here with you."

"She had to leave. There's so much work to do now, and she couldn't just sit with me all day."

Elizabeth decided she would be having words with the woman who had left Jenny alone and helpless. Better yet, she would let Mr. Darcy do it. "Come, let me help you into bed."

It took the better part of an hour before Jenny was settled in a clean shift with some degree of comfort. Elizabeth felt exhausted by the day's exertions, but the girl was restless, though each movement caused her pain.

Elizabeth said, "You must be bored after sitting there in bed all day. Would you like me to draw a picture of you?"

Jenny's eyes brightened. "Oh, yes, Mrs. Darcy! No one has ever drawn me."

Wincing at the appellation, Elizabeth said, "Then this shall be the first." Fetching the box of drawing supplies she had seen in Charlotte's room, she laid out a piece of paper. She had no great talent for drawing, one more of the many ways in which she would never meet Mr. Darcy's definition of a truly accomplished lady, but could usually manage a recognizable likeness. If it kept Jenny entertained, that was all she could ask.

Darcy struggled with the straps of the saddlebags. Rain dripped from the brim of his hat, and his wet gloves made little headway on the tight buckles. With an angry hiss, he pulled off his right glove and stuffed it in his pocket, then returned to the slippery straps.

His horse whinnied impatiently. Darcy said through his teeth, "I am in total agreement with you." He would rather have been almost anywhere else, but the only refuge that beckoned was more dangerous to him that floods or thunderstorms. If he went into the parsonage now, he would not be answerable for his actions, not after holding Elizabeth's sweet shape so intimately against his body for the last half hour. He gave a furious yank at the strap, and the buckle gave at last, pinching his forefinger hard enough to make him grit his teeth.

At least she seemed to believe him about Wickham, and he had manfully pretended to be unaware of her silent shaking that betokened muffled sobs. He had not taken the least advantage of his position, even when she had finally rested back against him. And still, when they arrived, she would not meet his eyes and could not leave his company quickly enough. What more did she want from him?

Thank God he had insisted on purchasing that cloak for her. It had not kept her dry, but from the quick glimpse of her wet dress when she removed the cloak, it was probably all that had preserved his sanity. If he had held her across his saddle in nothing but a clinging, near transparent dress that hid little of what was beneath it, he doubted he could have been held accountable for his actions. Even imagining it made his blood run hot.

Fortunately for his throbbing finger, the second strap did not prove as stubborn as the first. With an effort, he hefted the heavy set of saddlebags over his shoulder. Had the shopkeeper put lead bricks in with the barley? His boots sank deep in the mud as he carried it to the parsonage, shoving the kitchen door open with his free shoulder. His muddy boots squelched on the stone floor.

The cook, a stout woman of middle years with a permanent frown etched on her face, turned on him. "Track mud into my kitchen, will you, then?"

Darcy ignored her and dropped the dripping saddlebags on the broad work table with a loud thump. "Barley, dried peas, flour, parsnips," he said curtly.

"No doubt ruined," she muttered. "Useless."

Under normal circumstances, Darcy would have leveled a disdainful stare at such insolence and then given orders for the offender to be dismissed without a character. Disrespect was not tolerated among the staff at Pemberley toward anyone, much less the master, and it was beneath his dignity to argue with servants. It was the cook's ill fortune that on this particular day at this particular moment Darcy was more than ready to take out his anger on any available target.

"You will keep a civil tongue in my presence," he snapped. "If the food I have been served in this house is representative of your skill, then it is remarkable that you have been kept on at all, and you may be certain Mr. Collins will be hearing from me about it."

"*He* likes my cooking well enough."

"While the paucity of dishes laid out at supper last night might have been excused given the unusual circumstances, the food itself was indefensible - the roast burnt, the ragout watery, the cakes lumpy, and the pudding indigestible. The tea barely deserved the name. It is astonishing if no one has yet broken a tooth on one of your rolls. I would expect better of a scullery maid."

"I'll have you know that Lady Catherine de Bourgh herself recommended me!"

"Then I will make a point to tell my *aunt*, Lady Catherine, of my opinion as well. And if I am forced to eat one more tasteless dish in this house, you will be relieved of your position, and that woman -" he pointed in the direction of a village woman turning a haunch of meat by the hearth "- will take your place and your wages. And I am certain *she* would have no difficulty producing palatable food from what I have brought."

He stormed out, uncaring of the incessant rain. What was wrong with him? He had never spoken to a servant in that manner in his life. But the answer was clear enough. Elizabeth Bennet was what was wrong with him, Elizabeth and this impossible situation in which they found themselves. He should have sent her straight to London on the stage from Tunbridge Wells no matter how scandalous it would have been for her to travel on her own. He *would* have done so if it were not for the dangers she might encounter arriving unexpectedly. If only he could have squared it with his conscience to abandon the destitute villagers, he could have taken her there himself, but responsibility for his tenants – and by extension, his aunt's tenants – had been bred into him since he was a boy.

No, there was no way out… for either of them.

Elizabeth had finally tiptoed out of the bedroom after Jenny fell into an exhausted sleep. If she had remained, she might have joined the girl in slumber, even in the uncomfortable hard-backed chair. Instead, she went downstairs to the sitting room. Sally, discovering her there, put another log on the fire and timidly asked if the young miss if she should set the table for dinner.

Elizabeth was in fact quite hungry, but the prospect of a meal sitting across the table from Mr. Darcy was discomfiting. "Where is Mr. Darcy?"

"I don't know, Miss. He went out somewhere on his horse."

Perhaps she was in luck. "In that case, it would be lovely if you could bring me something warm to eat in here. Mr. Darcy will no doubt wish for something on his return."

Sally bobbed a curtsey and left. Elizabeth moved her chair closer to the hearth where the flames were now engulfing the new log, filling the room with a welcome warmth. She unplaited her still-wet hair and spread it out to dry. It had been an exhausting day in more ways than one, between embarrassing herself with her clumsy riding, the surprisingly civil time in town with Mr. Darcy, then being drenched and forced to ride so close to Mr. Darcy that she could feel the warmth of his body pressed against her own. Her stomach clenched at the thought. She pressed her fingertips to her temples, recalling his words about Mr. Wickham. How could she have misjudged so badly? She wished she could go to sleep and not wake up until Charlotte and Mr. Collins returned, whenever that might be.

The maid returned carrying a tray which she set on the small table by Elizabeth. "Soup, miss, and some hot tea."

"Perfect," said Elizabeth. "Tell me, has there been any word about whether the river has started to go down?"

Sally gave her a slightly peculiar look. "They thought it had, but then with the storm this afternoon, it's worse than it was before. It'll be days before it settles, Cook says."

Elizabeth dismissed her, then turned her attention to the soup. For once, she was looking forward to it, though the food at the parsonage was always of indifferent quality except when Charlotte prepared a dish with her own hands. Her lips twitched at the irony. The one thing she had regretted about missing dinner at Rosings yesterday was the chance to enjoy a decent meal.

She decided that hunger must indeed make the best sauce, since the soup seemed so tasty that she finished the entire bowl and wished she had more. The bread for once was tender and crusty rather than rock hard. Even the tea tasted like, well, tea, but that was a major improvement over the flavor of tar that usually accompanied tea at the parsonage. She smiled contentedly, running her fingers through her hair to separate the locks that still clung together.

⌒∞⌒

Darcy made a point of exhausting himself before returning to the parsonage. He found the straying mare, then checked on the villagers staying in the barn, talking to each one about the state of their particular cottage. By the time he decided that there was no more to do, he doubted that even Miss Elizabeth Bennet could draw a reaction from him.

Doubtless she was already abed. He entered quietly, but Sally was there to take his coat and hat. He accepted a candle from her to light his way to Mr. Collins's room where he had the luxury to strip off his clammy clothes in favor of a housecoat that barely reached his wrists. Still, it was dry, and that was all he could ask at the moment. A glass of brandy would not come amiss, either. The bottle he had found the day before in Mr. Collins's study barely deserved the name, but it was better than nothing.

He was almost to the study when he noticed a light in the sitting room. Was Elizabeth still awake after all? Could she possibly have been waiting for him? He paused a moment before presenting himself at the open door. The sight before him took his breath away.

She was fast asleep in the wingback chair by the fire, legs tucked beneath her and her dark curls loose. Her slippers were neatly lined up under the chair. The dying firelight flickered across her features and lent luster to her hair.

How could she look so innocent and yet so seductive at the same time? He drank in the sight of her. It was the first time all day he had felt able just to look at her, which had long been one of his greatest delights. She stirred in her slumber, half-smiling as if at something in a dream. If only he had the right to wake this sleeping princess with a kiss - but he did not, at least not yet.

He was sorely tempted to sit in the chair across from her and simply watch her sleep, letting his imagination go where his lips did not dare, but it was not right to take advantage of her vulnerability for his own pleasure. But he also could not leave her there where anyone could walk in and find her unable to defend herself. He would have to wake her so that she could go up to bed.

"Miss Bennet," he said softly, and then repeated her name a little louder. There was no response, so he drew closer to her chair. It would always be *her* chair in his mind now, somehow imbued with her essence. "I am sorry to disturb you, Miss Elizabeth, but you cannot remain here. You must go upstairs to bed." In his mind, he added, *preferably with me.* Just being in her presence had restored his sense of humor - and a few other senses as well.

She was obviously sound asleep. If she was half as tired as he, it was no surprise. He placed his hand on her shoulder, careful to touch only where the fabric of her sleeve covered it, despite the tempting expanse of warm skin just an inch away. He gave her arm a little shake, but though the corner of her mouth twitched, she did not open her eyes.

What now? He could not leave her and he could not stay. He could, of course, fetch Sally to stay with her, but he wanted to keep this moment private. No, what he *wanted* to do was to carry her up to her bed so that he could hold her sleeping form close to him for those few minutes. That, of course, was a good reason why he should not do so.

His gaze began to travel slowly down her body illuminated in the flickering firelight, from light to shadow, from draped fabric to tender skin, from her slender neck, past her gently rounded shoulders to the curves that he longed to cradle in his hands... no, this would *not* do. He had somehow managed to act the part of a gentleman with her all day despite extreme provocation. It would not be the end of the world for him to carry her upstairs, and it just might save him from worse, especially if his imagination kept going as it was.

Before he could talk himself out of it, he returned upstairs to place the candle in her room and turn down the covers of her bed, firmly not thinking of how she would sleep between those very sheets. No, he was *not* going to think of that, not at all. It was merely a bed like any other, a piece of furniture covered with a mattress and a few linens, not a shrine to the goddess he could not help worshipping. But those fortunate sheets were allowed to touch her all night long; how could he not be just a little envious, when he would give almost anything just to have her sleep in his arms? Not that it would stop with sleeping, but....Angrily he shook his head. He must *stop* this nonsensical thinking.

He returned to the sitting room, half fearing that she might have awakened while he was gone, but she had not moved. He drew near, then paused. Good God, was he actually *savoring* the moment of anticipation? He was further gone than he had thought. But savoring the moment could hardly injure her, and it was certainly giving him a great deal of pleasure.

He bent down, close enough to hear her even breathing, and slid one arm behind her shoulders. It was trickier finding a route for his other hand with her legs folded in the chair, and he kept a close eye on her face, ready to stop in an instant if she awoke. It also kept him from thinking about where his hand was, at least mostly. After all, he was supposed to be helping her, not enjoying her body. It was just that it was *such* an enjoyable body that it was hard not to notice it.

She made a little sound as he straightened, but settled into his arms like a dream. She fit there like a dream, too. Her natural warmth was augmented by her time in front of the fire. His arm was ensconced between her shoulders and the curtain of her hair which shifted with every step he took, showering him with the scent of honeysuckle and roses. Her chest moved with each sighing breath, and her head was a pleasurable weight on his shoulder. She was his Elizabeth, and that was all there was to it. Why could she not see it?

He started up the stairs, taking each step slowly to avoid jostling his precious burden, not that she seemed in any danger of waking. It was worse than that – she was shifting in her sleep, nestling ever closer to him, just as he had dreamed of her doing. His eyes widened slightly as he realized exactly which portions of her anatomy she was pressing against him as she nuzzled into his shoulder. What in heaven's name had made him decide to wear a thick housecoat rather than just his shirtsleeves? He would be able to glory in her every movement then, but no, he had decided to be proper. Sometimes propriety was distinctly overrated.

Propriety was also distinctly hard to recall when his every instinct was telling him to explore her face with his lips, committing the feeling of it to memory before moving on to meet her own. He could barely think why that was such a bad idea, but he was quite sure he had been resolved on it. It was torture to do no more than to hold her in his arms, and yet he hoped it would never end.

All too soon he reached her room, dimly lit by the one candle. Good Lord, he was alone with Elizabeth in her bedroom, and she was nestled close to him – and he was supposed to put her down and walk away. He was going to be a candidate for sainthood by the time this was over. Crossing to the side of the bed, he lowered her gently until her back rested on the sheet, then slowly and reluctantly began to pull his arms out from beneath her.

He was almost free – what a terrible word that was, free, when applied to something so distasteful as separating himself from Elizabeth – when she stirred. Holding his breath, he watched as her eyes fluttered open for the merest second, then closed again. She shifted onto her side, facing toward him, and clasped his hand so that it was trapped between her cheek and the pillow. With a sound of contentment, she rubbed her face against his hand as she drifted back into a deep sleep.

Only his arm that had supported her legs was now free. What in God's name was he supposed to do now? Did gentlemanly behavior really demand that he pull his hand from her grasp by force when the incredible silkiness of her cheek rested warmly against it? He had not sought out the position; she had definitely taken his hand, albeit without knowing to whom it belonged. Or perhaps on some level she *did* know, in some part of her that had never believed in George Wickham's lies, that knew she belonged with *him*.

But he could not stand there bending over her forever, so he lowered himself until he sat on the floor beside her bed, his hand still in hers. God help him, but he did not have the strength to pull himself free, not when it felt so unutterably right. He should not be watching her, though – she would not have given him permission to do that – so he closed his eyes against the temptation, resting his head against the side of the mattress, his entire being concentrated into that small part of him she held so close.

Chapter 6

ELIZABETH'S DREAMWORLD HAD taken her to the Netherfield ball, which for some reason was being held in the oversized dining room of Rosings Park, where a troupe of acrobats were performing. She was dancing with Mr. Darcy, but not in a country dance. Instead, she was in his arms for that scandalous London dance, the waltz. They whirled around the dining room, miraculously now empty except for an acrobat performing impossible feats of tumbling on a tightrope strung between the chandeliers. Somehow the acrobat transformed into a young child who fell from the tightrope, her body flipping in slow uncontrolled circles as she screamed and screamed....

Startled out of sleep, Elizabeth sat up abruptly in bed, her heart pounding. A child *was* screaming, "No! No! No!" And was that really Mr. Darcy's back disappearing through the door of her room? No, she must have dreamed that part.

She threw off the counterpane and stood, reaching for a dressing gown that was not there. Of course it wasn't; she was still wearing her dress. Her mind must still be fuzzy from the dream, she decided as she hurried into the passageway toward the source of the screams.

Jenny's bedroom was only faintly illuminated by moonlight through the window. It was a moment before Elizabeth realized that Mr. Darcy was kneeling beside her bed, trying to speak to the girl. Jenny's fists were in her mouth, but somehow not muffling her shrieks. She was staring at the woman in the other bed as if she were a creature out of nightmare.

Remembering the night terrors Lydia had suffered at a similar age, Elizabeth sat beside Jenny and gathered her into her arms. "Hush, Jenny. It was just a bad dream. It is over now. I won't let anything happen to you. I am here and Mr. Darcy is here to keep you safe." She continued in the same vein with soothing repetitions until Jenny's screams subsided into sobs. She met Darcy's eyes over the girl's head.

He motioned to the woman. "Fetch us a light."

Once she was gone, Jenny seemed a little calmer. Elizabeth pushed the girl's hair behind her ears. "See? Everything is well, and you are safe in bed."

Tears still running down her face, Jenny said, "Is it true, what she said?"

With some foreboding, Elizabeth said, "I don't know. What *did* she say?"

"That my mama is... isn't coming back."

Elizabeth closed her eyes in sympathy with the girl's pain. "No one can tell that for sure. It has been a whole day since anyone saw her. Could she swim?"

Jenny buried her head in Elizabeth's shoulder. "N..No, but maybe she got to the other side somehow and can't get back to us here."

On the other side of the bed, Darcy was shaking his head. Elizabeth, surprisingly conscious of Darcy's eyes on her, said, "I suppose it is possible."

"She can't be gone. She just can't." Jenny's sobs began anew. "That means they'd all be gone, wouldn't it?"

Having no consolation to offer, Elizabeth just stroked her hair. How terrible it must be for her to hear the news so unexpectedly in the middle of the night! She spared several uncharitable thoughts for the woman who was supposed to be taking care of her.

As if on cue, the woman returned, her hand cupped around the flame of a candle which she used to light the lamp by the bed. It provided little illumination in normal circumstances, but after sitting in the dark, the room seemed suddenly bright.

Elizabeth could see now that Darcy was still dressed as well, wearing one of Mr. Collins's housecoats over his waistcoat and trousers. When had he returned to the parsonage? It must have been very late, since she had been in the sitting room eating her soup, and then... and then what? She must have fallen asleep, but then how had she come to be in her bed?

A lively doubt seized her. As her suspicious glance met Darcy's, he flushed and turned away, rising to his feet and going to talk to the young woman in hushed tones.

That housecoat. It had not been her imagination. She had seen Darcy leaving her room when she was awakening, and he was wearing that housecoat. But what had he been doing in her bedroom while she slept? Had he only just brought her up to bed? That was a shocking enough thought, that he might have carried her in his arms. It was not as if it would be much more damning than riding with him that afternoon, but it felt more intimate somehow, especially when she remembered dancing in his arms in her dream. The timing of bringing her upstairs must have been remarkable to fit so closely with Jenny's screams – or had it been?

And what in the world was she doing even thinking about this while comforting a child who had lost her entire family? Fortunately, fatigue seemed to be overwhelming Jenny's sorrow, her sobs now interspersed with quiet moments. Sooner or later the girl was bound to fall asleep.

It was at least a quarter hour later when Elizabeth gently released Jenny's head onto her pillow, but when she looked up, Mr. Darcy had already left the room.

Back in Mr. Collins's room, Darcy checked his pocket watch. It was almost three in the morning. He must have slept half the night beside Elizabeth's bed. How could he have done such a foolish thing? He had meant only to close his eyes for a minute. Sheer physical exhaustion was no excuse, not when it came to spending the night in a lady's bedroom. Men had been killed for less. If Elizabeth ever found out, she would be furious.

But Elizabeth already knew; that much was almost certain of it from the reproachful look she had given him. Devil take it, why must he always be making things worse with her no matter how hard he tried? How was he to face her in the morning?

The situation between them was becoming more untenable by the hour. If the river was calmer tomorrow, he would find a boat and row Elizabeth across to Rosings, then consult with his aunt as to the care of the tenants. He did not like to think of the treatment Lady Catherine would mete out to Elizabeth. Informing his aunt of his intention to marry Elizabeth was something he was dreading himself, and he was far more accustomed to her fits of pique and resentment. And, of course, as soon as he and Elizabeth were with anyone of their acquaintance, the question of their relationship would have to be addressed, and that was something he would prefer to delay as long as possible.

First thing in the morning he would check the river. If it was still a torrent, he would have to come up with some other plan.

Sally brought hot chocolate and rolls to Elizabeth in the morning in what had to be a sign that life in the parsonage was gradually returning to normal, even if she felt rather like Noah on the ark. It gave her new sympathy for that biblical gentleman living through forty days and nights of torrential rain.

"How is Jenny this morning?" Elizabeth picked up a roll and tried to break it open, only to have it tear easily into two pieces. It looked light and flaky. Obviously things were not as much back to normal as she had thought. Cook's rolls usually bore a distinct resemblance to cannon balls.

"She was awake for a bit earlier, but now she's asleep again, miss." Sally straightened the counterpane on the bed.

Elizabeth tasted the roll. It was deliciously buttery and smooth. "Who made the rolls today?"

Sally gave her a frightened look. "Cook did, miss. She don't let any of the others cook for you and Mr. Darcy."

"Do not fret; the roll is excellent. Have you seen Mr. Darcy today?"

"Yes, miss. He went down to the village with some of the menfolk early this morning to see what can be salvaged."

"In this weather?" Elizabeth gestured to the window and the severe thunderstorm raging outside.

"It wasn't raining then, and the river looked to be going down a mite. I'm sure they're being very careful, miss."

Once dressed, Elizabeth went down to the sitting room to work on Charlotte's basket of mending for the poor. Ordinarily she might have chosen to read instead, but having discovered that there was little she could do to assist in the current crisis, she did not at all care for the new feeling of uselessness it gave her. She was accustomed to taking her part in household affairs, but there was no call at the moment for arranging flowers, directing the gardener, or making a purchase in Meryton. Here at Hunsford she had accompanied Charlotte in caring for her chickens, but her friend had managed the accounts, planned the menus, organized the household, and directed Sally and Cook in their tasks. The housekeeper did most of that work at Longbourn, and although Elizabeth supposed she could learn how to do so with as much facility as Charlotte had, her lack of knowledge of the supplies kept her from making an attempt.

Mr. Darcy had been the one to realize that food stores were running low. He had sent out the cart to fetch more, and when that failed, he had done it himself. He would have known even less than she had about the arrangement of the household, and he could not have been trained in these tasks any more than she was. Still, he had arranged to house the villagers in the neighbor's barn when she had not even realized there was such a barn, and now he was directing the efforts in the flooded village. All she had done was to entertain Jenny and attend to Charlotte's seemingly endless supply of mending. When she had tried to feed Charlotte's chickens the previous day, Cook had informed her testily that it had all been taken care of. She might have attempted to visit the displaced villagers in Charlotte's stead, but Mr. Darcy had been quite clear that she was not to be alone with them.

Sorting through the basket of old clothes, she put aside the wool socks with moth holes that were on the top. Jane had always teased her over the messiness of her darning, a task Elizabeth disliked and had never put much effort into learning to perform well. Instead she found an old shirt whose hem was partially ripped out. Sewing a basic seam was definitely within her capabilities. Threading a needle, she set to work.

The light was poor, even sitting right next to the window, and her eyes were already feeling the strain when she heard loud voices coming from the kitchen. Resolving that it was time for her to take more of an interest in the proceedings, she put aside the shirt and marched to the kitchen door.

The creature in the kitchen would most likely have been revealed to be one of the village men if the thick layer of smelly mud that covered him were removed. Cook faced him, hands on her hips. "Out of my kitchen this minute! And no, you cannot destroy our good clothesline in that filthy river!"

"What seems to be the matter here?" Elizabeth asked.

Cook turned a glare on her. "He can't have our good clothesline. Mrs. Collins wouldn't stand for such nonsense."

Elizabeth looked at the man. "What do you need it for?"

"River's going up again. Need to clear out what we can, but the river's too fast to go into without a rope. Mr. Darcy said to get more rope."

Cook sniffed. "Mr. High and Mighty Darcy always knows best, I suppose, so you might as well take it before he comes storming in here himself. It's on the shelf in the shed."

The man turned to leave, but Elizabeth said, "Is Mr. Darcy is still down by the river, then?"

The man guffawed. "Can't rightly say *that*. He's *in* the river up to here." He indicated a line across his chest. "Without a rope, more fool he. Wouldn't want to be the one to tell her ladyship if he don't make it out." Chuckling at his own wit, he shambled out of the kitchen.

Elizabeth felt a ridiculous urge to run after him and find out for herself what was happening by the river, but her presence would only be a hindrance to the efforts. Surely he must have been exaggerating the risk. She did not want to think about that. Since mending would only give her time to brood, she decided instead to check on Jenny.

Jenny was awake now, sitting up in bed with her arms wrapped around the wooden dog, staring blankly at the opposite wall. Her first words on seeing Elizabeth were, "Is Mr. Darcy back?"

Elizabeth blinked in surprise. She had not thought the girl to have a particular attachment to Mr. Darcy, or even to know his name, for that matter. "Not yet. Is there something I can do for you? Would you like something to eat?"

The girl shook her head. "Just your husband."

Not that again. Elizabeth had supposed someone would have disabused the girl of the notion, but at this point it would probably do more harm than good to correct her. "And why are you so eager to see my... Mr. Darcy?"

Jenny's mouth drooped. "I'm not supposed to tell."

What sort of nonsense was this? If the girl had not been through so much already, Elizabeth would have tried to coax the secret from her, but under the circumstances, she could only wait to find out. She would have some choice words for Mr. Darcy on his return, that was for certain – assuming he did return. Her chest felt tight.

Determined to give no sign of her distress, she sat down beside Jenny's bed and drew out a loop of string she had made earlier. "Do you know how to play scratch-cradle?"

Teaching Jenny to make the string figures took the better part of an hour, and Elizabeth was pleased to see her laughing at the silly mistakes that Elizabeth made deliberately. It was during one of those episodes that she heard footsteps behind her.

It was Mr. Darcy. He looked as if he had recently been used as fisherman's bait. Elizabeth's relief at the sight of him was enough to rob her of words.

Jenny gave a little bounce in bed, then winced in pain. "Did you find her?"

Darcy handed her something swaddled in a towel. "She is very wet."

As Jenny eagerly cradled the bundle, Elizabeth swept her eyes over Darcy. His coat was only damp, as was to be expected from being in the rain, but under it he appeared to be soaked to the skin. She looked up at him archly. "She is not the only one."

Darcy glanced down at his clothes. "No, she is not," he said with a fragment of a smile. Then he added more formally, "Please excuse my appearance, Miss Bennet. I can only plead that my errand was of some urgency."

"Indeed," she said gravely.

He bowed to her, looking rather silly making the formal effort in his disheveled state, then departed. To her surprise, she was disappointed. It was most likely simply a desire to scold him for taking risks.

Jenny was weeping openly over the bundle, where a slip of the towel revealed a painted doll. Elizabeth fetched a rag that Jenny used to dry the crudely carved shape as carefully as if it had been a live infant.

Elizabeth could see she was no longer needed. In a moment of inspiration, she returned to the sitting room and rummaged through the pile of mending until she discovered a torn piece of sprigged muslin large enough to make a dress for the doll. She spread it out on a side table and was contemplating how best to go about it when a firm knock sounded on the front door.

A moment later, Sally timidly entered the sitting room. "Colonel Fitzwilliam is here, Miss Bennet."

With a glad smile, Elizabeth straightened. "Show him in, please."

"Miss Bennet." Colonel Fitzwilliam bowed, his straight hair was plastered close to his head and his trousers splashed with mud. Still, he was a very welcome sight.

"This is a delightful surprise," she said. "I had not thought anyone would be able to reach us from Rosings yet."

"My route was hardly a direct one. I had to ride clear to the coast to find a bridge that was passable, and even there, my horse was knee deep in water on the approach. I hope you have not suffered unduly here. We have been worried on your behalf at Rosings."

Elizabeth laughed. "I imagine Mr. Collins has not allowed a moment of silence on the topic! But we have managed quite well here despite the circumstances."

"I am very glad to hear it." The colonel crossed to the hearth and held his hands out in front of the flames for a minute to warm them, then he turned to her with a grave expression. "I do not suppose you have had any word of Darcy."

"I have had many words both *of* him and *from* him," she said. "I believe he is coming down the stairs now."

"He is here?" He hurried toward the door just as Darcy appeared in it, wearing Mr. Collins's ill-fitting but dry housecoat. To Elizabeth's surprise, the colonel embraced him. "Darcy, thank God. We thought you had been carried off in the flood."

Darcy appeared taken aback. "Why would you think such a thing?"

"You disappeared without a word from dinner and never returned, and then we discovered you had taken your horse out just before the river spilled its banks. What on earth were we to think? But I am glad you thought to take shelter here." He stepped back, as if suddenly remembering Elizabeth's presence. "You cannot have been alone here all this time."

Elizabeth laughed. "Alone? Hardly. We have been well chaperoned by Sally, Cook, and a little girl with a broken leg, not to mention fifty or so villagers who took refuge here from the flood. And here is Sally now with a pot of hot tea. May I pour you a cup?"

The morning newspapers arrived as usual in Meryton on the early coach. Mrs. Long, who always read the page dedicated to intelligence of the *ton* over a cup of tea, appeared at Mrs. Phillips' door a scant half hour later with the offending paper in hand. After that lady made a shocked perusal, it was decided that this called for an immediate visit to Mrs. Bennet.

Mrs. Bennet was not in the habit of rising with the larks. She was firmly of the opinion that any event so discourteous as to occur before noontime was not worthy of her attention. As a result, she was still in her bedclothes when Mrs. Phillips and Mrs. Long arrived at Longbourn. However, the ladies were determined, and having convinced Miss Mary Bennet through their high distress and furious looks that the apocalypse must be at hand, Mrs. Phillips claimed a sister's privilege and breached the final defense of Mrs. Bennet's bedroom door.

She carried the newspaper as her battle standard, shaking it in the air until she tossed it on Mrs. Bennet's lap. "Well, sister, would you care to explain *this*?" she demanded.

Mrs. Bennet's nervous complaints about her dishabille were ineffective in halting the approaching forces. "Whatever do you mean?" she said querulously.

Mrs. Phillips struck a pose and pointed dramatically at one particular item in the newspaper. Mrs. Bennet, who was more short-sighted than she cared to admit, had to hold it close to her face and squint to make out the fine print. On first comprehending it, she sat quite still, unable to utter a syllable, staring blankly at the bearers of such astonishing intelligence. The shock was such that she did the unthinkable and rose from her bed while the day could still be called young. Grasping the newspaper, she hurried downstairs, crying Mr. Bennet's name as she went.

Mrs. Bennet's nerves had been Mr. Bennet's constant companions these many years, but in native self-defense, he had learned to tell the difference between her usual vapors and when she was in true distress. Her wild-eyed appearance in the door of his library suggested the latter. This did not, in fact, make him any more sympathetic to her, just more careful in watching for potential flying objects.

"Yes, Mrs. Bennet?" he said.

"Look! Look at this!" she cried, waving the newspaper in front of him so rapidly that it would have been impossible for him to read even the headlines.

"What, precisely, am I to look at?" he asked, prying the newspaper from her fingers.

"At that! Oh, Mr. Bennet!"

Since his wife had made no indication what *that* she was speaking of, Mr. Bennet glanced down the page. It is a truth universally acknowledged that no matter how many words might appear in a page of newsprint, one's own name will somehow immediately spring out, and so it was with Mr. Bennet. He read, frowned, put on his spectacles and read again, and finally set down the newspaper with an extraordinary gentleness which indicated how much he wished to tear it into little pieces. Even a natural indolence as strong as his could not stand for an insult of this magnitude.

He placed his hands on his desk and rose slowly to his feet. "Mrs.

Bennet, please be so kind as to instruct Hill to pack a bag for me immediately. I will be traveling to Rosings Park on the next post coach."

Chapter 7

COLONEL FITZWILLIAM DOWNED several cups of tea in rapid succession while sitting by the fire as Darcy related the various events of the last two days to him. "Today I had some of the men working to salvage what they could from their cottages, but then the water started to rise again. I had hoped that the river would be calm enough today that I could take Miss Bennet across to Rosings in a boat, but between the current and the detritus in the stream, it seemed unwise."

Elizabeth, now past the relief of discovering that Darcy was unharmed, had returned to her annoyance at the risks he had taken. "More unwise than going into the river yourself without a rope?" she said with mock sweetness. "The water must have been quite deep at the mill."

Darcy shot her a look out of the corner of his eye. "It was safe enough with the cottages breaking the current."

The colonel cocked his head. "Why do I think that Miss Bennet might not agree? But I still do not see why you did not return to Rosings yesterday."

"We had quite enough difficulty getting to Tunbridge Wells!" exclaimed Elizabeth.

The colonel pursed his lips. "You went with Darcy?"

"I could not leave her here alone." Darcy's tone brooked no argument.

"Not to diminish the importance of your efforts, cousin, but have you considered how it may appear to others?"

"There is very little to consider." He cast a serious look at Elizabeth. "Whatever our wishes might be, the situation is quite damning, and has been ever since the villagers discovered us alone together."

He could not possibly be suggesting... Could he? "I cannot agree," said Elizabeth hotly. "The opinion of Lady Catherine's tenants cannot possibly affect a part of society so wholly unconnected to it."

"Not so unconnected," said the colonel, "once they tell their family members in service at Rosings, who will spread the word to whomever they can. Lady Catherine's servants may be well-disciplined, but they are not known for their loyalty. It is thoughtful of you, Miss Bennet, to attempt to avoid the entanglement. Many women in your position would take advantage of the situation. Still, the entanglement exists, and the question, Darcy, is what are you going to do about it?"

Darcy gritted his teeth. Trust Richard to get it precisely backward! "Richard, I appreciate your concern, but you do not fully understand the situation. I have matters well in hand."

Richard frowned. "You are not the one who will suffer for it."

Elizabeth rose to her feet in a swish of skirts. "Colonel Fitzwilliam, please allow me to assure you that your cousin has been a perfect gentleman. We have, as I said, not been alone, and therefore there is no reason to worry about my reputation. If you will excuse me, I will go tell Cook we will have one more for dinner."

"Elizabeth," Darcy said tiredly to her retreating back. "I wish that were true, but there have been times we have not been chaperoned. The maid was not with us when the villagers first arrived, and there is no one who could vouch for where either of us were last night." And it was just as well there was not; having someone vouch that he had spent half the night in her room would not help at all.

She looked back over her shoulder, her eyes narrowing. "Indeed," she said with great deliberation. "There is no one who could vouch that you were not in my bedroom last night. No one at all." She did not have to add, 'Not even you.' She swept out of the room.

Richard let out a low whistle. "A perfect gentleman, eh?"

"Don't start," Darcy warned.

"I'm sorry, but you really do have to marry her, you know."

"Of course I have to marry her! *I* am not the one you need to convince."

Richard blinked in surprise. "Oh, come now. Don't be ridiculous. Of course she'll marry you."

"Funny. That isn't what *she* said." Darcy massaged his temples. "She will have to, though, whether she likes it or not."

"If she doesn't want to marry you, what on earth were you doing in her room last night?

"Where did you get the idea I was in her room?"

The colonel gave him a level look. "If that is the way you wish to play it, all I can say is that I hope no one saw you. It will be bad enough that everyone will know that you were forced into the marriage without adding more fuel to the fire."

"With luck, it will look as if we were already engaged. The announcement should have been in today's newspaper, or tomorrow's at latest."

Richard raised his eyebrows. "How did you manage that?"

"I sent off a note yesterday to my secretary when I was in Tunbridge Wells."

"You sent a note to London but you could not let us know you were alive?"

Darcy, unaccustomed to defending himself against his usually agreeable cousin, snapped, "I had no idea you were concerned, and I had enough to worry about without that! Richard, if you have nothing better to do than to criticize everything I say and do, I hope you will find your way back to Rosings quickly."

The colonel bit back a reply and turned to stare into the fire. He should have known better than to challenge Darcy. Still, after two days of uncertainty as to whether Darcy was even alive, and then a long, uncomfortable ride today, it was hard to settle into his customary deference to his wealthy cousin. He could not afford to turn Darcy against him, but sometimes the bit chafed, all the more so when Darcy insisted on ignoring the rules of propriety that bound the rest of society. One of the chief arguments for finding an heiress to marry was that he would no longer have to bend his will to that of his wealthy relatives. Darcy was among the best of the lot, there was no doubt, but it would be better still to be independent.

At least Darcy seemed to accept that he had a responsibility to marry Miss Bennet. That was the crux of his anger, after all. He himself was accustomed to Darcy doing whatever he pleased, but it was another matter when a sweet and lovely girl like Miss Bennet was injured by his cousin's heedless behavior. He wondered whether Darcy's sudden concern with the niceties of when the engagement was announced actually had to do with concern for Miss Bennet's sensibilities or whether it was simply to avoid any hint of scandal that might reflect on Georgiana in her upcoming first Season.

Richard seized on the question as a safer topic, not to mention one which did not cause him pain. "Has Miss Bennet been presented at Court? You can hardly marry a woman who has not been presented."

"Not yet, but she will have to be. That is another difficulty – I will have to find someone to sponsor her."

"Is there anyone in her family who could do it?"

Darcy made a scornful sound. "God forbid. That is the last thing I would wish for. No, I will have to find someone. Lady Catherine is hardly likely to agree to take on that particular task. One of my cousins might be brought up to scratch."

Richard doubted that, given how many of them Darcy had managed to offend over the years. "My mother might be willing, given that it would mean she would not have to sponsor Georgiana, since that would necessarily fall to your wife." He did not particularly like the taste of that phrase in his mouth.

"Georgiana will be delighted in any case, simply because this will mean putting off her come-out for another year," Darcy said dryly.

"At least someone will profit as a result of this predicament!"

Darcy gave him an odd look. "You refer to presenting Miss Bennet?"

He had not been, but it would hardly be wise to point that out. If Darcy did not already understand the effect his high-handed ways would have on Miss Bennet's lively spirit, it was not Richard's place to tell him. The material advantages of the match would certainly outweigh the personal incompatibility, but he doubted Miss Bennet would find pleasure in spending time with her husband. There it was again – another phrase he did not like to consider. He had liked it much better when he had thought that Darcy would find an attachment to Miss Bennet as imprudent as he himself did. In truth, he had not at all minded watching Darcy for once wanting something he could not have.

Instead, he said, "I take it Miss Bennet is unaware of the announcement?"

Darcy looked away. "I have not told her yet. I have been waiting for a calm moment to raise the issue, but there has been a dearth of calm moments. Hopefully she will understand the necessity of it."

Miss Bennet's melodic voice came from behind him. "What am I to understand the necessity of?"

Observing the sudden tension in Darcy's stance, Richard said, "If you will be so kind as to excuse me, I should see to... to my horse." It was an embarrassingly weak excuse, but he could think of nothing better.

Darcy said, "Richard, it is raining, and I would rather you remained here."

Elizabeth's lips twitched. "Perhaps the colonel might find the kitchen or the dining room diverting. The maid is preparing a bedroom for him."

"I thank you." Richard wondered how she would adjust to unquestioningly obeying Darcy's decrees. He had been bred to it. She seemed accustomed to more independence.

Darcy said, "I was not aware that there was another bedroom."

"There is not, but I can easily return to my old room. Jenny will be happy for the company."

"Jenny? Who may that be?"

Elizabeth darted a mischievous look at Darcy. "Jenny is the young lady for the sake of whose happiness Mr. Darcy felt it necessary to risk drowning himself."

Another young lady, one to whom Darcy was apparently attached? This was getting worse and worse.

Darcy, apparently noting his disturbance, said, "Jenny is a child, a peasant girl newly orphaned in the flood. I rescued her favorite toy." He turned his gaze on Elizabeth. "I had not realized you would object to the prospect, Miss Bennet."

"I object to foolhardy behavior as a general principle!"

"It was the prospect of my drowning that I thought you would not object to," Darcy replied dryly.

Elizabeth's eyes glinted with amusement. "That is indeed a very different question, sir."

Richard cleared his throat. "Dare I hope that your manservant could assist me in making arrangements for some clean attire? I had not anticipated being away overnight when I left Rosings."

As he had hoped, this distracted Darcy from dangerous topics. "Unfortunately, there is only the maid and the cook, but if you will accompany me upstairs, perhaps we can arrange for something."

Darcy without a valet! This had some possibilities for amusement.

⚭

Elizabeth was relieved when Darcy took himself off to check on the tenants staying in the neighboring barn. He had been oddly Friday-faced since his cousin's arrival, and she had not missed the warning look he had given Colonel Fitzwilliam just before his departure. Still, the colonel was always agreeable company, and she looked forward to a pleasant hour of conversation with him after the tensions of the last two days.

To her surprise, he fell silent for a few minutes, then said, with an unusually serious countenance, "I have been discussing your future with Darcy."

"Not that again!" Elizabeth exclaimed.

"I share his concern for your reputation – and for his. I do not wish to see either of you unhappy."

She strove to keep her tone level. "And you think I could make him happy? Has he told you his opinion of my family, of my low connections which would be such a degradation for him?"

"I am aware of his sentiments toward them. I am also aware that only the strongest of emotions could bring him to overlook them."

"So, naturally, in deference to his strong emotions, you feel that I should marry him."

"I did not say that, just that I cannot see any way out of this for you that does not require you to marry."

Her heart sank. "I believe this is a conversation I should be having with Mr. Darcy."

"Perhaps. Then again, perhaps not. Perhaps you should be having it with me."

She shot him a quizzical look. "I appreciate your concern, but I hardly see how it involves you."

He stood and moved restlessly across the room to the hearth. For a moment he seemed preoccupied with examining the mantelpiece, then he said, "Miss Bennet, you must marry. The question is whether you must marry Darcy, or whether another gentleman would suffice."

Perhaps all the men in Darcy's family had a predisposition to ridiculous assumptions. "I have not the pleasure of understanding you," she said carefully.

He leaned his elbow against the mantelpiece, bearing a striking resemblance to his cousin at that moment. "If marrying Darcy is not palatable to you, I am offering myself as another option."

Her cheeks grew hot. Could he be serious? Was there something odd about the air in Kent that caused men to propose to her at the drop of a hat? "I fear you are jesting with me, Colonel. Did you not explain to me just a few days ago that you needed to marry an heiress? I have no fortune, as you must know." It felt as if that conversation had taken place in another lifetime.

"I am aware of that, but in this particular circumstance, that may not be an obstacle. I will admit that I do not at present possess the means necessary to establish a family in the manner which I would prefer, but I think it likely that my father would be prepared to remedy that situation in order to maintain Darcy's status as an eligible bachelor."

"Why would your father care about Mr. Darcy's marital status?"

He sighed. "In a family such as mine, marriages serve as alliances, both financially and politically. Darcy has great value in the marriage mart. He could make a very favorable connection, one which would be to the benefit of my family. It is unlikely that I could find a bride who would offer as much, since I am just one more penniless aristocrat among many. I have no prospect of inheriting, as my elder brother already has three sons and a fecund wife. With no disrespect meant to you, my father would prefer to settle money on me than to give up his plans for Darcy."

"I might be good enough for his son, but not for his nephew? I find this difficult to credit." Not to mention that it was hardly complimentary to be told that the earl would pay to remove Darcy from her influence.

He shook his head. "It is not a judgment on you, but rather on what would most benefit the Fitzwilliam family, a matter of practicalities."

"By those standards, should not *I* do better to marry Mr. Darcy? He does, after all, have a great deal to offer."

The colonel smiled. "My father would think you a fool not to jump at the opportunity, and if a fortune is what you desire above all, then he would be right. If I thought that was what you wanted, I would not have made this offer. Since you are a lady of good sense, I assume you may have other reasons for refusing my cousin."

"May I ask on whose behalf are you making this offer? Is it to please your father?"

"Good Lord, no. His attitude makes it possible for me to consider it, but it would not prompt me to anything I did not already wish to do."

"I see." Elizabeth did not, in fact, see. While complimented by his offer, she could not help but view the calm nature of his presentation as a suggestion of disinterest on his part. She stabbed the needle into the muslin doll dress.

"Perhaps you wonder at the dispassionate nature of my offer. I am well aware, perhaps more than you are, that you must marry either my cousin or me. Whichever you choose, you will no doubt end up seeing both of us since we are often in company together. I prefer not to say anything that would be difficult for either of us to forget should it turn out that you elect to marry Darcy."

Elizabeth bit her lip. His words, while spoken lightly, had enough of an edge to make her wonder what lay beneath them. What a strange situation this was – Mr. Collins had said she might never have another offer, yet now she had a choice between the wealthy Mr. Darcy and the son of the Earl of Matlock! In terms of whose company she would enjoy more, there was no question in her mind, yet she felt as if there was more to this than the colonel had said. "Does Mr. Darcy know about your plans?"

"No." He looked remarkably unconcerned by this. "I doubt the idea has even crossed his mind."

"I cannot imagine he would be pleased by the intelligence."

"Most likely not. He seems rather relieved that the matter of marrying you has been decided for him. Poor fellow – he has had a difficult time of it trying to decide what to do about you. He feels the weight of the family's expectations."

Elizabeth fixed her eyes on her stitching. "And there is the little matter of his belief that my sister was not good enough for Mr. Bingley."

"Do we not all have relatives we must blush for?"

Elizabeth noticed he did not seem surprised by this information. "I wonder, then, that you chose to tell me how Mr. Darcy had saved Mr. Bingley from a disadvantageous match, if you knew that the lady involved was my sister."

He looked chagrined. Taking a seat beside her, he said, "You have caught me out. I told you that story quite deliberately with the intention of turning you against Darcy."

Her eyes widened at this impudent admission. "I had thought you were fond of him."

"I am. That does not always mean that I agree with him."

"And what benefit was it to you that I should be angry with him?"

He drummed his fingers on the edge of the chair. "There was no benefit for me. I hoped only to protect you from a potentially embarrassing situation."

"I must be particularly slow-witted today, for that makes no sense to me at all."

"Of course not. In order to explain myself, I would have to raise a subject unfit to discuss with a lady, so instead I am choosing to be obscure."

"Could you perhaps find it in your heart to be slightly less obscure?"

He looked away, then said with a certain resoluteness, "Marriage is not the only thing a gentleman can offer to a woman he admires."

Now she was truly shocked. "You do not mean that he would have asked me to be... that he would have offered me *carte blanche*?"

"I *hope* he would not have. However, I had never seen him so taken with a lady, and yet he seemed so convinced that marriage to you was impossible. He is not accustomed to being denied anything he desires, and so I feared what he might say if he thought you were favorably inclined toward him. I have no doubts as to what you would have said in response, but I hoped to avoid the situation arising. I have a powerful dislike for embarrassing scenes."

"You will be relieved, then, to know that Mr. Darcy chose to take the honorable route despite my despicably low connections." Inexplicably, she felt annoyed that the colonel suspected Darcy of less honorable plans. Darcy might have said things he ought not to have, but she could not imagine him making such a dishonorable suggestion to her.

He smiled, returning to his old amiability. "I would not have put it that way, but yes, I am glad of it, for both of you, and if you do desire to marry my cousin, you will have my very best wishes, and I will never raise this subject again."

Realizing her own manners had been at fault, Elizabeth said quickly, "I am very grateful for and touched by your offer. Will you allow me a little time to consider it?" Almost as soon as the words had left her mouth, she wondered at them. Two days ago she would have been delighted to receive an offer from the colonel. Why was she hesitating now?

"Of course. I know I have taken you by surprise and that the circumstances are less than propitious, but I will remain hopeful of a happy outcome. In the meantime, I shall enjoy the unexpected pleasure of your company, which is made even more delightful by comparison to that which is currently found at Rosings Park."

Elizabeth accepted the redirection of both the conversation and her own thoughts with relief. "I can only imagine! May I inquire whether you have been profiting from the constant stream of wisdom which issues from

Mr. Collins's lips?"

He laughed. "I would refer to *that* as a flood, rather than a stream, and it puts the torrents outside to shame. Even my aunt seems to begin to tire of his compliments." His expression sobered. "Lady Catherine, like all of us, has been very worried about Darcy. She did not go so far as to put on black, but she has given up hope, fearing all her plans for Anne's future were for naught. Not, of course, that Darcy ever had any intention of marrying Anne, but Lady Catherine only hears that which she wishes to hear."

"I imagine that if she had any hint of what was happening here, she would have commanded the waters to part so that she could rescue him from my clutches."

The colonel chuckled. "Most likely she would have simply assumed they would part as soon as she drew near."

"Indeed. She is already a true proficient at giving commandments and has no need to practice." Elizabeth tied off a thread, then examined her attempt at a doll dress. By some miracle, it actually resembled a dress. She hoped it would fit Jenny's doll. Cocking her head to one side, she said, "I do believe this elegant attire requires some trim to be truly fashionable. I wonder if Mrs. Collins has any bits of ribbon in her rag bag?"

Darcy returned in time for dinner with the welcome news that the water had receded slightly and that a few of the cottages furthest from the riverbank might be habitable soon. "I hope they will be; the barn is overcrowded, and tempers are beginning to flare."

Colonel Fitzwilliam inquired about the damage while Elizabeth helped herself to small portions of several dishes in the first course. Cook had somehow managed to find enough provisions to prepare a variety of dishes. No doubt the ham came from the stores in the cellar, but Elizabeth wondered about the presence of the chicken ragout, and whether it indicated that Charlotte might arrive home to discover one chicken less than she had left. Taking a tentative taste, she discovered it to be tender and well-seasoned with a delicious tang to the sauce.

The colonel apparently reached the same conclusion. "I shall stop feeling any pity for you for being stranded here, Darcy. Had I realized the kitchen staff here had such talents, I would have arranged to be trapped here for dinner more often."

Darcy cleared his throat and gestured to Sally. "Ah, yes. Sally, you may tell Cook that tonight's dinner is acceptable."

"Acceptable?" exclaimed the colonel. "It is a sight better than what is served at Rosings!"

"Acceptable," Darcy repeated firmly, dismissing Sally. "Have no fear; Cook and I understand one another tolerably well."

Elizabeth arched an eyebrow. "Have we *you* to thank, then, for the disappearance of tasteless dinners and bread that could serve as building stones?"

Darcy shook his head, but with a slight smile. "Some people simply appreciate a challenge. She did not choose to expend her best efforts on Mr. Collins, since he noticed no difference."

Colonel Fitzwilliam drawled, "You actually spoke to a mere cook? Darcy, you shock me!"

Elizabeth, seeing that Darcy looked somewhat offended, said, "Mr. Darcy has done an admirable job of managing a difficult situation here. The tenants have much to feel grateful for."

Darcy looked at her, his face unreadable. "You have also risen to the challenge admirably, Miss Bennet, especially with young Jenny. She showed me the picture you drew of her. She is very proud of it, and rightfully so."

"You flatter me, sir. What little talent I have for drawing lends itself more to caricature than to portraiture. It is fortunate for me that Jenny is not a critical audience."

"I thought you captured her likeness quite well."

"The drawing served its purpose, which was to convince her to sit still so as to avoid injuring her leg further." Elizabeth was surprised to be exchanging pleasant conversation with Mr. Darcy. Perhaps it was the presence of his cousin that allowed him to be more civil.

Nonetheless, she was conscious of the discomfort inherent in spending an unchaperoned evening with two gentlemen, each of whom had offered her his hand in marriage, reaching the conclusion that the efforts of the day might have fatigued her sufficiently that anyone would understand her need to retire from their company as early as possible. The fact that those efforts had primarily been on the part of Mr. Darcy rather than herself, and that making doll clothes was not in fact particularly tiring work, did not seem particularly relevant. Besides, she had not yet finished the novel loaned to her by Charlotte which sat waiting on her bedside table, and if she stayed up late reading by candlelight, who would be the wiser?

As it happened, the novel could not hold her attention that evening, not when she had so many decisions to make. The thoughts crowding her head demanded to be heard. She had been shocked to discover that Mr. Darcy considered his proposal to be still an open question, if not an expectation. Colonel Fitzwilliam would no doubt expect an answer to *his* offer the next day, and she had no idea what to tell him.

Two days ago she would have accepted him with pleasure. She liked and esteemed him, and believed she could learn to love him. His income, while not sufficient for the lifestyle he had been raised to, seemed perfectly satisfactory to her, and neither his breeding nor his manners could be questioned. Yet it seemed somehow improper to accept him in light of Mr. Darcy's proposal, unwanted as it might have been, but if interfering with his cousin's desires did not trouble the colonel, she could not understand why it should bother her.

Still, the colonel had *not* in fact proposed to her two days ago, and had not done so until he decided that he or his cousin must marry her. Darcy, on the other hand, had spoken when nothing forced his hand. Did this mean that the colonel was more concerned with preventing Darcy's marriage than with marrying her? She knew he admired her, but he had also admitted that his father's wishes played some part in his decision. Did that speak for him or against him? Taking his family's views into account displayed a pleasing sense of duty, but hardly indicated strong feelings on his part. She thought he would be disappointed if she refused him, but not heart-broken, but she could not say the same for Darcy.

Her heart began to thud in her chest. Was that what felt so troubling in all this? Darcy had said nothing further about his feelings for her, but instinctively she knew that he had been hurt, badly hurt, by her refusal. It had shown in his tight-lipped looks, his long absences – perhaps even in his foolhardy behavior risking himself to rescue Jenny's doll. Yet he had still shown concern for her, buying her the cloak in town and assisting her when she could no longer face riding the mare. Even then, he had not taken advantage of her when he could have. She could not deny that if she were only to judge on depth of the gentleman's feelings, Darcy would come out ahead.

It was one thing to refuse him, but would it be cruel to him if she married his cousin, where he would have to see her with another man at family occasions? She might not like him, but it was another matter to deliberately make him unhappy. After misjudging and hurting him by believing Wickham's lies, was she now to end up coming between two men who had such a long history of friendship? That was an idea she did not care for in the slightest. Yet why should she be forced to refuse an excellent offer just because it might hurt Darcy? Annoying, aggravating man!

She snapped the forgotten book shut and put it aside. It was unfair that a fluke of the weather should have placed her in such an impossible situation. As one who disliked having her choices dictated to her, she would have preferred to believe that the gentlemen overstated the risk to her reputation, but argue as she might, in her heart she knew they were correct. If it were only the two gentlemen and Lady Catherine who knew of her situation, it could have been covered up, but Maria Lucas could not keep a secret if her life depended on it, and it was beyond reasonable expectation that Mr. Collins would remain silent on a matter such as this. Between the two of them, word would reach Meryton that Mr. Darcy had spent two nights alone with her, and that would be the end of her respectability.

Now she wished she had not come upstairs so early. After being trapped indoors all day by the inclement weather, she needed some fresh air, to walk, to move, but instead she was trapped by her own device, with only her thoughts for company. In the end, the best solution she could find was to wrap a shawl over her dress, open the casement window a few inches, and sit beside it with an unopened book in her hand.

Despite his sudden sense of foreboding, Darcy had somehow managed to respond appropriately when Elizabeth had said goodnight to them at a ridiculously early hour. He had thought things had gone rather well at dinner. He had managed for once to participate in a conversation with her instead of sitting silently and watching her laugh with Richard. She had even praised his efforts and defended him to his cousin when he had despaired of ever hearing a positive word from her, but then she had excused herself at the first possible moment. Had he once again misread her?

Becoming aware that his cousin was eyeing him oddly, Darcy crossed to the sidebar and poured out two generous helpings from the decanter. "It barely deserves to be called brandy, but it serves the purpose." He offered one to Richard.

Richard raised his glass in a silent toast. Taking a careful sip, he made a wry face. "I have drunk worse, but it is not up to *your* usual standards, that much is certain."

"I doubt I could ever become accustomed to rough brandy and ill-fitting clothes. I have developed a far greater appreciation for both my valet and my tailor in these last few days. I could not live like this." Darcy swirled the brandy in his glass, more out of habit than any hope of a pleasant aroma. "In that way, I will be grateful to reach Rosings Park." He would not mind, though, a delay of another day or two to accustom Elizabeth to his company before having to inform her of the announcement of their engagement.

"I plan to return there tomorrow by the same route I took here. Do you think Miss Bennet would be able to make the ride?"

Darcy's body grew warm at the recollection of holding Elizabeth in his arms as they rode together, her curves resting against his thigh, but that was not what Richard meant. "An hour, perhaps two, on a good road would be the most one could ask of her. I expect with a few lessons she could be quite competent on horseback, but there is not even a decent sidesaddle here."

"Not everyone is as fond of riding as you are."

Somehow Richard's comment sounded critical to Darcy's ears. "I know that. It is a useful skill, that is all I meant."

"When do you plan to tell her about the announcement?"

Darcy took a sip of the brandy, then swallowed it quickly as the sharp taste burned his tongue. "Tomorrow, I suppose. Before we return to Rosings, in any case. They may have seen it there."

"If they have not, my father will have, and I wager he will be on the doorstep within two hours of reading it. Are you ready to face a united front from him and Lady Catherine?"

"I do not care what they say. Nothing will stop me from marrying her."

Richard set down his brandy and straightened his shoulders. "There is one thing that might. I made her an offer of my own today."

For a moment Darcy could not believe he had heard him correctly, then he half-rose from his chair as fear and betrayal churned through him. "How dare…. What did she say?"

"She asked for time to consider it. As for how I dared, well, I have as much right to pursue my own happiness as you do."

Elizabeth had refused him point-blank, but she had not refused Richard. Elizabeth and Richard. Good God, anything but that! "It cannot be. The announcement has already been made."

Richard shrugged. "It would be easy enough to explain as a misunderstanding. The name, you know – someone heard Fitzwilliam and thought of you, not me. No one would doubt it, especially with your history of avoiding entanglements."

The sharp edges of the chair arms were biting into Darcy's fingers as he clenched them tightly, almost as tightly as he had clenched his teeth to keep in the words that threatened to escape him, words that could never be taken back. Richard and Elizabeth. Richard holding Elizabeth in his arms. Richard kissing Elizabeth. His gorge rose. "Why? You never evinced any interest in marrying her until you heard I wanted to. Is that it? I would not have thought it of you, *cousin*."

"Or do you mean that you would not have thought it possible that any woman might choose me over you?"

It was true enough, but Darcy was too far blinded with pain and anger to care. "You *knew* I was planning to marry her!"

"I also knew she did not seem happy with the arrangement, so I offered her a different option. This is not about you or me, Darcy. It is purely up to her."

That was what frightened Darcy the most. "You may believe that if it gives you comfort. I thought I could trust you," he bit out as he rose to his feet. He had to remove himself before he lost control completely.

Richard stood as well and grasped his arm as Darcy tried to pass him. "For God's sake, stop and *think* for a minute! Think about *her*! You are entranced by her spirit. What do you think will happen to that spirit after she spends years listening to your insults about her family and living with your expectation that everyone will always fall in with your plans? I am accustomed to living in your shadow. You decide to stay at Rosings, so we stay at Rosings. You decide to leave, so we leave. You decide to marry Miss Bennet, so she has to marry you whether she likes it or not. It does not even occur to you that we may have wishes of our own. No, you are the Master of Pemberley. The world runs to your command. Well, Miss Bennet is not yours to command. Did you even try to woo her, or did you just assume she would be grateful for any attention you paid her? That she would not mind your comments about her family, or how you are degrading yourself with this connection? Do you even care what happens to her, as long as you get what you want?"

"You know her family is not the equal of ours!"

"Of course it isn't, but *I* can acknowledge that to her without making her feel degraded and humiliated!"

Darcy stared down at Richard's fingers gripping his arm, trying to fight back the urge to lash out with his fists. "Let me go," he said icily.

Richard released him. "Just think about it, Darcy," he said tiredly.

Darcy did not want to think about it. He strode out of the room and left the parsonage, slamming the front door closed behind him.

Chapter 8

CHARLOTTE COLLINS WAS exhausted. She had been relieved initially when Colonel Fitzwilliam offered to find a way to check on Elizabeth, but she had not realized how difficult it would be to manage to keep the situation at Rosings from deteriorating into a disaster. The colonel had seemed to manage his aunt almost effortlessly despite her worry over Mr. Darcy, which had allowed Charlotte to focus on keeping Maria from panicking over being stranded at Rosings and preventing Mr. Collins from aggravating the circumstances with well-intentioned sympathies that served only to distress Lady Catherine even further.

In the absence of Colonel Fitzwilliam, though, Lady Catherine's veneer of calm cracked. She reduced two maids to tears with a brutal and undeserved tongue-lashing, then turned her ire on Mr. Collins, criticizing everything from his posture to the manner in which he wore his cravat, making the poor man try franticly to say anything that might please her ladyship. Anne de Bourgh had pronounced herself quite unwell and took to her bed, indubitably to avoid her mother's rage, since Anne had been the only person at Rosings who seemed not to care about Mr. Darcy's disappearance.

At dinner, Charlotte was forced to maintain the conversation with her ladyship by herself, since both Mr. Collins and Maria had been thoroughly cowed into silence. This, of course, meant that Lady Catherine vented her spleen at her, roundly criticizing everything from her housekeeping to her appearance to her family background. It was almost enough to break through even Charlotte's calm, but somehow she managed to maintain her composure. She wished that Colonel Fitzwilliam would hurry back. She would be happy to see *anyone* beyond the current company.

❧

Mr. Bennet's mood had only worsened after he had been forced to abandon his beloved library for the rigors of the unknown. By the time he reached Rosings Park, he was furious. He was barely civil to the footman who opened the door to his knock as he demanded to see Mr. Darcy at once.

"Mr. Darcy is not here," the footman said curtly.

"Oh, yes, he is," Mr. Bennet snapped. "I had a letter from my daughter not two days ago telling me so. Tell him Mr. Bennet demands to see him immediately."

"I regret that I am unable to do so owing to his absence."

"Where might I find him, in that case?"

"I cannot say, sir."

"You cannot say? Then I will see Lady Catherine de Bourgh instead."

The footman seemed on firmer ground here. "Her ladyship is not receiving visitors at present."

"This is not a social call. I require information from her ladyship, and I require it immediately."

"If you will wait here, sir, I will see what I can do."

Mr. Bennet cooled his heels for a few minutes in an ornate dining room, but his hopes to be led to Lady Catherine were destined to be frustrated. Instead, the butler appeared to repeat the same information he had already received: Mr. Darcy's whereabouts were unknown, and Lady Catherine would not receive him. Only when Mr. Bennet refused to leave did the butler agree to seek further counsel on the matter.

A quarter hour later the door once again opened, and to Mr. Bennet's astonishment, he was greeted by none other than his former neighbor, Mrs. Collins.

Charlotte stopped abruptly. "Mr. Bennet! I had not expected to find *you* here when Jamison said there was a caller."

"I am sure you did not," said Mr. Bennet grimly. "It seems we are both in places where we are not expected. Is Lizzy here as well?"

"No, she is not." As Charlotte smoothed her hands over her skirt, Mr. Bennet noted that she appeared fatigued and unhappy. "She is, I presume, still at the parsonage, on the other side of the river."

"It does not matter. I am here to see Mr. Darcy."

Charlotte's face grew pale. "Have you had word of him?"

Mr. Bennet snorted. "So to speak."

"Where is he? Is he injured?" Charlotte wrung her hands as she spoke.

"I am trying to find out where he is, and I have no idea whether he is injured, though I think it quite possible that I may do him an injury myself!"

"Mr. Bennet!" Charlotte paused, then began again. "I should explain myself. You find us in some disarray here. The river that lies between Rosings and the parsonage burst its banks two days ago, washing out the only bridge, while Mr. Collins and I were dining here. Mr. Darcy disappeared just before the flood began, and we fear the worst, for there has been no word of him since. Lady Catherine is naturally quite... distraught, and Miss de Bourgh has taken to her bed, which is why the butler asked me to speak to you in their stead."

"And Lizzy, is she safe?"

"I cannot see why she would not be. She did not join us for dinner owing to a headache, so she remained at the parsonage. It is on high ground, and our maid is there to care for her. This morning Colonel Fitzwilliam set out to check on her, but he has not returned. No doubt he had to travel farther than expected before he found a way across the river."

"Who, pray tell, is Colonel Fitzwilliam?"

"My apologies; he is Lady Catherine's nephew and Mr. Darcy's cousin."

Mr. Bennet nodded slowly. "So, Lizzy cannot be reached, Darcy is missing, and you seem oddly surprised to see me."

Charlotte's expression grew puzzled. "I had not expected it, though Mr. Collins and I will be happy to have you as our guest, and I am sure Lizzy will be pleased to see you."

"I suppose, then, that you know nothing of this as well." Mr. Bennet took a folded sheet of newsprint from his pocket and handed it to Charlotte.

Charlotte unfolded it and perused it in her usual careful manner. A smile broke over her face. "Oh, Lizzy has been quite the sly one! She hasn't said a word to me of this." Then her smile abruptly disappeared. "Oh, no. Poor Lizzy! And she has no idea he is.... lost."

"I would not waste my time worrying about *that*, my dear," Mr. Bennet said dryly. "I would venture to guess that you will find Darcy with Lizzy."

Charlotte pressed her hand to her chest. "Of course! This would explain where he was going that night. We knew only that he rode out after dark, despite a warning that the roads were unfit for travel, but given this," she held up the announcement, "he is probably perfectly safe at the parsonage."

"Perfectly safe until I get my hands on him," grumbled Mr. Bennet. "I do not like learning of my daughter's engagement from a notice in the newspaper, and I like even less the idea that *he* has spent the last two days alone with Lizzy."

His companion, however, was not paying attention. She was re-reading the announcement and biting her lip. "But what shall I tell Lady Catherine? She is frantic about Mr. Darcy's disappearance, but if she were aware of *this*, it might be even worse."

"He is better off dead than engaged to my daughter?" Mr. Bennet demanded, his objections to the match forgotten in this new indignity.

Charlotte allowed herself a slight smile. "I am certain we will both hear far more than we wish on the subject of Lady Catherine's wishes."

A new pounding sounded from the direction of the front door. "Perhaps that is the colonel, with news from the parsonage," said Charlotte.

A man's voice bellowed, "Where is he, damn his eyes?"

Charlotte turned back to Mr. Bennet. "On second thought, that would *not* be Colonel Fitzwilliam."

Elizabeth let the light breeze from the window play over her hot cheeks. The rain had stopped, but the air remained moist, almost as she imagined sea air would be. Someday she would like to visit the sea. It was a pity to be so close to it here in Kent, yet not to see it.

The sky was beginning to clear as well. As she watched, a thin crescent moon scudded out from behind the patchy clouds, making the grounds of the parsonage into a quilt of light and shadows before it was once again swallowed up and blurred into the merest suggestion of light. To the west, the sky blazed with stars, and Elizabeth entertained herself with imagining new constellations from the patterns they made.

The crash of a door slamming broke the stillness of the night. A shadowy form emerged from the front of the parsonage, striding rapidly toward the row of trees that lined the property. She recognized Mr. Darcy by the set of his shoulders. Reaching the trees, he stooped to pick something up - a stick? - and weighed it in his hand. Then, with an abrupt motion, he drew back his arm and flung it hard. It flew away from the house and out of her sight, but Elizabeth heard the crack of wood meeting wood.

After repeating the action with another stick, he looked up at the sky, raking both hands into his hair, then holding his head between them. He stood that way for long enough that Elizabeth realized she should not be watching him when he believed himself to be unobserved. She looked away self-consciously, but her eyes were drawn back to his shape, now crouched down near the ground as his hands collected something too small for her to make out.

So the restrained Mr. Darcy did have limits to his self-control. She would not have believed it had she not seen it herself. What had brought him so close to the edge that he had allowed this side of himself to emerge? Had his calmness in her presence been nothing more than a pretence?

He disappeared then behind the line of trees. Elizabeth found herself straining to hear anything of his passage, but the only sound reaching her ears was the chirping of the crickets. He could not go far in that direction; the path there led down to the river. Would there be enough light to see his way safely and avoid the high water?

The sound of a small splash came, then a second and a third. A pause, followed by more splashes at varying intervals. Her lips curved as she wondered what Mr. Darcy was throwing into the river. More sticks, or had he moved on to rocks? The splashes sounded heavier than what she imagined a stick would create.

She leaned her head back and closed her eyes. He had, all unknowing, given her a tiny glimpse of his soul as he poured his - what? - anger, or frustration, or sheer bad temper out into the empty night. What did she actually know of him, of the man he was beyond his curt manners and proud behavior? She had been wrong about Wickham's tale; what else might she be wrong about?

Darcy's rude behavior at the Meryton Assembly could not be denied. She had heard his insults herself. She could not say whether it was typical of him or not; although he had been proud and distant on other occasions in Hertfordshire, she could not recall other insulting behavior. He had not been so distant here in Kent. Which was the true Darcy?

Colonel Fitzwilliam had confirmed her fears that Darcy had been instrumental in separating Jane from Bingley, and she did not think the colonel would create such a tale with no basis. From what Darcy had said in his proposal, his poor opinion of her family and her low connections would seem to be the cause. She felt the heat of anger just thinking about his words. True, his station was above hers, but it did not follow that hers was anything to be ashamed of!

Opening her eyes, she shook her head to clear it. Anger was not useful in her present situation. She needed to assess this rationally, if for no other reason than to prove to herself that she was not always so foolish as to accept a story like Wickham's as truth simply because he flattered her vanity. Mr. Darcy had been so far from flattering her that she would have believed any ill of him, yet he was the one who truly admired her, not Wickham, who was soon to marry Miss King. How had she missed that so completely?

Just then his figure emerged from the trees, making her aware that at some level she had been watching for him. He approached the house more slowly than he had left it, his pace almost reluctant. He paused twice to look at something around him, though it was unclear in the darkness what had drawn his attention.

He was but a short distance down the garden path when he looked up. By his sudden rigidity, she knew he must have seen her. How mortifying to be caught spying on him! How could she have been so foolish to remain in the windowseat where she must have been perfectly silhouetted by the candlelight? At least she was still dressed with her hair up. The mere idea of him seeing her in her nightdress with her hair loose sent a frisson of sensation through her. It was bad enough that he had spotted her curled up in the windowseat in what could hardly be considered a ladylike pose.

She had to repress an urge to scamper back into the darkness – that would only make her look ashamed of herself. Instead, she forced herself to nod in what she hoped to be a gracious manner and to raise a hand in brief salute.

He hesitated, then swept her a low bow such as would be proper for a duchess at the very least, or perhaps a fairy tale princess. The only suitable reply she could think of would be to drop a handkerchief out of her window, but that would send altogether the wrong message. Still, the idea made her smile. At least there was no trellis, so she was safe from the role of the princess in the tower.

For a moment she wondered if he might speak to her, but then he continued up the path and around the house. She told herself it was fortunate, since neither of them would want attention drawn to her position. It would look too much like she was seeking him out.

The encounter left her even more restless. She blew on the window glass to create a fog, then drew a design in it, a spiral that tumbled into itself. She needed to find a way to distract herself. Perhaps she should write Jane a letter, though there was a great deal she would need to leave out.

The light tap at her door came not quite as a surprise, more an inevitability. She pressed her hand to her mouth for a moment, then, with a resolution that surprised her, she patted her hair into place and wrapped the shawl more firmly around herself before opening the door.

As she expected, Darcy stood on the other side. He stepped back and bowed to her, his expression serious. "Miss Bennet, would you be kind enough to grant me the honour of a few minutes' conversation? Not here, of course – perhaps in the sitting room?"

"If you do not object, I would prefer to walk outside. I have been indoors all day."

"As you wish. The skies have cleared enough that you can see the stars – but I suppose that you have already discovered that."

She glanced over to the window with a hint of a smile. "It did not pass unnoticed."

He relaxed slightly. "I will await you downstairs, then."

Elizabeth cast a glance at the hook where her detested bonnet hung. If he could go out without a hat, so could she. "I will come now." It would be interesting to see if he said anything about her lack of bonnet and gloves – and after all, no one would see her except him.

There was a flash of something in his eyes, but he merely held the door open for her. With a nod, she followed him down the dark passageway to the steps. No sound came from Jenny's room, but downstairs Elizabeth noted that a light still burned in the dining room. She wondered if it was Sally at work or Colonel Fitzwilliam. She hoped for the former. Until the thought of the colonel discovering them crossed her mind, she had not realized how very furtive they would appear, leaving the house alone together at this time of night. At least with the roads in their current condition, no one would consider elopement a possibility! She could not help giving a soft laugh at the thought as Darcy opened the front door for her.

He closed the door behind him quietly. "Something amuses you,

Miss Bennet?"

"Only a bit of silliness." When he continued to look at her inquisitively, she said, "Slipping out of the house at night with a gentleman is supposed to indicate an elopement. I was picturing a hapless pair of lovers returning to the house and saying, "We tried to go to Gretna Green, but the bridge was out." As I said, just foolishness."

Darcy chuckled. "No, I believe Gretna Green is quite out of the question tonight, but we can still take a walk. Do you have a preference in direction?"

She considered. For propriety's sake they should stay within view of the house, but she longed to escape further, and she had been alone with Darcy so much in the last two days that she knew she would be safe. "Is it too muddy to go down by the river?"

"No more than anywhere else at the moment. The path is clear for a short way, and the river is quieter tonight."

She folded her hands behind her back to obviate the question of whether he should offer her his arm. There was no point in taking risks, after all. "Then let us go there."

They walked side by side without a word for several minutes until Elizabeth said, "For a gentleman desiring a conversation, you are remarkably silent."

"You are, of course, correct. I am better at silence than conversation, and I have been trying to decide where to start."

"It is traditional to start at the beginning," she said with mock gravity, teasing to hide the anxiety his words engendered in her.

"The beginning is the problem in this case. Very well, Miss Bennet, I have realized that some of what I said to you two nights ago may have come out in a manner other than I intended. I have," he said dryly, "something of a gift for expressing myself in a manner that sounds offensive when I mean nothing of the sort."

"We all have our unique talents." She gave him a sidelong glance, but could not read his expression in the darkness.

"In that case, *your* gifts must be far superior to mine! But my point is that I did not mean to insult your family when I tried to enumerate the obstacles my affection had to overcome, but I fear that is what I did. While there is an inequity of income and, to some extent, status, I know your family is as dear to you as my own is to me." There. He had said it.

Elizabeth's eyebrows rose. "Some dearer than others, of course," she said with a teasing inflection.

He glanced at her, wondering if she referred to his aunt's disagreeable behavior. It was true that his relations could be just as embarrassing as hers. "I should also mention that, while my relatives may have had other plans for my marriage, I am fortunate in that I need answer to no one but myself in my choice."

"But there are, of course, my low connections and how they will affect your standing in society." She was not, after all, a princess in the tower awaiting her knight; she was lowly Cinderella, though she would hardly label Darcy a prince.

How should he handle this? He remembered Richard's words about acknowledging inequality without degrading her. "You would think me either a fool or a liar if I claimed it would have no effect, but those who would judge me by it are not ones whose opinions I value. In fairness I should tell you that I am not well received in the *ton* as it is, in part because my family name still bears some slight taint from the manner of my parents' marriage, since all the bridges between *them* and Gretna Green were intact. The larger part is owing to my gift of giving offense, and also because I have never been able to bring myself to care who receives vouchers to Almack's and who does not. The *ton* tolerates me because of my fortune, and I tolerate them because I have a sister who must be launched into society soon. If you were hoping I could offer a better entrée into the *ton*, I am sorry to disappoint you."

To his relief, Elizabeth laughed. "Of all the concerns I have considered in this matter, I have not given the *ton* even one thought."

"I am glad." Some ridiculous sense of honor compelled him to say, "My cousin is well accepted in the *ton*."

She stopped and turned to face him. "Why are you telling me this?"

"It is probably unwise of me to point out his virtues, but it seems only fair to tell you the truth. I would not want..." His throat tightened to the point where he no longer knew if he could manage to say the words. Finally, in a low, half-strangled voice, he said, "I would not want you to be unhappy."

To his utter astonishment, this time she tucked her hand in his arm as she began to walk again. He had not offered her his arm because he thought it would make her uncomfortable, so it was her decision. He could not understand it, but was grateful for small miracles.

"You are very generous, then. I take it that Colonel Fitzwilliam has told you of our conversation?" She seemed to be choosing her words with unusual care.

"He did." Darcy did not trust himself to say anything more on that topic. "Along with some commentary on what he considers to be my failings."

Elizabeth was grateful now for the darkness. "Oh, my. That sounds…. unpleasant."

"It was unexpected. We should stop here, or your feet will become acquainted with the river's new path."

"The water is higher than I had expected."

"But calmer than it was this morning."

"Except, perhaps, when someone throws rocks into it?"

There was a long silence. "It seemed preferable to fisticuffs."

"Infinitely preferable."

"Besides, fighting with Richard is pointless. At rough and tumble fighting, he would win. In a boxing salon, I would triumph. Pistols – he would win. Swords – I would win. There is no sport in it. One learns these things, growing up together." He tried to keep the bitterness from his voice, but suspected he had not been fully successful. "He thinks that I expect everyone to fall in with my plans regardless of their own desires."

"Do you?"

"At times, yes. It is part of my role as master of Pemberley. Richard does not perceive that there are also times when *I* have no choices." Now he definitely sounded bitter.

"Such as?"

He took a deep breath to calm himself, but it did no good. "Do you think I *wanted* to leave you with him this afternoon and to check on the tenants instead? I knew that he admires you and that the two of you would be laughing and joking together while I was in the midst of chaos and filth, trying to make sure that no one had succumbed to illness. It happens after floods – a day or two later, they develop bloody flux, and some of them die. I saw it happen at Pemberley once, and my father told me it is common. He thought it was some ill humour native to flood waters, but it did not stop him from doing his duty even when it put him at risk, not until he himself became ill. Fortunately, with excellent care, he recovered eventually." He could not hide his anger. "Yes, I would have *much* preferred to stay in the sitting room with you. But I could not."

"I see." After a moment she added, "And you exposed yourself to the flood waters as well this morning."

"Perhaps you think I should have directed them from the bank, allowing them to take risks I was not willing to. I am sorry; I should not be saying any of this to you. Particularly if you and Richard...." He did not finish.

Elizabeth surprised herself. "I do not think it likely that you will need to worry about that."

"You do not?" His astonishment and relief were apparent. "But you seem to enjoy his company."

"I like him quite well – but not his proposal. It is just... well, let me explain it differently. If I were to discover that one of my sisters cared deeply for a gentleman whom I also admired, it would not matter to me how much I liked him. Even if I knew he did not care for her, he could be nothing more than a friend to me. Had I been particularly intrigued by Mr. Bingley – which, incidentally, I was not - I would never have considered him as a suitor because I knew how much Jane cared for him. Perhaps it is different between gentleman, but I cannot see my way clear to it." She hoped she was not making a mistake in saying this, but he had been very honest with her, and she owed him the same in return.

His free hand closed over hers as it rested on his arm. "Thank you. You have spared me from a most unpleasant night of reflections."

Although he clasped her hand gently, the strength of his fingers was apparent. His hand, warmer than she would have expected, enclosed hers almost completely in a way that was simultaneously comforting and disconcerting, leaving her senses off balance, poised between a desire to lean closer to him and an equally powerful urge to flee.

Her choice to leave aside her gloves had been a serious mistake. No wonder everyone expected young ladies to be gloved, if this sort of sensation was what could be expected from bare-handed contact with a gentleman! And it seemed more intimate by the second.

Hastily she said, "That does not mean anything else has changed, simply that I do not see that particular option as open to me."

"I understand." This time, though, his voice sounded somewhat empty. He released her hand. "Should we return to the parsonage?"

Back to the suffocating stillness, back to the tensions and polite rules? "Only if all the suitable stones are already in the river."

It was a moment before he laughed. "I suspect there may be a few I overlooked last time. Would you like one?"

"Yes, please."

She took her hand from his arm as he scuffed about the ground with his boots, pausing occasionally to collect something. It was definitely a side of Mr. Darcy that she would not have expected.

He returned and held out his full hands. "For milady's pleasure."

Apparently Cinderella had transformed back into the fairy tale princess. Elizabeth leaned closer, but could make out nothing but a jumble of shapes. She selected one at random and hefted it in her hand, feeling the irregular shape and weight of it before stepping forward and tossing it in the swollen river. It disappeared into the darkness and landed with a gratifying plop. She dusted off her hands. "Definitely satisfying," she announced.

She felt rather than saw his smile as he said, "It can be useful on occasion." He drew back one arm and hurled a rock upstream. The splash sounded impressively far away.

"You seem quite practiced at that!" she said.

"Richard and I used to have contests on who could throw the furthest."

"Who won?"

"The honors tended to be divided, so we had to work even harder at it."

"Well, you may be reassured that you could easily defeat me with either sword or pistol as well as throwing rocks and riding horses, though I would prefer to avoid contemplation of fisticuffs."

"And in what skill could *you* defeat *me*?" He handed her another stone.

She cocked her head to one side. "Teasing. I fancy my skills at teasing exceed yours."

"You are quite right. I would be sorry sport at that, though I am happy to serve as a target any time you wish to practice. I rather enjoy being teased, at least by you."

"See, you do have some rudimentary skills in that regard, but it is good of you to concede defeat so easily." She threw the stone, though judging by its sound it went no further than the last.

"That is because you have defeated me in so many ways, Miss Bennet." His voice was amused now, but still she felt a pang.

"It was *quite* unintentionally done, I assure you." The surface of the water in front of her grew brighter and more turbulent as the moon broke through the clouds once again.

"I am sure it was. I know you well enough to believe you would not deliberately injure anyone."

Elizabeth bit her lip. It was so much harder to keep her distance from him when he was gentle. If he had ever spoken to her like this before, she might not have disliked him so much. And it had been easier to speak freely when she could not see him so clearly. Now, with the moonlight casting shadows on the sharp lines of his face, the safety she had found in the darkness fled as well. "I fear you are too kind to me. The night is become chilly; perhaps it is time to return."

"As you wish." He did not offer his arm as he fell into step beside her, and she felt the lack of it, even though the path was clearer in her view now.

When they were almost back to the house, he said in a constrained voice, "I apologize if I have offended you. I did not mean to do so."

"No, you did nothing at all to offend me. You are simply not the person I once thought you to be, and it confuses me." She aimed for a light, pleasant tone.

He opened the door for her. "I will have to hope that is an improvement."

She laughed. "Given my past opinion of you, I would have to say it is to the good. Good night, Mr. Darcy." She dipped a curtsey.

"Good night, Miss Bennet." He bowed, then watched her retreating back thoughtfully.

Chapter 9

ELIZABETH BROKE HER fast in her room in the morning since all the options awaiting her downstairs would be uncomfortable at best and possibly much worse. If both Mr. Darcy and Colonel Fitzwilliam were already there, she suspected there would be tension. If it was the colonel alone, she would have to find a tactful way to refuse him. If it was only Mr. Darcy – well, then it would depend on *which* Mr. Darcy it was. The silent, staring Darcy? The dryly humorous one? Or the insulting one, or the flirtatious, or the playful, or the one in pain, or the darkly dutiful Darcy, or perhaps one she had yet to meet? Vexing, complicated man! The colonel seemed comfortingly simple by comparison. If neither were there, she would sit in suspense wondering which would appear first. Staying in her room alone all day was beginning to sound appealing.

She would not be such a coward, though, so after finishing her hot chocolate, she took a deep breath and headed downstairs. She found Colonel Fitzwilliam in the dining room with the tray of rolls and pastries. He greeted her with his customary good cheer, which served as a reminder that his amiability would likely smooth the way through the difficult discussion to come.

Helping herself to a cup of coffee more to give herself something to do with her hands than out of any desire to drink it, she said, "Have you seen Mr. Darcy this morning?"

His raised eyebrow showed he was not unaware of the importance of the question. "He was up and away before I came down. The maid says he was off to the barn, whatever that might mean."

"The poor folk displaced by the flood are being housed in a neighbor's barn. Mr. Darcy has been most conscientious about seeing their needs are met." She wondered if he had left to give her the opportunity to refuse his cousin more privately.

"Ah, yes – Darcy is always the consummate landowner, even when the land involved is not his own."

"He seems to take his responsibilities very seriously." Was she actually defending him to his cousin?

"He seems to feel some responsibility to act as landlord here since our aunt tends to give her tenants advice when she should be giving them assistance. His father did the same when he was alive."

Elizabeth took a sip of her coffee, unable to think of a good way to lead into her prepared speech. Finally, she resolved to take the desperate measure of raising the subject out of the blue. "I have been giving a good deal of thought to your kind offer of yesterday. I cannot begin to tell you how honored I am to be the recipient of such an offer from you, nor how grateful I am for your concern for my well-being and reputation. You are truly one of the most amiable men of my acquaintance…"

He held up his hand to stop her. "Miss Bennet, although I am not practiced at such things, I can recognize the beginning of a refusal when I hear it. Shall we save ourselves the embarrassment of discussing it further and simply consider the matter closed?"

She let out a deep breath. "Naturally, if that is what you wish, but please permit me to say that I was very tempted, and under other circumstances would probably have accepted with pleasure."

"Under which circumstances -- Darcy's proposal or the question of whether you have been compromised?" He sounded as disinterested as if they were discussing a game of cards.

"Both, I suppose. I dislike the idea of having no choice about marrying, but I could never be happy knowing that my presence was causing a rift between you, and there is nothing you can say to convince me that would not be the case. You and Mr. Darcy seem more like brothers than cousins in many ways, and I will not be the one to interfere with such an old friendship."

"Does this argument extend to refusing Darcy as well?"

"From a logical standpoint it should, but in fact I have not decided one way or the other. I have greater faith, you see, in *your* ability to tolerate such a disappointment than in his. You sensibly guarded your heart against me when you thought nothing more was possible, so I am disappointing only a few hours worth of hopes on your part. Mr. Darcy has been struggling with this for many months. I am sure he will be able to forget me if that is necessary, but I suspect he feels it too deeply to be able to put it behind him if he were forced to see me married to you."

"You have captured our relationship in a nutshell, madam. I bend to the circumstance far more readily than my cousin does." His voice had an edge to it.

"I will add that to my list of comparisons. I understand you can triumph over Mr. Darcy with a pistol, but not with a sword, that you are his equal in throwing ability, and that your ability at fisticuffs outdoes his, but not at boxing. I confess myself a little baffled as to what the difference between fisticuffs and boxing might be, but I will take it on faith that there is one."

"Rules, Miss Bennet," he said with a rueful smile. "Boxing has rules, and fisticuffs does not."

Since he seemed cheered by her teasing, she said, "Are there other skills at which you differ?"

"There are many. He loses at cards – anyone can read his expression to know what cards he holds – but has the deep pockets to afford it if he chooses, while I do well at cards but cannot afford to play." He shook his head with a mock sigh, then sat up, abruptly alert, looking over her shoulder out the window.

"Hell and damnation!" He hurried around the table and took her by the arm, urging her away from the window. "I beg your pardon, Miss Bennet, but I must ask you to go above stairs immediately, and to remain there until Darcy returns. You must move quickly now."

Taken aback by his vehemence, she asked,"Why, what is the matter?"

"My father and my aunt are coming, accompanied, unless I miss my guess, by a solicitor. They believe you are engaged to Darcy, and this is going to be an *extremely* unpleasant scene."

"I am not afraid to face them!"

"But *I* am afraid to let you do so, because if I do, Darcy will take that sword of his and carve me into little pieces, and he would be quite correct to do so. It would be kinder to hand you over to a squad of Napoleon's soldiers. *Please* go, Miss Bennet."

"Very well," she said, mystified. "But why would they believe me engaged to Darcy when I am not?"

"Never mind that. Go now, and do not come down unless Darcy is here, even if I send for you, no matter what you hear me or anyone else say."

He urged her toward the staircase and called for Sally, instructing her to send a boy for Darcy without an instant's delay. Elizabeth was just out of sight of the stairs when the sound reached her of the front door slamming open without even the courtesy of a knock. She pressed herself against the wall where she could not be seen, listening intently.

The colonel drawled in a voice quite unlike the one she knew, "Why, sir, to what do I owe this honor?"

"Where is Darcy, damn him!" The roar must be from the earl.

"Out and about somewhere. Something about the flood." Colonel Fitzwilliam managed to sound utterly bored. "Would you care for some refreshment? I warn you, the brandy here is an insult to the name."

"Is that girl here?" Lady Catherine sounded as if she had eaten icicles for breakfast.

"The maid? How would I know?"

"That Bennet chit, you fool!"

"Her? She is most likely with Darcy. Do, please, make yourselves quite at home here – oh, pardon me, I see that you already have."

Lady Catherine snapped, "Did he tell you that they are engaged?"

She could not hear the colonel's response, but the earl could have been heard in the next county. "You should have stopped it, then!"

"I did my best. He wouldn't listen, so I tried proposing to the girl myself – even told her that my brother was sickly and I was his only heir. No luck, not even when I dangled a countess' title." Again, he used that languid drawl.

"You should have compromised her, you fool!"

No wonder Colonel Fitzwilliam had not wanted her present!

"Tried that, too, but Darcy doesn't let her out of his sight, day *or* night. I should know; I tried climbing in her window last night. Pity, though – she's a toothsome piece, and I wouldn't have minded a taste or two. Oh, well - can't have everything, you know."

Elizabeth's jaw dropped. What could he be playing at?

"You stay out of this, birdwit!" the earl snarled to someone - perhaps Lady Catherine? Elizabeth wondered if there would be blood on the floor by the time this was over.

The colonel said, "How did you find out so quickly? He only told me last night."

"The damn fool put it in the papers! We will have to say it was an error."

Elizabeth's hand flew to her mouth. How could it be in the papers? They had been stranded here this whole time!

"The papers? Probably the soliticitor. Darcy says he wrote him already about the settlement."

The sound of running feet overtook the conversation, then she heard Darcy's voice. "Good God, Richard! What is the matter?"

"You have guests," the colonel drawled.

Darcy made some sort of reply, then exclaimed, "Mr. Bennet?"

"None other," came the familiar voice, sharp with anger. "You seem to have forgotten my existence, so I thought perhaps you needed a reminder that my daughter is not yet of age, and you cannot and will not marry her without my consent -- which, I might add, I have no intention of giving, now or ever."

Elizabeth closed her eyes, then slid down the wall until she was sitting on the floor, her knees bent to her chest. Her father! He must have heard all of the terrible things the colonel had said. This had to be a nightmare.

"Doesn't matter," the earl snapped. "You aren't marrying her, Darcy. You know perfectly well I have plans for you."

The colonel said in a sing-song voice, "You have plans, Lady Catherine has plans – Darcy, you are *very* well planned for!"

That was it – Colonel Fitzwilliam was trying to draw his father's ire away from Darcy by playing the rake. Despite whatever had passed between the two men the previous night, apparently their old bond still held. The colonel was playing the role for both of them because he knew Darcy couldn't do it for himself, and from the ease with which he did it, Elizabeth suspected this was not the first time.

Lady Catherine had been silent too long. "He is marrying my Anne, and that is the end of it. That chit may have fooled him with her arts and allurements, but he is promised to Anne."

"Be quiet, Catherine! He can do far better than Anne."

"He *must* marry Anne! She needs him, and his mother and I planned it when they were in their cradles!"

"I don't care if all the saints in heaven planned it. He isn't marrying Anne. If she needs to marry someone, she can marry Richard."

"How lovely for me," the colonel remarked. "I rather fancy being master of Rosings Park, especially once you move to the Dower House, aunt."

"Ungrateful monster!" cried Lady Catherine. "*This* is the thanks I get for all I have done for you! I'll see you hung if you come near my daughter."

"What a charming family gathering this is," said the colonel. "Wouldn't you say so, Darcy?"

Elizabeth buried her face in her hands. The colonel had been right – it would be a relief if a squad of Napoleon's finest soldiers stormed the house. She hoped his antics were giving Darcy a moment to collect himself before facing the onslaught.

Darcy had apparently seen enough. "I thank all of you for sharing your opinions with me. I am certain you have only the best of motives. However, the fact remains that my choice of wife is exactly that – *my* choice. I owe no duty to anyone but myself. Mr. Bennet, I would like to speak to you privately. There are factors here of which you are not aware."

"I doubt it. That gentleman there has already been kind enough to inform us that you have been spending your nights in my daughter's bedroom. I have *nothing* to say to you. Now, where is my daughter?"

Elizabeth could only imagine the look of betrayal Darcy must be sending in the colonel's direction. His voice was quite clipped as he said, "I do not know what you have been told, but nothing untoward has happened between Elizabeth and me. She will tell you the same."

"Darcy, I know you will see reason." The earl was apparently changing tactics, now all oily politeness. "I cannot imagine you would risk Georgiana's reputation this way."

"My marriage will have no effect on Georgiana's reputation. Miss Bennet is respectable."

The colonel drawled, "You misunderstand him, Darcy. That was a threat. If you persist in marrying Miss Bennet, *he* means to ruin Georgiana's reputation in retaliation."

Elizabeth could not believe her ears, especially when this response was met not with a denial, but by silence. That was the end of it, then. She would not be marrying Mr. Darcy. She would never see him again. Suddenly, she found herself choking back a sob. When had she come to care about him? She bit down on her hand until it hurt. How could she expect Darcy to sacrifice his sister for her sake? He could not. No, she would leave here alone, with her reputation in tatters and nothing to show for it but an aching heart, all because Lord Matlock said so.

When Darcy began to speak, Elizabeth covered her ears with her hands. She understood why he had to renounce her, but did not want to hear him say it, or it would echo in her mind forever. But she could hear him anyway, speaking in that same distant voice she had heard the previous night. "You offer me the choice between ruining Miss Bennet's reputation or Georgiana's. I have given Miss Bennet my word, and I will not withdraw it."

Her hands were on her chest now, holding in her pounding heart. Had he really said that? She could only imagine how much it hurt him – and all for a woman who had not even accepted his proposal, but whom he would still not allow to be injured. It was too much to bear. Even the colonel seemed to be speechless in face of this.

Elizabeth could not stand it. Without a thought to the consequences, she picked up her skirts and raced downstairs. She reached Darcy's side and slipped her hand into his arm. "I am *quite* surprised at all I have just heard," she said with a false brightness. "My lord, of course you wish to see your nephew make a brilliant marriage, but he has proposed to me and I have accepted, and we have a number of witnesses to that. I will not release him from the engagement. Before you try to force *him* to break it, I urge you to consider the effects of a breach of promise suit. He would only have to pay me a settlement, of course, but everyone will know that he broke a publicly acknowledged engagement *after* compromising the lady in question. Under those circumstances, will any gentleman risk allowing his daughter to contract an engagement to him? I think not. While it might be more satisfying to you to see both your niece and nephew ruined, would it not be more sensible to concentrate your efforts on making a brilliant alliance for Miss Darcy, since Mr. Darcy's case is already quite hopeless?" She did not dare to look at her father.

The silence that met this statement was broken only by Colonel Fitzwilliam's slow clapping. "Oh, brava, Miss Bennet! Spoken like a Fitzwilliam born." He was sprawled in an upholstered chair with one leg hooked across the arm of it, a large glass of brandy in one hand. He gave a quick wink when he caught her looking his way. "I say, Darcy, is there any more of this ghastly brandy to be had? This was the last of the bottle, and I am not *nearly* foxed enough if I am to be forced to deal with my *family* all day."

She felt a rush of gratitude toward him for defending not only Darcy, but her as well, when he owed her nothing and had reason for resentment as well.

"There is another bottle in the study," Darcy said slowly, but he was not looking at his cousin. His eyes were fixed on her face.

It was at that precise moment that Elizabeth realized that, in her impulsive rush to defend Mr. Darcy, she had also utterly committed herself to marrying him. Her skin prickled with goosebumps as she met his gaze, her insides churning with the knowledge that she had just agreed to be his wife, flesh of his flesh, till death parted them. He would take possession of her body, and she would live by his side. It felt as if the wind had been knocked out of her and she had forgotten how to breathe.

"Did you mean that?" Darcy spoke just above a whisper, his words directed only at her, as if he had forgotten the presence of all the others.

For some reason, his doubt put her own worries to rest. They might still disagree on many things, but somehow they would work it out together, and that idea made her feel light as air and as if the sun had just come out. "I meant it," she said, then with a sense of daring she stood up on tiptoe and whispered in his ear, "About marrying you, that is – not the other part." Having no reputation left to ruin, she discovered, could be quite freeing.

A slow smile dawned on his face. He took her hands into his, a pulse of fire racing where their fingers entwined.

Then the colonel was standing, swaying slightly. "Oh, please, Darcy. *You* may be happy about gaining a leg-shackle, but is far too early in the day to subject *me* to your amorous displays."

The earl wheeled to face his son. "You worthless ingrate! You are a disgrace to the Fitzwilliam name."

Richard held his glass up as if to examine the contents. "A disgrace to the Fitzwilliam name? Dear me, my memory must be failing me. Why is it that the proud Fitzwilliam name is no longer as proud as it was? Could it be because...."

"Miserable cur!" shouted the earl.

Elizabeth lost track of the shouting match when her father approached them, his face hard. He made no acknowledgement of Darcy. Instead he took her arm in a painful grip and said, "We are leaving now."

"We cannot leave, not with...."

His face turned purple. "You *will* obey me. I have been far too lax with you, and I am paying for it now."

Darcy said, "Mr. Bennet, we have a great deal to discuss, but perhaps we could do so outside."

"I have *nothing* to discuss with *you*. Come, Lizzy."

"Please, I know you are angry, but can you not spare a moment listen to Mr. Darcy – and to me? This is not what it seems, and...."

"Enough. You are my responsibility and under my rule, and if I tell you to go, then you will go."

Elizabeth hardly recognized the man who stood before her. "But..."

Darcy stepped in. "Mr. Bennet, I ask you to allow me a few minutes of your time."

"You have no rights in this matter at all, and you will unhand my daughter!"

Looking bewildered, Darcy released her hand, searching Elizabeth's face as if for clues. "I have the greatest respect for your daughter, sir."

"Yes, you *respect* her all day and all night, I am told!" Mr. Bennet tugged Elizabeth's arm until she followed him out of the sitting room and then through the front door.

Elizabeth threw a helpless look over her shoulder at Darcy, who kept pace with them as much as the narrow corridor would permit. "Papa, that is not true. I do not know why Colonel Fitzwilliam said that unless it was to impress his own father. Mr. Darcy *could* have taken advantage of my defenseless situation, but he *chose* not to."

"That would explain why he announced your engagement without speaking to me first, I suppose." Mr. Bennet's voice dripped sarcasm.

Once outside, Darcy strode around them until he could face Mr. Bennet as he pulled Elizabeth along. "There were pressing reasons for that, which I would be happy to explain to you if only you would allow me to do so!" His veneer of calm was beginning to break.

Mr. Bennet ignored him and continued to head down the road toward the ruined bridge.

Elizabeth tried again, speaking more gently this time. "I do not understand. This is not like you." Although her father had been forced to hear terrible things about her – untrue things - she would not have thought anything could put her usually easy-going father into a state like this. What could have happened to him?

Her father ignored her just as he had Mr. Darcy, which only concerned her more. That was unlike him as well. Could he be ill, or fevered in the head?

"Mr. Bennet, while I understand your desire to take your daughter away from here, I fail to see how it is in her best interest for us not to discuss what is to happen next. I would have been much happier to ask your permission first, but that was impossible at the time. Any delay in the announcement would have resulted in damage to Miss Elizabeth's reputation and rumors that I had only married her out of necessity. If it appeared that our engagement predated the floods, she would be protected."

"And it never occurred to you, not once, that I might refuse my permission?"

Darcy glanced at Elizabeth in confusion. "No, sir, it did not. Your daughter was compromised by my presence, but through no fault of mine. I am well able to provide for her, I am of good family, I love her, and I now also have a responsibility to marry her. If I were to refuse to marry her, you would have every right to be furious with me, but I am *not* refusing!"

"Oh, yes, I have seen your *good family*, Mr. Darcy, and you will forgive me if I want my daughter to have nothing whatsoever to do with them. I would rather see Lizzy disgraced and alone than treated with such disrespect. Perhaps your ten thousand pounds a year would be enough to convince any other father, but you have nothing to offer her that *I* value. You have likely already ruined her life, and that is more than enough."

"Papa, please! I *want* to marry him." There was an edge of desperation in her voice. How much of this outrageous insolence Mr. Darcy would tolerate before deciding that she was not worth the trouble? "He is a good man!"

Mr. Bennet stopped a few feet from the edge of the flood waters where an old man in rough homespun manned a rowboat. "When you are of age, I cannot stop you from marrying whomever you please, but until then, you cannot marry anyone without my permission. I do not give my permission. That is the end of the matter."

Darcy's face paled. "Do you plan, then, to place a retraction in the newspapers?"

Mr. Bennet's lips thinned. "No, that would simply draw more attention to the matter."

"Thank you, sir." It was clear the words cost Darcy a great deal. "Then we can wait, if necessary, until Elizabeth is of age. When will that be?"

Elizabeth cast a despairing look at her father. "Not until December. Boxing Day – I was a Christmas baby."

"I will call on you at Longbourn in a few days, and we can discuss this further then."

Mr. Bennet's face turned even more red. "You will do nothing of the sort, Mr. Darcy. You do not have my permission to call on Lizzy. If you set foot on Longbourn property, I will have you brought before the magistrate for trespassing. You will not write to Lizzy or attempt to contact her in any way."

"Sir, I do not question your authority to set whatever rules you choose, but that will simply cause more talk and more harm to your daughter!"

Elizabeth shook her head at Darcy. Surely her father would eventually come to his senses again, and arguing with him now seemed only to make matters worse. "We do not need to decide everything now. There will be plenty of time discuss this later." She hoped he understood her message that rational argument would not sway her father at the moment.

Mr. Bennet put a hand on Elizabeth's back and propelled her into the rowboat, apparently uncaring that this required her to step into water nearly a foot deep. She gasped as icy water rushed into her low half-boots, soaking through her stockings in a matter of seconds. She clambered into the boat, which rocked precariously until she sat down on one of the rude boards. It tipped once more as Mr. Bennet stepped over the gunwale.

Darcy visibly fought to calm himself. "I will hope for a better resolution than seems possible at the moment." Then emotion seemed overcome him. "My heart is yours, Elizabeth, and nothing can change that. I can be patient until December if I must. Wait for me, I beg of you, no matter what may come."

Hot tears welled in her eyes as the boatman used his oar to push off from the water's edge. She tried to form the words to tell him she would wait, but her voice had deserted her.

His eyes still fixed on Elizabeth, Darcy said to the boatman, "Return here after you have taken them across."

The man spat in the water by way of response and pulled on the oars.

Elizabeth turned to look at Darcy over her shoulder as the boatman fought his way through the still choppy waters laden with loose branches and debris, pushing away obstacles with his oar. It took only few minutes to reach the other side.

Darcy watched Elizabeth and Mr. Bennet until they disappeared from sight on the lane to Rosings Park. He rubbed a tired hand across his face, hardly able to believe what had just occurred – the joy of Elizabeth accepting him willingly, then having her torn from him, perhaps for months. He would need to find some way to communicate with her, but that would have to wait until he had dealt with his family. Wearily he turned away from the river and trudged back up the hill to the parsonage.

To think that only an hour ago, Elizabeth had been worried about how she would gently and politely refuse the colonel's offer of marriage! A day ago she would have been relieved to be taken away from Darcy. So much had changed since then. Her father had become a virtual stranger to her. She risked a glance at him, but his face was still stony, with no sign of his usual amusement.

The walk to Rosings seemed to take longer than usual, and not just because her feet squelched in her half-boots with each step. She had not even the hope of dry stockings when they reached Rosings; all her clothing apart from what was on her back was still at the parsonage. Would she have to travel all the way to Longbourn with wet feet? What was it that Darcy had said once – 'what is fifty miles of good road? I call it a very easy distance.' Half a day's journey would not seem easy with cold, wet stockings.

Looking back on that conversation, she wondered how she had ever missed his references to a possible match between them. She had been blind. Now, when she could finally see clearly, it was too late.

Mr. Bennet led her straight to the stables where an open carriage sat ready outside. "Hitch up the horses. We will leave directly," he announced to the groom.

The groom mumbled his assent and shuffled into the stables. Elizabeth tried to curl and uncurl her toes in hopes some of the water would run out her boots, but it did not help.

The groom had just gone for the second horse when Charlotte came hurrying toward them. "Lizzy, I am so happy to see you! Are you well? Is it true that Mr. Darcy was with you? Did Colonel Fitzwilliam reach you?"

Elizabeth essayed a wan smile. "Both gentlemen are safe at the parsonage." If they could be called safe while the earl and Lady Catherine remained in towering rages.

"You are not leaving already?"

Mr. Bennet snorted. "Do you think I would remain here one minute longer than necessary? Were it not ten miles to the posting house, I would not even have paused here."

"But will not Mr. Darcy...."

Elizabeth shook her head at her friend. "Best not to even mention him."

"You have not fallen out with him, I hope?"

"Not I." Elizabeth nodded toward her father.

"Well, I for one am very happy for you. I always felt he admired you, but you have been very sly with me."

"I will write to you, I promise. Please give Mr. Collins my thanks and tell him that I enjoyed my visit greatly and am sorry it is to be cut short."

"Into the carriage *now*, Lizzy," said Mr. Bennet.

Charlotte pulled off her gloves. "Here, Lizzy, take these, and my bonnet, too. You cannot travel as you are. I am sorry that the gloves will be large for you, but it is better than nothing."

Elizabeth had not even given a thought to her disgraceful lack of outdoor attire, not that her father had given her a choice about it. "But will you not need them to return to the parsonage?"

"I can borrow a bonnet from Mrs. Jenkinson, I am sure." Charlotte untied her bonnet and placed it in Elizabeth's hand.

"Thank you, Charlotte." With a regretful glance at her friend, Elizabeth stepped up into the carriage. "Could you send my belongings to Longbourn when the opportunity arises?"

"Of course."

The road was rutted from all the rains, making the carriage jostle uncomfortably. Elizabeth wished the sides were higher so that she could lean her head against them. If she could close her eyes, she could pretend none of this was real.

After perhaps a quarter of an hour, Mr. Bennet said briskly, "Well, Lizzy, have you nothing to say for yourself?"

His countenance now seemed as calm as ever, which stirred her own anger. How dare he treat her like a misbehaving child, and then expect everything to go back to normal once they left Rosings? No."

"No?"

Elizabeth enunciated each word slowly and carefully. "No, sir, I do not."

"It is not like you to sulk," he chided.

"It is not like *you* to refuse to listen!"

"Lizzy," he said in a warning tone.

She turned away to hide the tears pricking at the corners of her eyes. "You have made up your mind already. You have been judge and jury without stopping to hear the evidence, and I have been hauled off like a criminal to jail. You will have to forgive me if I seem disinclined to chat."

"Was not the public announcement of your engagement without a word to me reason enough for me to judge?"

"What public announcement? I have no idea how you heard about the engagement, especially as it did not even exist until this very morning!"

"I *heard* about it, if you choose to put it thus, from your mother, who had it from her sister Phillips, who had it from Mrs. Long, who read it in the morning newspaper – *yesterday's* morning paper, which is very timely indeed for an engagement that did not occur until today!"

She remembered then that Colonel Fitzwilliam had said something about an announcement in the papers at the beginning of that horrible encounter with the earl, and that Darcy himself had said something of the same to her father later. *They* must have known something about it even if she did not. Had Darcy been so certain of himself as to place an announcement before he had actually proposed to her? It made no sense. Everything she knew of his character suggested that he would have wanted to follow the usual procedure and speak to her father, yet somehow the announcement was there, and he had not even told her about it. Was he so certain she would give in to him eventually, or did her opinion simply not matter to him? She could make no sense of it, but her sudden doubts drained her of her righteous indignation. She struggled to recall what Darcy had said about it – something about protecting her reputation.

"I did not know about the announcement."

"Ha! So that is how your fine Mr. Darcy shows his respect for *you* as well as for me! How could you think to marry a man who would not even consult you on something of that magnitude – and before you were even engaged, by your own report! You are well rid of him, Lizzy."

"I am *not* rid of him. I am sure he has an explanation."

"An explanation he could not be bothered to give even to *you*?"

There was nothing she could say to that. Darcy's behavior in the last few days had been enough to convince her that he did not act on impulse nor without reason, but her father had no cause to believe that. She would not condemn Darcy out of hand without hearing his explanation, not after having made that mistake when Wickham had filled her ears with his lies.

Fortunately, they soon reached the town and pulled up to the post-house. There would be an hour's wait, but there was no privacy either at the post-house or in the coach itself for further conversation. Elizabeth was grateful for the reprieve. She would prefer to be squeezed between half a dozen passengers than to be alone with her father.

When they arrived in London, to her surprise, Mr. Bennet hired a hackney coach to take them to the Gardiner residence on Gracechurch Street instead of arranging to catch the coach to Meryton. They arrived at her uncle's house just before dark. From her aunt's reception of them, it was clear her father had not warned them of this visit in advance.

Jane ran to embrace her, shedding happy tears at the sight of her beloved sister. Mrs. Gardiner offered refreshments, but Elizabeth said that all she required was dry footwear and a place to rest. It was not so much that she desired to lie down as that she wished to be away from her father. She wondered vaguely how he planned to explain their odd arrival to the Gardiners, but could not bring herself to care.

It was almost amusing; after three days of desiring above all else to escape from the parsonage, now that she had done so, she wanted nothing more than to return to it. No, it was not the parsonage - she wanted Darcy. He would understand what she was feeling and would make her feel better about it, and beyond that, he would somehow find a way to solve the problems she faced.

Instead, she had Jane, who exclaimed with sympathy over the white, shriveled skin of her feet when she finally was able to remove her half-boots in the privacy of Jane's room. Her sister wanted to chafe warmth into them, but Elizabeth said, "No, I must wash them first. It is flood water, and that can carry disease." Just what Mr. Darcy would say, she thought.

"There was a flood in Kent? Is everyone safe?"

"Everyone you would know. Some poor villagers were washed away." What would little Jenny think now that Elizabeth had vanished just like her parents? She could only hope Mr. Darcy would think to explain it to the girl. "There was a little girl with a broken leg that I helped to care for. The rest of her family died in the flood."

"The poor child! And did you have to leave because of the floods?"

"I had to leave because our father refused to allow me to remain there." The words brought back the bitterness of the betrayal, and the tears she had hoped to hold in check broke free. She covered her face with her hands and sobbed.

Immediately Jane's arms were around her. "Dearest Lizzy, what is the matter? What happened?"

"So much. So much has happened. I do not even know where to begin."

Jane pressed a handkerchief into her hand. "You must tell me, though – I am imagining the most terrible events!"

Elizabeth hiccoughed a laugh through her tears, then mopped her eyes. "It is not so much terrible as terribly shocking. Today, for example – today I refused an offer of marriage from the second son of the Earl of Matlock and accepted an offer from Mr. Darcy, and met the earl himself who was horrible, so horrible to everyone. I have had my reputation quite ruined, and then our father swore that he not only would not permit me to marry Mr. Darcy, but that I may not see him, speak to him or write him. And *that* was just this morning!"

Jane gaped at her, then laughed. "Oh, Lizzy, you had me fooled for a moment! I thought you were serious."

"I *am* serious. That is precisely what happened. And now I am here, engaged but forbidden to see my betrothed, and completely at odds with our father who seems to have gone completely mad!"

"You are truly engaged to Mr. Darcy?" Jane sounded disbelieving. "But I thought you disliked him."

"I did, but – oh, Jane, it would take me half the night to tell you everything that has happened! And I do not know how I will ever face our father again, or even our aunt and uncle after he has told them his version of it – he has misunderstood *everything* and refused to listen to me. It was as if some demon took possession of him. He would not even allow Mr. Darcy to explain anything to him. It was in every way horrible!" Elizabeth's hands shook as she held the handkerchief.

Jane, on seeing her beloved sister so uncharacteristically distraught, begged her to lie back in her bed while she fetched her some tea and a hot brick for her feet. Elizabeth, too miserable to care what anyone did, obeyed her.

Chapter 10

JANE RETURNED CARRYING a tea tray. "The maid left a ewer of hot water so that I can wash your poor feet."

"There is no need for that. I am not ill; I can do it myself."

"But it will make *me* feel better if I can do something to help." Jane poured a little milk into Elizabeth's teacup without needing to ask, then lifted the teapot.

"Very well." Elizabeth watched the steaming tea fall in a smooth line from the spout into her cup. Water, water, everywhere. Then, realizing she had been less than courteous to her sister, she sat up and added, "Thank you."

Jane placed the ewer, bowl and towel next to the bed, then knelt on the floor. She took Elizabeth's foot in her hand and held it over the bowl. When she poured a little of the hot water over the arch of her foot, it felt like a burn to Elizabeth, and she could not help recoiling a little. "They must be even colder than I realized," she said.

Setting the ewer aside, Jane dipped the towel into the bowl, then gently massaged her sister's foot with it. Without looking up, she said, "We dine in an hour, but I told our aunt that you were practically asleep and would probably not come down. I hope that was right."

"Bless you, Jane! I have been trying to think of an excuse. I do not think I can face all those accusing eyes yet."

"I cannot imagine that our aunt and uncle would condemn you unheard."

"I would not have thought our father would either!"

Jane shook her head. "I am certain he must have meant well. Perhaps there is something we do not know yet that would justify his behavior. It is hard to imagine, though – Mr. Bingley thought so well of Mr. Darcy that it is hard for me to imagine him proving to be an utter blackguard."

"He is not a blackguard! There *is* a blackguard, but his name is George Wickham."

"Mr. Wickham! I cannot believe it. His address is so gentlemanly."

"His behavior does not always match his address, apparently. That is another thing I learned." Elizabeth leaned back. Perhaps someday her feet would actually be warm again.

The door to the room eased open. Mrs. Gardiner's face appeared in the opening. "Oh! I am so sorry to enter without knocking, Lizzy. I thought you were asleep, and I was looking for Jane."

"Come in, Aunt," Elizabeth said with resignation. "You are always welcome, of course."

Jane looked up from her ministrations. "Lizzy came all the way from Kent with wet shoes and stockings." The very slight reproach in her voice was as close as Jane ever came to criticism.

"I was not given another choice, and I had no dry shoes with me in any case. Jane, I hope I may borrow something of yours. We left Hunsford with nothing more than the clothes on my back." With a pang, she realized her cloak had been left behind, the one Darcy had given her. Charlotte would not even know it was hers. Somehow that loss seemed worse than the rest.

"What was the great hurry?" Mrs. Gardiner asked.

"That I cannot tell you. You will have to ask my father. Has he not told you the whole sad story?"

"No. He has been closeted with your uncle almost since his arrival."

"Well, when they determine my fate, I will no doubt be informed of it. If I am fortunate, I will not be dragged bodily away without a reason this time."

"Take care, Lizzy; that speech savors strongly of bitterness. Your father is concerned for your reputation."

Elizabeth pushed herself back to an upright position. "And have I not reason to feel bitter? He has allowed Lydia and Kitty to run wild. They have been alone with officers more often than I can count. Both are confirmed flirts that no decent man would consider marrying, and *that* troubles my father not a whit. But when *I* contract an engagement with an eminently respectable and wealthy gentleman of good family, and through no fault of my own am left alone with him by an act of God, he refuses his consent - refuses even to *talk* to him - because he does not like the fact that an announcement was put in the paper too soon! At least there *was* an announcement, which is better than the kind of disgrace Lydia and Kitty are likely to bring onto us. Mr. Darcy was, if anything, overly careful. I fail to see why I should be treated like a fool and a criminal for agreeing to a very eligible offer." She burst into tears at that last reminder.

Mrs. Gardiner sat next to her and squeezed her hand. "So it is true, then, that you are engaged to Mr. Darcy? Mr. Darcy of Pemberley? It is beyond my comprehension, since I have seen Pemberley. It is more than just a very fine house richly furnished; the grounds there are delightful, and have some of finest woods in the country. Unless Mr. Darcy has somehow managed to gamble off his entire fortune, I cannot see what the problem could be. You have told us he is proud – could it be his treatment of that nice Mr. Wickham that your father objects to? Even that, while reflecting poorly on him, is hardly dastardly."

Elizabeth closed her eyes and rubbed her temples. "There was no ill treatment of Mr. Wickham. That was all lies."

Jane dried Elizabeth's feet with a fresh towel. "Lizzy, you have not touched your tea. Please drink a little; you will feel better. There are some raisin cakes, too."

"I am not hungry."

"When was the last time you ate?"

Elizabeth knew that tone. "This morning." The last sustenance she had taken was the coffee she drank with Colonel Fitzwilliam at the parsonage. Her father had purchased food for them at a posting house, but Elizabeth had been too distraught to touch a bite of it. "And please, I do *not* want to go down for dinner. I will eat something here if you wish."

Mrs. Gardiner met Jane's eyes. "As it happens, my husband just asked for a tray of cold meats to be brought to his study in lieu of dinner. The children have already eaten in the nursery, so it is just the three of us. We can all have our soup up here."

There was no point in resisting.

Eventually, Elizabeth succumbed to Mrs. Gardiner's gentle probing and revealed most of her story. She was careful to leave out certain parts, such as what she had learned from the colonel about the role Darcy had played in separating Bingley from Jane. That was something that still needed to be resolved between them, though her inclination now was to assume that Darcy's motives had been good, even if she disagreed with his actions. There was no reason to tell them all of the details of what had passed between her and Darcy, either. Riding double with him had made sense at the time, but she did not think she could adequately convey the situation that had forced them to it. Jane had been shocked enough with the mere fact that Darcy had spent the night in the same house with her. Her precious memory of being held tight in Darcy's arms was one she knew to keep to herself.

"So, you see, we had very little choice but to make the best of a situation that was compromising by its nature. Mr. Darcy could easily have taken advantage of me, but he chose not to." At least not much, she corrected silently.

Jane said hesitantly, "Did our father explain himself later?"

"No. He only asked if I had anything to say for myself, as if I had done something wrong. I was not temperate in my response."

Mrs. Gardiner frowned. "That may not be the wisest tack to take, Lizzy. I understand why you are resentful, but I fear that your anger may only lead your father to be more stubborn in his position. If he thinks you have accepted the situation, he may eventually be persuaded to listen to you."

"I will *not* renounce Mr. Darcy! If I must wait until I am of age to see him, then I will wait, but I will not pretend otherwise."

"I am not asking you to lie, my dear; merely to make it easier for your father to see both sides of the question."

"So he can be as unfair to me as he likes, and I must be all sweetness in return?"

"He *is* your father and you must be ruled by him. My suggestion is only to set the scene so that it is more favorable to you."

"I will consider it," Elizabeth said petulantly. "More likely he will retreat back to his library and forget all about it if he thinks I have accepted his dictates."

"Would it be better to be continually at odds?" When Elizabeth had no reply for this, she added, "But let us wait to discover more. Your uncle has no doubt gained a further understanding of your father's motivations, and may be able to enlighten us. There must be more to this matter than meets the eye. As you say, this is out of character for him."

"If I write a letter, will you send it to Mr. Darcy for me?"

Mrs. Gardiner bit her lip. "No, Lizzy, I cannot," she said gently. "Not when your father has expressly forbidden it."

Elizabeth looked away. It had been her one hope.

After a mostly sleepless night, Elizabeth decided that her aunt's advice had some merit. Wearing one of Jane's dresses and her slippers, she went downstairs to breakfast with the appearance of calmness, though she could not bring herself to smile at her father. She ate enough to alleviate the concern of anyone who might be observing her habits. She listened without comment as the others discussed their plans for the day. Her father made no reference to the previous day or anything related to Kent.

After breakfast, she gave in to the importuning of her young cousins to tell them a story. She was a particular favorite of theirs for the fantastic tales she wove for them, and if this day's imagining was somewhat paler than usual, they did not complain.

Once the children were back in their nursery for lessons, Mrs. Gardiner suggested a shopping expedition with her two nieces. "We will need to purchase a few sundries for Lizzy since we do not know when her trunks will arrive."

"I imagine Charlotte has already sent them to Longbourn, since there was no mention of stopping in London," Elizabeth said equably. "But I will not need anything if I am to go home in the next few days, and if I am to stay longer, I imagine the trunks can be sent on here from Longbourn."

"You are welcome to stay for as long as you like," her aunt said warmly.

"Thank you. I am always happy to see you, but I believe it is not up to me." Elizabeth glanced at her father.

Mr. Bennet lowered the newspaper he was reading by just a few inches. "I have not decided when we will return." His gaze returned to the paper.

Mrs. Gardiner shrugged lightly. "Well, then, you and Jane will need to fetch your bonnets and gloves. I will lend you a shawl, Lizzy. I do not want you to take a chill!"

Elizabeth tactfully chose not to point out that she had spent the previous day outdoors without a shawl. At least she had Charlotte's bonnet and gloves, and today her feet would not be soaking wet. Her half-boots were still a bit damp despite sitting in front of the fire all night, but a pair of warm woolen stockings would prove a suitable barrier.

When the two sisters returned downstairs, now prepared for their excursion, they found Mrs. Gardiner still in the sitting room conversing with their father.

Mr. Bennet folded his newspaper and laid it aside. Rising from his chair, he approached Elizabeth and held out his hand. "I will take that letter, Lizzy."

Elizabeth lifted her chin. "What letter?"

"The letter to Mr. Darcy that I am quite sure you have secreted somewhere about your person -- the one you are hoping to post while you are out and I am not watching."

At that moment, Elizabeth detested him. Slowly she reached into her pocket and drew out an envelope, but instead of handing it to him, she darted behind him and pushed it directly into the hottest part of the fire. Her aunt seized her hand, beating out the sparks that remained on her glove.

Elizabeth looked dispassionately at the singe marks. She would have to buy a new pair for Charlotte. "Shall we go now?" she asked with false brightness.

Mr. Bennet held out a hand to stop her. "Not until I have your word that you will not attempt to write to Mr. Darcy or to contact him in any way, either directly or through someone else."

Elizabeth raised her eyes to his. "And if I do not give you my word?"

"Then you must remain in your room until such a time as you are prepared to give it."

The smile with which he delivered his ultimatum goaded Elizabeth's fragile temper beyond its breaking point. She removed the gloves and her bonnet and slapped them down on a small table. "Then I will be in my room. You may keep these hostage as surety that I will not sneak out. Of course, that would make no difference to *you*, since you have no objection to my being exposed to the entire world, but *I* have better manners than to go outside bare-headed. Perhaps you would do best to tie my hands behind my back."

Mrs. Gardiner put a restraining hand on her arm. "Lizzy, your father does not mean…"

Elizabeth cut her off. "Do not worry. I will be perfectly well. If he intends to starve me into submission, I can trust Jane to sneak a few stale bread crusts and water to me."

Mr. Bennet said dryly, "Kindly spare us the drama, Lizzy."

"Why should I? After all, it is apparently the only thing which I am allowed," she shot back as she stalked out of the room.

Mrs. Gardiner pursed her lips. "Oh, Thomas, that was not well done. I would have been willing to watch her while we were out."

Mr. Bennet crossed his arms. "She must learn to obey me."

"What has happened to you? Did the fairies swap the real Thomas Bennet for a changeling when you were in Kent? I can understand that you do not look forward to your Lizzy leaving home to live halfway across the country, but all you are accomplishing now is keeping her with you a few months longer, while making sure that when she finally does leave, she will never look back!"

"It is *my* family, and I will run it as I see fit." He shook out the newspaper and sat down behind it once more.

Mrs. Gardiner met Jane's eyes and indicated the door with a tilt of her head. Before they left the house, Jane glanced over her shoulder up the stairs. "Perhaps I should spend a few minutes with Lizzy first."

Mrs. Gardiner shook her head. "It is best if we give this as little notice as possible – least said, soonest mended." But once the front door was closed behind her, she let out a long breath through her teeth. "After that little scene, I have half a mind to write to Mr. Darcy myself!"

With a little hitch in her voice, Jane said, "I don't understand *why* he won't let her write to him."

"I wish I knew. Your uncle knows something of it, but he tells me it is not his confidence to share. Something will have to change, though."

The dinner table that night was set for four. Mr. Bennet took this in with one keen look as he claimed his place. "Is Lizzy still sulking, then?"

Mrs. Gardiner exchanged a glance with her husband. "Since you said she was not to leave her room, I had a tray taken up to her."

"I did not mean that she could not take meals with the family!"

"If that was your intention, it was not clear to me; nor, I daresay, was it to Lizzy." Mrs. Gardiner appeared completely preoccupied with spooning out a portion of the ragout. "Perhaps you might explain it to her."

Mr. Bennet waved away this obviously distasteful suggestion. "Later, perhaps."

Elizabeth was not, in fact, sulking. Since she was forbidden to write to Mr. Darcy, she naturally spent the entire afternoon penning a letter to him. Since he would never receive it, she took pleasure in the utter freedom to write whatever she pleased, including a lengthy indictment of her father, the terms of which would have shocked anyone of her acquaintance. She had then moved on to discussing all the things that puzzled her about Mr. Darcy, asking him the questions she had either never thought to or never dared, and then, in his absence, answering them for herself. On Jane's return three hours later, Elizabeth met her with ink stained hands, sore fingers, and a pen which had been so often mended as to be practically useless, but in much better spirits for having cleared her thoughts through writing them.

Her good humor did not last long, since Jane was inclined to hover, which made Elizabeth want to shred all the linens and tear around the room like a mad tiger. Since she loved her sister, she instead expressed a desire to do some quiet reading. After assuring Jane at least half a dozen times that there was nothing she either needed nor desired to be fetched, Elizabeth was finally able to breathe a sigh of relief when Jane went down to dinner.

Her dinner tray, which Mrs. Gardiner had evidently prepared with her own hands, included a tiny vase filled with snowdrops and crocuses. The evident vote of sympathy cheered Elizabeth somewhat, but the prospect of remaining trapped indefinitely in her room was making her uneasy. How long would her father continue this charade? In his current frame of mind, she feared that she would give in before he did, and then she would never forgive him – or herself.

She wondered if her father would visit her at some point, but when a knock finally came on the door, it was her uncle who stepped inside. It was unusual enough for him to come by himself; usually her aunt was the one who had direct dealings with her. Of course, she had no idea which side he was taking in this quarrel, so she decided to proceed with care, especially when she saw the very unusual sight of a wine decanter on the tray he carried.

When she offered him a seat, he said, "Would you mind if I closed the window? It is a little cold in here for me."

"Of course not." She had left it open all afternoon as the one bit of freedom she still possessed. Not that the sooty miasma of London could qualify as fresh air, but at least it could move freely.

Once he had wrestled the casement closed, he unstoppered the decanter and filled one wineglass. "Would you care for a glass?" he asked.

"Am I likely to require it?" she asked dubiously. Under normal circumstances, her uncle was a temperate man and would have been more likely to offer her lemonade.

He smiled as if at a private joke. "That I cannot say, but *I* certainly will before we are done."

"This is going to be unpleasant, then." Her heart sank.

"Less so for you than for me, my dear. I am the one who has to make the difficult explanations. You need only listen."

"Then I will take that glass of wine."

He raised an eyebrow, but poured for her without question, then settled back in his chair. "You are no doubt quite baffled by your father's vehement opposition to your entanglement with Mr. Darcy."

"To my *engagement*, you mean? I admit I am."

"To your engagement, then, if you will. Having talked to your father at length last night, during which we imbibed rather stronger spirits, I can tell you that his objection is not so much to Mr. Darcy as to his family, and to the assumption that Mr. Darcy must resemble his family in behavior."

"His family? To the best of my knowledge, he has only a sister, and she is no older than Lydia. What could be objectionable about her?"

"To be more precise, he has a powerful dislike for the Earl of Matlock."

Elizabeth could not help but laugh. "I can certainly credit that, but I am not proposing to marry Lord Matlock, and it is not as if my father would be likely to find himself in the company of Mr. Darcy's uncle."

"True, but you underestimate the depth of the animosity he feels. His grievances against Matlock – Lord Matlock, I should say – go back many years."

"Years? But they just met!"

Mr. Gardiner took a long sip of wine. "No. They met again for the first time in years. They were at school together, or rather *we* were at school together."

"He has never mentioned Lord Matlock."

"I am not surprised. Lizzy, you have grown up without brothers, so you are perhaps unaware that, although we may manage to force a veneer of civility on young boys, they are in truth young savages, and I can attest to that as a former young boy myself." He smiled at her. "Then we send those young savages away to school with other young savages, and we pretend that what occurs at those schools is something other than uncontrolled savagery. Unfortunately, it is often precisely that."

"So you were all young savages together."

"Matlock – Lord Matlock, but you must forgive me, as he was called simply Matlock at school, since he had inherited the earldom when he was still in short pants – was a poor scholar but excelled at savagery, a talent I gather he still possesses. Your father was several years younger, bookish and small for his age, and had no older brother or cousin there to protect him. He quickly became one of Matlock's favored victims." He fell silent for a few minutes.

Finally Elizabeth said, "And you?"

"I arrived two years later, and your father and I became fast friends. He had no friends at all before that – Matlock had seen to that. Matlock's great talent was for humiliating the younger boys, and none of them would dare cross him. I was of very little interest to the others since I was not a gentleman born like the rest of them. My father had bribed my way into a school for gentlemen's sons because he thought it would stand me in good stead in later years. In any case, Matlock targeted me as well, but not to the same extent. I was too easy a target since everyone knew I was nothing but a cit. That was the nickname he gave me – the Cit. It was quite mild compared to some of the other nicknames boys were given. The ones he gave your father were rather worse."

A memory came back to Elizabeth. "Birdwit. He called him birdwit."

"Yes. Birdwit instead of Bennet, you see. Birdwit and the Cit – that was what he called us. It rhymed so nicely. Birdwit was perhaps the least offensive of the names your father was called, and the names stayed with him throughout his school years, since naturally the other young savages followed Matlock's lead. I do not wish to tell you about the many humiliations, both public and private, that Matlock forced upon your father, but you must understand that they were constant and vicious. I would not wish to see such things inflicted on Napoleon Bonaparte, much less on a helpless young boy. At times I feared that Matlock would accidentally kill your father with one of his 'games,' and I know that at times your father hoped that he would just to end his suffering."

Horrified, Elizabeth covered her mouth with her hand.

"Needless to say, we both survived, as many boys before and since have done, and we eventually outgrew our savagery by our last years at school, as most boys did. Matlock was an exception in that he retained his savagery till the end, perhaps because he had come into too much power too young, or perhaps it was simply his nature to be cruel. From what your father says, he has not changed much."

"From the little I saw, I would have to agree," Elizabeth said. "His behavior was abominable."

"Yes. Well. So your father read of your engagement in the papers, and went off to confront the unmannerly and brash Mr. Darcy who cared nothing for his opinion – yes, I know, Lizzy, but can you not see how it looked that way from the announcement? But instead of finding Darcy, he discovered Lord Matlock was uncle to your Darcy, who cared nothing for your father's opinion, just as Matlock would have. Meantime, when Matlock discovered that the woman who had entrapped his precious nephew was the daughter of a man he held in such contempt, he flew into a rage. He accused him of being too weak to control his own daughter, and of letting his women rule him – well, you can see where this would go. He topped it off by telling everyone within earshot, which apparently included a neighbor of yours from Meryton, all the humiliating things he had forced your father to do at school, things that no gentleman would wish to have known about him."

Elizabeth buried her face in her hands. It was too horrible to contemplate.

"And that, my dear, was the company your father kept until he reached you the next morning, determined to demonstrate that he was not a wheyfaced weakling who could not control his daughter, and equally determined to keep you safe from Matlock's disdainful nephew. I do not condone his behavior toward you -- from what my wife tells me, it was appalling – but I hoped to give you a little more understanding of why he is being quite so unreasonable about your situation."

"I… Thank you." Elizabeth's voice was strangled. She drank some wine to cover it, but swallowed a bit too much, leaving her coughing.

"Well, my dear, I hope that was only the wine, and that you are not catching a cold from that drafty window. Your father does not know that I planned to tell you this; he thinks I am trying to reason with you. He would be mortified to discover that you knew any of this history, and I hope you will not tell him."

"No. But can you tell me what he plans to do with me? Am I to stay here indefinitely? What is he telling everyone about Mr. Darcy and me?"

"I do not know what his plans are for you, and I doubt that he does either. I suspect he brought you here simply because he knew I would understand what had happened, rather than as part of some greater purpose. Whatever he decides, I have faith in your good judgment. Since you agreed to marry Mr. Darcy, I will assume he is not like his uncle."

"No, he is not. He is scrupulously fair and honest to a fault. He was trying to protect me from his uncle."

"Well, I am glad to hear that, and I hope that at some point your father will be able to as well. But I will wish you goodnight now, my dear."

After he left, Elizabeth spent a painful half hour staring at the ceiling as she tried to assimilate this new view of her father. Was this why he always refused to travel to London for the Season, but instead hid in his library at Longbourn? She had sometimes wondered why he was so prone to disparage even his own family. Perhaps he had grown so accustomed to insults that he saw them as natural.

Chapter 11

THE NEXT MORNING, Elizabeth awoke with a headache, which she attributed to her distress at being trapped in her room and her uncertainty about what to do about her father's dictum, but by breakfast-time, she found it painful to swallow. After a fit of coughing that brought a concerned Jane to her side, even Elizabeth had to admit that her usually strong constitution had failed her this time. She had fallen victim to a cold.

Jane fetched Mrs. Gardiner, and soon Elizabeth was tucked into bed with a warm brick at her feet and a pile of handkerchiefs beside her. "There is no need to fuss. It is merely a cold and will pass. It is just that I so despise to be ill," Elizabeth said.

Her words fell, as she expected, on deaf ears. Jane insisted on sitting with her during most of her waking hours, but from what little she said of the family below, that might have been as much from her desire to avoid the continued tension between Mrs. Gardiner and Mr. Bennet over the subject of Elizabeth.

Her father's contribution to entertaining Elizabeth while she was ill was to send a message through Jane that he hoped her sickness would pass quickly. She had not expected anything else; he had never shown much interest in their childhood illnesses. Jane took it harder, since she still held out hopes for a reconciliation between the two, and it grieved her to see any fault in someone she loved.

On the third day of Elizabeth's illness, Jane appeared with a letter in her hand and a troubled demeanor. "I have received a letter from Mary," she said.

"And what is the news from Longbourn?" Elizabeth croaked.

"Mary says..." Jane turned the letter between her fingers. "She says that our mother has been very distressed since receiving word from our father that the engagement between you and Mr. Darcy was nothing but a fabrication. She moralizes at length about the sort of person who might place such an announcement as a prank without any thought for the consequences to the two principals, so I assume that is what they believe happened."

"Well, *that* is an original explanation, I suppose. I expected something of the sort."

"But it isn't true!"

"I am well aware of that, but given that our father wants to keep me away from Mr. Darcy, he has no choice but to deny the engagement. If our mother were to believe that Mr. Darcy wanted to marry me, she would do anything in her power to bring us together, even if it meant marching me to his doorstep."

"But she detests Mr. Darcy! It is all a misunderstanding, of course, but she took against him that first night at the assembly."

Elizabeth gave a wan smile. "She may detest *him*, but her feelings would be very different about his ten thousand pounds a year. She would marry me off to Satan himself if he had such a fortune and was nephew to an earl." A bout of coughing lessened the sting of her last words.

"He cannot expect us to lie to her on his behalf!"

"Be careful what you say, Jane, if you do not want to find yourself joining me in my prison cell! Either he assumes you will be biddable, or he plans for you to stay here where you can do no harm."

"Lizzy, you must try to talk to him again, and I will as well. Perhaps between us we can make him see reason."

Elizabeth sneezed into a handkerchief, then turned her face away. "It would make no difference. He will never give his consent. He means for me to have to choose between him and Mr. Darcy."

"He may yet change his mind."

"If our uncle and aunt have been unable to convince him, we stand no chance. No, all we can do is to wait quietly until my birthday, and then I will marry Mr. Darcy... assuming he has not changed his mind or been persuaded by his aunt and uncle against allying himself with a family such as ours. He might already have done so, but I will remain in ignorance of it for all these months since he cannot tell me of it." She used the handkerchief to mop the ready tears from her eyes.

"I cannot believe he would be as fickle as that."

"We will have the answer to that in December and not a moment sooner."

"He is an honorable man, and too violently in love with you to think of changing his mind."

Elizabeth sighed. "You are no doubt right, Jane. Being ill always makes me feel that everything is hopeless."

Jane sat silently, unfolding and folding her letter. "Will you truly choose Mr. Darcy over our father?"

"I would laugh if it did not pain my throat so much. A week ago, I would likely not have done so, but now everything has changed. Our father, by trying to keep me away from Mr. Darcy, has made it impossible for me to remain at home, so Mr. Darcy, who deserves better, wins by default."

Jane eyed her sister shrewdly. "I think it is more than winning by default. I think you care more than you wish us to believe."

Elizabeth was in fact tolerably well acquainted with her feelings by this time. She knew how much she longed for Mr. Darcy to ride up on that huge horse of his and rescue her from her tower, wrap her in her cloak and in his arms, and ride away with her to... well, anywhere would do, as long as she was with him.

Within a few days, Elizabeth's health was improved enough that her aunt suggested that she come downstairs while the maid changed the linens and aired out her room. Mr. Bennet made no comment on her presence out of her room, and, with a little encouragement from Mrs. Gardiner, Elizabeth said nothing either, but continued to spend time in the sitting room and dining with the family. It seemed that her father had fallen back into his usual lethargic lack of interest in the affairs of his daughters, but she suspected that the mere mention of Mr. Darcy would produce the return of the late tyrant. So she said nothing and did not suggest leaving the house, but her spirits chafed at her lack of knowledge about her father's plans.

She had almost resolved that he intended for her to remain in London indefinitely when Mrs. Gardiner, apparently also growing tired of the uncertainty, raised the question directly as they sat down to dinner.

"It depends upon Jane and Lizzy," Mr. Bennet said. "If they are prepared to undertake to stay silent on the subject Darcy or any engagement, and if Lizzy is ready to give her word that she will not contact him, then we can return to Longbourn."

Elizabeth kept her face blank. "Am I to lie to my mother, then?"

Her father smiled broadly as if he had just won a bet. "That will not be necessary. Your mother was delighted to hear that I had changed my mind about travelling to Brighton. She and your younger sisters have already left Longbourn and will spend a month by the sea, or perhaps I should say by the militia, since that factor seems to be more important to them. Since *we* will be at Longbourn, you need not worry about telling your mother anything. By the time they return, you will already be gone on your Northern tour. After that – we shall see."

Elizabeth's cheeks grew hot as she tried to hold back her rage. "You censure *me*, yet you allow them to go to Brighton with the militia, when you know how improper Lydia's and Kitty's behavior will be. With so many soldiers to tempt them and without us to hold them back, they will be even more imprudent than they have been at home!"

Mr. Bennet shook his head soothingly. "They will be silly wherever they are, and at least this way we shall not have to observe it."

"We shall not, but the world will see it! Their unguarded behavior already affects our family's respectability in the world. They will soon be the most determined flirts that ever made themselves and their family look ridiculous! And you have put them in temptation's way when you know that my mother will do nothing to check their behavior!" She would have gone on, had not Jane's restraining hand descended upon her arm.

Mr. Bennet raised his eyebrows. "She does nothing to check them at home, and they seem to have survived so far."

Her fingernails bit into her palms as she clenched her hands into fists. How could he be so careless of Lydia and Kitty, yet so intolerant of her engagement? But it was not a matter of rationality, she knew, so much as an inability to admit he might have been mistaken. No matter how angry she was, she could not afford to give him reason to become more entrenched in his position, so she said nothing more. Her appetite had completely fled, though. Conscious of her aunt's concerned gaze, she choked down a few bites to keep up appearances, but the food seemed to sit like a brick in her stomach.

After dinner, she told Jane and her aunt that she wished to be alone, which they agreed to, though not without a number of worried glances. Elizabeth took the opportunity to sit down in her room with pen and paper, and spent over an hour painstakingly drafting a letter. It took three attempts before she was satisfied. She put the letter away in a drawer without sealing it.

At breakfast the next day, she calmly but distantly told her father that she was prepared to accept his conditions. He raised his eyebrows in a teasing manner, but she made no response either in word or expression. Finally he announced that they would depart for Longbourn the following day, then finished his coffee and left the room.

Mr. Gardiner looked down at the scrap of paper in his hand, then up at the imposing edifice before him. Lifting his cane, he rapped on the door with it.

The door was opened by an elderly butler whose face appeared to be carved from stone. Mr. Gardiner proffered his card. "I wish to speak to Mr. Darcy."

"One moment." The butler creaked away, then returned a few minutes later. "Mr. Darcy is not at home."

Mr. Gardiner had expected this. "Kindly inform Mr. Darcy that I have a letter for him from Miss Elizabeth Bennet."

"Yes, sir."

Mr. Gardiner swung his cane under his arm. Darcy House reeked of money and good breeding. He wondered if his brother-in-law had been correct in his assessment of Darcy. Lizzy was very young, after all.

Instead of the aged butler, a tall young man hurried toward him, dressed in clothes that would have been elegant if they did not look as if he had been sleeping in them.

"Mr. Darcy, I presume?" Mr. Gardiner held out his hand. "Edward Gardiner, at your service. I believe you know my niece, Elizabeth."

Darcy looked at him searchingly, but shook his hand without hesitation. "Please come in, Mr. Gardiner. I apologize for keeping you waiting. Will you join me in the sitting room?" He seemed not to know what to do with his hands. No doubt he was accustomed to a servant showing guests in. The butler stood a good six feet behind him, looking discreetly appalled.

"Thank you." The sitting room confirmed his expectations with expensive furnishings, but at least they were elegant, rather than simply showy.

As soon as they were both seated, Darcy said, "You have word for me from Miss Bennet?"

Mr. Gardiner wondered if Darcy was being deliberately rude or just desperately worried. "I have a letter she wrote to you, but it is not quite what you might expect."

Darcy stiffened, suddenly looking ten years older. "I see."

"She wrote it under unusual circumstances. Her father has forbidden her to contact you, but she knows I have some sympathy for her position. She left the letter to you on my desk, unsealed, with a note asking me to read it and determine for myself whether I thought it appropriate to send it to you. She gave as a reason that it seemed cruel to leave you in suspense as to her intentions. While I was reluctant to go against her father's expressed wish, it seemed a reasonable point." He removed the letter from his pocket, noting how hungrily Darcy watched his every move. "She clearly went to some effort to make her letter as innocuous as possible in order to give me no grounds to object to it, so you will find it quite stilted, not at all in Lizzy's usual style." He leaned forward and held out the letter.

Darcy took it, then held it in his hands for a moment as if fearing what might be inside. When he finally opened it, he scanned quickly through the brief missive. He rubbed his hand over his mouth, then rose abruptly and strode to the window where he read it again, then stood with his head bowed. After a long pause, he said, still looking away, "I must apologize for my rudeness. I had thought this might tell me of an end to my hopes."

Mr. Gardiner blinked. "You thought she might have changed her mind?"

"I feared it." Darcy's voice was low.

"Because of her father's opposition? I cannot think of anyone less likely to give way under pressure than Lizzy. Do you not know how very stubborn she can be?"

At that, Darcy looked up, the ghost of a smile crossing his face. "It has come to my attention once or twice."

Mr. Gardiner decided to venture a test. "I don't suppose you would care to explain to me the meaning of that little sketch at the bottom of the page. The one where she is standing by a river with a large pile of... something."

"That?" Darcy looked down at the letter, and for a moment looked almost happy. "I think it is her way of saying she is upset about the situation. Once, when I was angered about something, she found me throwing rocks into the river."

"And that would explain why there are enough rocks by that river to rebuild Hadrian's Wall, I suppose."

There it was, that hint of a smile again. "She seems to think she will require quite a few." He returned from the window and sat down once more, looking calmer than before. "I may need a small mountain of them myself."

"I am not surprised."

Darcy appeared to be wrestling with something. "Elizabeth says in the letter that I can trust you implicitly, as she does."

Mr. Gardiner raised an amused eyebrow. "I know. I did read it, after all."

"Can you advise me as to what I should do?" The words came out in a rush. "I am not well enough acquainted with Mr. Bennet to know how best to plead my case. Should I write to him and explain myself, or try to meet with him, or should I just stay away? I do not even know what his objection to me is." He shrugged helplessly.

"I think his objection is less to *you* than to his assumption that you must be similar in character to certain of your relatives. He has an intense dislike for Lord Matlock."

"He is in good company in that. I would be hard put to name half a dozen people who do *not* have an intense dislike of my uncle."

Mr. Gardiner chuckled. "I see you have no illusions about him."

"Have you ever met my uncle, sir?"

"Yes, I have. Many years ago."

"Then you know how hard it would be to retain any illusions about him. But what have I ever done to make Mr. Bennet think that I am anything like him? Has he so little faith in Elizabeth's judgment?"

"I doubt it is that reasoned an opinion. But to return to your question, I do not think you would harm your case by writing to him, but I would not expect it to lead to a change of heart on his part. He seems determined to think the worst of you."

Darcy's lips formed a thin line. "Then I must learn to be patient. If you ever have the opportunity, please tell Elizabeth that I will find her on December 26, with a special license in my hand."

"Well, do keep me informed of your plans. My wife and I are very fond of Lizzy, and we would be sorry to miss her wedding day."

"You may depend upon it, sir. And in the meantime, would you be willing to let me know from time to time whether all is well with her... or do I ask too much?"

"I would be happy to do so. We must invite you to dine with us soon. My wife will be anxious to meet you."

"Thank you, sir. I cannot thank you enough – you do not know how greatly you have relieved my mind."

Mr. Gardiner thought he actually had a fairly good idea.

Longbourn House usually teemed with activity and noise, but it was oddly silent when the three Bennets returned. To their surprise, they were greeted by Mary.

Mr. Bennet looked over his glasses at her. "I thought you were to be in Brighton."

"I preferred to stay here where I can read and practice my music in peace. I find no enjoyment in such frivolous pursuits as balls and parties, and I think that flirting with soldiers shows a disregard for reputation unsuitable to a young lady, so Brighton has no appeal for me."

Shocked, Elizabeth said, "Did our mother agree to leaving you here alone?"

Mary shrugged, her lips tight. "It was her idea. She said that if I planned to moralize on their pleasures the entire time, she would rather that I did not come. It has only been a few days, and I have enjoyed the quiet."

Elizabeth exchanged a glance with Jane. "*We* will be glad your company, Mary."

Mr. Bennet immediately disappeared into his library, while Jane and Elizabeth chose to refresh themselves first. Although Elizabeth's bedroom had not changed since her departure, she discovered that it seemed smaller, as though she no longer fit in it.

Her trunk, sent from Hunsford, had been placed at the foot of her bed. She opened the lid to discover that it had not yet been unpacked. On top of the neatly folded clothes was a note from Charlotte.

> *Dearest Lizzy,*
>
> *I hope I have managed to locate everything of yours, but if I have missed anything, I will bring it when I next come to visit. I have included a cloak which Mr. Darcy insists is yours, although I do not recognize it. I saw him for only a few minutes before he and Colonel Fitzwilliam departed for London, not long after you left. I cannot blame them for*

taking flight; Lady Catherine was beside herself with rage, and Lord Matlock as well. Mr. Darcy seemed in very poor spirits, and I was glad the colonel was with him. It seems so quiet here now that our parties only consist of Lady Catherine, Miss de Bourgh and my sister. Maria will remain here longer than we expected; Lady Catherine has decreed that she shall stay through the summer. We dare not mention your name for fear of Lady Catherine's wrath falling on Mr. Collins for the crime of being your cousin.

The coach is waiting for your luggage, so I will write more later.
Charlotte Collins

Elizabeth read this missive twice, lingering over the part about Mr. Darcy's poor spirits, wishing she had been there to comfort him.

She put the letter aside, then hurriedly moved the top layer of dresses and laid them on her bed with little care for the meticulous folding Charlotte had done. She burrowed through the trunk until the heavy wool of the cloak was revealed. She gathered it to her, and with a sound that was almost a sob, sat in the rocker and hugged it tightly, burying her face in it. It still bore the scent of leather and horses, taking her back again to that hour in his arms when she had felt safe.

Longbourn was indeed a different place in the absence of Mrs. Bennet, Lydia and Kitty. Its usual noisy chaos was replaced by civilized conversation. The only thing that remained unchanged was that Mr. Bennet continued to seek refuge in his library every day, seeing his daughters only at dinner. From the outside, it might seem as if nothing had changed between him and his favorite daughter, but the teasing and warmth that had once characterized their relationship was a thing of the past. Mr. Bennet still made jests, but Elizabeth no longer shared the joke with him.

To Elizabeth's great relief, it did not take Mary long to realize that something was being kept from her. When she raised this question, Elizabeth readily agreed that it was true, and that she herself was unhappy about it and would like to tell Mary the full story, but that their father had forbidden her to discuss it. As she expected, Mr. Bennet was sufficiently displeased to be lectured at repeatedly by his middle daughter that he eventually lifted the ban where Mary was concerned, and Mary was treated to two very different versions of the same story, one from her father and one from Elizabeth.

Elizabeth anticipated a dramatic increase in morality lectures from Mary as a result of her new knowledge, but to her surprise, the converse occurred. When Mary, accustomed to being the least considered and valued of the sisters, discovered that Elizabeth and to some extent Jane were in parental disfavor while she herself was not, she responded by becoming protective of them. Elizabeth, who did not question her own actions to the degree Mary seemed to believe, found Mary a more pleasant companion and one whom she could confide.

Elizabeth's other happiness was in the absence of the militia in general and Wickham in particular. She could no longer imagine finding any pleasure in flirting with handsome young men. She avoided even the usual parties in the neighborhood, not out of any distaste for the company, but because she was sure to be asked about the announcement, and she did not care to lie to her friends about the state of affairs. She found sufficient to interest her in the vicinity of Longbourn, and often went out walking for hours in the silence that allowed her to rest her thoughts on those days in Hunsford with Mr. Darcy.

She was relieved to receive a letter from her aunt a few days after their arrival which mentioned in passing that Mr. Gardiner had found time to deal with all the correspondence that had piled up on his desk during their visit. It was little enough to know that Darcy had received her note, for she could barely call it a letter, but she took consolation in the fact that Mrs. Gardiner did not mention anything amiss in the delivery of the letter, and that her aunt did not seem distressed with her for having made the request. If she was surprised by the degree of subterfuge in her aunt's reply, it did not last through the next day when her father summoned her to his library.

He held a letter in his hand. "Mrs. Collins wishes you to know that the pigs found their way into the garden, causing severe depredations, to the despair of Mr. Collins. She also mentions that Jenny, whomever that might be, is now able to hobble about on crutches and is to live with her aunt at Rosings. The village is apparently being rebuilt slowly." He dropped the letter onto his desk. "The remainder of her letter consists of messages from Darcy. Kindly inform Mrs. Collins in your reply that I will be reading any correspondence you receive, and that if she wishes you to see it, she will refrain from such discussion. Is that clear?"

"You read a letter sent to me?" Elizabeth struggled to keep her voice level.

"I was apparently correct to do so. That will be all, my dear."

If only she could snatch the letter from his desk and run off with it! Perhaps she could lure him away and return for it later. "Jane wishes to know if you would like to join us for some tea."

With an exaggerated sigh, he picked up the letter and tore it across, then into quarters, then once again. For good measure, he tossed the fragments into the fire.

Helpless fury burned inside her. "I will tell her that you have no interest in tea," she said icily. *Or anything else to do with me*, she thought.

Chapter 12

ON ELIZABETH'S RETURN from one of her walks, she spotted a figure in uniform approaching Longbourn on horseback. At first she thought it was one of the officers who had returned for some reason, but as he drew closer, she realized his uniform did not match that of the militia. The face under the black bicorne hat seemed simultaneously familiar and strange, and it was not until he dismounted in front of the house that she recognized Colonel Fitzwilliam.

She had never before seen him in regimentals, and it made him appear quite a stranger to her eyes, but she approached him with pleasure. Her discomfort in refusing his proposal was quite forgot in the happiness of seeing someone who knew the truth of her engagement.

She hailed him by name, and he swept her a bow so extravagant as to make her laugh. "Colonel, this is a delightful surprise. I had not thought to see you at Longbourn."

"Although I will never complain of your charming company, I confess the object of my visit is to speak to your father. I left him with quite the wrong impression that morning at Hunsford – I had no notion at the time that he was your father – and I felt it was my duty to attempt to mend the damage I had done."

"That is very good of you, but most likely he will refuse to see you. He is not precisely reasonable on the subject of that day."

"That is what Darcy said as well, but as it happens, he *cannot* refuse to see me. I am, after all, an officer in His Majesty's service, and I come bearing a letter to him from no less a personage than the Secretary at War himself." He leaned closer and said in a confiding tone, "It is, in fact, merely a letter of introduction to serve as a character reference for me, but Lord Palmerston did direct me to deliver it to Mr. Bennet, and I must do my duty to King and country."

She laughed, as he had no doubt intended. "I cannot stand in the way of a soldier performing his duty, but I would expect a very cold welcome indeed if I were you."

"Your father holds no terrors for me. You have met *my* father; can yours do anything worse?"

"I suppose not! But since I will not be allowed to speak to you once he is aware of your presence, may I inquire as to whether you have any news of Mr. Darcy?"

"Does he know that I am here, do you mean? He is aware I planned something of this sort, though not the details. This concerns my honor, not his."

Elizabeth felt her cheeks grow warm. "But is he well? I have heard nothing since I left Hunsford."

The colonel tapped his crop against his leg, considering the matter. "He is well enough, though I cannot say that he is happy with the situation. He keeps rather a grim visage these days."

"I feared as much. I am forbidden to send him messages, but will you tell him you saw me?"

"If that is what you wish." He bowed slightly.

With a rush of embarrassment, she recalled that the colonel might have mixed feelings about facilitating communication to Darcy. "I should have said this immediately, had I not been taken by surprise, but you must allow me to express my gratitude for your efforts to turn Lord Matlock's wrath away from both Mr. Darcy and me. It was very generous of you. And if you were ever to decide to sell your commission, you could have a bright future on Drury Lane! Had I not known you had been perfectly sober before their arrival, I would have believed you to be quite foxed!"

His eyes crinkled as he grinned. "You do me too much honor, Miss Bennet. I would be much better suited to play the jester."

"I hope that day had no lasting consequences for you." It was something that had worried her.

"Nothing of note. I am forbidden access to Matlock House, but losing the opportunity to enjoy the charming company of my father is not much of a punishment."

"I would imagine not! But I should take you to *my* father, for if he finds me talking to you, *I* will be made to regret it," she said lightly.

He dropped his voice. "I deeply regret being the source of conflict between you. You always spoke of your father with affection, so this must be painful for you."

His sympathy and consideration threatened to breach the walls that held back her feelings of betrayal, so she responded in a teasing tone. "I prefer to think of it as opening my eyes to his shortcomings. But come, I will announce you to my father. You are fortunate that my youngest sisters are away; they are mad for any gentleman in a red coat."

"I will keep my sword to the ready so that I may defend myself if necessary," he said with a laugh.

She led him into the house, past the open sitting room door where all conversation abruptly ceased, and then to the library. She knocked on the door before opening it. When her father looked up, she told him with all the sweetness she could muster, "Colonel Fitzwilliam to see you." She waited for the explosion.

"I know no Colonel Fitzwilliam," he grumbled.

Elizabeth hid a smile, realizing no introduction had been made at Hunsford. She stepped back and waved the colonel in, then closed the door behind him and waited for the explosion.

Richard was prepared to be amiable in face of all provocation, but he was surprised when Mr. Bennet stood and held out his hand.

"You have the advantage of me, Colonel."

So he did not recognize him in uniform. "We have met, sir, but under rather unfortunate circumstances which precluded a formal introduction. Richard Fitzwilliam, at your service." He made a formal bow.

Either his voice or his name was apparently enough to make a connection in Mr. Bennet's mind, since his eyes narrowed and he withdrew his hand. "I wonder at your insolence in presenting yourself here."

"I can understand your sentiment, sir, and it is precisely that which I came here today to address. I deliberately gave you a very misleading impression that day, unaware of your relationship to Miss Bennet. I am afraid you saw a show which was intended to impress a different audience. It would have been beyond insolent had I known your identity."

Mr. Bennet's lip curled. "It was beyond insolent in any case. Say what you have to say, and then leave."

"I do not blame you for distrusting me, sir, given the circumstances of our last meeting. In your position, I would do the same. I presented myself as a drunken rake with no respect for your daughter and proceeded to impugn her good name, when in fact I was stone-cold sober and have the greatest respect for your daughter, and everything I said about her was a fabrication intended to avoid a different sort of unpleasantness."

"I do not care about your reasons."

"But *I* ask of your justice a chance to defend myself. Since you have no reason to believe me, I came prepared with character references from individuals you are likely to find more trustworthy." He placed two sealed letters on the desk in front of Mr. Bennet. "The first is from Lord Palmerston, my superior at the War Office, and contains his frank assessment of the strengths and weaknesses of my character. Being uncertain of your political leanings, I took the precaution of also obtaining one from Mr. Perceval in case you are more inclined to place your faith in the opinion of a Tory. I hope you will agree with me that they are both known to be honest men."

Mr. Bennet did not touch the letters. "Compared to other politicians, that is true, but all you have convinced me of is that you are exceedingly well-connected, which I already knew."

Richard gave a disarming smile. "Had I wished to prove my connections, I would have asked Wellington to write to you. I was his aide de camp for a time, but I wished to avoid the unnecessary delay of having someone track him down in the wilds of Spain. But if I know Lord Palmerston, you will see the extent of his frankness in his letter. It will not be uniformly positive."

"Regardless of what they say, I have no wish to talk to you. I will thank you to leave my house."

"With due respect, Mr. Bennet, I will not leave until you have heard me out."

"Must I have my servants expel you forcibly?"

Richard leaned forward and placed his fingertips on the edge of Mr. Bennet's desk. "If you believe your servants will forcibly expel a commissioned officer in His Majesty's service who is offering you no threat, then I invite you to do just that. Since I doubt you have such servants, the quickest way to rid yourself of me is to listen to what I have to say."

Mr. Bennet crossed his arms and leaned back in his chair. "I see you are very like your father."

"*Touché*, sir – you know just where to strike. You are, however, quite incorrect. Have you known him to come to your home and seek to clear his name?"

"No, but I doubt there is anything he would not stoop to do if he felt it in his best interest."

"You give him credit for more subtlety than he possesses, then. I understand that you were at school with him, so I imagine you know how he prefers to resolve problems."

Mr. Bennet's mouth twisted. "So he told you all about that, did he?"

"Of course he did. He does not care that his behavior then was dishonorable, nor that he is breaking the code of honor by speaking of it now. Surely you did not expect better of him? If so, I will be disappointed in *you*, Mr. Bennet. I thought you more perspicacious than to expect honorable behavior of him."

"What great respect you show for your father!" commented Mr. Bennet mildly.

"I give him the respect he is due. Have you ever read a description of a Spanish bullfight, Mr. Bennet? The bullfighter respects the bull owing to his strength and the danger he offers, not because the bull has any honor. And when the bull is ready to charge, the bullfighter fools him into charging at a waving red cloak instead of at him. A bullfighter who did not feint with a red cloak would be a dead bullfighter. What you saw that day in Hunsford was my own version of waving a red cloak in front of a maddened bull. My father came in determined to destroy your daughter, but instead ended up attacking me, and to a lesser extent Darcy – and I am, after all, somewhat inured to his attacks from years of practice."

"Destroying my daughter's good name seems an odd way to protect her."

"Consider my audience, sir. Your daughter and Darcy both knew what I said was not true. As for my father and Lady Catherine, I told them what they were already convinced was the truth, that your daughter had entrapped Darcy with her arts and allurements. That is where it would have ended, except that you were not my father's pet solicitor as I had assumed, but rather a concerned father who did *not* know that I was playing the fool. And that, Mr. Bennet, is what I came here today to tell you, so that you would know that the fault was mine for lying, and that your daughter's behavior was irreproachable, because whatever you may believe of me, I do not allow an innocent woman to take the blame for my failings."

"Or perhaps your true reason for coming here was to promote the engagement with Darcy by exculpating him. It will not work. I remain opposed to it."

Puzzled, Richard rocked back on his heels. "Why do you think I would suddenly be promoting the match?"

"Oh, come now. He is your cousin and your friend, and likely your moneylender as well."

"He is my cousin and friend, but that does not mean... Sir, have you *talked* to your daughter about what happened at Hunsford between the three of us?"

"To a certain extent."

"Well, if you speak to her further, you might discover that I was *not* a proponent of the match; in fact I tried to dissuade her from it. I support the engagement only in that your daughter must marry *someone* to preserve her reputation, and since Darcy is the only one she will accept, then she has to marry him. I would rather see her married to Darcy than ruined and alone."

"Let me guess – now you are waving a red cloak in front of *me*." Mr. Bennet's tone oozed scorn.

"Oh, think what you will! I have told you what I came to say, which is that your daughter is innocent of all wrongdoing. Good day, Mr. Bennet." He stalked out of the room, as annoyed with himself for his loss of composure as at Mr. Bennet's insinuations.

"There he is," Elizabeth whispered to Jane by the sitting room door. "I hope father did not upset him too much. He is such an amiable gentleman."

The colonel strode down the passageway until he reached the two ladies, his usual genial expression back in place. "You need not have worried for me, Miss Bennet. Your father only threatened to throw me out once, and I did not even need to draw my sword," he teased.

Elizabeth released the breath that she had been holding. "I am glad of that. Blood is so very difficult to clean off the carpet. Colonel Fitzwilliam, may I present to you my sister Jane? And you are safe with her as well; it is only my younger sisters who are mad for a red coat."

Jane held out her hand, and he bowed over it in a courtly manner, going so far as to kiss her hand lightly. "Now that is a pity," he drawled, his eyes fixed on Jane's face.

Elizabeth, accustomed to the stunned expression most gentleman took on when they first met Jane, merely laughed. "Will you come in and take some refreshment with us?"

"I would be honored to, but if I am not mistaken, I am expected to quit the premises without delay."

"Nonsense. Would you have me be so inhospitable as to set you on the road without even a bite to eat when you have already ridden all the way from London?" Elizabeth laid a hand on his arm.

"When you put it that way, I feel obliged to accept," he said.

As Jane led the way and took the seat by the teapot, the Colonel whispered in Elizabeth's ear. "Is she the one Bingley admired?"

She nodded. In a conversational tone, she said, "Jane has also just returned home. She has spent the last few months in London with our aunt and uncle."

Colonel Fitzwilliam picked up the hint and asked Jane about her time in London, comparing notes on her favorite haunts there. Elizabeth allowed the two of them to dominate the conversation, tension still coiled inside her as she waited for the inevitable confrontation with her father.

It came sooner than she expected when he emerged from the library a quarter hour later, an open letter in one hand and his glasses in the other. He paused in the sitting room doorway, taking in the cozy domestic scene. "So you are still here," he said.

Colonel Fitzwilliam stood. "I allowed the ladies to convince me that it would be rude not to partake of the refreshments they had set out, but I will not overstay my welcome."

Mr. Bennet waved away his assertion. "Not so quickly, please. Had I realized how very entertaining these letters would prove, I would have read them sooner."

Elizabeth closed her eyes, wishing herself far away. Being forced to observe as her father amused himself at the colonel's expense was the last thing she wanted.

As the colonel reseated himself, Mr. Bennet placed his spectacles on his nose and opened the letter. "I was particularly taken by this part: 'Although Colonel Fitzwilliam gave distinguished service during his years in India, it is unlikely that he will advance beyond his current rank. While he has always performed his duty, his lack of enthusiasm for military offensives on the Continent has been noted. While I, having worked closely with him, have no doubt as to his loyalty, I do not anticipate placing him in a combat position unless he chooses to return to India, which I believe to be unlikely.' And this is your character reference? Tut, tut, young man!"

The sudden rigidity in the colonel's expression told her that this intelligence was unexpected. But he recovered quickly. "I did tell you he would describe my flaws as well as my sterling characteristics."

"These are telling flaws indeed – disloyalty and – shall we say cowardice?"

"Father!" Elizabeth cried. "That is untrue."

Colonel Fitzwilliam's hand had fallen to his sword hilt, but he slowly unclenched his fingers. "If you call it cowardice that I cannot ride cheerfully into battle against my kinsmen and friends, then indeed I am a coward, but as that letter says, I have *always* done my duty. I have killed as many French soldiers in battle as any other officer; you will have to forgive me if I do not triumph in it."

"A French sympathizer in His Majesty's service? I am shocked indeed!"

Elizabeth stood. "That is beyond enough, sir! Amuse yourself as you like, but I will not have you insult a guest in this house."

Mr. Bennet ignored her completely. "Well, Colonel?"

"I believe I saw a bottle of smuggled French brandy in your library, and Miss Bennet is charmingly attired in a style that I believe originated in Paris. Does that make you a traitor for supporting England's enemy? Our very word for good society – the *ton* - is French, and most ladies can speak at least a smattering of French. Many of our fashions originate in France. Yet we are supposed to delight in killing the French. We are all students of hypocrisy – or perhaps I should say *l'hypocrisie*."

"But *you* apparently take it a step farther than drinking French brandy. Perhaps you are an admirer of Bonaparte."

"I am no Bonapartiste, but I do sympathize with the French people. They have suffered enough in the last thirty years, even before the tyrant Bonaparte came on the scene. My mother is French, and when the political situation allowed, I have visited France with her. I speak French as well as I do English, which is why I am of particular use in the War Office. It is the current fashion to view all the French as demons. I do not, and have been forced on more than one occasion to defend my honor because of it, but I am *not* ashamed of my sentiments."

Shaking his head, Mr. Bennet folded his glasses as placed them in his pocket. "Matlock married to a Papist. Who would have believed it?"

"A very, very wealthy Papist heiress, precisely at the time that his estate was in desperate need of money." The colonel was all amiability again.

Elizabeth noticed then that Jane's hand clutched the colonel's arm. Her face was ashen, but her voice was steady as she said, "I cannot bear this talk of politics on such a beautiful day. Colonel, perhaps you would care to see our gardens? The flowers are delightful this year."

He looked down at her in surprise. "That would give me great pleasure, Miss Bennet. Miss Elizabeth, will you join us?"

Elizabeth found her voice. "In a few minutes, perhaps."

Jane kept up a smiling monologue as she and Colonel Fitzwilliam left the room. Elizabeth looked accusingly at her father.

"Lizzy, of all the unfortunate occurrences in Kent, the worst has been the complete disappearance of your sense of humor. For what do we live, but to make sport for our neighbors and laugh at them in our turn?"

"Laughing at others can sometimes be very hurtful. I do not find insulting a perfectly amiable gentleman amusing. Regardless of what you believe, Colonel Fitzwilliam has been very kind to me."

"You will have to forgive me if I assume that if Lord Matlock's son was kind to you, it was because he found it to be in his best interest."

"He is not responsible for the sins of his father. Perhaps he takes after his mother."

"Just because he feels sympathy for the poor, poor Frenchmen who are doing their utmost to kill as many Englishmen as possible."

Elizabeth began to make a retort, then stopped as a thought occurred to her.

"What is it?"

"I was thinking about what he said to me when he saw the earl approaching the house. He told me to hide because he would rather see me face Napoleon's guns than be in the same room with his father with no one to protect me."

"That is the most sensible thing I have heard of him so far. The worst bullets can do is to kill you."

Elizabeth gave him a sharp glance, but said nothing.

"But I will say, Lizzy, that was a remarkable set-down that you gave Lord Matlock. I was proud of you."

It was an olive branch of sorts, but Elizabeth was not sure if she wanted to accept it or not. "I should join the others."

She circled the house without catching sight of Jane and the colonel, nor did she find them in the arbor or the formal garden. The only other likely place was the small wilderness beyond the ruined wall. She turned her steps there and was only a few feet from the wall when a sound came that she had not heard in far too long. It was the sound of Jane laughing freely, not a forced or polite laugh, but a real, joyous laugh. The murmur of the colonel's voice followed and Jane laughed once more.

Elizabeth could not recall such gaiety in her sister since Mr. Bingley had left Netherfield. Jane had been sad throughout the winter and during Elizabeth's stay at Hunsford, and after that, Jane's spirits had been equally oppressed by the conflict with their father, even though it did not involve her. Between the two blows, Jane's natural good humor had been replaced by a quiet sadness.

If Colonel Fitzwilliam could give Jane a few minutes of happiness, Elizabeth had no desire to interrupt the *tête-à-tête*. Her own appearance would only bring up the painful subject of their father. She crept quietly back into the garden, then took care to lose herself in the shrubbery for at least a quarter hour.

She did not have a chance to speak to the colonel alone until he was ready to depart. As the groom brought his horse, the colonel said, "I hope my visit did not make matters worse for you."

"Not at all. I just wish sometimes that I could go back to before all this happened, but of course one cannot step into the same river twice – and it would be very unwise to try when the aforementioned river is in flood. But I am sorry for my father's inexcusable behavior."

"You need not apologize – your sister has already done that at length, despite my protests, and quite charmingly as well." He took the reins of the horse in one hand. "I must say, Bingley was a *fool* to leave her. Darcy as well, but Bingley even more so." He shook his head in disbelief.

Elizabeth laughed. "You will get no argument from me on that score, sir. I am glad you can still believe that after meeting with my father today."

He swung up into the saddle with a practiced grace. "As I said earlier, you have met *my* father, Miss Bennet. Until we meet again!"

Chapter 13

ELIZABETH USUALLY ENJOYED summertime, since it gave her so much freedom to ramble and explore, but this year it seemed that she was simply marking time. Her tour to the Lakes was now the object of her happiest thoughts; it was her best consolation for all the uncomfortable hours which the discontentedness of her father made inevitable.

The trip was almost upon her when Hill, her face white, announced a most unexpected visitor. "The Countess of Matlock is here, Miss Lizzy."

Elizabeth dropped her embroidery in an untidy heap.

"Jane, Mary – you should not stay here. Truly." Elizabeth sounded half-strangled. She moved to stand behind her chair and gripped its back, her knuckles showing white. It was a poor defense, but it was the best she had.

Mary merely looked quizzical, but Jane, who knew more of Elizabeth's confrontation with Lord Matlock than Mary, said, "We will not leave you to face this alone."

Before Elizabeth could importune them further, Hill showed in an elegant lady of about Mrs. Bennet's years, wearing a fashionably cut gown of green silk. "The Countess of Matlock."

Lady Matlock surveyed the room with a glance and moved directly to Elizabeth. "*You* must be Elizabeth! I may call you Elizabeth, *n'est-ce pas?*

Elizabeth gripped the chair back more tightly, glancing from side to side with a certain desperation. How had Lady Matlock recognized her? A description of her appearance would have fitted Mary equally well. "I would be honored, Lady Matlock."

"Ah!" The countess spread her hands in front of her. "You want to know how it is I knew you. It was simple; Richard told me you have met my 'usband, and you are the only one who looks as if you expect me to pluck all your feathers and serve you for dinner." She pronounced her son's name *Ree-shar* in the French manner, and it was a moment before Elizabeth realized of whom she was speaking. Leaning forward and using a confidential tone, Lady Matlock added, "You need not fear. I am nothing like my 'usband, *vraiment.*"

Making an effort to loosen her fingers, Elizabeth said, "I mean no disrespect to Lord Matlock."

Her visitor trilled with laughter. "Ah, but I *do*! Come, sit by me, *cherie*. We must become better acquainted, you and I, since you are to be my niece." She gracefully seated herself on the sofa and patted the space beside her.

So this was where Colonel Fitzwilliam had learned his amiable manners. Elizabeth sat as instructed, albeit with a nervous glance at Jane. "Thank you, madam."

"Richard has told me all about you. You have quite charmed him! Darcy, of course, he only scowls, the poor boy. I knew immediately that I must meet the lady who has captured my nephew's so elusive heart."

Elizabeth could not suppress a smile. "It was quite unconsciously done, your ladyship."

"But of course it was! Darcy would never have taken notice of you had you been one of those young ladies who fawn over him so embarrassingly! He hates that so *very* much."

"I was as far from fawning as possible! My behavior toward him could only be described as impertinent."

Lady Matlock tapped Elizabeth's cheek with her folded fan. "Then we shall do splendidly together, you and I. We shall be impertinent, and Darcy will stop scowling all the time and learn to smile again. I wish you did not have to wait until Christmas!"

"So do I, Lady Matlock, but my father thinks otherwise."

Lady Matlock frowned, the feathers in her elaborate coiffure bobbing indignantly. "Your father, he is the ogre, yes? The one who refuses to let poor Darcy see you?"

Elizabeth wondered whether it would be more polite to agree that her father was an ogre or to argue the point. "He means well," she said without conviction.

"I would hope so, for if he does not, he is merely a fool, and for a man it is perhaps better to be an ogre than a fool, *n'est-ce pas*? Richard is with him now, I believe."

At that moment the two gentlemen appeared. Lady Matlock looked at Mr. Bennet appraisingly. "Ah, *you* must be the ogre, then!" she exclaimed in apparent delight, her accent making even this sound like a compliment.

Mr. Bennet made a perfunctory bow. "At your service, madam. But you need not fear; I have already whetted my appetite for human flesh upon your son, so you are quite safe from me."

The colonel looked amused as he claimed the chair nearest Jane. "Fortunately, my wounds are something less than mortal."

The rest of the visit proceeded as unremarkably as a visit from a countess to the house of a country gentleman of small fortune might be expected to do. With the absence of her mother and youngest sisters, there was little to embarrass her. Mary was too much in awe to speak, and Mr. Bennet limited himself to the occasional sardonic comment.

When at last Lady Matlock's carriage pulled away, after that lady had pressed upon Elizabeth many invitations to call on her when she should be in London, Elizabeth was surprised to discover that Colonel Fitzwilliam, who had ridden to Longbourn rather than travel in the stifling carriage, had remained, standing between Jane and Mr. Bennet.

"I hope you are satisfied," Mr. Bennet said dryly to him, "though my restraint was not due to anything *you* said, but instead came from my own conviction that any woman unfortunate enough to be married to your father deserves pity, not censure."

Colonel Fitzwilliam chuckled. "True, though she has not lived with my father for many years. She fed him poison once, you know, and withheld the antidote until he signed the papers granting her a separate household. It is a well-known story."

Mr. Bennet clasped his hands in front of his chest. "Truly a lady after my own heart! – although *I* fail to see the need for an antidote. Do give her my compliments. And now I believe *you* were leaving, sir."

"True, although, I will be leaving your home only a short distance to bespeak a room at the inn. Miss Bennet has informed me that there is an assembly in Meryton tonight, and was kind enough to invite me to attend."

Mr. Bennet removed his glasses and placed them in his waistcoat pocket, then surveyed the colonel from head to toe. "Am I to understand that you are in the habit of gracing country assemblies with your august presence?"

"No, but your eldest daughter is remarkably beautiful, and I *am* in the habit of accepting such invitations when they come from ladies of remarkable beauty." He bowed toward Jane, who colored prettily. "I hope you will do me the honor of dancing the first set with me."

As Jane nodded, Mr. Bennet said, "On the contrary. I think you accepted because you delight in annoying me."

The colonel assumed a thoughtful expression. "Delight is perhaps the wrong word. Better, perhaps, to say that it simply comes naturally to me." He winked at Elizabeth. "Miss Elizabeth, since I have already requested the honor of the first set from your sister, may I hope that you are free for the second?"

Elizabeth looked straight at her father as she said, "I will look forward to it, sir."

At the assembly, Colonel Fitzwilliam immediately became the subject of discussion among those who attended. Word that he was unmarried and son to an earl circulated at an astonishing pace, followed by rumors of more dubious origin, including that he was courting Miss Bennet and in line to be a General. In a moment of wicked amusement, Elizabeth considered mentioning his fictional sickly elder brother, but refrained.

The colonel danced twice with Jane and Elizabeth, once with Mary, and once each with two young ladies whom Elizabeth felt certain had been pointed out to him by Jane as being the most in need of some gentlemanly attention from the son of an earl. She had not seen Jane in such good looks and spirits since Mr. Bingley had decamped from Netherfield, and she was grateful to the colonel for his part in it.

"It was at an assembly such as this that I first set eyes on Mr. Darcy," Elizabeth told the colonel during a break between sets.

"And he fell violently in love with you." The colonel handed glasses of lemonade to Elizabeth and Jane.

Elizabeth laughed. "No, indeed. He said I was tolerable, but not handsome enough to tempt him to dance, and that Jane was the only pretty woman in the room. And in my hearing, no less!"

"Trust Darcy to say something foolish! No wonder you took such a dislike to him. Apparently you tempted him afterwards, though."

"It seems so, though I cannot imagine why. I was *very* impertinent to him."

"He no doubt thoroughly deserved it. On the subject of

impertinence, may I hope that my presence has not caused speculation that could make you uncomfortable?"

"No, especially since they seem to be linking your name with Jane's, not mine. Your presence tonight is sure to be a nine days' wonder here, but fortunately, I will be leaving Longbourn in two days, travelling with my aunt and uncle to the Lake District. By the time I return, I imagine the fuss will have died down. The gossips will have found someone else to talk about."

Elizabeth had no idea how correct her prediction would prove to be.

"I wonder what Colonel Fitzwilliam said to our father before they joined us," said Elizabeth as Jane tugged a brush through her hair that night.

"You will be amazed at my daring, Lizzy! I asked him directly about that. Apparently, he said that although our father might insult *him* with impunity, secure in the knowledge that he would not retaliate against his cousin's future father-in-law, rudeness to his mother did not fall into the same category."

"And I am certain he said it in such an amiable manner that it was impossible to take offense!"

"Yes, he is a very amiable gentleman." Jane fell silent, and Elizabeth knew she was thinking of a different amiable gentleman who had disappointed her hopes. "But still, he can be firm, and he knows his own mind."

It was just as well that there would be few chances in the future for Jane's path to cross that of Colonel Fitzwilliam. Elizabeth did not want her sister to be disappointed in love yet again.

The Gardiners' carriage rattled on the rutted road as the travellers departed from Meryton. Elizabeth gloried in the luxury of being alone with her aunt and uncle. "You cannot begin to imagine how glad I am to leave Longbourn behind! I am looking forward very much to the Lakes, but I do not think I could have borne another day at home."

Mr. Gardiner cleared his throat. "I have some disappointing news about the Lake District, Lizzy. Since I must be back in London sooner than expected, we decided it would be wiser to substitute a contracted tour, so we will be travelling no further than Derbyshire. The scenery there is second only to the Lakes, and it will also give us the opportunity to visit the town where your aunt spent some of her childhood."

Elizabeth was excessively disappointed by this news. She had set her heart on seeing the Lakes, but she did her best to mask her dismay. "But even this morning you spoke about visiting Windermere!"

"I admit to practicing a little deception," said Mrs. Gardiner with a slight smile. "We have known of this change in destination for several weeks, but feared that your father might not allow you to join us if he knew we planned to travel so close to Pemberley. We will send a letter in a day or two informing him of our change in plans."

"I imagine Derbyshire is large enough that Mr. Darcy and I are unlikely to cross paths by accident, but you are no doubt correct." Elizabeth picked at a loose thread in her glove as she allowed a fraction of her bitterness into her tone. It would be hard to know he might be so nearby and unable to do anything about it. On the other hand, there was no reason to believe he would be in residence at his estate; he might be anywhere. Realizing that her words might have sounded reproachful, she added, "I am so glad you invited me to join you. Without this journey to look forward to, I do not know how I would have survived the last month."

Mrs. Gardiner patted her hand. "I am so sorry, Lizzy. I had hoped that once you were back at Longbourn, your father would be more understanding."

"He no longer gives me orders, although I am still not allowed to contact Mr. Darcy. What I cannot bear is his mockery."

"His mockery?"

"Oh, it is nothing new. He has always said that his daughters were silly and ignorant, and I paid no attention because he would say that I was quicker than the rest, and my flattered vanity insisted he must be speaking in jest. But it is no longer amusing to be told I am silly, especially when *he* is the one who is choosing to remain in deliberate ignorance. I am sorry; I do not mean to spoil our trip with my complaining. I want to hear all about what we will see in Derbyshire." She forced herself to smile.

Her aunt nodded understandingly. "If that is what you wish, but I hope you know I am always happy to listen to anything you would like to say."

Elizabeth's throat was too tight for speech, so she limited herself to a quick nod of her head.

Mr. Gardiner, his brows slightly drawn, said, "We have an

ambitious itinerary planned. We will visit Oxford, Blenheim and Kenilworth on the way, and of course in Derbyshire there will be a great deal to see – the Peak, of course, as well as Dove Dale, Matlock and Chatsworth."

The mention of Matlock brought Colonel Fitzwilliam immediately to mind. Was she doomed to spend the entire trip faced with reminders of her situation, when she had hoped to put it from her mind in the beauties of the Lake District? "It sounds delightful," Elizabeth said firmly.

Chapter 14

THE HUMAN MIND is a curious thing, and there can be no surprise that Elizabeth, having resolved that the possibility of an accidental encounter in Derbyshire with Mr. Darcy was ridiculously remote, could not keep herself from hoping to see his tall form every time they rounded a curve in the road. By the time the travellers had reached Lambton, the town where Mrs. Gardiner had passed her childhood, Elizabeth was heartily sick of the constant cycle of wishful thinking and disappointment. On discovering that Pemberley lay not five miles from the inn where they were staying, her anxiety rose even higher.

Her first concern on arriving in the neighborhood was that her name might be recognized among the local people who had heard about the engagement of the Master of Pemberley, but that proved not to be the case. For her other worries, she applied to the chambermaid when she retired that night, asking her if Pemberley were not a very fine place and whether the family there often ventured to Lambton. On receiving the disappointing news that the Darcys were seldom seen in Lambton, she hoped to put all her thoughts to rest by asking whether the family were down for the summer. The chambermaid replied in the negative, but instead of providing Elizabeth relief from her ruminations, this intelligence caused a new depression to strike her spirits.

The following morning, she prepared herself to meet her aunt and uncle's plans for the day with a semblance of enthusiasm, but was completely undone when her aunt expressed an inclination to see Pemberley itself. "My love, should not you like to see the place where you are to live? It seems a shame to pass it by when we are here in the vicinity," said Mrs. Gardiner.

Elizabeth could not hide her distress. She felt that she had no business at Pemberley without Mr. Darcy, and that her visit could be seen as seen in the light of an unpleasantly avaricious curiosity. She could not think that her name would be unknown *there*, where every person's life was so entwined with Mr. Darcy's. What would *he* think if he discovered she had been there?

Her aunt made some attempt to argue with her, but on seeing that Elizabeth's mind was made up, she conferred briefly with her husband, who proposed a plan for driving into the Peak. Elizabeth quickly acquiesced to this idea.

They set out shortly thereafter, and Elizabeth settled herself back in the carriage seat to enjoy the rugged scenery that surrounded them. She was surprised when the carriage halted by a lodge, and her uncle stepped down to speak to the keeper. When he returned, he instructed the driver to turn into the woods through a set of large, ornate gates just past the lodge, causing Elizabeth to look at him with curiosity tinged with suspicion.

"This appears to be a private road," she said.

"We have to make a brief stop at Pemberley," her aunt said apologetically. "I am sorry, my dear, but we had already made arrangements, and it would be terribly rude if we did not appear at all. We do not need to linger, just to stop long enough to explain that we will not be able to take the tour. You may remain in the carriage if you wish."

Heat rushed into Elizabeth's cheeks. Two months ago she would have argued, or at least disagreed, but she had since lost faith that her opinion would make a difference. Besides, she was only a guest on this journey and had no right to complain if she disliked the itinerary. She folded her hands in her lap, doing her best to hide her distress, and said, "Very well. If you wish to take the tour, I will not stand in the way."

Relief blossomed in her aunt's face. "Thank you for understanding, Lizzy. I had not anticipated that you would wish to avoid the place."

"Do they know who I am?"

Mr. Gardiner said, "I merely said I was bringing a small party with me."

"I would prefer it if you did not tell anyone there of my connection with Mr. Darcy."

Her aunt smiled, looking much happier about the prospect than she would have anticipated. "We will not mention it to a soul."

Elizabeth took several deep breaths, hoping to slow her racing heartbeat. If she had no choice in the matter, she might as well make the best of the situation, and she could not deny a certain curiosity as to her future home. As she gazed out as the carriage reached the crest of a hill, her eye was instantly caught by the large, handsome stone building, standing well on rising ground, with a stream that broadened into a small lake before it. She caught her breath in delight. Despite all the praise she had heard of Pemberley, she had not expected such beauty. She had been determined to be pleased by it for Mr. Darcy's sake, but such natural elegance reflected even more praise to him. To think that she would live in such handsome surroundings someday! Her aunt and uncle were instantly forgiven for bringing her there against her will, but she felt at that moment a new grievance toward her father. But for him, she could be arriving here today as Mrs. Darcy.

The carriage drew up a short distance from the house. As she stepped out, Elizabeth's gaze was drawn by the lofty Palladian portico in the front. As her eyes adjusted to the size of the house, she realized there was a dark, elegantly clad figure standing at the foot of the steps. Her heart suddenly began to race. She blinked twice, telling herself she must be imagining things, but his broad shoulders and his stance were achingly familiar, as was his brisk gait as he began to move in her direction. With an inarticulate cry, she ran to him.

Propriety was completely forgotten in her sudden joy and relief as she flew into his embrace. His arms tightened around her until her feet almost left the ground, but Elizabeth did not care. Half laughing, half crying, she pressed her face against his chest until she could feel the weave of the superfine cloth of his coat on her cheek, and she only wished she could hold him closer still. She could hear him murmuring her name, but she herself was beyond speech, almost beyond thought as she found solace in the refuge of his arms, and with it the release of all the pain of the last weeks. She could hear his heartbeat matching her own, and she wished the moment would never end.

Reality was slow to return, and when it did, Elizabeth chose to ignore it as long as possible, preferring to keep her present happy position rather than obey the laws of propriety which suddenly seemed extraordinarily foolish. After all, if the proper Mr. Darcy did not object, why should she? The thought made her laugh, and she tipped back her head to look at him.

His expression was one she had never seen before, a mixture of heartfelt delight, tenderness and something else she could not name. He leaned his forehead against hers, an intimacy that robbed her of what little breath remained.

A thought suddenly crossed her mind. "You do not seem surprised to see me."

He shook his head slightly and laughed low in his throat. "True. I am delighted, overjoyed, and pleased beyond measure to see you – but not surprised."

"But how...." she began, but then realized she did not care how he had known.

"Your uncle was kind enough to tell me you would be here today."

"My uncle?" Suddenly many things made sense – the Gardiners' disregard of her wishes to avoid Pemberley, the odd looks she had seen them share, and even the change in destination from the Lakes.

"Yes." Darcy sounded amused. "The same uncle who is taking great care to look in every direction but this one."

"Oh. Of course." Now acutely aware of the inappropriateness of her behavior, she reluctantly disentangled herself from Darcy, even though it felt like she was losing something very precious. "I'm sorry; I was not thinking of appearances."

"Do not apologize for this. *Ever.*" His voice was low and intense as he pulled her back into his arms. "You cannot know what it means to me that you are so happy to see me."

From behind her, Mr. Gardiner's voice said pointedly, "The proportions of the arches are quite fine. As for the balustrades, are they not reminiscent of the ones in the drawing of Woburn Abbey that hangs over my desk? Oh, Lizzy, there you are. I had quite forgotten that we had brought you with us today."

Darcy released her, looking slightly shamefaced. "My apologies, Mr. Gardiner, for allowing my feelings to overrule my better judgment."

Mr. Gardiner made a shushing sound. "Not to worry, lad. No one thinks the less of you for it."

Elizabeth turned to embrace her uncle, pressing a kiss on his cheek. "Thank you, thank you. I cannot thank you enough."

"Your happiness is all the thanks we have ever wanted. And we will keep our promise not to tell a soul here of your connection to Mr. Darcy – but I think that they will all have guessed by now." He winked at her.

She laughed. "But why did you not tell *me*?"

His face grew sober. "Although we disagree with your father, we did not wish to encourage you to disobey him. As long as you did not know why we were bringing you here, you were not disobeying. I believe we can turn *that* responsibility over to Darcy now."

She looked back and forth between her uncle and Darcy, who was brushing off his hat which had fallen to the ground during their embrace. "What do you mean?" she asked.

"Only that Darcy understands that you are to have no reason to contact him."

Darcy took her hand in his. "I intend to already be with you whenever you might wish to contact me."

"If you are expecting me to complain about that, you will be waiting a long time!" It felt so right to have his hand around hers, even though it raised little flutters in her stomach.

"Good." Darcy leaned toward her and spoke softly in her ear. "I have not had the opportunity to court you as you deserve to be courted. This is likely to be my only chance to do so before we marry, so I intend to make the most of it."

"But how did this come to pass?"

Mr. Gardiner chuckled. "Darcy has become a regular visitor to Gracechurch Street, where we have shared whatever news we had of you. Your aunt and I have grown quite fond of him, so when we made our plans to visit Lambton, we decided to mention it to him. You can imagine the rest."

Darcy said, "Mr. and Mrs. Gardiner have been extraordinarily kind to me. I credit them with preserving my sanity on more than one occasion. And now, I hope you will all honor me by coming inside for a tour of the house."

"Thank you," said Mr. Gardiner. "I confess that I have been looking forward to seeing Pemberley after hearing my wife praise it so frequently."

Elizabeth hesitated. "Does your staff know who I am?"

Darcy smiled down at her. "Yes, but my housekeeper has instructed them to treat you as they would any other guest."

"Thank you; I do not think I could do my future role justice at the moment."

His warm breath moved against her ear as he spoke. "I am glad you do not mind, but I did it for purely selfish reasons. My time with you is too precious to share with them."

Elizabeth was in a daze as Darcy took them on a tour of the house, taking in only the elegance of the furnishings and the sweeping vistas from the windows. Although she usually had an excellent sense of direction, she could not have retraced their steps had she tried. She kept turning to look at Darcy, sometimes even touching his arm, finding it hard to believe that he was truly there. She had never seen him like this – warm, affectionate, at ease. His pride in Pemberley shone from him, but there was no haughtiness in his manner toward the Gardiners. They might look like people of fashion, but if he had been to Gracechurch Street, he must know the truth of their status. She had thought he would want little to do with her relatives in trade, but instead he seemed truly pleased to see them, and even said that he hoped they would stay at Pemberley on any future trips to Derbyshire.

He concluded the tour by showing them a private suite of rooms, richly decorated in a Rococo style different from the subtler elegance of the rest of the house. Elaborate gold stucco work wound up the walls of the sitting room, while ornate porcelain sculptures of pastoral gentlemen in white wigs and ladies in full skirts were clustered on the mantelpiece. A dressing room lay between the sitting room and a large bedroom in matching style.

Darcy took Elizabeth's hand. "These were my mother's rooms, and they will be yours. They have been closed up for years, but I thought you would like to see them, so I had the staff ready them. They are in sore need of updating, but any changes must be to suit your tastes. I hope you will feel free to tell me what you would like. I want you to be happy here."

She laughed at his worried look. Did he truly think that she might be disappointed in Pemberley simply because the décor in these rooms was old-fashioned and out of style? At Longbourn, most of the furnishings were far older than this. "I cannot imagine being unhappy at Pemberley. These rooms are indeed very grand. I feel as if I am visiting a royal palace!"

The lines on his face relaxed, allowing a small smile to appear. "We can talk further of this later. Come, there are some refreshments in the saloon, and then perhaps you would like to see the grounds."

They discussed their plans over an extensive offering of cold meat, cake, and a variety of all the finest fruits in season. Darcy told them that he was completely at their disposal for the next two days. "The rest of my party, in a visit that was planned before I knew you would be here, will be joining me after that. My sister will be among them, along with a few who can claim acquaintance with Elizabeth – Mr. Bingley and his sisters.

Georgiana is particularly anxious to meet you; she has been longing to make your acquaintance since I first told her of meeting you in Hertfordshire."

Although disappointed by the idea of sharing him with a larger group, Elizabeth said, "I will be glad of the opportunity to meet her." She hoped Mr. Bingley's presence would not prove disruptive. Even if Jane claimed not to mind, Elizabeth had not yet fully reconciled herself to Darcy's actions in separating Bingley from Jane.

After tea, Darcy led them on a circuit of the grounds. He had walked this way a thousand times, but this time it was as if he was seeing it through new eyes - the picturesque walk by the side of the water, every step bringing forward a nobler fall of ground or a finer reach of the woods. Elizabeth's delight in the artful design of the park pleased him not only because of his love of his home, but as a sign that she would not be displeased to live there. Pemberley was lovely, and to him no other county could match the beauty of Derbyshire, but he had wondered more than once what Elizabeth would think of the stark, hilly landscape, and whether she would be homesick for the gentler Hertfordshire countryside.

By far the best surprise of the day had been how obviously glad she was to see him. Mr. Gardiner had been right about that as well. Early in their acquaintance, Darcy had expressed his concern that Elizabeth might be convinced to call off their engagement owing to her father's opposition, especially since he had just barely won her consent in the first place. Strong though his own attachment was, he was well aware that hers was much less and of far shorter duration. Mr. Gardiner had disagreed, though, saying that in this particular circumstance, Mr. Bennet's opposition would likely work in Darcy's favor. "If he had tried to persuade her to end the engagement, she might have considered it, but by forbidding it, he is pushing her into your arms. I think you will find her attachment to you to be stronger rather than weaker."

Darcy could see how this might well be true, but he had thought it would be more a determination on Elizabeth's part to follow through with their engagement rather than true attachment. That was all that was necessary for now; no matter how much he longed for her love, he had accepted that winning her affection might have to wait until after they were married. After all, how could she develop tender feelings for him when she could not even communicate with him? He had not dared to believe it possible until he saw Elizabeth running to him, her eyes alight. What a moment that had been! He would never forget it, no matter how long he lived.

The Gardiners again showed their tact by following them at a distance, allowing the opportunity for private discussion which earlier had been lacking. Elizabeth found herself in the unusual position of feeling tongue-tied. She had imagined conversations with Darcy so often in the last few months that she hardly knew what to say to the real man, but merely having her hand rest on his arm was an undeniable pleasure. Still, she felt unaccountably shy in his presence.

"Your uncle tells me that your father remains fiercely opposed to our engagement."

"Yes, though I sometimes think it is as much out of stubbornness as anything. He hates to admit he was wrong about anything."

"Has it been very difficult for you?"

His concern was nearly her undoing, as the sense of betrayal and pain she had felt these last months threatened to overwhelm her. Feelings such as these were not something she confided in anyone, not even Jane or Charlotte, and the idea of doing so with Darcy, no matter how tempting, was frightening. "I try to focus on the things that bring me pleasure, not the ones I cannot change."

"I regret that my presence in your life has caused a rift between you and your father. I know you value him," Darcy said gravely.

"The rift was caused by my father, not by you. I have never been blind to the impropriety of his behavior as a father, but for many years, I was so grateful for his affectionate treatment of me that I endeavored to forget what I could not overlook. Now my eyes have been opened. I had hoped at first that his attitude would change with time, but now I think he has taken the matter to such an extreme that he can no longer admit to making an error."

"I wish I could do something to help. I have written to him several times, but he has not responded. He may not have even read my letters, but I felt obligated to try."

She tightened her hand on his arm. "He never mentioned it to me. Thank you for making the effort."

"You must know by now that there is nothing I would not do to make you happy."

Warmth settled into Elizabeth's stomach, along with a flash of physical awareness of him. This man, who was still half a stranger, would be her husband, flesh of her flesh. She could feel the telltale blush rising in her cheeks. "It is fortunate for you, then, that I tend to high spirits. Otherwise you might be very busy."

He chuckled. "I would be happy to be occupied in such a good cause. But I also have not had a chance to thank you for taking the risk of accepting me."

"Whereas I should be apologizing for taking so long to make up my mind!" she teased.

He gave a small smile, but the look in his eyes bespoke greater warmth. "Some things are worth the wait." He halted, and the next thing she knew, his hand was resting lightly on her cheek, and his gaze had fallen to her lips. "Elizabeth," he whispered. "It has been driving me mad that I have not been able to do this."

She knew what was about to happen, but even so, the intimacy of his lips gently caressing hers was a shock. Her entire body seemed to pulse in time with his kiss, as if she had suddenly come alive after a long sleep, the skin on her arms tingling as if a storm was coming. Most shocking, though, was how the firm warmth of his lips seemed to spiral deep inside her, tugging at her core. Almost involuntarily she swayed toward him, then realized what she was doing. Taking a step back, she gasped, "My aunt and uncle!"

Darcy gestured behind them, his eyes remaining fixed to Elizabeth. "Still safely around the bend."

He was correct; the path had taken a sharp curve, the woods hiding them from the older couple behind them. "Did you plan this?" she said in mock accusation.

He had the grace to look guilty. "Only a few minutes ago."

Her moment of fear past, Elizabeth found her lips aching to touch his again, but just then, the Gardiners appeared behind them. Darcy offered her his arm again as if nothing had happened, but somehow everything had changed.

Neither of them spoke for several minutes, and afterwards Elizabeth would have been at a loss to describe the path they took. Her cheeks were hot, and she could hardly bring herself to look at Darcy, but she felt his presence beside her with every fiber of her being. Good heavens, if a mere kiss disrupted her so deeply, what would happen when they were married and matters went far beyond a kiss? Based on the glimpses Elizabeth had caught over the years of amorous young farmers and milkmaids, she knew this had been a fairly chaste kiss, yet it had still affected her profoundly.

She stole a glance up through her lashes at Darcy. She could not read his expression, but there was something almost distant about it. It made her uncomfortable, so she said archly, "You are very quiet, sir."

The distance faded, and his eyes smoldered at her, rendering her oddly short of breath. "I am reminding myself of all the reasons why it would be a mistake to elope. Given that I am something of an expert on why elopements are a poor idea, it is a testament to your power that I should even give it a second thought, much less have to dissuade myself from it."

"While I agree that elopement is not the solution, I am intrigued to hear you describe yourself as an expert on the subject. Is there something I ought to know about?" The idea that he might have considered marrying another woman left her feeling vaguely ill.

"I have lived with the consequences of my parents' elopement all my life - my mother's regrets over the loss of the position in the *ton* that would have been hers had she not been forced to elope, and my father's distress over the consequences of the scandal. After her death, the whispers died off. It seems that society has more exacting standards for women than for men in this matter."

So it had not been another woman after all. Elizabeth was embarrassed by how relieved she felt. It might also explain his powerful concern for her reputation. "Is that why you were so eager to have matters settled between us at Hunsford?"

He considered. "Not as such, but I could not ignore the fact that any delay would besmirch your reputation. Then, when we were in Tunbridge Wells, we passed some of my acquaintances from the *ton*. I saw how they were eyeing you, and I realized it had begun already. Hoping to minimize the damage, I sent off the notice of our engagement, not realizing the price we would both pay for it when it came to your father's attention."

Elizabeth chose her words carefully. "I have wondered why you said nothing of that to me."

"What I told myself was that, although you had not yet accepted that you would have to marry me, you would likely do so given a few days' time, and that with luck I might have the opportunity to soften your opinion of me so that it would not come as such a blow to you. But it was more about my wounded pride, I fear. I was still smarting from your refusal, and could not face the anger you would have felt if you thought I had forced your hand. But I can tell you in all honesty that I did *not* do it to force you to marry me. As far as I was concerned, we had both lost any choice in the matter the previous day, but I knew you saw it differently."

"At that point, I did not want to see it at all. Loss of reputation was perhaps preferable to marriage to a man whom I considered detestable, but I hoped to avoid both, although I knew on some level that you were correct. Still, my own pride revolted at being forced into that or any other match. I heartily dislike having my choices taken away from me, as my father has discovered." To Elizabeth's relief, they entered a dark grotto that, despite its natural appearance, had no doubt been constructed to complement the landscape. More to the purpose, the sudden plunge from sunlight into shade would disguise her expression.

"That, of course, was part of my dilemma," Darcy said, his voice quiet, yet echoing off the rough rock walls around them. "I wanted you to *desire* to marry me, and that seemed more impossible each day. The best I could hope for was that you would decide you had no choice but to accept my offer. Your liveliness and sparkle had drawn me to you, yet I could see that my presence was smothering those very qualities I loved in you. I did not want you to come to me unwillingly, yet everything I tried seemed only to drive you further away." His pain seemed to fill the cool air of the grotto.

Unable to bear how much he had been hurt through their misunderstandings, she turned her face into his shoulder. "I wish I had understood more." Her voice was muffled by the superfine fabric of his coat.

His arms tightened convulsively around her. "You cannot know what joy you gave me when you marched into that sitting room like an avenging Amazon and announced you were going to marry me."

Tears burnt in Elizabeth's eyes as she remembered what had happened next, and before she knew it, a sob choked her. The surprises of the day and the overwhelming relief of finding herself in his protective embrace had shaken her more than she cared to admit. She tried to hold it back, telling herself that this was a foolish time to cry, now that she was finally with him, yet the salty tears insisted on pouring down her cheeks anyway. "I am sorry; I am not usually such a watering pot!" Her voice shook.

The pressure of his lips on her forehead soothed her even while it made her feel hot inside. "No, I am the one who should be sorry, my sweetest Elizabeth," he murmured. "I never meant to hurt you or to cause you the least distress, yet I have done so, time and again. I do not know how you can ever forgive me."

"I forgave you as soon as I realized your true intentions. My father was the one who truly hurt me, not you." Her last words were barely audible.

Darcy's arms tightened, then he released her just long enough to lead her to a rude stone bench carved into the grotto wall. It was wide enough that they could have sat with a proper distance between them, but instead he put his arm around her and drew her close beside him. "You are too kind to me. I was to blame for the situation arising in the first place. Were it not for me, your reputation would not have been in danger, there would have been no announcement, and your father would not have come to Kent and discovered us together."

Even through her tears, she managed a shaky laugh. "So you caused the flood that stranded us together? I never knew you had such power over the weather!"

"I could not prevent the flood, but it was my choice to go charging over to the parsonage at night, knowing you were there alone. I knew your your reputation could be harmed if word got out of it, but I blithely assumed we would be engaged and therefore above reproach before anyone knew of it."

"So, it would have been more respectful on your part to stay away, leaving me alone to face the village ruffians?"

Darcy's arm around her tightened. "Do not even joke about that. It is hard enough to know how little I can do to protect you once you return to Longbourn."

He was, she thought, all too prone to take responsibility for things far beyond his control. "I have managed to survive quite well thus far, sir! I am not as frail a creature as you might think." She mopped her tears with a crumpled handkerchief from her pocket.

He spoke quietly in her ear. "Your uncle is just beyond the entrance to the grotto."

Startled, Elizabeth looked up. Mr. Gardiner was looking directly at the two of them, without condemnation, but also standing his ground in a manner which showed his intention to watch them. He could not have said more clearly that he would allow Darcy to comfort her, so long as it went no further than that. Embarrassed, she hid her face in Darcy's shoulder until she could control herself once more. "Oh, what must he think of me!"

"He understands how much you have suffered. He has been very good to me, which I do not deserve when I was the one who once condemned your low connections. It has been a lesson to me."

His words provided a balm to her. She had worried often in these last months that Darcy might expect her to keep her relatives at a distance. That he might grow fond of them was an unexpected gift.

It was the happiest day Darcy had experienced in months. Coming as it did after such a prolonged period of gloom, it was all the more valued. While Elizabeth's tears over her father pained him, it was outweighed by the satisfaction of being able to give her comfort. Later, as her usual high spirits began to emerge, he was once again absorbed into the joyous and light-hearted place the world could become when Elizabeth's liveliness lit it. He had missed her teasing ways and the brilliance of her fine eyes, her quick intelligence so unlike the languor in fashion among ladies of the *ton*. To think that this would someday be his to enjoy constantly! He was determined to think only of that, not of the months of separation which they would suffer after her departure from Derbyshire. Sometimes he even succeeded in doing so, keeping the darkness at bay for a brief time.

The hardest part was fighting the constant temptation to take her into his arms. Those brief moments of holding her soft body against his had been intoxicating, and were it not for the presence of the Gardiners, he would have held her in his embrace for hours. Ah, why was he lying to himself? He would have done far more than hold her. Every sinuous movement of her lithe body, every unconsciously seductive gesture she made, every sparkling laugh tempted him into ever more dangerous desires to caress her soft skin, to claim her lips, to make her moan with pleasure from his touch. When one of her dark curls escaped from its binding, he could not look away from where it bounced against her neck, imagining how she would look with her hair loose and spread across his pillow. During their walk, he had been haunted by the vision of her legs, outlined through the thin muslin of her skirt when the sun was behind her. The urge to carry her off and make her forever his had been well-nigh unbearable, and the painful restraint he had showed in limiting himself to a chaste kiss was enough to qualify a man for sainthood. Fasting for weeks and wearing a hair shirt would be nothing in comparison. Still, he would happily tolerate that torment in exchange for the consuming delight of Elizabeth's company.

Although he had wished the Gardiners far away dozens of times that day solely so that he could have Elizabeth to himself, he was also grateful for the leniency Mr. Gardiner had demonstrated in overlooking the moments when he could no longer restrain himself from even a chaste touch. Many chaperones would not have tolerated such breaches of propriety towards a young lady under their care, but Darcy suspected Mr. Gardiner of having sympathy toward his position, and Mrs. Gardiner seemed content to follow her husband's lead.

The day ended far too soon, even though the Gardiners had extended their visit through an informal dinner and well into the evening. When Mr. Gardiner announced that it was time for them to return to the inn, no amount of preparation for the moment had prepared Darcy for the wrenching sense of emptiness that swallowed him at the prospect of being separated from Elizabeth. He would see her again in the morning, but the hours between now and then suddenly seemed like an endless stretch of bleakness.

His eyes automatically went to Elizabeth's, so he did not notice Mr. Gardiner directing his wife out the door. That gentleman then came to him, blocking his view of Elizabeth, and clapped him on the shoulder. Leaning forward, he said quietly, "You have five minutes, lad, not a second more."

As Darcy tried to make sense of this, Mr. Gardiner exited the sitting room and closed the door, leaving him alone with Elizabeth. Then he understood, astonished that even the sympathetic Mr. Gardiner would go so far, but prepared to be quite grateful for it. Later. Right now he had more important things to think about.

Elizabeth's flushed cheeks told him she had some idea what was happening. Fortunately her blushes were enough to curb the insatiable voice in Darcy's mind that was informing him quite explicitly of what might be accomplished in five minutes. Not wanting to waste a second of their precious time, he took Elizabeth's hands in his. Turning them over, he brushed his lips against the palm of first one hand, then the other. Her shiver in response only made him want more. "Your uncle says we have five minutes." His voice sounded hoarse even to his own ears.

Good Lord, how was he to take this slowly when she was looking at him in that unconsciously seductive manner? His body was already responding as he drew her into his arms, her familiar scent of lavender wafting over him. She trembled as her soft curves came into contact with his body, and for a moment Darcy was unsure whether it was fear or anticipation that she felt. Then her hands found their way around his neck, drawing him even closer, her hint of an arch smile tempting him to find his pleasures within.

Elizabeth's heartbeat pounded in her ears as she vaguely wondered why her lips were already tingling when Darcy had not even touched them, but then he remedied that with a kiss so tender that it made her heart ache. Her body ached as well, but in a very different manner, and she pressed herself against him more tightly in an attempt to fill the void within her.

Darcy reacted instantly, his lips brushing hers as soft as a whisper. Elizabeth's eyelids drifted closed as she focused on the delicate sensation as the tip of his tongue traced a line between her lips. A tingling sensation in the pit of her stomach threatened to engulf her. Without conscious thought she allowed her lips to part at his sensuous urging, and she was shocked at her own eager response to the unexpected intimacy of his tongue exploring her mouth. She could taste the warm sweetness of port and a tantalizing hint of something like cloves, sending fire sweeping through as she clung to him.

Instinctively she responded, meeting his ardor with her own burgeoning passion. Even though it felt as if her entire being was centered in the spot where their mouths met, somehow she was aware of the warmth of his hands exploring her back, tantalizing her with light touches as he stroked downward toward her hips. A melting warmth spread inside her at his every caress until she felt nothing in the world mattered beyond this astonishing sensation. All she wanted was to be even closer, until nothing could come between them. She arched against him, and Darcy's response was to hold her even tighter.

The sharp knock at the door barely registered to Elizabeth until Darcy's lips were no longer on hers. She opened her eyes to see the sharp angles of his face, his eyes dark with passion and his breathing uneven.

He touched her cheeks lightly with both hands. "My sweetest, loveliest Elizabeth," he said softly.

Her mind still would not formulate words, but she managed to remember to step away from him as the door opened.

Mr. Gardiner stepped into the room just as Darcy was straightening his cravat. "Our carriage is waiting, Lizzy."

Darcy offered her his arm. "May I see you to your carriage?"

"Of course," Elizabeth murmured. As she rested her hand on his elbow, she took advantage of his proximity to lay her head against his shoulder. She felt the brief pressure of his kiss on her forehead.

Their hands clung as he handed her into the carriage. As they drove away, Elizabeth was grateful that her aunt and uncle did not try to engage her overmuch in conversation. Her mind and her heart were still at Pemberley.

Chapter 15

THE FOLLOWING MORNING, Darcy appeared at the inn before breakfast with the intention of spending as much of the day as possible with Elizabeth. She had spent much of the previous night reliving his kisses with enough pleasure that she found herself blushing when he first entered the room. But if it was hard to meet his eyes at first, she quickly overcame that as he took advantage of every possible opportunity to touch her arm or the back of her hand, each caress reminding her of the fire between them. If only she could kiss him again!

The plan for the day called for a visit to Dove Dale, a journey made swifter and more comfortable in Darcy's elegant and luxurious carriage. They stopped twice en route at Darcy's recommendation to view a scenic vista, and Elizabeth again had the feeling he was watching her with unusual intensity.

She had seen illustrations of Dove Dale and heard her uncle wax eloquent about the famous trout stream that ran through it, but nothing had not prepared her for the loveliness of the valley with its thickly wooded slopes and towering pinnacles of rocks. She turned in place, taking in the sight.

Beside her, Darcy rested his hand lightly on the small of her back. "Does it meet with your approval?"

"How could it not? No one could resist such beauty." She had never realized a touch on her back could provoke such sensations.

"No one, indeed," Darcy murmured, but he was looking at her, not at the dale, and his thumb was tracing sensuous circles on her spine. "The usual path lies this way."

Engrossed in her response to his touch, Elizabeth could hardly attend to the view. Noticing that her aunt was eyeing them suspiciously, Elizabeth decided it was time for a safer subject. "So, is Mr. Bingley to marry your sister?"

His hand stopped its covert caresses and he glanced down at her, a line furrowing his brow. "No. Why would you think that?"

"Oh." Elizabeth toyed with her bonnet ribbons. "In a letter last winter, Miss Bingley hinted that an announcement was imminent, and so when you told me they were travelling together to Pemberley, I assumed it must be true."

He frowned slightly. "That was merely a matter of convenience, since I was travelling ahead of them. At one time I had hoped for such an arrangement between them, but nothing came of it. Bingley has no particular interest in Georgiana, nor she in him."

"I imagine there is no shortage of young ladies eager to attach Mr. Bingley's affections." Elizabeth strove to keep any bitterness from her voice.

"Indeed, though they have had little fortune in that regard of late." He was silent for a minute. "Your aunt and uncle tell me that your sister still holds Bingley in a tender regard."

"It is true, but she does not believe anything will ever come of it."

"Is her preference for him widely known?"

"Everyone in Meryton knows of it."

"No wonder you resented me so much for my part in separating them," Darcy said flatly. "I intended no harm. I had observed your sister attentively during the ball at Netherfield, and while her manners were open, cheerful and engaging with him, I saw no symptom of peculiar regard in her. She seemed to receive Bingley's attentions with pleasure, but not to invite them by any participation of sentiment. Her countenance was open and serene, and it did not appear that her heart would be easily touched. I thought she would forget him quickly."

"Jane's feelings may be but little displayed, but they are no less fervent for that."

"Remarkably fervent feelings on both of their parts, for an acquaintance that spanned no more than six weeks' time! I did not mean to injure your sister, much less you, when I advised Bingley against the match." He sighed, then said in a calmer voice, "I tried to tell him that I was wrong on my return to London from Rosings."

"You did?" A wave of relief rushed through her. She had worried so much about how they would resolve their differences on this front. Then she realized what he had *not* said. If he had truly wanted to share the knowledge with Bingley, what could have stopped him? "I take it, then, that you did not actually tell him," she said carefully.

"I did tell him, but he did not believe me. He came to confront me over our engagement, calling me a hypocrite and more. When I raised the question of your sister, he thought it was for self-serving reasons. He told me I was not worthy to speak her name, then walked out. We have not been on good terms since that day." His voice was a little too even as he spoke.

Elizabeth hated to see his pain. "Surely he would not be coming to Pemberley if he had taken serious offense."

Darcy shrugged, his expression bleak. "The arrangement had already been made, and I doubt Bingley's sisters would allow him to rescind his acceptance. They are always seeking excuses to visit Pemberley. I hoped it would give me the opportunity to speak to him further about the matter. If he does not believe me, perhaps he will listen to *you*."

"Does he know I am here?"

Darcy shook his head. "I told no one, not even Georgiana. I did not want to risk word getting to your father."

Elizabeth gazed up at the tall rock formation towering over them. How could such a pillar of rock be natural? It looked as if it had been carved by a giant sculptor.

She did not want to think about her father. She would have to deal with him again all too soon.

Darcy found it oddly satisfying to have Elizabeth standing beside him as they waited for his guests' carriage to pull up to the front steps, but he noticed the tell-tale nervous sign of Elizabeth rubbing the fabric of her skirt between her fingers. He wondered if it was the prospect of meeting Georgiana and seeing Bingley once more that troubled her, or whether it was taking a wife's place by his side to greet their guests.

If only she were truly his wife! He could not bear to think that in a week she would be returning to Hertfordshire and would be completely out of his reach for five excruciatingly long months. He was more certain of her now than he had been after their separation at Hunsford, but he also knew better what he was would be missing. Her presence brought light and laughter into his life, and the mere act of being able to rest his eyes on her brought him joy.

And her kisses! By heaven, she was a fast learner. Mr. Gardiner had generously allowed them five minutes again the previous night, and this time there had been no hesitation on her part. She had come straight into his arms and kissed him as if she had been waiting for it all day. *He* certainly had been – all the little touches he had stolen during the course of the day had only whetted his appetite for her, especially when he caught glimpses of her response. The little shivers, blushes, and the widening of her eyes all spoke to the sense that he was having an increasing impact on her physically, and by God, it sent thrills straight through him.

But these were not safe thoughts when his guests were about to arise. Fortunately, he had the distraction of worrying about how his sister and friend would respond to Elizabeth's presence there.

Georgiana's face peered out the window as the coach drew up, and she gave him a happy wave. She was the first to step out of the carriage when it drew to a halt, and she hurried forward to him, then halted abruptly at the realization that he was not alone.

He kissed Georgiana's cheek, then said, "May I have the honor of presenting your future sister to your acquaintance?"

His sister's eyes widened. "You are Miss Bennet? What a wonderful surprise! Oh, I am so happy to meet you at last!"

Darcy could not hear Elizabeth's response, since Miss Bingley and Mrs. Hurst were already upon him, exclaiming their delight at returning to Pemberley. Mrs. Hurst noticed Elizabeth's presence first and tugged on her sister's sleeve. A look of disdain crossed Miss Bingley's face, but she quickly covered it with a false smile and greeted her "dearest Eliza" with enough civility to be embarrassing. At least she seemed to have recognized that Elizabeth would henceforth be the one issuing invitations to Pemberley and had decided to pay off her debt of incivility.

Bingley stood behind his sisters, making no effort to move forward to shake Darcy's hand. "Darcy," he said coolly.

So he had not been forgiven. "Welcome to Pemberley, Bingley. I am sure you remember Miss Elizabeth Bennet, do you not?"

Bingley's coolness vanished when his sisters finally made room for him to greet Elizabeth. "What a delightful surprise, Miss Elizabeth!" he exclaimed with unaffected cordiality. "I had no idea you would be joining us here. I hope your family is in good health?"

It was a painful contrast to his treatment of his old friend, but Darcy was grateful that at least Elizabeth was to be spared Bingley's anger. "Please come in," he said to the party in general. "We have two other guests I would like you to meet."

In the saloon, Darcy introduced the Gardiners. Mrs. Gardiner, taking the lead, was all warmth when she spoke to Georgiana. When she remarked to Bingley that she was delighted to meet him at last after hearing so much about him from her nieces, he blushed furiously, looking as if he would have liked to ask more.

Miss Bingley acknowledged the introduction with the barest of nods, then turned immediately to speak to Mrs. Hurst. Even that lady wore an embarrassed smile at her sister's poor manners. Mrs. Hurst curtsied and made a civil greeting, but showed no eagerness for conversation, which might have been attributed to fatigue from her journey were it not for her sister's behavior.

Mrs. Gardiner, however, seemed not at all troubled by the snub. She was all civility as she spoke to Bingley's sisters in a clear voice that could be heard by all of the party. "What a pleasure to see you again! I was *so* glad to make your acquaintance when you called on our dearest Jane. It was such a pity you could not stay longer on that occasion."

Bingley looked confused, then said, "You were at Longbourn then, Mrs. Gardiner?"

Mrs. Gardiner beamed at him. "No, this was at our home on Gracechurch Street, in February, if I am not mistaken. Yes, it must have been February, because Jane had been with us just over a month then. But it was only the briefest of visits; I believe the ladies had another engagement."

If Darcy had any doubts as to whether Mrs. Gardiner had an ulterior motive in her words, they were confirmed by one look at Mr. Gardiner, who was observing Bingley with great attentiveness.

Bingley turned first to Caroline, who now appeared to be examining a portrait miniature above the mantelpiece, then to Mrs. Hurst, then back to Mrs. Gardiner. "Miss Bennet was in London?"

Sensing an imminent explosion, Elizabeth stepped in quickly. "Yes, Jane was there for several months. Miss Darcy, you must be fatigued after your long journey."

Georgiana faltered, "Not at all. Well, perhaps a little." She cast a timid glance at Darcy, who nodded encouragingly. "Perhaps I might retire for a short time."

Miss Bingley was instantly by her side. "An excellent idea, Georgiana dearest! I think we could all use a little rest."

Without a word, Darcy rang the bell, then asked for the guests to be shown to their rooms. Bingley followed quickly after the ladies.

Mrs. Gardiner sighed, putting a hand to her brow. "I am sorry, Lizzy! I should not have said anything, but when they pretended never to have met me, I could not keep my peace. Do you suppose they expected me to dissemble for their sakes? Poor Jane! It is clear Mr. Bingley was never told of her presence in town."

Elizabeth touched her aunt's arm. "I am glad you did, for otherwise *I* might have said something." She cast a quick glance at Darcy as if expecting disapproval.

Darcy tried to look reassuring, a challenge given his own annoyance with Miss Bingley's ill-bred behavior – not least because he suspected he might have behaved much the same a year ago – and the demoralizing sense that his brief idyll with Elizabeth had come to a premature end. If Bingley had been angry before, he would be outraged now. At Elizabeth's worried look, he said, "He was bound to learn of the deception sooner or later. It is just as well to have the matter out in the open."

Any hope that the matter could be smoothed over was quelled by the tense atmosphere at dinner. Bingley drank too much and spoke to no one but Elizabeth and the Gardiners. Miss Bingley acted the part of the martyr, while Georgiana looked as if she wished she could disappear. Were it not for Georgiana's companion Mrs. Annesley and Mrs. Gardiner engaging in well-bred discourse, sometimes assisted by Elizabeth, the party would frequently have been reduced to awkward silence. It was a far cry from the cozy meals Darcy had shared with Elizabeth and the Gardiners.

It was even worse when the ladies withdrew. While Darcy had no objection to Mr. Gardiner's company, Bingley was in a dangerous mood, and Mr. Hurst was as usual well in his cups. Even the best companions in the world could not have made up for being separated from Elizabeth. With so few days remaining before she left Lambton, Darcy wanted to spend every available moment with her.

Bingley pronounced with great care, "I suppose *you* knew as well, Darcy." Although the comment was seemingly unrelated, no one had any doubts as to what he referred to.

"Your sister told me of it, yes, and I should have told you. I was under the misapprehension that Miss Bennet was pursuing you in obedience to her mother's commands rather than as a result of her own sentiment."

Mr. Gardiner said, "You were mistaken, but understandably so. While I myself have no doubts of Jane's sentiments, it is likely that, had she felt otherwise, she still would have been instructed to behave in the same way."

"You still should have told me! It was my decision to make, not yours!" Bingley's fists were clenched by his side.

Hurst lifted his head from the back of his chair. "Wha's that?"

None of the men paid any attention, and Hurst's head slumped back again.

"You are quite right," said Darcy in a clipped voice. "I should have told you. I was in error not to have done so."

"That is easy for you to say now that the cat is out of the bag!"

"I tried to tell you this in May, but you did not wish to hear it."

Bingley subsided a little at this reminder, and settled into brooding over his port while Mr. Gardiner carried on a determined conversation about fishing.

Darcy was quite out of patience with Bingley by the time they rejoined the ladies. Not even the balm of Elizabeth's presence could soothe him, especially when he considered how the larger company precluded his opportunity for those precious five minutes alone with her. Still, he had duties as the host, so he laid forth for the company the plans he had made for a picnic on the following day.

Miss Bingley and Mrs. Hurst were in raptures at the idea, but Darcy was not surprised when Mrs. Gardiner said that they had friends in Lambton whom they had been neglecting. "With so many other ladies present, though, I see no reason why Lizzy cannot join your party if she wishes," Mr. Gardiner said.

Darcy thought he would never manage to repay Mr. Gardiner for all he had done.

⌒⌒⌒

The picnic at Pemberley was different from any Elizabeth had ever attended. There were six large baskets filled with delicate pastries, lobster patties, the finest fruits, cold meats, cakes, and at least four different wines, all served to them by a pair of uniformed servants. Costly damask cloth covered the ground to protect the ladies from a dangerous blade of grass. Elizabeth resolved that if this was Mr. Darcy's idea of a picnic, she would have something new to teach him.

Elizabeth devoted her time to an attempt to draw out the shy Miss Darcy, which was less successful than it might have been since Miss Bingley would chime in whenever the girl actually said something, causing her to go silent again. At least Mr. Bingley seemed in slightly better spirits, if he was not quite his usual amiable self. Through it all, Elizabeth could feel Darcy's eyes on her, and it would give her a dizzying boost of joy when she looked in his direction and their eyes met.

When the meal was done and the carriage drawn up, Darcy held Elizabeth back from entering it with a touch on her arm. When all the other ladies were seated, he said in a tone that brooked no argument, "Elizabeth and I plan to walk back. Bingley, may I trust you to see the ladies back to Pemberley House?"

As Bingley agreed, Elizabeth raised an amused eyebrow at Darcy, since this was the first she had heard of this plan. Not that she objected -- some time alone with Darcy, even if it was along a public lane, was precisely what her spirit needed.

Once the carriage was out of sight, Darcy steered her off the lane, then across the moor for a few minutes until they reached a well-worn path into a small copse. "I hope you do not mind. It will give us more privacy. It leads back to the lane again before we reach the house."

"No, indeed. I wish it were more private still," Elizabeth said without thinking, since they could still be seen from the lane and she wished she could be in his arms.

"You should be careful what you wish for," Darcy said roughly. "Especially since you will get your privacy in a moment when our path takes us behind that copse and into the shadow of the rise. There you will find a very private hollow."

"Indeed? And I suppose you planned this as well?"

"I am *trying* to behave like a gentleman, Elizabeth."

She slipped her hand into his elbow. "I do trust you, you know."

"Even after I announced that we had planned to walk? Thank you for not contradicting me."

Elizabeth laughed. "I was not always so compliant with your wishes, was I?"

"During those days we were stranded at the parsonage? No, you certainly were not. In fact, there were moments when it seemed that if I wanted you to do something, the best way to accomplish it would be to tell you to do the exact opposite."

"Yes, I was feeling rather contrary and quite embarrassed to be so perturbed about our situation when all those poor people had lost homes and loved ones!"

"Yet you were all kindness to them, especially to Jenny. You even tolerated *me* in her presence!"

"Poor Jenny. I wish I could have said good-bye to her before I left. It must have seemed to her as if I did not care. I hope she is doing well."

Darcy's brows drew together. "Mrs. Collins has not kept you informed?"

"Only that Jenny was to live with her aunt at Rosings. My father will not allow me to read Charlotte's letters if she speaks of you, so she rarely mentions anything about that time."

"Jenny did go to live at Rosings, but once she was able to walk, or perhaps I should say run, Lady Catherine objected to the noise so young a child made in the house. Her aunt did not want to give up her position, having worked at Rosings all her life, so Jenny perforce was sent to an orphanage."

Elizabeth stopped in her tracks, horrified by the thought of Jenny in one of those terrible places. "How could she? Poor, poor girl! It would have been better for her had she died with her parents. Oh, I cannot bear it!"

"If all has gone well, she should no longer be there. I gave orders for her to be taken from the orphanage, and to find a family who will care for her."

"You are so good! But how did you even know what had happened?"

"Mrs. Collins wrote to me last month, concerned that nothing was being done to rebuild the village, and many of the villagers still required assistance. She hoped I could intercede for them with my aunt and convince her to devote some resources to the situation. Since Lady Catherine is still more inclined to berate me than to listen to me, I instead sent my steward's assistant to lead the recovery efforts. I asked him to check on Jenny's well-being."

"Thank heavens you did! I know there are many children condemned to those horrible places, but somehow it is worse to think of a child who became dear to me there."

"How could I not help Jenny? Albeit unwittingly, she played a role in bringing us together." Darcy's voice was tender.

"Do you remember how she called me Mrs. Darcy?" She tightened her hand on his arm, moving as close to him as she dared. "So much happened in those few days, and my life has been so very different since then." Unaccountably, she felt the urge to cry.

"I wish..." He did not finish what he had started to say, but his expression was stern.

With some anxiety, Elizabeth said, "Is something the matter?"

"No, all is well." He sounded gentler now, and then he laughed.

"What is so amusing?"

"I am laughing at myself, for reasons that I had best not share."

She stopped and gave him a mock glare. "Can you not trust me with your secrets?"

"No, this one I should not tell you, Elizabeth. Believe me." He laughed again, his voice low.

"I want to know, or I shall imagine the most terrible things!" She tugged teasingly on his carefully knotted cravat, creating disarray where there had been perfection.

"If you insist, minx! It is my own personal conundrum. The first day you were here, when I asked you whether it was difficult for you to be with your father, you kept your feelings hidden. It made me want to kiss you until there could be no doubt that you are mine. Just now you were open with your feelings, and I was so glad of your trust that it gave me an almost uncontrollable urge to kiss you. So it seems I am fated to spend all my time wanting to kiss you senseless."

"A truly terrible fate, sir!" Elizabeth proclaimed with due solemnity. "How will I ever survive it?"

"You should not laugh at a desperate man," he growled back teasingly. "Do not think it has not crossed my mind that the one way to force your father to let me marry you sooner would be to seduce you. In fact, there are probably no more three or four minutes per day when that idea does *not* cross my mind."

"Mr. Darcy!" Elizabeth was half-scandalized, half-tempted to throw herself into his arms. "You can lay that thought to rest. You would, after all, need *my* cooperation."

He looked at her searchingly, then closed his eyes tightly. "You really do not know, do you?" he said in an odd voice.

She crossed her arms over her chest and smirked. "What do I not know?"

"That you are a powder keg of passion just waiting for a spark. I can feel it whenever I touch you. Good God, it would be so easy to make you want more, and I do not trust that I would have the strength to stop."

Elizabeth lurched back a step. He might as well have slapped her across the face, or perhaps dug her heart out with a dull knife. No, that would be less painful than this, because she would be dead and never have to face him again. "Why not just say I am a shameless wanton and have done with it?" she said icily. "I had not realized that your opinion of my morals was so low. This is the estimation in which you hold me! I thank you for explaining it so fully. Good *day*, Mr. Darcy." She turned and hurried in what she hoped was the direction of the lane as quickly as her legs would carry her, but there was no way to outrun the pain.

"Elizabeth, wait! That is not what I meant!" Darcy's feet crashed through the underbrush behind her.

She picked up skirts and ran into a small grassy clearing, tears of humiliation burning in her eyes. She could not believe this was happening, that he had said such a horrible thing. Then his hand clamped around her arm, causing her to stop so abruptly that she tripped over a hidden root. He grasped her around the waist before she could fall, but she tried to twist away from him. Then they were both on the ground, Elizabeth lying half underneath Darcy, the scent of damp earth and dried leaves rising around her.

"Are you hurt?" he demanded, clutching her wrists.

"I am *fine*," she panted through clenched teeth. "Now let me *go*."

"Not until you listen to me! That is not what I meant. Elizabeth, when we are married, I will go down on my knees every night to thank God for your passionate nature. I cannot begin to tell you what it means to me that you respond to me. It means that we *belong* together, you and I, not that your morals are lacking or anything else. God knows I respond the same way to you, and always have. All you have to do is to look at me, and I go up in flames. Good God, sometimes I think your father is right to keep us apart because it may be the only way to keep me in check!"

Unsure of what to believe, Elizabeth stared at him as if the answer might be written in his shadowed eyes. Above her, his breaths were short and harsh, his dark hair falling around his face. "Are you quite done taking the Lord's name in vain?" she said tartly.

"God, no," he breathed as he lowered his head and captured her waiting lips. This was no gentle exploration but a fierce claim. His tongue invaded her mouth, fencing with hers and demanding an equal response. Her lips throbbed with a burning need as she accepted his claim and met him half-way. His kiss seemed to fill her entire being, but then she became aware that his body was moving over hers, his chest brushing tantalizingly against the tip of her breasts in a way that sent surges of lightning through her. Involuntarily, she arched her back, struggling for more of his touch, but he had pinioned her wrists to the ground beside her and one of his legs had somehow found its way between hers, so she could do no more than writhe beneath him, shocking herself by sucking greedily on his tongue.

He growled his pleasure, but before she could get her fill of him, he tore his mouth from hers. At first she thought he meant to pull away from her, but then his teeth nipped at the sensitive skin of her neck, leaving behind an delightful ache as he moved on to explore the hollow at its base. His tongue probed at it excitingly for a moment, then he was running his lips over the exposed tops of her breasts.

Elizabeth closed her eyes in response to the flood of sensation he created as his lips traced a burning path across her. Just as she thought it could get no more intense, his tongue dipped beneath the neckline of her dress, and she forgot everything but the captivating need within her. Then he shifted, and with a jolt she felt his hand cupping her breast, the heat of it coming right through the muslin of her dress and the light chemise beneath it. The shocking delight of that intimacy intensified the pulses of sensation from his exploring lips, which were now pushing aside her neckline and nibbling her newly revealed shoulder. This was heaven.

When his thumb drifted across the tip of her breast, it created a surprising shock of pleasure, but that was nothing to the intense surge of sensation as he then began to trace tiny circles over that excruciatingly sensitive spot. When he moved on to toying with nipple, rolling it between his fingers, she gasped, moaning helplessly as sharp pangs of passion arched straight to the very core of her being. She was on fire with the intensity of it, with answering pulses of pleasure echoing from below. But no, that was not an echo, but his leg pressing up against her most private parts, and God help her, she was arching against him, succumbing to her need as her very essence dissolved into a seething cauldron of desire.

She whimpered when he stopped stimulating her breast, and she opened her eyes to see his face above her, his eyes burning, his leg still between hers. "*That* is how I want you," he murmured, "with your eyes filled with desire only for me. And *that* is why I could seduce you, because you are innocent of what passion can do to you and because you *trust* me - - which is also precisely why I am *not* going to seduce you, even if it kills me." Abruptly he released her wrist and rolled onto his back, his fists pressed against his forehead.

It took a moment for his words to penetrate through the clamor of her senses. When it did, she wavered between dismay at her behavior and a sudden desire to laugh over the folly of it all. Amusement won. Raising herself on one elbow, she tasted the corner of Darcy's lips with a delicate kiss. "I hope you will manage to avoid death, since it would be a pity if you never had a chance to show me all the *other* things I am innocent of," she murmured provocatively.

He did not open his eyes, but one arm snaked around her waist and pulled her against him. "I do not know if you are trying to tempt me or to torture me," he grumbled.

"Most likely both." She rested her head on his shoulder. It felt so natural to be there, her body seeming to fit perfectly against his, even as she still thrummed with sensual need.

"When I discovered Wickham with Georgiana in Ramsgate," he said in a conversational tone at odds with the tension in his body, "I was at first furious with her for allowing him liberties. It was not until later that I realized what an impossible predicament she was in. A young man is trained in the art of seduction, and the more he practices it, the more his friends proclaim him to be a fine fellow indeed. Young girls, meanwhile, are kept in complete ignorance, so they know nothing of what can be done to them until an expert seducer comes along. If she trusts him, as Georgiana trusted George Wickham, it will be too late when she realizes what he is doing, and even if she somehow does realize it, he is stronger than she. And then we have the unmitigated gall to blame *her*? Would we send a young boy with a wooden sword into battle against Napoleon's troops, and then censure him for losing the battle?"

Elizabeth considered this radical notion to the degree to which she was able, limited by the longing that still consumed her. Her hand, almost of its own volition, slipped under his topcoat to rest palm down on his waistcoat. To her surprise, he stiffened even further.

"Of course," he continued, "Perhaps one can hardly blame a man when he is confronted by such natural seductive talent as *some* women possess."

"Such seductive talents as either hiding or displaying their

168

feelings?" she teased.

"Precisely what I meant."

Elizabeth stayed in Darcy's arms as long as possible, but they could not linger long, knowing they were expected. They walked hand in hand like children, their fingers entwined, stopping frequently for kisses that were not in the least bit childlike. When they at last came in sight of the house, Darcy said, "Perhaps it would be best for me to drive you to Lambton without stopping inside." He removed a tiny twig from her hair. "It might be difficult to explain some of the interesting green streaks on the back of your dress. You might wish to change before your aunt and uncle return to the inn."

"Oh, no!" Elizabeth attempted the impossible feat of trying to see her own back by looking over her shoulder. "I had not thought of that."

"I do not believe that either of us was doing much *thinking* at that point."

She laughed. "If I recall correctly, it seemed that you enjoyed *not thinking*."

His gaze dropped to her lips. "It is not too late to go back to the hollow."

"As if you would permit it even if I agreed!"

"I am *very* sorry to say that you are correct," he said. "Sorrier than you can know."

Chapter 16

THE NEXT MORNING Darcy waited impatiently as his guests dawdled over breakfast. It felt as if days had passed since he had last seen Elizabeth, even though it was only yesterday that he had left her at the inn, after first ascertaining that she could make it safely to her room to change clothes before her aunt and uncle saw her. She had invited him to remain and have tea with her, but Darcy had deemed that too dangerous. Inns had beds, and after the afternoon they had spent, any equation that included Elizabeth, a bed, and no chaperone was asking for trouble, so he had merely kissed her hand in the common room of the inn and bade her a reluctant farewell.

Finally his guests finished their breakfast. He knew better than to say he was going to see Elizabeth, since then half the party would wish to join him, so instead he told them that he would be tending to business and would see them at dinner.

At the inn, he found only the Gardiners waiting for him. In response to his questioning look, Mrs. Gardiner said, "Lizzy is in her room, reading letters newly arrived from Longbourn. I will tell her you are here."

But before Darcy could agree, Elizabeth appeared in the doorway, her eyes red and unmistakable signs of tears on her cheeks. What had happened? Had he somehow hurt her the previous day? Had her aunt and uncle found her in her stained dress after all?

He moved toward her in concern, but she gave him only a distracted look and instead approached her uncle, holding out to him two sheets of closely written paper.

With a frown, Mr. Gardiner began to read. His wife said, "What is the matter, Lizzy? Is it bad news?"

"It is in every way dreadful." Elizabeth said to her aunt, with a despairing glance in Darcy's direction. "Lydia has left all her friends – has eloped – has thrown herself into the power of --" She paused, closing her eyes. "Of Mr. Wickham. They are gone off together from Brighton."

The sound of that detested name moved Darcy into action. Placing a supportive hand under her elbow, he guided her to a bench and urged her to sit. Taking his place beside her, he took her icy hands in his. "Is there anything you can take for your present distress? A glass of wine – shall I get you one?"

"No, I thank you," she said, her voice trembling. "You know Mr. Wickham too well to doubt the rest. She has no money, no connections, nothing that can tempt him – she is lost forever." She burst into sobs. "When I consider that I might have prevented it! I who knew what he was. Had I but explained some part of what I learnt to my own family, had his character been known, it could not have happened."

Mrs. Gardiner handed her niece a handkerchief. "But is it certain, absolutely certain?" she asked.

"Oh, yes! They left Brighton together on Sunday night, and were traced almost to London, but not beyond; they are certainly not gone to Scotland. My father is gone to London, and Jane writes to beg my uncle's immediate assistance. But how is such a man to be worked on? How are they even to be discovered? I have not the smallest hope. It is all, all too late."

Darcy gripped her hands tightly. "It is *not* too late. Your sister is *not* without connections, as Wickham is no doubt aware. As for discovering them, I have some ideas where to start."

At first she seemed not to understand him, but then she shook her head. "I cannot ask you to involve yourself, not in this. Not with *him!*"

"I am already involved in it. I will not allow Wickham to trifle with my future sister, and you may be certain that he is counting on precisely that."

Mrs. Gardiner touched her husband's sleeve, drawing his attention to the conversation at hand, then said, "Mr. Darcy, if you have some idea how to locate Lydia, we would be very grateful to hear it."

"I know several of his associates who may have information on his present whereabouts. That is where I plan to begin, at least. If that should fail, there is a gentleman attached to Bow Street who has assisted me with confidential inquiries in the past. He has a network of informants, and may be able to discover them."

Mr. Gardiner nodded slowly. "Then let us discuss how best to proceed."

⌒⌒⌒

Darcy could have found it in himself to wish inefficiency upon Mr. and Mrs. Gardiner, for despite the hurry and confusion of their preparations for their unexpected departure, every minute that they remained was one more minute he could spend with Elizabeth, even if it was only watching her write notes on her aunt's behalf. Unfortunately, a mere hour saw the whole completed and the separation upon them.

It felt as if part of him was being torn away. He had known that their days together would be brief, but this unexpected foreshortening of their time was wrenching. He had only just begun to feel more confident in her attachment to him, and now her worry for her sister seemed to predominate over her feelings for him. He understood, but that did not mean he had to like it.

He could not bear it that Elizabeth was in distress and there was nothing he could do to ease her pain, at least not at the moment. Even if – no, *when* he found Wickham and made him marry Lydia, Elizabeth would still have the pain of knowing her sister was wed to a reprobate and faced a future that was uncertain at best. He seriously doubted Wickham could make any woman happy for more than a very brief period, and Lydia's unhappiness would hurt Elizabeth. God, how he *hated* problems he could not fix! And it was even worse when they involved the woman he loved.

It was too much. As soon as Elizabeth set down her pen, Darcy took her by the hand and led her into the small private parlor. Beyond caring about propriety, he closed the door behind them. After all, if anyone wished to complain about his behavior, he would be perfectly happy to do the honorable thing and marry Elizabeth this very minute. In fact, he half-hoped someone *would* make a fuss. Anything would be better than to be plunged back into the awful limbo of complete separation without even the consolation of news or letters, knowing Elizabeth to be in pain. Closing his eyes, he embraced her tightly. For almost the first time in his acquaintance with her, he did not even want to kiss her, just to hold her in his arms and never let her go.

He could feel her tension, but as she rested her head on his shoulder, her body seemed to relax a little. "I wish I could do more to help," he said.

She slipped her arms around him, her hands pressing against his back. "Do you know what is worst?"

He could imagine too many possibilities for that. "Tell me."

"I am frantic about Lydia's safety, of course, her loss of reputation, and about how this will affect both you and my family, but the thing that bothers me most is that I have to leave." Her voice quavered at the end.

He leaned his cheek against her hair. "My dearest! If it were not that I would sound horribly selfish, I would be saying the same thing."

Her shoulders were shaking now. "I do not care what my father says. I will try to find some way to write you."

"Only if you can do so safely. I do not want you to bear further punishment for my sake. It is only five months – and if I say that often enough, perhaps I will even start to believe it."

She made a sound that was half laugh, half sob.

Mrs. Gardiner's voice came from outside the door. "Lizzy? Are you there?"

Since Elizabeth was now weeping openly, Darcy said, "She is here." He could not bring himself to release her, even though he knew he should.

The door opened and Mrs. Gardiner peered through. To Darcy's relief, she seemed able to ignore their improper position. "I am sorry, but the carriage is ready."

Darcy nodded jerkily and slid his arms down until he held Elizabeth's hands in his. He kissed her gently on the forehead, and in a voice only she could hear, he said, "Remember yesterday. Remember that I will always love you. Remember me."

She nodded jerkily, unable to speak, tears still flowing from her eyes as Darcy handed her into the carriage. He watched the carriage pull away, not moving until it was completely out of sight. Then slowly, as if the last hour had aged him ten years, he mounted his horse and rode back to Pemberley.

Elizabeth's subsequent journey to Longbourn accompanied by the Gardiners was filled with the keenest of all anguish, from which she could find no interval of ease or forgetfulness. Her aunt and uncle offered what comfort they could, but there was little that they could say to help her.

They travelled as expeditiously as possible. The scene when they arrived at Longbourn was chaotic. Mrs. Bennet and Kitty had been brought home from Brighton by Colonel Foster two days after Lydia's elopement, and Mrs. Bennet had taken directly to her bed. Mr. Bennet had left for London the following day, leaving Jane and Mary responsible for the four young Gardiner children as well as their distraught mother. Kitty was of little help, complaining constantly of her desire to return to Brighton. The arrival of Elizabeth with Mr. and Mrs. Gardiner was greeted with great relief on Jane's part.

In the afternoon, the two elder Miss Bennets were able to be for half an hour by themselves. Elizabeth instantly availed herself of the opportunity to tell Jane about meeting Mr. Darcy at Pemberley and his plans to aid in the search for Lydia. She forbore to mention the presence of Mr. Bingley.

Jane said, "I feel so very guilty for keeping your engagement a secret from our mother. We gave our word to our father, but I cannot help but think the knowledge would be a great comfort to her in this time. I shudder to think how desperate I would feel if it were not for that, thinking we would be forever shamed and eventually penniless. Your marriage will not only guarantee us a roof over our heads after our father dies, but it will lend some respectability to the rest of us. Kitty, Mary and I would be doomed to spinsterhood if our only connection were to Lydia, but as the sisters-in-law of Mr. Darcy, we will still be marriageable, if somewhat tarnished by all this."

Her words struck Elizabeth to the heart. Why, after all, was she still keeping it a secret? Her father was not there, and when she had given him her word, this situation was yet undreamed of. She thought of what Darcy might say, and that strengthened her resolve. "You are quite right, Jane! I had not thought of it that way. Come, I will tell her at once."

"But how will you explain having kept it secret for so long?"

Elizabeth thought for a moment. "I have an idea for that." With that, she marched straight to her mother's dressing room, where she found Mrs. Gardiner sitting with her weeping mother.

"Mama, there is something very important I must tell you," Elizabeth said firmly. "While we were in Derbyshire, I saw Mr. Darcy, and he and I are engaged. We meant to keep it a secret until I spoke to my father, but in his absence, it is only right that you know the truth."

This startling intelligence had the effect of stilling Mrs. Bennet's sobs, and she stared at her second daughter in astonished disbelief. "Is this another of your jokes, Lizzy?" she said fretfully. "It is cruel of you to try my nerves so at such a time as this!"

It took Elizabeth a moment to recall that her mother believed the announcement in the paper to have been a joke. "It is not a trick. Mr. Darcy and I are engaged, and we plan to be married at Christmastime."

Mrs. Bennet turned her face to Mrs. Gardiner. "Can this be true, sister? Why did you not say anything?"

Mrs. Gardiner said soothingly, "It is true that they are engaged. Edward and I agreed to keep the matter confidential until such a time as your husband gave his permission."

Fanning herself, Mrs. Bennet said, "Of all the foolishness! Of course he will give his permission. Ten thousand pounds a year! Oh, my dearest Lizzy, come and give me a kiss! How very clever of you to find and secure him!"

"I assure you, I had not the least expectation of seeing Mr. Darcy in Derbyshire." At least that much was completely true.

Mrs. Bennet sat up. "Oh, but we must tell everyone the good news! Then they will stop gossiping about poor dear Lydia."

Elizabeth had not thought the matter through to this point. "No! We must not tell anyone. Er, Mr. Darcy would be most displeased if he discovered that anyone had been told without my father's permission. He is very proper, you know, and we must not displease him!" She noticed her aunt's look of repressed mirth at this prevarication.

Her mother's eyes grew wide. "Of course we must not displease Mr. Darcy! Oh, but it will be so terribly hard to keep it a secret. How I long to tell my sister Phillips! I cannot wait to see the look on Lady Lucas's face when she hears the news. Charlotte's marriage is nothing to it, nothing at all! Ten thousand pounds a year!"

Mrs. Bennet's raptures were such that it was nearly half an hour before she again recalled Lydia's plight. "Oh, but that hardly matters now! Everything will all sort itself out nicely, I am sure. Mr. Wickham is sure to want to marry her now that it will make Mr. Darcy his brother! After all, they were such good friends when they were younger, and now they will be able to make up their quarrel!"

Mrs. Gardiner and Elizabeth exchanged bemused looks at Mrs. Bennet's convenient restructuring of the truth.

෭෨

Elizabeth's next step was to acquaint Mary with their mother's new understanding of the situation, lest she let something slip about having already known about the engagement.

Mary closed the book she had been reading. "I am glad you told her. I had wondered how we would explain Colonel Fitzwilliam's visits. He is almost due to call, if he keeps to his usual schedule."

"His usual schedule?"

"He seems to visit about once each fortnight, and it has been almost that long since he was here last."

Elizabeth counted backwards in her head. "He called while I was away?"

"Yes, he offered to take Jane and me to tour the park at Ashridge. It was truly lovely. He says he will take us to Wimpole Hall another time. He thinks I would enjoy seeing the library there."

Colonel Fitzwilliam had been very busy, it seemed. "That was very kind of him. What is that book you are reading? I do not recognize it."

Mary held it out to her. "It is by Mary Wollstonecraft."

Her sister's taste in reading had evidently taken a surprising turn. Elizabeth examined the spine, expecting to see the title of one of Mrs. Wollsonecraft's novels. Instead it read 'A Vindication of the Rights of Women.' She raised her eyebrows. "A new interest?"

"Colonel Fitzwilliam recommended it. He thought I would be interested in her views on the education of women."

It would certainly provide some balance to the sermons that constituted Mary's usual reading material. "I will look forward to hearing what you think of it, then."

∽∾

Later, Elizabeth asked Jane, "What has been happening in my absence? Mary can speak of nothing but Colonel Fitzwilliam!"

Jane blushed. "He has been very kind to her. He always takes the time to compliment something about her appearance – her hair or the color of her dress – and it has made her much more attentive to how she looks. But then he always seems to know what people need to hear. He was very kind to some of the wallflowers at the assembly as well."

"Well, if he somehow managed to convince Mary to read a book by a fallen woman such as Mrs. Wollstonecraft, he clearly has quite an influence. I am convinced she must be half in love with him!"

Jane looked away. "He *is* very amiable. I can see why you liked him so much."

Elizabeth began to suspect that more than one of her sisters was developing a *tendre* for the colonel. She hoped Jane at least would know to protect her heart this time.

Chapter 17

DARCY HAD DEBATED whether to send Mr. Gardiner a note requesting a private meeting instead of calling on him. The latter carried the danger of encountering Mr. Bennet and revealing Mr. Gardiner's connection to him, but when he attempted to take the wiser course of writing, he found he could not bring himself to put pen to paper. Why should he have to avoid Mr. Bennet as if he were the villain of the piece? If Elizabeth's father wanted nothing to do with him, well, there was nothing to stop him from walking away.

Thus it was almost three hours after he had received intelligence about Wickham's location that he rapped on the door of the house on Gracechurch Street. The manservant there recognized him from his prior visits, taking his hat and gloves even before telling his master of Darcy's arrival.

The house was compact enough that Darcy could hear him at the door of Mr. Gardiner's study saying, "Mr. Darcy is here to see you, sir."

There was an almost imperceptible pause before he heard Mr. Gardiner say, "Show him in."

When Darcy entered the study, Mr. Gardiner rose to his feet from one of the pair of red leather chairs in front of the hearth. The other chair held Mr. Bennet, who sat frozen with a glass of brandy raised halfway to his mouth.

Mr. Gardiner came forward to shake his hand. "I am glad to see you, Darcy. I was just thinking that your ideas might be helpful in deciding our next course of action. Have you been able to learn anything yet?"

Darcy bowed slightly in the direction of Mr. Bennet, taking in his narrowed eyes, then turned all his attention back to the more approachable face of Mr. Gardiner. "I have had some success. I have located them, and I plan to make contact with Wickham tomorrow to discover his plans."

Mr. Bennet put down his brandy snifter none too gently. "Where are they?" he growled.

Darcy said evenly, "They are staying in a shared room at a boarding house whose reputation leaves much to be desired."

"But on what street, what is the direction?"

Darcy paused, glancing at Mr. Gardiner. "I prefer to deal with Wickham alone at this point. If good fortune is with us, Miss Lydia may be prepared to return here, in which case the direction is unimportant."

Mr. Bennet heaved himself up from his chair. "How dare you waltz in here and then refuse to tell me where *my* daughter is?"

Mr. Gardiner reached out a restraining hand to his brother-in-law. "Darcy has offered his assistance in this matter. He is acquainted with some of Wickham's former associates."

"How does he even know what happened?" Mr. Bennet said through gritted teeth.

"That is hardly important now. What matters is that he can help us."

"Help us by refusing to let me see my daughter? Lydia is *my* responsibility, not his. I will talk to Wickham, and if necessary, I will fight him."

Darcy felt his calm slipping. "If anyone fights Wickham, it will be me, since I have the better chance of winning. The point is moot, though; if challenged to a duel, Wickham will not appear. This is not the first time the situation has arisen. He has no honor to defend."

"Then I will talk to him and try to make him see reason."

That was the last straw. "You will have to pardon me, Mr. Bennet, if I have some doubts as to whether you are the best person to speak to a potential son-in-law. You may have failed to drive *me* away, but Wickham is a different story. He is looking for an excuse to flee, and all you will be left with this time is a ruined daughter."

Mr. Gardiner stepped between them. "That is enough from both of you! We all share the same goal, which is to rescue Lydia from her present situation. We cannot afford to squabble among ourselves. Now, let us leave your disagreement about Lizzy aside and concentrate on what needs to be done. Come now, I want you to shake hands."

Neither man moved, and finally Darcy shook his head slowly. "I will agree to put other matters aside for the time being, but that is all I can do. Because you are Elizabeth's father, I have forgiven you for your behavior toward me in Kent, for refusing to hear me out, and for separating me needlessly from Elizabeth. For Elizabeth's sake, I have even chosen to overlook your repeated slights to my honor. You can do what you like to me, secure in the knowledge that I will accept it. But this is not only about me. You have hurt *Elizabeth*, hurt her badly, and *that* I cannot forgive."

"I have been *protecting* Lizzy, and I have no need of your forgiveness for anything I do!"

Mr. Gardiner held up his hands. "I think it is safe to say that both of you feel you are trying to protect Lizzy, even if you disagree on the means. In the meantime, we need to work together if we wish to resolve Lydia's situation."

Darcy drew in a deep breath. "My apologies, sir," he said tightly, aiming his comment toward Mr. Gardiner. He ignored Mr. Bennet's snort in the background.

Mrs. Gardiner bustled in, her good humor a relief in the dark study. "Mr. Darcy, I just learned of your arrival. I hope your journey was unremarkable. No, do not answer that now. Please come to the sitting room where we may all sit down and share what we have learned."

Darcy followed her gratefully, aware of Mr. Bennet stalking on his heels. Instead of selecting the sofa he had used on his previous visits to the Gardiner home, he chose to sit beside Mrs. Gardiner, who inquired about Georgiana's whereabouts. By the time he had finished his reply, the others had joined them.

Mr. Bennet continued to glower. "I am desolated to be obliged to interrupt this charming reunion, but I find myself in need of an explanation of how Darcy comes to be acquainted with both this matter and with you."

Mrs. Gardiner looked delighted at the opportunity. "You are no doubt already aware that we had travelled no further than Lambton, where we had planned to spend several days visiting friends from my childhood, when Jane's letters reached us, informing us of Lydia's plight. But I am getting ahead of my story! I had longed to visit the grounds at Pemberley again, and as chance would have it, despite reassurances we had received that the family was away, it turned out that Mr. Darcy had arrived ahead of schedule. When he discovered our presence, he naturally wished to speak to Lizzy, and my husband and I decided it was an excellent opportunity to see what sort of man he was. He introduced us to his sister, a charming young lady, and we met on several occasions. The matter of Lydia, when it arose, could not be hidden from him."

Darcy leaned back in his chair, impressed at her ability to create a misleading tale without once telling an untruth. "Miss Bennet was quite distraught, and naturally I could not rest until I knew the cause."

Mr. Bennet's narrowed eyes focused on Mr. Gardiner. "How very *interesting* that you should choose to disregard my wishes."

"Thomas, this is neither the time nor the place," said Mrs. Gardiner sharply. "Mr. Darcy has offered us his assistance, and I for one am grateful for it."

Darcy decided that the better part of valor was to say his piece before Mr. Bennet had the chance to go on the attack again. "As I have already told the gentlemen, I have located Wickham and Miss Lydia. If all goes well, I will speak with them tomorrow. Wickham, of course, is well known to me, but I hoped you might have some suggestions as to how I should approach the matter to Miss Lydia, since I have no significant acquaintance with her."

Mrs. Gardiner passed a tray of pastries to her husband. "Perhaps I should go with you. Lydia might be more inclined to attend to my suggestions."

Mr. Bennet snorted again. "As if she listens to anyone."

Darcy accepted a pastry to be polite, then set his plate aside. The prospect of food had no appeal at the moment. "I will need to negotiate a settlement with Wickham. He is likely to be more reasonable if he believes I am working on my own, since he would expect me to be more disinterested than her immediate family. His demands might well escalate if he knows you are involved."

"His demands?" said Mr. Bennet sharply. "You seem to be assuming he will need to be bribed."

Darcy inclined his head. "Wickham never misses a chance to improve his own situation at the expense of others. I wish I could say otherwise, but the fact that he has located himself in a part of town unsuitable for a gentleman's daughter strongly suggests that he has no honorable intentions toward her. If so, he will not change his mind without a significant incentive."

Mr. Bennet leaned forward. "All the more reason I should be the one to negotiate with him. Any payment will come from me."

Darcy opened his mouth to reply, but Mr. Gardiner spoke first.

"There is no point in discussing who will foot the bill when we do not yet know if there will be one. There will be plenty of time for that later." He shot Darcy a warning glance. "I hope you will keep us informed of your progress."

"Naturally." He rose to his feet. "Thank you for your kind hospitality."

Mrs. Gardiner pointed back to his chair. "Oh, please do not go yet, Mr. Darcy. We had so little time to get to know one another in Lambton."

Mr. Bennet shifted in his chair, looking as annoyed at this blatant manipulation as Darcy felt. Nevertheless, he followed her instructions. "It would be my pleasure, madam."

"I hope your journey to town was not unpleasant."

"Not at all. I arrived before the rain began, so I made excellent time."

"I just arrived yesterday, since I travelled with Lizzy to Longbourn. I fear that the children were not at all happy to see me; they had hoped for an extended holiday with their dearest Aunt Jane!"

"I hope you found Miss Bennet in good health."

"Apart from a natural concern for the situation and for her family's distress, yes, she was quite well. Is any of your family in town at present, Mr. Darcy?"

Out of the corner of his eye, he saw Mr. Bennet sit up straighter. "I cannot say. I have kept to myself since my return, but I imagine that any of them who have the ability have moved to the countryside for the summer. London loses much of its appeal in the warm weather."

Mr. Bennet laughed shortly. "Is that why I have seen so much of your various relatives at Longbourn? It certainly was not for the charm of *my* company."

Darcy regarded him quizzically. If the visitor had been Lord Matlock, he doubted Mr. Bennet would make a joke about it. "My relatives do not keep me informed of their whereabouts, but I have heard nothing about travels to Longbourn."

"Am I to believe that your charming cousin in the red coat has not been carrying messages to you from Lizzy? I am not quite so gullible, young man, as to believe that he is suddenly so enamored of my eldest daughter that he cannot stay away above a fortnight."

"Your eldest? No, it is Elizabeth that Richard... well, no matter." Darcy was going to have some choice words for his cousin about his visits to Elizabeth behind his back.

"And then there was the call that Lady Matlock paid to my daughters," Mr. Bennet said icily.

"Yes, Elizabeth mentioned that to me, but I cannot believe you found my aunt anything but charming."

At Mr. Bennet's snort, Mrs. Gardiner stepped in. "Is Lord Matlock still firmly set against your marriage to Lizzy?"

This hardly seemed a safe topic for conversation, but perhaps it was best to get it out into the open. He hoped Mrs. Gardiner knew what she was doing. "To the best of my knowledge, he has not changed his mind, but his opinion would make little difference to me, were it not for his extraordinary talent for convincing other people to do his dirty work for him." He looked directly at Mr. Bennet. "He was quite pleased when he heard you had refused your consent and planned to keep us apart – especially as he had no power to stop me himself."

Mr. Bennet raised an eyebrow, radiating dubiousness. "So your family's opinion means nothing to you, then?"

"I see no reason to consider my uncle's opinion, since he never considers the opinions of others himself. The members of my family whose opinions do matter to me are more likely to assume that I am the best judge of whom I should marry. Once they were reassured that Elizabeth was not a fortune hunter, they rallied behind me. It is only Lord Matlock, Lady Catherine de Bourgh, and you who persist in opposition." Darcy hoped the Gardiners at least appreciated what it cost him to say this in a calm manner that belied his inner turmoil.

Mr. Bennet clearly had no appreciation of it. "Matlock may not be the only clever manipulator in your family. Tell me, did Wickham run off with Lydia on your orders?"

"Good God, no." Darcy's reaction was automatic, even before he realized the depth of the insult he had been paid. He steadied himself by gripping the armrest of his chair until his fingers hurt. "Either you have no idea what you are saying, or you have far more in common with my uncle Matlock than I had realized. Mrs. Gardiner, Mr. Gardiner, I hope you will understand that I must be on my way. I will be certain to inform *you* when I know more of the situation." He bowed stiffly and left the room before anyone could respond.

He heard Mrs. Gardiner's light footsteps following him down the passageway, but he did not stop, unable to trust his own temper. He had already yanked open the front door when her hand descended on his arm. "Please, Mrs. Gardiner, it is best for me to be alone right now."

She tightened her grip reassuringly, then released him. "I understand. But please remember that I know both of you, and I believe this can be resolved, however little it might appear that way at the moment."

He nodded jerkily, fearing he could not answer in a civil manner, then left.

⁂

Mr. Gardiner poured himself a glass of brandy and another for Mr. Bennet. "Thomas, I am glad you will be returning Longbourn tomorrow. I will, of course, keep you informed about every development."

"You prefer yon pup's assistance to mine?" Mr. Bennet's tone was cool and distant.

"At the moment, yes. I understand that you are angry, but it is foolish to risk the only lead we have toward finding Lydia. Also, anything you say now is likely to rebound against you later when Lizzy is married to Darcy."

Mr. Bennet's lips thinned. "Not if she comes to her senses first."

"She is not going to change her mind. I have seen the two of them together, and frankly, I have not seen any reason why she should *not* marry him. Whatever you may think, he is not like Matlock. No one at Pemberley had a word to say against him. He has a temper – who among us does not? – but as you saw today, he does his best to keep it in check, even when provoked quite outrageously."

"Did he not provoke me equally outrageously by suggesting I was serving as Matlock's pawn?"

Mr. Gardiner did not reply immediately, instead gazing into his brandy as if it held the answer. "The question is whether he said it to provoke you or because it is true."

The silence in the room was complete for several minutes, then Mr. Bennet set down his brandy snifter with unusual delicacy. "There is still time for me to catch the last post coach to Hertfordshire. Excuse me."

"Don't be a fool, Thomas! Look at it rationally. You were angry with Darcy when you sought him out at Rosings, but when have you *ever* refused to hear a man out, much less virtually imprisoned one of your daughters? Was that what you had in mind when you went there, or was it only after Matlock's insults that you chose that course? Is it reasonable that

183

you have restricted Elizabeth so greatly when she has done nothing beyond accepting the proposal of a man she believed you would have every reason to approve of, while at the same time you allowed thoughtless Lydia to run wild with the soldiers in Brighton? Explain to me, if you will, how you have come to behave so uncharacteristically if it was not for Matlock's taunts. Do not forget, I know him of old as well, and I know what he can do. How many times did we see him set one boy against another in the same manner, even though they had been the best of friends the previous day?"

"Do you expect me to *rejoice* in Lizzy's new connection to Matlock?" Mr. Bennet spoke through gritted teeth.

Mr. Gardiner shook his head, looking suddenly older than his years. "No, I do not. But I also did not expect you to sacrifice Lizzy's happiness to your desire to avoid him. I would have thought that if Matlock were dead set against the marriage, you would have rushed them to the altar to show him he has no power over you. *That* would be taking revenge against him. *This* is playing into his hands."

"And why are you suddenly on *their* side?"

"Thomas, I am on *your* side as well. I never took against Darcy as badly as you did, since I had never met him previously or dealt with Matlock at Rosings, and I give Lizzy some credit for good judgment. Still, I assumed he was likely a disagreeable sort until I met him. He is nothing like Matlock, and if anything he dislikes him as much as we do. Believe me, I did my share of snooping in Lambton asking about Darcy's typical behavior, talking to people who owed nothing to him, and I heard very little to object to. His mother was not well liked, but Darcy himself seems to be respected."

"*I* still do not like it."

"Just give it some thought. How can it hurt you to actually speak to the boy for a few minutes?"

Mr. Bennet was relieved of the necessity of a response by the entrance of a maid announcing that dinner was ready.

⁂

The following day, Elizabeth was making her very best effort not to listen to Mary's moralizing about the loss of Lydia's reputation. Kitty had already stalked off in disgust. It was with some relief that she saw Jane enter the sitting room and ask Mary to take her place at their mother's bedside, as Mrs. Bennet, unable to boast about the future Mrs. Darcy, had returned to bewailing her lost Lydia. Mary agreed reluctantly, and Jane waited for her to leave the room before indicating to Hill that she could show their guest in.

"A guest? I thought there was no one left who would be seen in our company," Elizabeth said, but this puzzle was explained when it was not one of their neighbors but Colonel Fitzwilliam who entered the room.

"This is an unexpected pleasure," she said, wondering if Darcy had sent him.

"For me as well," replied the colonel. "I had thought you were still on your journey to the Lakes."

So he had not spoken to Darcy, and Mary had been correct in thinking Colonel Fitzwilliam planned to continue his visits in her absence. Elizabeth glanced at Jane, whose cheeks were delicately flushed. If the colonel had thought her absent, then he must have called to see Jane. Just as a happy new suspicion began to fill her mind, she remembered their circumstances and the likely effect on her unmarried sisters. "That was the plan, but circumstances necessitated an earlier return."

Jane gestured to a chair. "Please sit down, Colonel. I am afraid you do not find us at our best today. Our mother is unwell, and our father is in London, so I am grateful that Elizabeth is back sooner than expected."

"I am sorry to hear it. I hope your mother's illness is nothing serious."

Jane glanced down at the floor. "We do not believe her to be in any danger, thank you. I am sure she will be sorry to have missed the opportunity to meet you. Did you travel from London today?"

Elizabeth realized with dismay that Jane intended to avoid the subject of Lydia entirely. Perhaps she hoped to keep it a secret from him, but that was highly unlikely, given Darcy's awareness of the situation. "Colonel Fitzwilliam, my sister is being very tactful, no doubt in hope of avoiding any distress to you. I believe you are acquainted with Mr. Wickham?"

"To my sorrow."

"A fortnight ago, he convinced my youngest sister, who is but 16 years old, to elope with him. They have been traced to London, but no further. She has no dowry to speak of, nothing to tempt him."

"Does Darcy know?" The colonel's amiable mien showed an unusual harshness around the lips.

"I believe he has joined the search for them in London."

185

The colonel frowned. "I had thought him still at Pemberley. Regardless, you may be certain that I will be offering my assistance as well. I have some resources that may be of use in locating your sister."

"I thank you, though I did not tell you in hopes of receiving help, but rather because I thought you would wish to know the truth of the matter."

"You are quite correct." He drummed his fingers rapidly on his thigh, clearly already lost in thought about what steps to take.

Jane was blinking rapidly, her eyes unusually shiny. Elizabeth moved to her side and took her sister's hand in both of hers. "Dearest Jane, I am so sorry! I did not mean to distress you!"

"It is nothing." Jane's voice trembled slightly. "I am sorry, Colonel. What you must think of us!"

"Hush, Jane. He knows what Wickham is. Others may think ill of us, but *he* will not."

To Elizabeth's astonishment, Colonel Fitzwilliam knelt at Jane's feet. "Miss Bennet, your sister is correct. This does not change my respect for you in any way. I am not at liberty to disclose the details, but Wickham has caused difficulties for my own family. He is a force of nature, spreading destruction wherever he goes, but it is no reflection on your own goodness." Not taking his eyes from Jane's face, he hunted in his pocket, then handed her a handkerchief.

Elizabeth was beginning to feel distinctly *de trop*. It was bad enough to find herself in the middle of such a scene, but when it included a man who had proposed marriage to her a mere four months previously looking tenderly on her dearest sister, it was even more embarrassing. Had the situation with Lydia been less dire, she would have been tempted to laugh.

As it was, Elizabeth was trying to invent a reason why she might need to withdraw herself to the other side of the room when Hill returned holding an envelope. "A letter for you, Miss Elizabeth."

"Is there mail from London?" Elizabeth asked. Personal letters were well and good, but it was news from Gracechurch Street that she hoped for.

"Only this."

At least it gave her an excuse to leave Jane's side. She took the letter absently, then, seeing it was in her aunt's handwriting, broke the seal and opened it with greater alacrity. She had seen Mrs. Gardiner only two days ago. What could merit a letter already?

It was quite brief, and she read through it twice before slowly folding it again, tapping it thoughtfully against her other hand. "Hill, I will be needing the small trunk in my room. I will be travelling to London on the morning stage."

Jane looked up from her tête-à-tête with the colonel. "To London? But why?"

Elizabeth held out the letter to her. "Mrs. Gardiner feels it is important for me to be there at my very earliest convenience, but she does not say why, except that she does not believe that our father will be returning here tomorrow after all. I mislike leaving you here to deal with our mother, but I assume our aunt has some good reason for her request." The only other time she recalled this level of mystery from her aunt was regarding their trip to Pemberley. Perhaps this also involved Darcy somehow.

The idea that she might be able to see him sent a surge of relief through her, almost enough to make her weep. It had been only a week since she had bidden him farewell in Derbyshire, but it felt like much longer. So often in these last few stressful days she had longed for his presence and the comfort of his arms around her.

The colonel resumed his seat. "Miss Elizabeth, did you say that you plan to take the stage to London?"

"Yes, that is how we usually travel. Our carriage is not suited for long journeys, and the horses can rarely be spared." She smiled impishly at him. "Let me guess – you are about to tell me that your life and limbs will be in serious jeopardy if your cousin ever discovers that you allowed me to travel by stage. Do not worry; I will tell him it is all my fault."

He laughed. "If it were only a matter of facing a pummeling from him, I could meet that with equanimity. However, in this case he would be in the right, which is far more annoying. I hope you will be merciful enough to spare me the ensuing self-flagellation by permitting me to arrange for a private carriage."

"I appreciate the generous offer, but you must know that I cannot allow you to go to such an expense on my behalf."

He winked at her. "Nonsense. I intend to make Darcy foot the bill, and he will be more than happy to do so."

Chapter 18

THE COLONEL WAS better than his word. While Elizabeth packed, he made arrangements with a livery stable in Meryton for a carriage and driver to take her to London that very afternoon, even hiring a maid from the inn to chaperone her. He rode beside the open carriage the entire way, enlivening her journey with occasional anecdotes that prevented her for the most part from ruminating on the reason for her aunt's summons.

At Gracechurch Street, he walked her to the door and remained long enough to be introduced to Mrs. Gardiner and receive her thanks for the safe delivery of her niece, but declined an invitation to enter. "I must be on my way, as I am hoping I can still meet with Darcy today. I may be able to render him some assistance in this matter."

Elizabeth opened her mouth to express her gratitude, but her aunt spoke first. "If you are seeking Mr. Darcy, why, he is here in our sitting room. Are you certain you will not come in?"

"In that case, how could I refuse?" The colonel straightened his coat.

Elizabeth had already forgotten his presence, instead peering over her aunt's shoulder and longing to move past her to reach Darcy. It was not until they reached the door of the sitting room that it occurred to her with a flash of foreboding that her father was likely to be there as well. Her smile froze on her face at the sight of Mr. Bennet in his favorite chair.

Darcy, his expression one of surprise and heartfelt delight, was at her side in a few quick strides. For a moment she thought he intended to embrace her, but he pulled back just in time, taking her hands in his instead. Their fingers twined together as she drank in the sight of him, even while waiting for the protest certain to come from her father.

Mr. Bennet was eyeing them with no great pleasure, but in response to Elizabeth's worried look, he said dryly, "There is no cause to fret, Lizzy. We are managing to be relatively civil today, at least most of the time. But what brings you here?"

Elizabeth decided that discretion was the better part of valor and deliberately misunderstood him. "Colonel Fitzwilliam was kind enough to arrange for a private carriage. He rode beside it the entire way."

Mrs. Gardiner came to her rescue. "I wrote to Lizzy and asked her to come," she said tartly. "I hoped she might have better luck than I have had in keeping the peace."

Colonel Fitzwilliam bowed in Mr. Bennet's direction. "I am an uninvited guest. I happened to be calling when Miss Elizabeth received Mrs. Gardiner's letter. She was planning to take the public stage alone, which I did not think would meet with Darcy's approval."

Darcy, it appeared, was not listening to his cousin, instead occupying himself with gazing into Elizabeth's eyes, a slight smile on his lips. "Thank you for coming," he said softly, for her ears alone.

Elizabeth wanted nothing so much as to be in his arms, but she dared not even touch his cheek for fear of her father's reaction. Instead of the tender words she wished to say, she said only, "Your cousin made the journey an easy one. He has taken very good care of me today." Only when she saw the furrow between his brow did she realize that he might not be pleased that she had been accompanied by Colonel Fitzwilliam. She added, "Jane was disappointed to be deprived of his company so quickly. Apparently he has become a regular visitor at Longbourn."

Colonel Fitzwilliam took a glass of wine offered to him by Mr. Gardiner. "Mr. Bennet, your daughters shared with me some of the particulars of why you are in London. I hope you will permit me to offer you my assistance in locating Miss Lydia."

Mr. Bennet pushed his glasses up on his nose. "I appreciate that *you* had the courtesy to ask my permission before taking action, but it is unnecessary. The fugitives have been located."

Elizabeth's eyes flew to her father's face. "Is she here? Is she safe?"

Her father merely raised an eyebrow. Darcy said, "She is well, but she refuses to leave Wickham, insisting that they will be married at some point, and that it does not matter when that should take place. Wickham admits privately that he has no intention of marrying her, but he is willing to do so under certain circumstances."

Mr. Bennet said, "So you now find us addressing the crux of the matter, which is the question of whether Darcy or I can be more obstinate about footing the bill. Sit down, Lizzy; you will give me a stiff neck from looking up at you."

She obeyed, but allowed Darcy to lead her to the loveseat where he sat beside her. "You are both firm in your resolve," she said carefully, "but I must admit that in my experience, Mr. Darcy can be more persistent than most of my acquaintance."

Her father raised his glass. "Stubborn as a mule is how I would describe it."

The colonel laughed. "Very perceptive of you, I must say!"

Darcy said evenly, "It is my responsibility, and I will meet it as I see fit."

Colonel Fitzwilliam leaned toward Mr. Bennet as if to speak confidentially, but his tone was audible to everyone in the room. "If this is a matter of his *responsibilities*, I can only advise you to retire from the field now. Darcy is utterly hopeless on this subject."

Mr. Bennet chuckled. "How very kindly your cousin speaks of you, Mr. Darcy."

Darcy shifted to glance at Elizabeth, then back at Mr. Bennet. "I had not realized that you and my cousin were on such friendly terms."

"Why, what could I possibly object to about the good colonel? True, he has threatened to run me through, slandered my daughter, and raised his voice to me, but apart from *that* he has been a perfect gentleman," said Mr. Bennet genially.

Elizabeth leaned toward Darcy. "He is skipping the part when he tried to run your cousin off the grounds at Longbourn, as well as a few other key details." She lowered her voice. "But if he is teasing you, that is an improvement greater than I could have hoped for."

"So I gathered," he whispered back, taking her hand once again, as if he could not help himself. At Mr. Bennet's pointed frown, he would have released it, but Elizabeth tightened her grip.

Mrs. Gardiner inquired politely after the family at Longbourn, and from the discussion that followed, Elizabeth could ascertain that her father had no intention of returning home quickly. She wondered how much of a role Darcy's presence had in changing his mind, and how the Gardiners had explained their acquaintance with him. She would have to wait to ask her aunt these questions.

Darcy did not take an active role in this part of the conversation, and in fact barely seemed to be attending to it, since his eyes rested on Elizabeth the entire time, his expression warm.

Mr. Bennet watched the interplay with a sour expression, then said abruptly, "I take it your father is no longer with us, Mr. Darcy."

Darcy looked surprised by this question, as well he might be since he could not otherwise be in possession of Pemberley, but he still replied civilly. "I am sorry to say he died some five years ago."

"And no doubt devoted to Lord Matlock till the end."

Darcy and the colonel exchanged puzzled glances. "My father and my uncle were never friends."

"Oh, come now. Your father was high in Matlock's favor at school, and later married his sister. That does not sound like enmity to me."

"Married his sister to spite him, you mean," said Colonel Fitzwilliam with a laugh. "You must have heard the public version. My father wanted my aunt to marry a dissipated old marquis with deep pockets, but she threw herself on the mercy of her childhood friend Darcy, who eloped with her solely to prevent the match. By all reports, my father was livid."

Mr. Bennet's upper lip curled. "Forgive me for thinking that beyond unlikely, given that they were friends."

"Perhaps at one time they were friends; I do not know," said Darcy evenly. "All I know is that my father was sent down from Cambridge and that he blamed my uncle for it, believing he had caused it deliberately. I do not know the details, but he harbored a grudge until the day he died. My uncle never acknowledged their marriage, and if he happened to encounter either of them in town, he gave them the cut direct. I would never have known my cousin here were it not for the efforts of Lady Matlock to bring us together."

To Elizabeth's relief, Colonel Fitzwilliam took this as a cue to relate various amusing tales of his childhood escapades with Darcy. With support from Mrs. Gardiner, he managed to keep the conversation along civil lines for half an hour. It was then past time for the gentlemen to take their leave since they had not been invited to dinner, although Darcy showed distinct reluctance to part from Elizabeth.

Elizabeth knew better than to try to obtain any private conversation with Darcy, communicating instead through glances and their joined hands. She longed for a little time with him away from the accusing eyes of her father. She knew better than to hope for it, though.

Despite the presence of the Gardiners, the room felt empty to Elizabeth once Darcy left. Foreboding filled her each time she looked at her father. She considered retiring to bed early in order to avoid being alone with him, but that would just delay the inevitable and give her a sleepless night as well. No, it would be better to face his wrath and whatever punishment he chose to mete out to her, even if it was to send her back to Longbourn in the morning. At least this time she could count on her uncle to inform Mr. Darcy of her departure, and would not have to worry about his reaction to her absence. Her anxiety rose with each minute that ticked by on the ornate mantelpiece clock. She found herself in the highly unusual position of wishing for some needlework; much as she disliked the exercise, at least it would have kept her hands busy and given her something of a distraction.

Mrs. Gardiner, apparently sensing the tension between the two, requested her husband's assistance with putting the children to bed. It was not the best of excuses since they all knew it was not the usual custom for the household, but Elizabeth said nothing while Mr. Bennet only raised an eyebrow.

Once they were alone, Mr. Bennet removed his eyeglasses and rubbed the lenses with his handkerchief, holding them up to the light to check for any remaining marks on the glass. He took longer than usual in folding the glasses and wrapping them in the soft cloth. Then he closed his eyes and rubbed the bridge of his nose with his thumb and forefinger, as if his eyes pained him.

Elizabeth sat quietly, her hands folded in her lap, but tension crawled through her neck and shoulders. This pause filled her with dread. It had felt so much easier to face her father when Darcy had been beside her. She fixed her gaze on the indentation on the cushion beside her where he had sat. If only she could conjure up his presence in reality!

"Well, Lizzy." Her father's hand finally left his face, and Elizabeth noticed for the first time how much older he appeared.

She could think of no appropriate response, so she said nothing, instead simply waiting for the scolding to begin.

"I suppose I must withdraw my objection to your engagement." His mouth twisted as if he had tasted something unpleasant.

Taken by happy surprise, she began to thank him, then reconsidered. His entire countenance told her this was a grudging concession. "I am glad of it, even if you do not seem to be."

"He left me damned little choice!" Mr. Bennet scowled as he rubbed his hand along the wooden chair arm. "Why else would he insist on taking charge of Lydia's marriage if not to force me to accede to his own?"

Unreasoning fury filled Elizabeth. "Why are you so determined to misinterpret everything he does? He would have done the same regardless of your attitude. He takes his responsibilities more seriously than you can perhaps imagine, and what is more, I think you *know* it! Would it be so hard for you to admit that he has even one redeeming feature?"

Mr. Bennet shrugged dismissively. "Very well, if you insist. Perhaps he is decent enough in his own way, but rich clothing and fine jewels will not make up for the lack of respect you can expect from him. He comes from a different world, and you will not be happy with him."

"I have not been happy at Longbourn of late! If we are to speak of respect, why have *you* shown none to me during all this? You do not know him at all, yet you insist on maligning him. You have a grudge against his uncle, that is well and good; but I defy you to show me even one way in which his behavior resembles Lord Matlock! Or perhaps you think *I* should be condemned forever as hopeless merely because my *mother* is silly? He is not his uncle, nor his father, nor anyone but himself! Tell me, do you think my aunt and uncle Gardiner's judgment to be as faulty as mine? They do not think ill of him, and they know him better than you do! But no, everyone else must be wrong, simply because they hold a different opinion from you!" Elizabeth had lost all judgment in her anger as the words she had held back all these months came tumbling out.

"I am giving you my permission to marry him," he said heavily. "Do not ask for more than that."

"Perhaps I should have taken a lesson from Lydia! She seems to have earned your consent much more easily, even though *she* is to marry a worthless, immoral blackguard!"

"Good night, Lizzy." Mr. Bennet pushed himself up from his chair.

For the first time Elizabeth noticed that his complexion had taken on a greyish tinge. She hurried to take his elbow. "Please, sit down," she said, in a very different tone. "You are not well. Perhaps some wine will help." The decanter was nearly empty, but she poured what little remained into a wineglass and handed it to her father. His breathing was shallow. Grimacing, he pressed his hand to his chest.

"Wait here – do not move." Elizabeth raced up the stairs, holding her skirt up almost to her knees to allow her to move faster. She found Mrs. Gardiner in the nursery, tucking her daughter into bed. Grabbing her aunt's arm, she cried, "Oh, please come! My father is ill, very ill!"

Mrs. Gardiner took one look at her niece's face and hurried after her.

More than two hours later, Elizabeth's feet were sore from her constant pacing, but she welcomed the pain. "It was my fault! I was so angry with him."

Mrs. Gardiner had responded to this so many times that she had given up repeating her reassurances that Elizabeth's actions had nothing to do with it. "Let us wait to hear what the doctor says. After all, he had an episode similar to this when he first arrived, and the next morning he was quite himself again."

"I should not have said such things to him. I know it!"

A heavy tread in the hallway presaged the return of Dr. Jenniston. Elizabeth clasped her hands together tightly as the heavyset gentleman appeared in the doorway. Mr. Gardiner set down the newspaper behind which he had been hiding.

"Well, well!" The doctor rubbed his hands together, smiling genially. "Mr. Bennet is resting comfortably now. A little laudanum and a few strategically applied leeches – only a very few! – seem to have done the trick. He will need to rest for at least a week, and nothing stronger than barley broth for him, no matter what he may say, Mrs. Gardiner!"

Mr. Gardiner said, "What is the matter with him?"

"Just a mild heart seizure, a very mild one indeed! He is a fortunate that you called for me so quickly, or it might have been very much worse. But as long as he does not exert himself overmuch, he should be with us for a good many years yet."

"Oh, thank God!" Elizabeth collapsed into a chair, feeling as if her heart might be having a seizure of its own.

"No need to fret, young lady. A cheerful smile from you will do more for him than any remedy I possess, I am sure! You may give him more laudanum if he complains of pain, and I will return to check on him in the morning. There is just a touch of the dropsy around his ankles, and if that does not improve, he may benefit from a little tincture of digitalis, sweetened suitably with a spoonful of honey. But that question will wait until tomorrow."

"That is excellent news," said Mr. Gardiner. "Will you join me in the study for a glass of madeira before you go, Doctor?"

"I don't mind if I do, sir! Now, don't forget, Mrs. Gardiner – nothing but barley broth!"

"Nothing but barley broth, I promise." Mrs. Gardiner laid her hand on Elizabeth's shoulder as the gentlemen departed. "I think we should see if your father is awake. Perhaps you would like to sit with him."

Elizabeth blinked back the tears that threatened to overflow onto her cheeks. "Yes. I would like that."

They found Mr. Bennet sleeping, but he roused at the sound of their whispers. Elizabeth was relieved to see that even though he looked pale and a little confused, his face no longer carried the greyish hue that had so worried her earlier.

Elizabeth kissed his cheek. "You gave us quite a scare," she scolded, but her tone was affectionate.

"Mmm. Sleepy."

"The doctor gave you laudanum."

"That... would explain... it."

She took his hand between both of hers. It felt clammy but warm. Impulsively she said, "I am so sorry that I upset you, papa."

"No, I... I should not..." His eyes drifted closed briefly, then reopened.

"Don't try to talk. You should rest. Shall I sit with you?"

There was only a moment's hesitation before he nodded. A few minutes later, the change in his breathing told Elizabeth he was asleep again.

◇

It was full dark when Elizabeth made her way downstairs to find her uncle writing at his desk in the study, a small flickering lamp leaving a pool of light in front of him.

Mr. Gardiner looked up at her approach. "How is he?"

"He woke about half an hour ago and took more laudanum, and now he is sound asleep again. My aunt is sitting with him now."

"Good. Rest is no doubt the best thing for him."

"May I ask your advice on something?"

"Of course." He placed his pen in the inkwell and turned his full attention to her.

"You know that some months ago my father forbade me to write to Mr. Darcy. Do you suppose that, under these changed circumstances, he would object if I wrote to tell him of tonight's events?"

Mr. Gardiner patted her hand. "No, I do not think he would mind, but it is unnecessary. I sent Darcy a note just after the doctor left, with the suggestion that he call here tomorrow morning."

Elizabeth felt a weight lift from her shoulders. "Thank you."

"Of course. This concerns him as well, since we will need to avoid causing your father any distress, and that will mean keeping Wickham away from him. Darcy as well, of course, but I have no doubt he will cooperate in protecting your father, while I cannot say the same for Wickham, or even for Lydia. I would like to wrap this all up as quickly as possible."

Elizabeth nodded. "That would be for the best."

The lamps were already lit when Darcy arrived home the following evening after a long day comforting Elizabeth, who was still distressed over her father's ill health and prone to blaming herself for it. It would only be a short leap from that to blaming *him* for the whole situation, so Darcy was determined to be with her as much as possible to circumvent that possibility.

Even his butler looked tired as he greeted Darcy. "Sir, Mr. Jackson is awaiting you in the breakfast room."

Meeting with a stranger had no appeal. He would have ordered him sent away immediately, except that his butler would not have admitted him in the first place without a reason. "Who is Mr. Jackson and why is he in the breakfast room?"

"He arrived here from Kent today, but he claims to be from Pemberley. The sitting room seemed unsuitable owing to a *person* he brought with him. The breakfast room seemed the safest place."

Jackson – that was his steward's assistant. Why was he in London instead of leading the recovery in Hunsford? Darcy was too tired to try to muddle through why the breakfast room would be safer than any other room. It was easier simply to go there and see.

The butler opened the door for him. Darcy only caught a glimpse of Jackson, a gangly young man who looked even more fatigued than his butler, before a large animal jumped at his leg. Assuming in the dim light that it must be a dog, he reached down to push it away, only to encounter a tangle of hair which was definitely not canine. Why on earth was a dirty child clinging to his leg?

"Mr. Jackson, no doubt you have an explanation for this." Darcy tried to control his temper.

The young man jumped to his feet and bowed. "I am very sorry, Mr.

Darcy. This is the child you asked me to take from the orphanage. I tried to find a home for her, as you directed, but she became, er, distraught. She turns into a wild animal when anyone tries to touch her. The local apothecary suggested that perhaps a London doctor might have some idea how to help her."

This emaciated wretch was Jenny? He could not see her face, since it was buried in his leg. "It does not appear to me that she is unwilling to be touched." It was hard not to sound disdainful when the untouchable child was clinging to him like a limpet, with his hand resting on her head.

"I... I cannot explain it, sir, but I swear to you, she even *bit* one woman who was trying to help her. I did not know what else to do. Had I realized that she would not respect your person, sir, I would never have brought her here."

With a deep sigh, Darcy kneeled on the floor, which forced the little girl to release her grip on him. His trousers were probably ruined anyway, so a scuffed knee would be the least of his valet's worries. And how was he supposed to know what to do with her if others had failed?

Now that he could see her face, his first thought was that Jackson had fetched the wrong child. This one had a peaked look with a face that was all eyes, and looked nothing like the little girl whom he had never seen standing upright. But it was her expression that made him recognize her – it was the same one she had worn that night when she had woken the house with her screaming – and the doll she clutched, who looked even worse than when he had rescued it from the flood.

"Jenny?" he said tentatively.

She nodded.

"What is the matter?"

She whispered something he could not make out. Darcy looked up at Jackson questioningly.

"That orphanage – it was a terrible place, sir," Jackson said apologetically. "I suppose they are all terrible, but this one, well, it was *terrible*."

It must have been terrible indeed if it rendered his steward's usually competent assistant unable to employ his native language. "No one will hurt you here, Jenny. This is *my* house, and everyone here works for me. Do you understand?"

She nodded again.

What did Jackson think that he was going to be able to do with her?

"Well, then, Jenny, I would say that you need a good meal and a bath and a warm bed to sleep in."

"No bath!" She clutched her doll to her with both hands.

Did the child not realize he was trying to help her? "Very well, then, no bath, just a good meal and a warm bed, and you will obey the maids and Mr. Jackson when they tell you to do something, unless it is to take a bath. If there is a problem, you can tell me about it tomorrow, and I promise I will listen. Do we have an agreement?" And tomorrow he would ask Elizabeth what he should do with her.

"As long as they don't take my dolly."

"No one will take your dolly, I promise. Now, Jackson will take you to the kitchens for something to eat." He stood up and brushed off his trousers. He certainly hoped Elizabeth would know what to do.

In the morning, Darcy concluded that his well-trained staff was no match for a stubborn four-year-old girl. In the interest of maintaining domestic tranquility among his servants – or so he told himself – he decided to bring Jenny with him to the Gardiners so that Elizabeth could see her for herself. It really had nothing to do with the fact that Jenny started sobbing uncontrollably when she found out he was going out for the day and leaving her behind.

Elizabeth, seeing Jenny for the first time in the light of day, was shocked by the change in her. Quickly realizing this went beyond her limited experience with children, she asked Jenny to stay with Mr. Darcy for a few minutes while she found her aunt and explained the girl's history.

Jenny initially shied away from Mrs. Gardiner, but upon hearing that she was Elizabeth's beloved aunt and Mr. Darcy's good friend, she seemed to decide that this made the lady at least provisionally trustworthy. Mrs. Gardiner, after gravely requesting the honor of an introduction to Jenny's doll, exclaimed, "Oh, your poor dolly! Her dress is torn and dirty. Should we fix that, do you think?"

The girl considered this briefly before agreeing.

Mrs. Gardiner said, "First, you will need to remove her dress and so that we can wash it, and then I can help you mend it when it is dry, but in the meantime, we will need to do something to keep your dolly warm." She paused, as if puzzled. "I know just the thing! My little girl has a doll not much bigger than yours, and we can borrow one of her doll's dresses for your dolly to wear while her own is drying. What do you think?"

"Oh, yes, Dolly would like that!"

"Excellent!" Mrs. Gardiner held out her hand to Jenny, who took it without hesitation and went with her out of the room. Her voice continued from the hallway. "If I found a wet washcloth for you, do you think you could clean your dolly a little? I am afraid it would make her very sad to be dirty when she is wearing a pretty new dress."

Elizabeth looked at Darcy with amusement. "Apparently she only needed the right touch."

Darcy said, "I suppose it is a step in the right direction if her doll is no longer filthy and ragged, but I would prefer it if she herself were the one to be cleaned."

Guessing at the true source of Darcy's ill humor, Elizabeth checked to be certain that the hallway was now empty, then put her arms around him. "I can understand why Jenny does not want you to leave her. I feel the same way every evening when you depart, even if I am sensible enough now not to cry about it."

"Do you truly miss me when I am gone?"

"What sort of silly question is that? Of course I do. Do you not miss me?"

He answered first with a kiss that fluttered her pulses. "Agonizingly," he said in a low voice. "Especially now that I can never be sure that your father will not have sent you away during my absence."

"He has not mentioned it, and my guess is that he wants me here for his own sake. Should he tell me to leave, I will not go without an argument."

"I am glad of it." He released her with apparent reluctance, then walked a few paces away.

It did not bode well if he was not interested in holding her. "Is something the matter?"

"No." Then, with a look at her hurt expression, he added, "Last night, your uncle told me that since no one could be spared to chaperone us, he expected me not to take advantage of that fact, especially given the scandal surrounding your sister."

"You sound angry."

His expression softened. "Not angry. He is right, and I should have known it without being told. I just do not like it, particularly when our time together is so limited. Still, I would far rather be with you and unable to touch you than not to see you at all. But more importantly, how is your father this morning?"

She knew he was only asking for her sake, but she appreciated it. "His spirits have improved enough that he is complaining about having nothing to eat but barley broth and telling us not to hover over him. The doctor seems satisfied with his progress."

An hour later, Mrs. Gardiner reappeared, holding two girls by the hand. One was her youngest daughter, Emma, and the other was a smiling Jenny, scrubbed pink, wearing a dress that must have been Emma's, her fair hair cut short and falling in soft curls around her thin face.

Elizabeth had been expecting something like this, but judging from Darcy's stunned look, he had not. "You look lovely, Jenny! Why, your hair is just like a fashionable lady's!"

Jenny giggled. "Emma wants hers cut now, too, but her mother says no."

"I helped, though," Emma retorted. "I did a good job, too!"

Darcy finally found his voice. "Mrs. Gardiner, you are a miracle worker. I cannot thank you enough. How did you convince her to bathe?"

"Jenny was perfectly happy to bathe as soon as we established that she could keep her doll with her. She doesn't object to washing, just to having her doll taken away. Apparently one of the older children at the orphanage stole her doll from her, and she did not get it back until your man insisted upon it to the matron. You, Mr. Darcy, are apparently the only person she trusts with her most prized possession." Mrs. Gardiner's lips were quivering with restrained mirth.

Elizabeth, feeling no such restriction, laughed. "That is no wonder, given that he risked drowning to bring her that doll!"

"So I have heard! Jenny told us about it in great detail." Mrs. Gardiner smiled down at her.

Emma asked eagerly, "Was there really a dragon that you had to fight your way past?"

"Just a river in flood, which is close enough to a dragon for my taste," Darcy said gravely.

Elizabeth took his hand. "I believe *I* was playing the role of the dragon at that point!"

Mrs. Gardiner released the two girls' hands. "Emma, I think Jenny would enjoy seeing your toys. Please take her up to the nursery with you."

The girls managed to leave the room with a certain amount of decorum, but once they were out of sight, Elizabeth could hear their running footsteps and giggles.

"Mrs. Gardiner, I will be forever in your debt," said Darcy with feeling.

"Nonsense. Emma had a glorious time turning a real, live rag girl into a princess. Jenny is a sweet girl."

"If only you could convince my staff of that!"

"She was frightened, that is all. She was beaten at that orphanage, you know – I saw the marks on her back. What do you plan to do with her?"

"My man is looking for a tenant family in her village willing to take her in. I will pay her expenses, of course. He only brought her to me because no one could manage her, and he feared I would object to strong measures being taken."

Elizabeth could not help laughing. "How very like you! You pulled her out from under a tree branch, so now you feel responsible for her for life."

Darcy frowned. "Do you object?"

"No, not at all. I think it is very kind of you."

Mrs. Gardiner said, "She was fortunate in finding you. Might I suggest that you leave her here for a few days while the arrangements are made?"

"I could not ask that of you! You are already caring for Mr. Bennet, and soon there will be Miss Lydia's needs as well."

"I am only being practical. I have a well-stocked nursery and a nursemaid who can manage five children as easily as four, and you have neither. My children will enjoy the novelty. It is the very least we can do after all you have done for Lydia."

Darcy opened his mouth to object, but Elizabeth spoke first. "My aunt is quite right. A man as generous as you needs to learn to accept generosity in others."

He looked puzzled by this, but said, "In that case, I offer you my thanks, Mrs. Gardiner. I will not venture to argue when you are both in agreement!"

Chapter 19

DARCY HANDED HIS hat and gloves to the Gardiners' manservant. "I came as quickly as I could," he said to Mr. Gardiner. "What is the matter? Has Mr. Bennet taken a turn for the worse?"

"No, nothing of the sort. I sent for you because he asked to speak to you as soon as possible."

Darcy stared at Mr. Gardiner. "Mr. Bennet wants to see *me*?"

"So he says. Alone, and without Lizzy's knowledge. I was reluctant to agree to that part, but I did not wish to agitate him, so I sent Lizzy out shopping with my wife. I trust you will do everything within your power to avoid distressing him."

Since Mr. Bennet as a rule seemed distressed by his very existence, Darcy thought himself singularly unqualified to avoid agitating him, but he would try. God knew how often he had tried already! "Of course. But would he not be calmer if you spoke to me on his behalf?"

"He insists on private conversation with you, and he called me an old fussbudget. I am not happy about it either, but I do not see how you can refuse."

"As long as he does not ask me to give up Elizabeth, I will do my utmost to agree to whatever he wishes." Unfortunately, that was probably precisely what Mr. Bennet wanted of him.

Mr. Gardiner clapped him on the arm. "Good lad. Go on up to him – the second door on the left."

Mr. Bennet looked better than Darcy had expected. He was sitting propped up by pillows in bed with a tray of tea by his side. "Ah, Mr. Darcy. Do sit down."

Darcy seated himself gingerly. He had never heard Mr. Bennet speak to him in so genial a manner, and it raised his suspicions even further. "I understand you wished to see me, sir."

"Yes, there is something I wish to ask you, but first, I hope you will tell me what in God's name is happening with Lydia and Wickham, since everyone here seems to believe they can fob me off with platitudes."

Darcy hesitated, aware that the Gardiners would prefer to keep the information from Mr. Bennet to prevent distressing him, but he could not justify a refusal to answer a direct question. "Wickham and I came to an agreement two days ago. In the end, he was more reasonable than I expected, no doubt due to the influence of Colonel Fitzwilliam's tendency to fondle the handle of his saber as we talked. My solicitor is drawing up the papers. The settlement includes a commission in the regulars. Wickham will be stationed in Newcastle, at the suggestion of my cousin, who is acquainted with the commander of the garrison there."

"When are they to marry?"

"Next week. Wickham has obtained a license."

"Is Lydia still with him?"

Darcy did not expect Mr. Bennet to like his answer, but avoiding the question would likely upset him even more. "No. That was part of the agreement. Initially I planned to bring Miss Lydia here, but since Mrs. Gardiner already has her hands full, I arranged for her to stay at a respectable boarding house with a hired companion who reports to me."

"I think you mean to say that the Gardiners felt that I would not stay obediently calm with Lydia under this roof."

Darcy gave a slight smile. "Something along those lines, sir."

"Ah, well. They're probably right. My daughters are a silly lot, though you picked the best of them." Mr. Bennet had a glint in his eyes that Darcy recognized.

He decided to take a risk. Raising one eyebrow he said, "Now I am worried. That sounded suspiciously like a compliment."

Mr. Bennet chuckled, a laugh which turned into a cough before it subsided. "Don't let it go to your head." He mopped his brow with a handkerchief, looking tired.

"You mentioned there was something you wished to speak to me about."

"Yes." Mr. Bennet closed his eyes and leaned his head back against the pillow. He was silent long enough that Darcy began to worry for his well-being, but then he sat upright again, his gaze alert. "I want you to marry Lizzy at your earliest convenience."

Darcy was certain he must have missed something. "I beg your pardon?"

"Oh, your face is a study! You heard me perfectly well. So, what is your answer?"

It had to be a trap. "May I inquire as to the reason for your sudden change of heart on the subject?"

Mr. Bennet coughed again, a little longer this time. "Wickham."

"Because I arranged for their marriage?"

The older man waved a hand at him dismissively. "No, not that. I need you to keep him in check. That fool of a doctor says another one of these heart seizures could finish me, and then Wickham would weasel Mrs. Bennet out of every penny in her settlement if there was no one to stop him. Can't have that."

"I am relieved," Darcy said dryly. "For a moment there I thought you might have actually come to approve of me, but if it is only that you now think better of me than of Wickham, I can rest easy."

"Don't make me laugh. It rattles my lungs. Will you do it?"

"Of course. I will arrange to have the banns called on Sunday."

"Your *earliest* convenience, Mr. Darcy." Mr. Bennet spoke sharply.

"Ah." Darcy could not recall the last time that he had felt speechless. He gathered his scattered thoughts. "Very well. Does Elizabeth know that this is your wish?"

"No. You tell her. Now let me rest." He sounded peevish.

"Of course." Darcy's hand was on the doorknob before he realized the reason for Mr. Bennet's sudden change of mood in the last minutes. He could not possibly be looking forward to losing his favorite daughter while he was in such straits. He turned back to face his future father. "I will ask Mr. Bingley for the use of Netherfield. Elizabeth will not want to be far from you right now."

"Drafty old place, Netherfield. Never liked it myself." Despite the complaint, Mr. Bennet no longer sounded annoyed, just tired.

"I promise to keep Elizabeth safe from the drafts." His words felt somehow weighted with significance.

"See that you do." Mr. Bennet's voice was so soft that Darcy barely heard it.

Darcy found his way down to the parlor without even noticing his surroundings, his mind whirling. He must write to his solicitor immediately and direct him to prepare the settlement. A clergyman. He needed a clergyman, and a license as well, but it was already afternoon, so

Doctors Common would be closed for the day. Tomorrow morning, then. He should send for Jane Bennet – Elizabeth would want her to be present – and likely for Charlotte Collins as well, as long as she could come without her pest of a husband. They could both travel to London and back in a day, or they could stay at Darcy House. He would have to tell Richard, and that would have to be in person. Richard most likely would not want to attend under the circumstances, but he would never forgive Darcy if he was not informed about it. And he had to tell Elizabeth... Good God, what if Elizabeth refused to accept an immediate wedding? Mr. Bennet would blame *him*.

Mr. Gardiner had clearly been pacing the floor as he waited. "What happened?" he asked, then caught a glimpse of Darcy's face. "Good Lord, what did he say to you? Sit down and have some madeira. You look white as can be."

Darcy shook his head absently. "I am perfectly well, though in need of a pen and paper."

"Come into my study, then." Mr. Gardiner held his tongue until Darcy was settled at his desk, his pen scratching on paper in a firm, neat hand. "Did he forbid you to marry Lizzy?"

Darcy did not look up. "No, now he *wants* me to marry her."

"Does he indeed? That is excellent news. Lizzy will be very pleased."

Darcy's fingers froze, the pen leaving a blot of ink. "Will she?"

"Of course she will! What sort of foolish question is that?"

"He wants us to marry as soon as we can." He dipped the pen back in the inkwell, then resumed writing. "He does not even wish for the banns to be called."

"Does he now? That is a change indeed! He must be more worried for his health than he has been admitting."

The pen quivered. Realizing that his hand was trembling, Darcy set the pen back in the inkwell and eyed it distrustfully.

Mr. Gardiner laughed in sudden comprehension. "Darcy, you are the last man in the world I would have expected to develop wedding nerves. Here, have some of that madiera. It will calm you."

"There is so much I must do first," Darcy said distractedly. "And I must ask Elizabeth if she is willing. Do you think she will be distressed by this rush into marriage?"

"Of course not, lad." Mr. Gardiner's chuckle was followed by the sound of the front door closing. "And if I am not mistaken, that will be my wife and Lizzy now. Shall I send her in to you?"

"Yes, please." Darcy made another attempt at writing, focusing his attention on his penmanship with great deliberation.

A few minutes later, Elizabeth slipped in and closed the door, her presence brightening the room and providing a soothing balm for his agitation. He wondered distractedly if he would always feel this mixture of relief and burning desire whenever he saw her, or whether it would be different after they were married. But no matter - as long as she was with him, all would be well.

"I do not know why," she proclaimed with a laugh, "but my uncle tells me that I should waste no time in consenting to whatever you wish." She kissed his cheek lightly, then his mouth, the caress of her soft lips lighting a smoldering fire in him, and he did not hesitate to return the gesture with interest, catching the back of her head with his hand. "He seemed very amused."

"He told you to consent to whatever I wished?" Darcy said in disbelief. The first image that came into his mind had nothing at all to do with her father's plans, and everything to do with making good use of the settee in the corner.

"That is what he said." Elizabeth's eyes sparkled up at him. "So what is it that you wish?"

When she looked at him with that teasing light, there was only one response Darcy could make. He drew her soft form into his arms, reveling in the sensation of her breasts pressed against his chest, and kissed her with all the passionate need he had been repressing since their interlude at Pemberley. Since she had arrived in London, he had only been able to kiss her that one time, and he had been aching for her touch.

"Oh, my," said Elizabeth breathlessly, her lips so near his that he could feel her warm breath tickling his cheek. "I do not think that was what my uncle had in mind."

"He did say you should consent to whatever I wished, did he not?" His hands still locked behind her waist, he stole a quick kiss for the sheer joy of being allowed to do so.

To his delight, she responded by deepening the kiss, one hand tangling in his hair, the other clutching his cravat. For a few minutes that was all that existed – her mouth for his exploration, her body pressed against his, his hands roaming the delicious curves of her back, and the only thing on his wayward mind was the overwhelming desire to make her his. But reason nagged at the back of his head, reminding him that this was neither the time nor the place, and he reluctantly lifted his lips from hers.

The only thing more delightful than Elizabeth's arch smile was when she wore it while her eyes were dark with desire for him. "So, what am I *supposed* to be consenting to?" she asked.

He could not bear to release her, so instead he drew her down until she sat on his lap, where he could hold her close enough that he could breathe in the warm scent of roses rising from her body. As long as he avoided looking down at her décolletage, he could brush his lips against the exposed skin of her neck. If he gave in to the temptation of looking down, he would lose any vestige of rational thought. He made a valiant attempt to force his mind away from Elizabeth's tempting body. "Your father made a very surprising request of me today."

"Oh, dear. That does not sound promising."

"Actually, although it came as something of a shock, I would have to say his idea is a good one." In fact, a quick marriage seemed an inspired idea at the moment. The very thought made his body throb with desire. Why did Doctors Common have to close so damned early anyway? "He wants us to marry as soon as possible."

Elizabeth looked away. "I know you mean well, but this is not a matter I can joke about."

"I am quite serious, my love, as was your father. It seems that he has accepted that I intend to marry you in any case, and given that he cannot prevent the match, he has decided it would serve his purposes best for it to take place now. He said it was because his declining health made him fear he would be unable to keep Wickham in line, but I think it is more that he realizes that, should anything happen to him, your mother and sisters would be unprotected. He wants us married so that I can protect your family should he be unable to do so."

Elizabeth paled. "The doctor told us he would recover and be with us for many years. Why is my father so worried?"

He tightened his arms around her, wishing he could make this easier for her. "Whether there is something he knows that we do not, I cannot say, but he does seem to fear a relapse. Your uncle had told me that under no circumstances was I to say anything that would distress your father, so I did not inquire. He seemed happier after I had agreed to his request."

"If it will relieve his anxiety, then of course we must do it," she said with her old determination. "We can have the banns called on Sunday if he wishes."

It was so close to what his own response had been that he almost laughed. With her in his arms and her consent obtained, he was happy to explain her father's instructions in further detail.

"This is a surprise, Darcy," said Colonel Fitzwilliam. "Can't remember the last time you were here. Is Wickham creating more problems?"

It was indeed a rare occurrence for Darcy to call at Colonel Fitzwilliam's austere bachelor lodgings, but the mention of it made Darcy wonder for the first time how his cousin felt about that fact. "Not that I am aware of. There are some new developments on another front, though." He briefly explained Mr. Bennet's change of heart, watching his cousin's face closely. "So, after all his opposition, now we are to be married in two days' time."

If Richard was troubled by the news, he showed no sign of it. "In two days? That is fast work."

"He would have preferred it even sooner, but I requested the delay to have time to make everything ready – the settlement, preparing her rooms at Darcy House, and whatnot. I doubt we will be staying in London long, though, since Mr. Bennet should be able to travel soon, and we will accompany him home."

"You will be staying at Longbourn? I wish you joy of it! It is a little too crowded for my taste."

"Mine as well, believe me. Elizabeth and I will stay at Netherfield, the house Bingley has leased. Bingley himself plans to return there soon." It would be like those days when Jane had lain ill at Netherfield, except this time he would not have to settle for a phantom Elizabeth in his bed.

Richard gave him a startled look. "I thought he planned to give up the place."

Darcy shrugged. "He changed his mind, both about the house and about marrying Elizabeth's sister."

Richard turned his back on Darcy to fetch the decanter from the sideboard. By the time he had poured out a glass, his expression was neutral. "Some port? Not up to your usual standards, of course, but decent enough. So Bingley is engaged to Miss Bennet?"

"No, but I believe he plans to make her an offer. She knows nothing of it yet."

Richard held up his glass. "To the lovely Miss Bennet, then."

"She is my next order of business. Since the wedding will be held at Mr. Gardiner's house so that Mr. Bennet can be in attendance, it will be quite small, but Elizabeth would very much like Jane to stand up with her. I offered to send a carriage to Longbourn for her."

"Good of you, but if you feel up to trusting me with your curricle, I can save you the trouble. A drive out into the Hertfordshire countryside would be just the thing to escape from the heat of London."

Darcy supposed this offer was Richard's way of telling him he had come to terms with Elizabeth's choice of husband. "I would not wish to put you to any trouble."

"Since when is it trouble for me to take advantage of your fine horseflesh while enjoying the company of a beautiful woman?"

"In that case, I accept your offer. Naturally, you are welcome at the ceremony as well, but I will understand if you prefer not to attend." Darcy avoided his cousin's eyes.

"How very kind of you," Richard drawled. "I wouldn't miss it for the world."

Chapter 20

AT FIRST JANE had been nervous, perched on the narrow seat of the curricle. She had never ridden in such a stylish vehicle before, nor so far from the ground in an open carriage. But Colonel Fitzwilliam had noticed her discomfort and made a joke about how he felt tiny when he stood beside one of the fashionable high-perch phaetons, and shifted to make more room for her so that she did not have to sit at the edge of the seat. She noticed his skill at handling the team; she was not accustomed to seeing a driver so responsive to his horses.

As always, she found him remarkably easy to converse with. She still could not understand why Lizzy had chosen Darcy over his much more amiable cousin, and wondered, not without guilt, if her sister had made her choice based not on her heart but on the need for one of them to marry well. If Bingley had lived up to her expectations of him, Lizzy would not have had to consider their family's future when making her decision. At least Lizzy did seem genuinely attached to Mr. Darcy, but that could be an act. She would need to see the two of them together to know for certain.

"Since you are aware that Lizzy is in London, I assume Mr. Darcy must be as well. Have they been able to meet?"

"Several times. In fact, there is a confession on that subject I must make to you."

Jane's stomach lurched, and it had nothing to do with the motion of the curricle. She did not want to hear about Colonel Fitzwilliam's heartbreak at Lizzy's hands. She could accept that her own romantic fantasies about him were hopeless since he could not afford a woman with her poor prospects, but it was harder to face that he cared for Lizzy more than for her. "I am eager to hear it," she said politely.

"I am taking you to London under false pretences. While my mother did in fact invite you and Miss Elizabeth to tea, it was only after she discovered that you would be coming anyway. I chose to tell your mother of the invitation as the reason you should be allowed to come with me because my instructions were to fetch you without telling your mother the true cause."

Jane's heart began to flutter. "What is the matter? Is Lizzy ill? Or my father?"

"Miss Elizabeth gave me a letter for you which explains the situation." He withdrew a folded paper from his pocket and handed it to her.

Darting a glance at him, Jane opened the letter and began to read. She gasped when she reached the part about her father's heart seizure, and she must have turned pale since the colonel placed his hand lightly on her arm and said, "He is better now."

Not for the first time, she wondered how he could tell so easily what she was thinking. Her eyes hurried through the rest of the letter. "They are to be married *tomorrow*?"

"Yes, and Miss Elizabeth very much desires your presence."

Her first thought, oddly enough, was for the colonel. How this sudden marriage must pain him, yet he had gone out of his way to fetch her and had even been reassuring *her* when he himself must be in need of comfort! Her earlier envious thoughts were banished now, replaced by a desire to protect him from pain. "Thank you for bringing me," she said slowly. "I appreciate the efforts you have taken so that I may attend."

"It is a pleasure and an honor to be of service." He sounded as if he actually meant it. In a lighter tone he added, "Even if it did require me to indulge in a bit of prevarication with your mother just as she was proclaiming how she knew she could trust me to bring you safely to your uncle's house."

She turned a grateful smile on him. "You gave her such delight by making her believe that the Countess of Matlock wished for my presence enough to send her son for me. You may be certain she will be sharing that story with everyone of her acquaintance!"

"I hope the change of plans does not cause you any distress."

"Not at all!"

"I am glad. You seemed a little subdued, and I supposed you might be disappointed."

How could she tell him she felt pain on his behalf? "I was taken aback to hear of my father's heart seizure."

"Of course." He looked at her with such sympathy that she felt almost guilty for misleading him.

"I am also a selfish creature, and I find myself sad to be losing my sister's companionship sooner than I had expected."

"That is a worry I can help allay. Darcy and your sister plan to spend a month or more at Netherfield so that she can be near your father during his recovery." He seemed to be watching her very carefully.

The mention of Netherfield did not cause her the pang of distress that it had so often since Mr. Bingley had left. "It is kind of Mr. Bingley to allow them the use of it." How odd it was – usually she found it difficult to speak his name, but this time it rolled off her tongue without a second thought.

He seemed unusually preoccupied with the horses as he steered them around a slow farm cart. "I understand that Bingley will be returning there soon as well."

For a moment she could not think at all. She had prayed for so long to hear this news, had longed for it and dreamed about it, and now that it was here, she felt nothing except embarrassment for all the talk and pitying looks that would now begin anew, just when they had started to wane. With Lydia's disgrace, Mr. Bingley would be that much less likely to seek her out. He might even start dangling after some other pretty girl who would at least have the advantage of knowing that he would eventually disappoint her hopes. She would not be able to avoid seeing him if Lizzy was living at Netherfield. To her astonishment, she realized she did not want to see him at all, and that distressed her most of all. She looked away from the colonel, pretending interest in the farm they were passing. At least she had the consolation that the colonel did not know what Bingley had meant to her.

With great care, Colonel Fitzwilliam said, "Darcy tells me there is a lady in the vicinity whom Bingley has found himself unable to forget, and whose acquaintance he intends to renew."

"Does he?" The uncharacteristically angry words escaped Jane's lips before she realized what had happened. "I wonder that any lady who had been abandoned so long would be willing to receive him again. I suppose he believes his fortune is enough to gain him forgiveness."

Colonel Fitzwilliam did not appear to be disturbed by her outburst. In fact, he seemed to be smiling, or at least as much as he could while tunelessly whistling. "Many ladies would tolerate a great deal for a fortune such as his."

She could not understand him. Was he laughing at her? She took care to speak in her normal, calm voice when she said, "Perhaps some might think it naïve of me, but I believe that true affection and respect are worth more than the largest income. Is something the matter, Colonel? You have gone quite pale."

His pallor was belied by his expression as he beamed at her. "I am *quite* well, thank you! I am merely suffering from an unaccountable urge to spring the horses, but I will not subject you to that."

Pleased to see him cheerful again, she said recklessly, "Why not? Is it too dangerous?"

He smiled broadly. "You do not *mind* if I spring the horses? It is not dangerous, at least not on such a good road. The horses are very well trained."

"I cannot say if I will mind, as it is something far from my experience, but I will never know if I do not try it." She could not understand what had happened to her normal reticence.

"In that case, you might wish to hold onto the rail."

Obediently she leaned forward and gripped it with both hands. "Very well, you may do your worst, sir!"

He hesitated. "Will you tell me immediately if you find it at all unpleasant?" At her nod of agreement, he shook the reins. As the horses shifted in unison to a smooth canter, the curricle surged forward.

The wind whistled past Jane's ears. It was an odd but exhilarating sensation to hurtle along at such a speed with no enclosing carriage. The countryside almost seemed to blur beside them, but her attention was captured by the colonel's intent expression as he drove, shifting the reins slightly from time to time, the team responding instantly to his instructions. Despite their speed, she did not doubt his command of the situation.

He reined the horses in as they came up behind a plodding stagecoach, deftly veering around it and onto the clear road ahead at a trot. "Well?" he said. His hair was becomingly tousled and his expression was boyish.

"It might be a bit much for everyday, but there is something pleasing about it. You drive beautifully. I was not in the least bit frightened."

His expression of satisfaction warmed her heart. He said, "Thank you. Darcy's team is a pleasure to drive. I have none so fine. Actually, I do not own a team at all, just my horse, but he has bravely carried me through several battles, so I cannot complain."

"Carrying you to safety seems of greater value than the ability to race along the highway in a fashionable equipage."

"Ah, but the fashionable equipage is enjoyable, is it not? Still, one can live without it. Tell me, Miss Bennet, would *you* consider an offer from a gentleman with little to offer except his affection and respect?

Jane's heart slammed against her ribs. She could not possibly have understood his question correctly. He was in love with her sister, and Lizzy had told her that the colonel needed to marry an heiress. How could he be offering for *her*? Or was her heart hearing only what she desired in a question that had been meant innocently? That must have been the case. The disappointment was bitter. It was exactly calculated to make her understand her own wishes, even though they were in vain.

But she intended to keep the colonel's respect, so she put on the calm face she employed to disguise distress. "Is that a theoretical question, Colonel?"

The corners of his mouth twitched. "For the moment, yes. After all, your father has made *quite* clear his opinion of gentlemen who offer for his daughters without speaking to him first. Fortunately, I know precisely where to find him."

Heat seemed to pour through her, and Jane was certain her cheeks must be scarlet. She looked down to hide the incredulous smile that insisted on showing itself. "But you hardly know me."

"Do you recall the day we met, and you walked with me through the gardens to the wilderness beside your house? By the time we left that wilderness, I felt I had known you all my life. When we danced together at that assembly, I realized that I found more pleasure in one of your smiles than I could recall experiencing in a day spent with any other lady." He paused, then began again, his voice rough. "Despite my profession, I am not a violent man. But when I learned Bingley intended to return to Hertfordshire, I wanted to run him through. That was when I first knew what it would cost me to see you married to another man."

"Yet you were the one to tell me of his return."

"Of course. I would not attempt to secure you under false pretenses. You deserve to know that you have a choice, especially since he has so much more to offer than I do."

"I beg to differ." And she looked up at him with her heart in her eyes.

They agreed to say nothing publicly until after Elizabeth and Darcy's wedding, since to do so would be to draw attention away from the bride and groom. This delay would also give Colonel Fitzwilliam time to speak to Mr. Bennet. Jane had the further motive for secrecy of being somewhat reluctant to share her news with Elizabeth, whom she thought likely to question the colonel's newfound devotion. Still, even if she could only hug the news to herself, she still considered herself the happiest woman alive.

Jane was glad of the decision when she saw the hubbub at Gracechurch Street. Elizabeth was making some hasty alterations to a silk dress of Mrs. Gardiner's that was to serve as her wedding dress, while Mrs. Gardiner worked feverishly to create a celebratory atmosphere in the house, taking advantage of the plethora of flowers readily available at that time of year. Mr. Darcy and Mr. Gardiner were closeted in the study with Mr. Darcy's solicitor, finalizing the marriage settlement. It had the appearance of a dumb play, since all this was done in near complete silence in order to keep any hint of stress from the invalid upstairs.

On hearing this, Jane immediately consulted with the colonel, fearing that the news of their engagement was likely to distress her father. "He is not likely to be pleased, given his sentiments toward your father. What if he suffers another heart seizure? I could never forgive myself."

The colonel took her gloved hand in his. "If you wish me to wait, of course I will do so. I do not anticipate that our news will trouble him, though. He has been quite cordial to me here, and he is afraid of the future. He will be relieved to have your future settled, just as he wanted Miss Elizabeth's settled as soon as possible. Also, he has been concerned about the effects of the scandal regarding your youngest sister, and to have a connection to an aristocratic family, impoverished or not, could do a great deal to ameliorate that."

"But how can we be certain? He was so angry over Lizzy's engagement, and he liked you no better than Darcy when you first appeared."

"I believe you may be surprised. I propose that we visit him together so that you can see how he receives me, and if you are still uncomfortable, all you need do is to stay in the room. Unless you leave the room so that I may speak to him alone, I will assume you wish me to remain silent."

Indeed, Mr. Bennet seemed pleased to see the colonel, and after a brief interchange of greetings with Jane and the usual questions regarding his recovery, he devoted most of his conversation to Colonel Fitzwilliam. "So, you found another excuse to visit Longbourn, did you, knowing I was safely abed in London?" If his expression was challenging, his amused tone belied it.

The colonel stretched out his legs, crossing them at the ankle. "Of course. It is all part of my plan to subvert your entire family. Why, they almost sympathize with the French now! And *you* have taken advantage of *my* absence to torture my poor cousin Darcy."

"Guilty as charged." Mr. Bennet's expression was more gleeful than guilty.

Richard shook his head with mock sadness. "So even now you remain unconvinced of his rectitude. What must he do to satisfy you?"

Mr. Bennet smirked. "Torturing your cousin is one of the few amusements left to me."

"And he is so very easy to torture," Richard agreed.

"That he is." The two gentlemen shared an amused look.

After several more minutes of their bantering, Jane excused herself, saying her aunt would be requiring her assistance. When the colonel did not move, Mr. Bennet turned a keen look on him. "So, is this an official visit or an unofficial one?"

"Definitely official. A pity; I had hoped to catch you unawares."

"I was not under the impression that you kept returning to Longbourn out of a desire to see *me*."

"No; although it was rather entertaining to have had the opportunity to threaten to run you through."

"So, are you asking my consent, my blessing, or something else entirely?"

The colonel gave a slow smile. "Neither, sir. I am *telling* you of my intentions. Miss Bennet is of age. You need not be involved at all, but since you objected so strenuously to poor Darcy announcing his engagement before speaking to you, I thought to save us all a scene by going at it the other way around."

"How very considerate of you. Jane may be of age, but would she still agree to marry you against my wishes? She has not my Lizzy's spirit."

Richard was enough of a card player to recognize a bluff when he saw one. "I don't know," he said cordially. "Shall we ask her?"

Mr. Bennet waved a hand at him dismissively. "Just keep her away from that father of yours."

"Since I stay away from him as much as I can, she would do the same, but there will be occasions when they must meet. I would not allow her to be alone with him, however."

"Keep her with your mother, then. I like her."

"I am glad of it, since Jane and I will likely be living with her. It will offer more comforts to Jane than I could afford on my own, especially after my mother drives me into debt by purchasing what she considers suitable clothing for her daughter-in-law's introduction to the *ton*. She has been looking forward to that for years."

"I will thank you to spare me any details of lace and ribbons," Mr. Bennet said dryly.

The two acknowledged lovers bade one another a tender farewell that afternoon, while the unacknowledged shared nothing beyond long look. Colonel Fitzwilliam clapped Darcy on the shoulder and told him he would stop in at Darcy House after dropping off the curricle there, as he needed to have a word with him.

"Tonight?" Darcy asked in a long-suffering voice.

"Would you rather it be tomorrow night?" Richard countered. "No, I thought not!"

Nonetheless, Darcy greeted him cordially when he arrived, looking more relaxed than Richard could recall seeing in some time. "So, how is the last night of bachelordom going?"

"Too slowly. Everything that needs doing has been done, and now all I have to do is to wait on the parson's pleasure tomorrow. And that cannot happen soon enough for me."

"My sympathies," said Richard. At Darcy's suspicious look, he added, "No, I mean it. I quite sympathize with your dilemma, since I am now in the same boat. Miss Bennet – Miss *Jane* Bennet – did me the honor of accepting my hand today."

Darcy's brows drew together. "What? I do not understand. I thought you wanted…. Well, I thought you wanted Elizabeth."

"And so I did, but I have since realized Elizabeth was just the precursor for me, the one who ensnared my attention because of her similarity to the woman I was waiting for. When I met my Jane, I had no doubts."

"But Bingley is planning to offer for her, and she has been waiting for that!"

"I realize this comes as a shock to you, but do be sensible, Darcy. When I first met Jane, she was pining for Bingley, yes. But he abandoned her without a word, and what woman wants a man who will not stand by her? I told her directly that Bingley planned to offer for her, and she still accepted me."

"This is quite a shock." Darcy shook his head as if to clear it. "I thought you had only met her a few times."

"That was enough. I would have waited longer, had you not told me of Bingley's intentions toward her. I did not intend to miss my opportunity by moving too slowly." As he had missed his opportunity with Elizabeth, though that had proved to be a blessing in disguise.

"You know that her portion is small? It will not provide enough for you to live in the style to which you are accustomed."

"And that is what is different. I wanted Elizabeth, I admit it, but only if she brought me money as well. With Jane, it seems irrelevant. All the money in the world could not compensate for losing her. We will make do somehow. I will be giving up my bachelor quarters and we will live with my mother, which will allow me to put some money aside while still providing Jane with the luxuries she deserves. And before you ask – yes, she does know I have little to offer her financially."

"That was the least of my concerns. If there is one thing I have learned in the last year, it is that Elizabeth and her sister are not mercenary. However, there is one matter I should mention. It has been my intention to settle some money on the remaining Bennet sisters to augment their portions, but obviously nothing could be done until I marry Elizabeth. Will it offend you if I still do so?"

Richard laughed. "Only you would ask that, Darcy. As a younger son, I cannot afford to be proud about where money comes from. But it would go into her settlement in any case, which would provide us both some peace of mind, I imagine."

"Well, then, there is nothing for me to say but to wish you happy and that you have better luck than I had when you speak to Mr. Bennet."

With a grin, Richard replied, "I already did that earlier today, and he gave his consent."

"He gave his consent, just like that?" Darcy sounded incredulous. "Damn the man!"

"I imagine he did so at least in part to annoy you. He does seem to delight in being perverse."

"How well I know it! I intend to be civil to him for Elizabeth's sake, but it will be a long time before I can forgive him for these last few months. But at least I have come to know the Gardiners, who have proved to be among the best people of my acquaintance."

"I would have never thought to hear you say that about people in trade, Darcy. Elizabeth has been good for you."

"There is no question of that. I only hope to make myself worthy of *her*." Darcy frowned. "In the meantime, I had best write to Bingley tonight. I do not expect he will want to travel to Netherfield under these circumstances."

Jane Bennet preserved her usual cheerful demeanor as she climbed into bed beside her sister that night for the very last time, though she was experiencing a startling mix of sentiments. It was hard to truly take in the significance of her last night with Lizzy when every thought was overset with the wonderful surprise of Colonel Fitzwilliam's offer. That morning she would have considered such a thing to be impossible, and now it was true! But on this important night she must play a different role, that of Lizzy's sister.

She tried to put her own joy out of her mind in her concern for her sister. "Lizzy?"

"Yes?"

"Are you worried about tomorrow?"

"I have not had time to worry, to tell you the truth. It has been so difficult to reach this point that I feel more as if my troubles are over. Apart from leaving you, I have no regrets. Is that wrong of me?"

"Of course not! Tomorrow should be the happiest day of your life."

Elizabeth laughed. "I hope not, since I plan to have a great many days that are even happier in the future! And I hope we will see each other very often. Will you come to visit at Pemberley? The Gardiners are to come at Christmastime, but it would make me happy if you stayed longer."

"Well..." Yesterday Jane would have been delighted with this invitation, but now she hoped to be married by then.

"Naturally, if you would prefer not to…" Elizabeth's cheery voice sounded forced.

"Of course I want to see you! It is just…" Jane, unpracticed at deception, felt wretchedly guilty at her inability to explain herself, especially on this night of all nights. What would Lizzy think? She screwed up her courage and said, "There is something I must tell you, something that happened today, and I hope you will not be troubled about it since I am very happy about it, so please try to be happy for me."

"Dearest Jane, you are babbling! What is the matter?"

Jane took a deep breath, then said quickly, "Colonel Fitzwilliam made me an offer today and I accepted him. I know you must think it very strange since he offered for you not so long ago, but I hold him in the very highest regard, and he had a reason for speaking so quickly and…"

"This is wonderful news!" Elizabeth hugged her tightly. "Quite unexpected, I admit, but how could you think I would not be happy for you? I am pleased for both of you – for your sake, for having found a man as amiable as you are, and for his sake, for choosing to follow his heart rather than his pocketbook. I so hated the thought of his marrying without affection! And I am *very* glad to hear that he no longer thinks of me. I never truly believed that he cared deeply for me, and you are so much better of a match for him. Oh, Jane!"

"You do not think less of me for it?"

"How could I think such a thing! But are you sure he is the one you want? I did not want to say anything before, but Mr. Bingley is intending to return to Netherfield, and I know he wants to see you. If you are accepting the colonel because you think you cannot have Mr. Bingley, you should not give up your chance of happiness with him."

"I know it must seem odd that I would transfer my affections so readily. If I had not met Colonel Fitzwilliam, I would likely still be pining for Mr. Bingley, but the reason I stopped thinking of him is not that the colonel took his place, but rather that he made me see what Mr. Bingley had been lacking all along. Do you remember the first time the colonel came to Longbourn? He was amiable, even when our father was being so unkind, but he did not back down. He did not hesitate to speak of his sympathy for the French, and he did not apologize for it. Mr. Bingley's amiability is such that he cannot bear to argue with anyone. The colonel is both amiable and knows his own mind, and that is far superior. He is not wealthy, but I know that I can depend on him, no matter what may befall us."

"I cannot argue with you on that point. Mr. Bingley is a good man, but he has not the colonel's strength of mind. He will make you very happy. And I am also delighted for a very selfish reason – because you will be marrying a man who is already a close friend of my almost-husband! Is it odd that I am perfectly calm about marrying him tomorrow, but that calling him my husband still seems like an impossibility?"

Jane giggled. "I feel just the same way!"

Chapter 21

MR. BENNET CAME downstairs on the day of the wedding for the first time since his heart seizure. If he did not seem in particularly high spirits, at least Elizabeth could discern no sign of either illness or displeasure.

The wedding party was a tight fit in the sitting room, even with most of the furniture moved aside, but somehow they managed to find room for all the principals as well as Mr. and Mrs. Gardiner and their four children. Jenny had refused to be left behind in the nursery, although she was still somewhat confused as to why this marriage was taking place when, as far as she was concerned, Darcy and Elizabeth had always been married. Still, her mother had always told her that the ways of the gentry were passing strange, so perhaps they all repeated their weddings at regular intervals. It made little difference to her, especially with the promise of cream cakes afterwards.

It was a touching ceremony in which no one could doubt the affection the bride and groom felt for each other, and both Mrs. Gardiner and Jane had tears in their eyes. After the vows were all said, the cream cakes devoured, and the bridal couple departed for Darcy House with many good wishes and warm embraces, Mr. Gardiner turned to his brother-in-law Bennet and said affectionately, "You old fraud."

"Me? Whatever do you mean?"

Mr. Gardiner chuckled. "That heart seizure was real, I grant you, but convincing those poor children that you had changed your mind about their marriage solely because you were nigh on your death bed and needed to protect your family? Would it have been so hard simply to admit you were wrong?"

"That boy is too certain of himself as it is," grumbled Mr. Bennet. "It'll do him good to be kept guessing."

His brother-in-law did not miss the lack of a denial of his accusation.

"As I said, you are an old fraud. Come, let us go to my study. I purchased some fine port for the occasion."

"As long as it is not barley broth, I will drink anything! I hope to never see another drop of that in my life."

Mr. Gardiner clapped him on the shoulder. "Well, then, if you are *very* good, perhaps you can even have some solid food, since you have made such a miraculous recovery. And this way we will not have to watch the *new* set of lovebirds bill and coo."

Darcy could hardly believe it. Mr. Bennet had looked so hale that Darcy had steeled himself for the possibility that he would change his mind and refuse to allow the wedding to proceed. But Mr. Bennet had not rescinded his permission at the last minute, and Elizabeth was now his wife. He had not breathed easily until the vows were said, and then the entire world seemed a much finer place to him.

Now she was sitting beside him in the curricle. Hoping to be able to kiss his new bride, Darcy had planned to use a closed carriage to give them privacy, but the morning had dawned unusually hot and humid, and a closed carriage would have been oppressively close. Nothing, though, could keep him from touching her hand or tracing a finger down the exposed skin of her arm, and it aroused him mightily when she shivered despite the sun burning down on them.

A little conversation might be the only thing to keep him sane on the journey to Darcy House. "Your father looked well this morning."

"I noticed that as well, although I admit to having a few distractions." Elizabeth gave him an arch smile.

"Do you know how long he plans to stay in London?"

"He has not said, but I assume he plans to remain until after Lydia's wedding next week."

Darcy was even feeling beneficent toward Lydia Bennet today. Through all the trouble she had created, she was ultimately responsible for Mr. Bennet's change of heart, and that had saved Darcy four long months of separation from Elizabeth. Yes, while he detested the connection to Wickham, right now he could not even muster annoyance with Lydia.

"Will we still be able to stay at Netherfield for a time, do you think?"

The same question had crossed his mind several times since hearing his cousin's news. "It might be best not to depend upon it. Bingley was unhappy with me already, and having had his hopes raised only to be dashed will not help."

"Surely he cannot blame you for failing to know Jane's true sentiments!"

"That he would likely forgive, but the conclusion he drew from our engagement was a different one. He believes that I discouraged him from marrying Jane because I did not think him good enough to marry my future sister."

"But that is ridiculous! You had not even thought of offering for me at that point."

"Oh, I had *thought* of it far too often; I was just able to convince myself that I would be able to forget you after I left Netherfield. By the time I saw you at Rosings, I knew the fallacy of that. I could not forget you no matter how hard I tried. Still, while Bingley's suppositions are far from the truth, I cannot prove that to him, and the fact that my cousin swooped in and engaged Jane's affections just when Bingley decided to return may confirm his suspicions." In a few days, Bingley's defection would no doubt be painful, but he would not let it ruin today. "I made a very serious mistake, and Bingley is paying for it."

"*You* made a very serious mistake? I may disagree with the advice you gave him, but it was just that: advice. Bingley is the one who made the mistake, not you."

"I knew he would follow my advice. Bingley is most unaffectedly modest. His diffidence prevented his depending on his own judgment, but his reliance on mine made everything easy."

"Yes, and your propensity is to take responsibility for everything, no matter whether it is in your purview or not. Your aunt's tenants, Jenny, Wickham, Bingley – as soon as someone crosses your path, they become your responsibility, and if anything happens to them, it is your fault. Pardon me, but Mr. Bingley is a grown man, and it was his choice to follow your advice and not his own heart."

"Are we having an argument not two hours after our wedding?" he asked mildly.

Elizabeth laughed. "If we are, I predict it is one we will have on a regular basis. I admire your sense of responsibility, but sometimes you do carry it to an extreme. You will have to accustom yourself to being teased about it. From time to time it is acceptable to do what you wish rather than what you think you ought to do."

"You are not the first person to say that, I admit. Very well, I will strive to do better." And very soon indeed, he thought smugly.

He reined in the horses in front of Darcy House. "Welcome home, my love."

Elizabeth tilted her head backward to examine the townhouse façade as Darcy handed her out of the curricle. The front door was already opening; his butler had clearly been watching for them in hopes of impressing the new mistress. Darcy ignored him, however. Instead, when they reached the doorway, he said in Elizabeth's ear, "The *responsible* thing for me to do now would be to take you on a tour of the house, introduce you to the staff, and allow them to serve us the elegant dinner they have no doubt been working hard to produce. But since you wish me to practice less responsibility, I am forced instead to do what I *wish*."

He swept her up in his arms and carried her across the threshold, but did not stop there. Over his shoulder, he said to the startled butler, "This is Mrs. Darcy. We do *not* wish to be disturbed."

"Of course, sir," the butler murmured.

Darcy was already carrying the laughing Elizabeth up the grand staircase and directly through his anteroom into his bedroom. He kicked the door closed behind them, then deposited his bride directly on the bed.

"You do not waste time, sir!" Elizabeth teased, but he could sense a hint of nervousness behind it.

"I am following your instructions, my dear," he said with mock austerity. "And right now what I wish to do is to show you what I would have done that day in the hollow at Pemberley had I trusted my self-control more. I have given this matter *substantial* thought." In fact, he had played it out in his mind more times than he could count.

Elizabeth raised a dubious eyebrow. "And you trust your self-control more now?"

He lost no time in joining her on the bed, raising himself on one elbow as he trailed his finger lightly from her chin to the base of her neck, and then lower until it was poised just above the neckline of her dress. "Yes." He plunged his finger between the delicious softness of her breasts, eliciting a gasp from her, then continued in a softer, more intimate tone. "Self-control will be much easier since this time I know I will not have to stop. Now, if you will be so kind as to cast your mind back to that day...."

"Very well, but your bed is much softer than the ground, and there is not a stick poking into my back."

He stopped her teasing mouth with a probing kiss as he removed his finger, but only in order to curve his hand around the temptation of her breast. "Perhaps you remember this part," he said conversationally as he allowed his lips to drift to her throat, planting light, tantalizing kisses along the sensitive skin until Elizabeth's breath was ragged and she tipped her head back, exposing more of herself to his explorations and mutely inviting him to turn his attentions lower.

God, he had dreamed of this so often since that day, of tasting the slight salt tang of the top of her breasts as his nostrils filled with the scent of rosewater and Elizabeth. Intoxicated by her nearness, he skimmed his thumb over the tip of her breast, feeling it tighten and grow hard. Her moan was all the invitation he needed to take advantage of her response, his fingers now toying with her nipple through the smooth silk of her dress, squeezing and rolling it until her body began to move involuntarily.

Seeing her response was not enough. He needed to feel her beneath him. Trapping her legs with his, he moved over her, brushing against her sensitized breasts, feeling the shock of it even through all the layers of clothing that separated them. Her hips rocked up to meet him. The motion against his hardness made him long to stop this slow seduction and take her right then and there, but he wanted to give her more than that.

And Elizabeth wanted more. No, she needed more, was desperate for more. Then she was kissing him as desperately as he was kissing her, his hands exploring her body, touching her in ways no man had ever touched her before, setting her every nerve afire. Her hands clutched him to her, digging into the firm muscles of his back as he nudged her legs apart with his knee, then took his place between them. She knew full well that her skirts and his breeches stood between them, but still she was overwhelmed by an odd mixture of intimate vulnerability and anticipation. Then his hardness rocked against her, rhythmically rubbing against her most private places, each movement sending through her a shock of pleasure so pure that it made her writhe against him. Instinctively she raised her knees to open herself more fully to him and the intoxicating sensations he was creating in her. It built and built until she felt as if there was nothing left of her but a well of exquisite need.

The intimacy of the moment was so great that it was almost a shock to look into his eyes, bare inches from hers. Her chest heaved as if she had been running a race. She tried to calm herself and let the storm inside her ebb, but then it intensified as Darcy laid his hand against the naked skin of her thigh. With a shuddering breath, she discovered that her skirts had pooled above her knees, exposing much of her legs to his view. What was more shocking was that she did not care. In fact, the heat in his eyes as he inspected them kindled a new fire inside her.

Without removing his hand, he settled himself beside her, lightly caressing her thigh. Then he spoke, in a voice no longer steady. "Had my self-control not begun to fail me, and had my conscience allowed it, this was where I would have asked to be allowed to satisfy you."

She laughed shakily. "You would have seduced me after all, then?"

His slow smile seemed to hold an enticing wickedness. "No, not that, just to give you pleasure. It will not violate you; you will still be a virgin, at least for the moment, if not precisely... untouched. And it would have helped you... ease the tension." His fingers traced burning circles on the sensitive skin of her inner thigh. "That is what I plan to do now."

Awash in need, Elizabeth could not think of anything that might ease her tension short of being struck in the head by a brick, and certainly did not see how more of this temptation could possibly improve matters.

The corners of his lips turned up, then he covered her mouth with a passionate kiss. But how could she focus on his kiss when his fingers were trailing up her inner thigh and then – oh, goodness – directly over her private parts. She was sure that she ought to want him to stop, but her body did not seem to agree, instead straining those same parts against his hand as if begging for more. She made the astonishing discovery that mere pressure was a torture of a new sort, sending her need for his touch spiraling. How could this possibly *relax* her, of all things?

He seemed to sense her need, his nimble fingers continuing their journey of discovery until finding a spot where his caresses elicited blinding waves of pleasure. Unable to help herself, she moaned, and Darcy ceased his kiss just long enough to whisper, "Oh, yes, Elizabeth, yes."

She forced her lips to obey her long enough to quaver, "How...."

"I adore you, and that is all that matters. Just feel."

And she did feel. She felt ragged with desire and wantonly desirous of more, and when one of his fingers slipped inside her, she could feel the shocking sensation through every inch of her body as he moved it in and out. Somehow he continued to stroke that incredibly sensitive spot, the one that made her writhe like a madwoman, yearning for something she did not understand.

Cool air wafted over her breast, and she realized vaguely that he must have pushed her dress off her shoulder. Then his mouth unexpectedly descended upon her nipple, and he was sucking at it and teasing it with his tongue and teeth, sending unexpected riptides of sensation through her. This new tension, compounding the effects of the dance of his nimble finger in her private places, rose into something near pain, and she did not know how she could bear another minute of it.

Then, without warning, the ache crested, a splendid flood of pleasure cascading through her, fountaining from the spot where he touched her all the way to her fingertips. She was shuddering uncontrollably with release, her body alive with sensation and responding to his lightest touch. Slowly the tide receded, leaving Elizabeth both drained and amazingly fulfilled at the same time.

He kissed her gently, then raised his head to meet her eyes. "My dearest love," he murmured. "That is what I wanted to do that day, to show you that we belonged together."

Overwhelmed by tenderness for him, she wanted to reply, but her muscles would not obey her. All she could do was to put her feelings into her eyes and hope that he understood.

"All is well. It takes a moment to recover," he said.

She sucked in a deep breath. "So… I see. But it is much better than being hit on the head with a brick."

He laughed. "I beg your pardon?"

"Just a random thought. Pay me no mind. I am full of nonsense."

Darcy could spare no more thought to the question, for his own dilemma was becoming a burning one. He had intended to remove Elizabeth's clothing so that he could feast his eyes and lips on her before consummating their marriage, and of course his own enjoyment would be heightened by removing his own. But pleasuring Elizabeth had proved even more arousing than he had anticipated, and his body was clamoring for satisfaction with a vehemence that left no room for dealing with tiny buttons and unlacing stays, much less for calling his valet to remove his boots and fashionably tight coat. Not when Elizabeth was warm in his arms, gazing up at him with dreamy, aroused eyes, and he ached to make her his own. He cursed the tailors and modistes who had dreamed up all these impossible layers of formal clothes and the fashionable set which demanded boots so tall and tight that a man could not remove them himself. Well, that particular fantasy of admiring Elizabeth's lovely body would have to wait until tonight if he was not to become a candidate for

Bedlam.

Elizabeth reached up to touch the tip of his nose. "You look so serious. Is something the matter?"

"No, not a thing." And it was true. "Except that I am in great need of more of your kisses, my love."

"What a fortunate man you are, then, for I am well supplied with them!"

He knew just how to chase that arch smile from her face and replace it with a look more appropriate for their wedding night – even if it was actually the middle of the afternoon. Experimentally he moved his fingers, still ensconced in her private places, and was rewarded when Elizabeth sucked in a sudden breath.

Yes, indeed, he was going to make her his, but he wanted her to be thoroughly aroused when he did so. Now he was the one smiling as he delicately caressed her most sensitive spot. "And now, my loveliest Elizabeth, since we are not after all in the hollow," He paused to run his tongue tantalizingly over her nipple, making her arch up toward him. "It is only fair to warn you to disregard anything I said about not seducing you, because ...." he trailed kisses along her bared breast before taking the peak completely into his mouth, sucking and nibbling at it as she groaned her pleasure, her hands entwining into his hair. He lifted his head just enough to release her nipple and said, "... because now I am quite definitely going to seduce you."

With those words, he plunged two fingers inside her. She gasped, her hips rocking up gratifyingly to meet his hand. If it was possible, it made him even harder and more desperate to possess her. With the last shreds of his self-control, he used his fingers to thrust in and out of her, preparing her for what was to come. His thumb drew tiny circles over her nub until she began to whimper and press herself harder and harder against his hand.

He could wait no longer. He stopped his ministrations only long enough to drop the flap on his formal breeches and free himself. Poising himself at her entrance, he kissed her deeply, exploring the sweet depths of her mouth for a long minute. As slowly as he could bear, he pushed inside her warm wetness, exulting in each moment, until he reached the last barrier. Then, with a final thrust, he made her his own.

Elizabeth winced, but did not cry out. He paused to kiss her tenderly for a moment, but she was so sweet, so tight and he was so hard that it was impossible to wait long. As soon as she began to return his kiss, he allowed himself to move, doing his best to be gentle. When she wrapped her legs around him with a sigh of pleasure, permitting him to go deeper still, his restraint broke. As she finally cried out, her flesh spasming around him, he found his bliss at last as he spilled his seed within her.

He would have stayed in that moment forever if he could, connected to Elizabeth in the most basic way possible, her soft body pressed against his in the last tremors of her pleasure. He had dreamed of this so long, and now it was real. There were no words for it. Raising himself on his elbows so as not to crush her, he said the only sensible thing which came into his head. "Are you well? Is there pain?"

Her eyes fluttered open, meeting his in a tender look. "Less than I was led to expect, and it was over quickly." She raised a hand to cup his cheek. "My love."

"Always yours, my dearest."

Elizabeth glanced down at herself, noting her skirts rucked up to her waist, the shoulder of her dress pushed down to expose one breast, and her hair coming loose. She looked up at him half-ruefully. "At least this time I will not have grass stains on my clothes."

"No. And tonight, when I come to you, we will not have all these accoutrements between us. But you may have the pleasure of knowing that I followed your sage advice by doing what I wished instead of waiting until then – and you are all that I ever wished for." His voice was low and intense.

She felt a deep upwelling of affection for him, and wondered how she could ever have failed to love him. Then a pattering against the windows drew her attention. Laughing, she said, "Look -- it is raining!"

"Good." He kissed her deeply. "I hope it continues until the Thames overflows its banks and traps us here for days."

⌘

It was a pleasure to watch Elizabeth even when she was doing something as mundane as selecting which roll to eat for breakfast. Her fine eyes flicked back and forth between the selections, then her slender hand hovered in the air for a moment like a hummingbird about to sip the nectar from a flower before it descended on her choice. The curve of her arm reminded him of how it had felt to have those arms around him last night, and then to wake in them this morning. Heaven.

His reverie was interrupted by the entrance of his butler, who presented him a silver salver with a card on it.

"Who the devil is calling at this hour?" He took the card and looked at it, then threw it down again in disgust.

"What is the matter?" asked Elizabeth. "Is it Lord Matlock?"

"Worse. George Wickham."

The butler bowed. "Shall I show him in, sir?"

"No. Better yet, I will tell him myself." Darcy tossed his napkin on his chair and strode past the shocked butler.

Wickham was awaiting him in the entry hall wearing that smirk Darcy so detested. The very presence of that man was polluting his house! "What is it, Wickham?"

"Why, I heard the good news and came by to give Mrs. Darcy my best wishes, of course."

Darcy silently glared at him, waiting for him to get to the real purpose of his visit.

The smirk grew wider. "And I have been thinking that the reputation of Mrs. Darcy's sister is a more valuable thing than when she was no more than your, shall we say, *somewhat* intended bride?"

"You will not get a penny more from me."

"Really? Well, I hope the scandal of Mrs. Darcy's sister does not affect Georgiana's marriage prospects too severely. You will be responsible for it, you know."

Darcy considered briefly. "No. It will be *your* fault, and I am done cleaning up after you. Good *day*." He turned to the butler. "Stephens, if that man is not out of this house of his own volition within one minute, he is to be thrown out." With one last look of distaste, he strode back to the breakfast room and Elizabeth.

Wickham's wheedling voice came from behind him. "Darcy, is this any way to treat your future brother?"

Darcy ignored him completely, apart from closing the doors to the breakfast room behind him.

Elizabeth wore an arch smile. "That was quick."

"I assume you heard it all." He stood behind her chair and bent to brush his lips against her neck. "I hope you are satisfied, even though I did not do what I truly wished to do, which was to pitch him out the door myself."

"An excellent compromise. Some things are better left to the servants." Her eyes sparkled up at him.

"Speaking of compromises, I agreed to your request to come down for breakfast so that the household could see you. To my mind, that means you should compromise and agree to return to our rooms immediately after breakfast." He continued his exploration of her neck and collarbone.

"But what will the staff think?" she teased.

"They will think that newlyweds have more important things to do than to eat breakfast." He captured her mouth with his, and Elizabeth was forced to agree that he could be right.

Chapter 22

DARCY'S BOX AT the Theatre Royal was full on the occasion of Mr. Bennet's last day in London, when that gentleman joined the newlyweds, Jane, Colonel Fitzwilliam and Lady Matlock in attending a play. Mr. Bennet seemed back to his usual self, with no hint of his recent illness, although Elizabeth had insisted that he walk up the stairs slowly. He had shown no sign of discomfort during Lydia's wedding the previous day either, even going so far as to laugh during Lydia's tirade when she accused Elizabeth of having cheated her of being the first in the family to wed. At least that matter was well settled now.

Darcy guided Elizabeth into the second row of chairs in the box, ceding the front row to their guests, which was not only good manners, but also meant he would be able to hold Elizabeth's hand during the play with no one the wiser. Even after a fortnight of marriage, he was still happiest when he could maintain physical contact with Elizabeth.

Richard and Jane were directly in front of them, alongside Lady Matlock and Mr. Bennet, who were engaged in a lively conversation as if they were old friends. Darcy could not make out Mr. Bennet's share of the discussion, but Lady Matlock trilled with laughter as she gave his wrist a sharp tap with her folded fan. "You *would* like it! Me, I am not so fond of the Hamlet. Why should it have so many deaths at the end? It would be much better if Mr. Shakespeare had allowed everyone to shake hands – except the evil king. He deserves his end, n'est-ce pas?"

Richard had been whispering in Jane's ear when he suddenly sat up. "Oh, charming," he said with heavy irony.

"What is the matter?" Jane asked.

He handed Jane the opera glasses. "The third box from the stage. My father."

Jane peered through the glasses. "Who is that lady with him?"

Lady Matlock had by now taken note of their conversation. "No one of importance. The latest whore, no doubt." She gave a dismissive wave of her hand.

"Mother!" Richard said disapprovingly.

"What is the matter? I am sure Miss Bennet knows what a whore is, n'est-ce pas? If not, I will be happy to explain it to her later." Turning her attention back to Mr. Bennet, Lady Matlock raised her fan to whisper something to him behind it. Mr. Bennet's response was a deep chuckle.

Richard winced and turned a pained look on Jane. "My apologies. The French can be very frank about certain subjects."

Elizabeth touched Darcy's sleeve. "I do not know if this is a good idea," she said softly, indicating her father with a movement of her head. "He is supposed to stay calm, but seeing your uncle even across the theatre could upset him."

Darcy thought it more likely that Mr. Bennet would be all too well amused by flirting with Lady Matlock under the eye of her estranged husband. "He seems unperturbed, but if that changes, we can leave at any point."

Just then the lights were extinguished, leaving only the halo from the footlights lighting the heavy curtain, which slowly rose to reveal the parapets of old King Hamlet's castle.

When the interval began, Elizabeth tried to convince her father to remain in the box. "Mr. Darcy will be happy to bring you a glass of wine," she said.

"Thank you, but I have been sitting long enough." Mr. Bennet offered his arm to Lady Matlock.

Darcy tried to stay close to Mr. Bennet in case Lord Matlock should put in an appearance, but the crush of people made it difficult. There were several strangers between them when he heard the familiar sneer. "Birdwit *again*? I thought we were rid of you."

Richard interposed himself between the adversaries. "This is a fortuitous meeting. Father, may I present to you Miss Bennet, who has lately done me the great honor of agreeing to be my wife? The announcement will be in the papers within the week."

"Another of Birdwit's daughters? Just because Darcy is making a fool of himself doesn't mean you have to. No doubt this one is penniless as well. Don't think that you'll be getting a farthing from me, boy."

Richard stiffened, then drawled, "I wouldn't dream of it, since the last I heard, you barely have a farthing to your name."

Darcy tried to elbow his way through to them. People were already beginning to stare and whisper.

Mr. Bennet said, "Fortunately, I do still have a few farthings to *my* name, most likely because *I* do not have to pay anyone to tolerate my company at the theatre. After all, why should I, when I can enjoy the company of *your* wife, *your* son, and *your* nephew? It's enough to make one wonder which of us is the birdwit. Now, if you will excuse us, we must be going."

Elizabeth tugged at his arm. "What did he say? I could not make it out."

Darcy smiled down at her fondly. "I will tell you later – but I think you need not worry about your father any longer."

With Mr. Bennet's health so much improved, Mr. and Mrs. Darcy decided it was safe to return to Pemberley where Georgiana still awaited them. It was hard to believe it had only been a few weeks since they had departed Derbyshire, each of them going their separate way and expecting not to see each other for months. Their stay there was brief, though, owing to the need to return to Hertfordshire for Jane and Richard's wedding, where they were privileged to hear on several occasions Mrs. Bennet's icy comments about how pleasant it was that she would finally be able to attend the wedding of *one* of her daughters. Fortunately, Jane's wedding was one she could boast of for many years, as it was attended by various titled relatives of the groom. That list did not, however, include the Earl of Matlock, who felt it pointless to travel so far from town simply to watch his younger son marry a girl of no distinction whatsoever. His absence caused no grief among those gathered to celebrate.

After receiving the intelligence of Jane Bennet's engagement from Darcy, Charles Bingley had a great many things to say to the man he had trusted above all others, some of them true, some false, but all of them angry. Given the choice of blaming his sister, Darcy, or himself, he elected Darcy as the least painful choice to carry the onus of his culpability in losing Jane Bennet. His intention was to put an end to their friendship, but he gave way under pressure from his sisters and maintained a civil relationship with the Darcys, although without the closeness of previous years. He never returned to Netherfield and soon after gave up the lease. A year to the day after Jane's wedding, Bingley announced his engagement to a delicately bred girl from York with golden hair and pretty manners.

Jenny flatly refused to return to Hunsford where, as she pointed out forthrightly, everyone she cared about was dead. Instead, she was taken into the family of the Pemberley steward as a ward, where her foster father could meet any misbehavior with the ultimate threat of reporting it to Mr. Darcy. She remained a thorn in the side of the steward's young assistant who often threw up his hands in despair at how to handle a spirited child who pestered him at every opportunity, until some dozen years later when he finally noticed that she was no longer a child. At that point she became a completely different sort of thorn in his side until he convinced her that she could do a much more effective job of pestering him as his wife.

Jane and Colonel Fitzwilliam lived in Lady Matlock's town house for several years while he continued his work at the War Office. When peace was declared, he sold his commission and took a position in the embassy in Paris at the personal request of the Prime Minister. To provide some companionship to Jane in France, they invited Mary Bennet to live with them. Mary's public presentation benefited substantially from the efforts of a French maid, and in that environment she was able to gain some of the confidence she had lacked in Meryton. She also provided more practice in English for a new generation of Fitzwilliams whose first words were in the French of their nursemaid. The family regularly spent summers at Pemberley, much to Elizabeth's delight.

With the Gardiners, they were always on the most intimate terms. Darcy, as well as Elizabeth, really loved them; and they were both ever sensible of the warmest gratitude towards the persons who, by bringing her into Derbyshire, had been the means of uniting them.

About the Author

Abigail Reynolds is a lifelong Jane Austen enthusiast and a physician. Originally from upstate New York, she studied Russian, theater, and marine biology before deciding to attend medical school. She began writing variations on *Pride and Prejudice* in 2001 to spend more time with her favorite Jane Austen characters. Encouragement from fellow Austen fans persuaded her to continue asking "What if...?", which led to seven novels in The Pemberley Variations series. She has also written two contemporary novels set on Cape Cod, *The Man Who Loved Pride and Prejudice* and *Morning Light*. In 2012 she retired from medical practice to focus exclusively on writing. She is currently at work on a new Pemberley Variation as well as the next novel in her Cape Cod series. She lives in Wisconsin with her husband, two teenage children, and a menagerie of pets. Her hobby is trying to find time to sleep.

www.pemberleyvariations.com
www.austenauthors.net

Acknowledgements

Many people assisted in the creation of this book. I'd like to thank Sharon Lathan, Rena Margulis, Susan Mason-Milks, and Deirdre Sumpter for their comments on the final version. Lee Smith Parsons suggested the title, along with the very tempting alternative "Pride & Precipitation." The talented Frank Underwood brought to my attention the painting by Merry-Joseph Blondel used in the cover image. My fellow Austen Authors (www.austenauthors.net) provided support, knowledge, and general encouragement. As always, conversation with my readers helped shape the work in progress. I'm grateful to live in an age where I can connect so easily to readers and other writers.

Made in the USA
Lexington, KY
21 September 2012